A Time For Love

In the dark they sank down on the bed with no words between them. The winds continued their death-dealing velocity.

Mara thought, *It's like the end of the world.*

The world was ending for her and with it, all her hopes and dreams of love and success, of springs to come and winters ahead.

She turned to Halloran, pressing herself against him.

"You once told me I'd come to you, and on your terms."

Her hand crept up the back of his neck, into his thick faintly curling wet hair.

"I'm here, John...and on your terms."

WINDSWEPT

ANN FORMAN BARRON

AVON
PUBLISHERS OF BARD, CAMELOT, DISCUS AND FLARE BOOKS

AVON BOOKS
A division of
The Hearst Corporation
1790 Broadway
New York, New York 10019

First Avon Printing, March, 1985

AVON TRADEMARK REG. U.S. PAT. OFF. AND IN
OTHER COUNTRIES, MARCA REGISTRADA, HECHO EN
U.S.A.

Printed in the U.S.A.

WFH   10   9   8   7   6   5   4   3   2   1

For my sister
Billie
with love

Love is a familiar;
Love is a devil;
there is no evil angel but Love.

William Shakespeare
Love's Labor's Lost
Act I, Scene 2

WINDSWEPT

Chapter 1.

〜 "I won't do it," Celia said quietly, her face white against the window opened on the sunny gardens below. "Lucinda knows I went with David and she suspects I love him. It's just her way of turning the knife in the wound."

Her younger sister, Mara, looked at her compassionately. God knows, thought Mara, she herself knew how painful it was to love without reciprocation. She adored their father, Archer Ashworth, and she never seemed able to please him, no matter how hard she tried.

"This," Celia added through tears, "on top of Papa's store failing after all these years, us having to sell the house and all our furniture is too much. It's too . . . humiliating!"

Celia was a virtuoso on the piano and Lucinda Ames had asked her to play at her wedding to David Donellan—David, whom Celia loved desperately and who had stopped calling when it was rumored that Archer Ashworth might be bankrupt.

A close observer would note that of the two girls, Mara had by far the stronger personality. It showed in the firm jawline, softened by a faint cleft in the chin, and in the fine but imperious straight nose. Though both sisters were beautiful, Mara was arrestingly so, despite the juvenile clothing she was forced to wear. Now she looked at her fair sister narrowly.

"Celia, you *must* do it," she said passionately, dark eyes flashing. "We can't let our financial misfortune beat us. As for humiliation, we're still the same people we've always been. Just because Papa's store is going under, we can't let them think it's destroyed us."

1

"Mara, Mara," Celia's voice broke, "you're too young to know how I feel. I think I would die watching them marry."

"I'm old enough," Mara responded bitterly. "And I know if you played the piano, it would show everyone that you didn't care and that we aren't crushed by Papa's so-called bankruptcy. You've got to do it for Papa's sake, Celia."

Celia looked at Mara with identical brown eyes, but Celia's were crowned by a mass of red-gold hair, like their father's, while Mara's resembled that of their French mother, Celeste Bonheur, with her delicate bones and masses of dark hair. There was but three years' difference in their ages. Celia was nineteen to Mara's sixteen.

Suddenly Celia began to cry hard. Her shoulders shook, and her younger sister came over immediately and embraced her.

"Don't cry, Celia. Hold your chin high and show the world you don't care a rap, not for David or about *Ashworth's*. You don't want Papa's smug, society sisters and our uncles to think we're weak. You know how critical they are."

"Yes, and all because they're sitting on a pile of Grandpa's money, while our darling papa tried to make something of his inheritance."

She was three when Grandpa Ashworth died, and although Mara couldn't remember him, she knew he had made a fortune during the war shipping cotton to England. He had owned a fleet of blockade runners and he had left all his money to his son and two daughters.

Celia wiped her eyes and looked back at the engraved invitation in her hand. It was well thumbed, mute testimony to her heartbreak.

Robert L. Ames invites you to attend the wedding of his daughter, Lucinda Alice, to David Pierce Donellan, at home, 2460 Wynhaven Way at 4:00 P.M. on June 2, 1897.

Though living in Richmond, Robert L. Ames was the owner of dozens of tobacco farms, among other enterprises. He was wealthy enough to indulge himself and his only daughter, Lucinda, in every luxury. Lucinda, who looked to Mara like a spun-gold Christmas tree angel, had attended the same exclusive school in Richmond that Celia and Mara attended. In fact, Lucinda and Celia were classmates. And now David Donellan was marrying money, for Robert Ames's interests were far-flung. He had investments in real estate in faraway Los Angeles, in nearer places like New York and Boston, and he was actively engaged in warehousing throughout the Southwest as well.

"Oh, yes, I knew David wanted money," Celia said defiantly, sensing Mara's thought. "But I can't seem to stop loving him. It's incredible to me that a man would put money first—before the love of a woman. And he *loved* me, Mara. I *know* he did."

Mara's heart twisted. Their father had never treated her with anything but coldness, for he held her responsible for his wife's death. And how Mara longed for *his* love. Only that strange, piercing watchfulness in which Mara sometimes caught him, made her think he was even aware of his younger daughter. She veered from the old hurt and moved away from her sister.

Celia, wiping her eyes, sank into a small chair nearby, as the curtains belled inward with a soft breeze, carrying on it the delicate fragrance of Virginia roses in full bloom. May was a time for joy, a month to revel in, yet Archer Ashworth and his family, including the girls' aunt, Felice Bonheur, their mother's younger sister, were filled with gloom. Ashworth's two sisters, Maggie Ashworth Robertson and her husband, Robert, and Julia Ashworth Quayne and her husband, Abel, made no secret of their mortification over their brother's financial debacle. Mara thought it a blessing that both sisters were childless. They were too sharp, impatient and self-centered to ever love a child, although they were loud in their praise of Celia's talent.

And here in their room, the Ashworth sisters sat, each of them in her own way, distraught over the bleak future. Their enormous and beautiful white-columned house, all their polished, gleaming silver, all the exquisite hand-rubbed mahogany furniture (much of it in the family for over a hundred years), must be sold at auction to satisfy Ashworth's creditors. His fine store in downtown Richmond, *Ashworth's*, would be sold and taken over by others.

Celia rose and went back to the window where she stood looking out on the riotously flowered gardens. Red-gold hair was piled high on her head in the latest fashion, with small tendrils about her ears. Thick and gleaming, it was in beautiful contrast to her deep brown eyes. Celia was every inch her father's daughter, tall, regal; even the curved sensual mouth was Archer's. Only the girl's eyes betrayed her French heritage. Even the aunts had the Ashworth hallmark in their luxurious red-gold hair. They were handsome, haughty women.

But Mara was her mother's child, and the aunts seemed to think it a great pity, always regarding her as somehow alien to the Ashworth brood. Mara didn't think they had ever really approved of Mama, though Aunt Julia said grudgingly that Celeste had been beautiful. Mara didn't think Aunt Julia ever realized what a compliment she was paying her niece when she railed out that Mara was almost twin to Celeste.

Celia's and Mara's wide-spaced dark eyes were features they had in common with their Aunt Felice, who had come from New Orleans to live with Celeste and Archer Ashworth after their honeymoon. Aunt Felice's features were not as exquisite as Celeste's, whose oil portrait hung above Ashworth's bed. And Mara knew Felice's coldness to her, her arbitrary decisions; her cutting remarks and meanness to her niece were silently backed up by her father. If her aunt hadn't been Mara's own flesh and blood, she could have easily mistaken her actions for jealousy.

Though Felice Bonheur had had a number of suitors through the years, she had never married. Now thirty-five, she seemed content to help with the keeping of Ashworth's house and fancied herself as rearing his two daughters. She seemed very fond of Celia, but Mara suspected her aunt's exclamations of pleasure in her sister were spoken as much to please Ashworth as through any genuine affection. Indeed, Mara suspected that, like herself, Aunt Felice nursed an unrequited love for her father.

"I should have let him do it—that last night when—when he wanted to," Celia said softly, looking out at the gardens they would soon have to leave. "If I were carrying his child he'd be marrying *me* now."

"Celia, don't talk like a fool!" Mara said roughly.

"We're going to hold our heads up. We're not going to let anything break us."

"But Mara, we don't even know what we'll be doing in a few more weeks or how Papa will make a living! We'll be objects of charity to Papa's sisters and their husbands—"

"Never! Where's your courage—the Ashworth pride?" Mara said it coldly with deliberate, biting contempt.

As Mara had intended, Celia straightened her shoulders as though struck, dried her eyes and gave her younger sister a hurt look. "All right. I'll play that wedding march *and* I'll look at David—oh, God, I'll look at him as if I cared not a whit."

"Spoken like an Ashworth! Lucinda's not nearly so beautiful as you, Celia. And someday, someone will come along that you'll love even better than you loved David."

"Never," Celia whispered low. "David is my heart."

The wedding day dawned clear and bright. All of Richmond and her June gardens were green and gold, scarlet and salmon pink, and dozens of blossoms wove a web of enchantment in the air. Celia, Mara, their papa and Aunt Felice were in their finest clothes. True to her word, Celia held her head high and smiled brilliantly at the many friends they met in the great Ames mansion. Mara was further comforted by the exquisite original gown Celia wore, for Mara had designed and made the gown herself, with the help of Sudie's nimble dark fingers.

When they saw David standing in the foyer with his best man and the ushers, Mara whispered *sotto voce* to Celia, "I never did trust him. He always looks like a mule eating barbed wire when he grins." She had hoped to make Celia smile.

Instead, her sister gave her an ironic glance and murmured, "You know he's the handsomest man in Richmond." And at that moment, David Donellan turned his eyes to Celia. They widened on her fabulously beautiful dress, then he smiled, slowly, warmly.

Mara watched her sister return his smile mechanically. Since she was sixteen, Celia, and even Mara who was three years younger, had had a steady stream of beaus, but they all had paled beside the tall, slate-eyed Donellan with his thick, dark brown hair. Mara grudgingly admitted he was charming, lithe and wide shouldered. He had always been kind to her, too, treating her as if she were a grown-up lady throughout the months he'd courted Celia. After he ceased to call on Celia last December after word seeped out that *Ashworth's* was bankrupt, she had teased and flirted with all her suitors but had chosen none of them. It did not bother Archer Ashworth, who adored his older daughter. He thought no man good enough for Celia and said so, often.

They entered the great salon with a hundred or more guests streaming in to take their seats in rented chairs before an altar of smilax, roses and golden tapers. Celia moved smoothly to take her place at the grand piano. The pale blue silk dress, of which Mara was so proud, framed her form sweetly. The piano glittered like glass in the late afternoon light. Celia's slender fingers touched the keys and Bach's *Jesu, Joy of Man's Desiring* rolled sonorously out over the people. Though not all had yet taken their seats, a hush fell over the guests.

Mara stood hesitantly just inside the door, her eyes moving over the people. She knew most of them well. Most had been guests at one time or another in their own great, red-brick Georgian home.

Suddenly her eyes riveted on her father where he was seated near the front, his hair still copper bright at fifty-five. He was such a handsome man, Mara thought proudly. And there was pride in him, too, directed at Celia as always, while her fingers moved swiftly over the keys. It was a fine instrument, but not so fine as Celeste Bonheur Ashworth's in the music room at home.

As she stood there looking at her beloved papa, she remembered the lightning rage that had shaken him only this morning. As usual, Mara had been the unwitting source of it. And she had been so happy!

She was the one who had persuaded Celia to perform this afternoon. And it was she who had carefully created the gorgeous dress Celia would wear. Now she was defiantly proud that the Ashworths would present a united front of cheer and lightheartedness among these people who whispered behind their hands about the bankrupt *Ashworth's*. And after arranging in her papa's library a vase full of his favorite scarlet roses, Mara bounced merrily out of the door and collided directly with him. It knocked the wind from both of them.

His arms shot out instinctively, closing about her. For an instant, they stood there. Then suddenly he was cursing and his hands were hard on her shoulders. He shook Mara violently until her hair spun like a dark veil about her shoulders.

"Goddamn you, Mara!" His voice was harsh and furious. "Must you always charge out of a room like a wild horse? You idiot, you could have broken both our necks! I'll teach you to—," and abruptly his hands flew up and cracked like a whip across her mouth and cheek.

Stunned, she stood with his one hand still cutting into the flesh of her shoulder. For a brief instant, his handsome florid face contorted and she thought he would strike her again. But at that moment, Celia called from the stairs, "Papa!"

Then suddenly Celia was beside them, her hand on their father's arm. "Papa, Mara's only sixteen!"

Then Mara was in her arms, her head tucked into Celia's shoulder, while the older girl upbraided her father. "I galloped myself when I was sixteen! How could you strike her? It was only an accident, Papa."

"By God, I've got a lot on my mind—our whole future and it's damned uncertain. My sisters Maggie and Julia and their husbands have it in their heads that I've disgraced the family. And they've made plans—," he broke off, then said coldly, "I've got too much on my mind to put up with Mara's stupid carelessness."

"I'm sorry, Papa," Mara said, refusing to cry. "I'll be more careful next time." As always, she was ruled by her tempestuous spirit, when she wanted more than anything in the world to please him!

"You always say that. See that you try harder," he said contemptuously before turning away from her. "Oh, Celia, I just learned that Will MacAdam—you remember the Colonel's son—and his associate are coming into town from Houston and I have to meet them at the train. They'll come to the Ames wedding with me. Julius will drive you, your Aunt Felice and Mara to the wedding and I'll meet you there." Without another look at his youngest daughter he went into the library.

As always, Mara had pushed back tears. White-faced and mortified, she retired with Celia to their big bedroom where Celia bathed her sister's reddening face with a cool cloth. "You know he really didn't mean to do that, Mara, darling," Celia comforted her. "It was purely reaction and surprise and he *is* terribly worried for all of us. We really don't know what the future holds and I'd hate to have to go live with Aunt Maggie or Aunt Julia."

"I won't have that opportunity, I'll wager," Mara said dryly. "They'd never offer me a home. I wonder what plans the aunts are making." Mara felt a great uneasiness over this information her father had just imparted.

Ashworth had another sister, Bonnie Ashworth, who had run away to Houston, the same city in the far Southwest where Colonel William Hunter MacAdam had gone years ago to recoup his fortunes. It had happened before Mara was born when Aunt Bonnie had been in her early teens. She had left under mysterious circumstances, and the family rarely mentioned her and then only in the most disparaging terms. Mara remembered once Aunt Maggie saying she had a letter from an old schoolmate who now lived in Houston.

"She said she saw Bonnie driving in a gorgeous carriage and it's rumored she owns interests in businesses and hotels. Do you suppose the featherbrain could possibly have married money?" Aunt Julia had laughed scornfully. *"Not Bonnie, or we'd have heard from her. I, for one, hope never to lay eyes on her again."*

Celia and Mara had talked often about their Aunt Bonnie. If what Aunt Maggie had said was true, she was evidently prospering, a fact that sat poorly with the stiff-necked sisters and their stuffy husbands, who attended church religiously while cutting the throats of lesser men in their business dealings. Or so Mara had heard Lucinda Ames whisper laughingly two months ago at the Westons' social, just when she thought Mara couldn't hear.

Mara had hidden her own smile to disguise just what she thought of her hypocritical aunts and uncles and their dealings in stocks and bonds. Mara remembered the countless times she and Celia had been invited to their childless homes, where they had indulged Celia immoderately while remarking on Mara's misfortune to have inherited her brunette mother's physical traits, rather than the coppery hair of her father.

"Her disposition, too," Julia had commented, looking at Mara. Then cuttingly, "Mad as a hatter and wild as a march hare, more's the pity. Sometimes I think she's just like Bonnie, God forbid!"

Though without meaning to, her aunts had done Mara a favor, for they had taught her not to cry; they had made her too proud to cry, despite her volatile nature. Mara was grateful for that, but it did not make her like them any better. The aunts knew, of course, of their brother's antipathy to the child and it strengthened their own, as it had Aunt Felice's. They never missed a chance to belittle or berate Mara and she avoided them whenever she could.

Now as Mara looked out over the enormous Ames salon, where the guests were still streaming in, she saw the aunts, their glorious hair piled high and gleaming richly in the candlelight that Lucinda Ames had chosen to use instead of her father's newest installation, electricity. They were smiling broadly at their companions as they seated themselves not too far from their brother. There was an empty seat beside Ashworth, just one.

Mara hesitated. Did she dare take it and try to make amends with him? A very tall broad-shouldered man was seated on his other side. She would risk it! He *might* smile at her and then—

"Mara, you'll have to sit elsewhere," he said coldly, looking up at her. "Will and I are waiting for John Halloran, Will's associate, to join us." Mara remembered Will MacAdam vaguely. Now the young man glanced at her sharply with narrowed eyes. Then he smiled, radiating a deep inner fire that puzzled her. She was drawn to his warmth and smiled back shyly.

Still she shrank away and returned to the rear of the room as Celia's expert fingers swept into Mara's favorite, Chopin's *Waltz in C Sharp Minor*. Ordinarily, this flashing, soaring music would bring goosebumps along her arms, but not this time. She sank into a seat beside strangers.

Why can't he forgive me? she wondered for the thousandth time as her mind fled from the elaborate ceremony that was soon to begin.

* * *

Looking back through her childhood, it seemed to Mara that her father must have resented her long before she was born, because Celeste had been so ill during her pregnancy. Mara had compounded her illness by arriving breech and a few weeks prematurely. Celia told her their father had not left their mother's side after he finally returned from one of his long buying trips abroad. Then his beautiful French wife had died giving birth to Mara.

Though Celia had been only three at the time, her memory was phenomenal and her questioning of Aunt Felice had reinforced it. Then in response to Mara's persistence over the years, the truth had slowly surfaced.

The doctor and two white-clad nurses had worked feverishly to save her. Celeste had screamed papa's name, "Archer!" over and over during Mara's agonizing birth, and Celia, crouching at the door, had heard it fade at the end to a gasp. Aunt Felice, who was barely seventeen, had stood by, her face white.

Ashworth had acted like a madman. When they showed Mara to him, he turned away, refusing to look at her. But Celia, who crept in unnoticed, had stared in wonder at her baby sister.

As the nurse held the baby to him Celia, in her child's voice, had cried, "Oh, Papa—do look! She's pretty, prettier than my dollie. Papa, what shall we name her?"

Aunt Felice had tried to shush her, but Ashworth flung himself away, blurting over his shoulder, "Name her whatever you like, Celia. She's cursed me by her coming." He paused, wheeled about and peered down into the small face, then quoted low, "Call her Mara, for the Almighty hath dealt bitterly with me. I went out full, and the Lord hath brought me home again empty, hath testified against me, hath afflicted me." With a short, derisive laugh, he was gone.

Celia told Mara that for a long week their father had stayed drunk and red eyed. Even during the funeral he swayed, his face set like a stone. Then in less than a month, he was gone on another long buying trip to Europe to buy more of the exquisite furniture, rugs, silver and crystal for *Ashworth's*. Often he would be gone as long as six months. This time he stayed nearly a year, leaving

Celia and Mara in the care of Aunt Felice and the two
starched nurses.

Celia, who adored her papa, said Mara was her only
comfort—Mara and Pleasance's tender, dark-faced family.
Pleasance and her late-in-life child, Sudie, and her tall,
black husband, Julius, had run the Ashworth house for
years, since long before Archer Ashworth had married Celeste Bonheur. Julius had been with him since childhood,
before the war, thirty-six years ago. Sudie was just Mara's
age. They played together and sewed the doll dresses Mara
designed. Mara loved her and her parents dearly.

Celia grieved but briefly for her mother, for she was so
taken with Mara, wheedling the nurses into letting the
two little sisters share a room. Like a tiny mother, she
would check Mara's covers and soothe her infant tears.

Aunt Felice had been short with her about this behavior
and muttered, "Celia, you are too young to worry so. Your
mama would not like it and neither would your papa."

But when Ashworth returned at last from Paris, Celia
was past four and acutely aware when he went out night
after night, returning late to tiptoe into their room and
kiss her cheek. She said she still remembered the strong
smell of whiskey and expensive perfume that always woke
her. When she was older, Mara asked if their papa had
kissed *her*, too. Celia evaded the direct question, but Mara
knew the answer. Her papa never kissed her if he could
avoid it.

On her thirteenth birthday Mara had daringly clasped
him to her, and he had brushed her cheek quickly before
striding away. It was on that birthday that she found her
name in the Bible, in the Book of Ruth, and she read what
her father had quoted when he named her that August day
long ago. She wept on finding the meaning of her name.

As she grew she became increasingly aware of her father's and her Aunt Felice's hostility toward her. And
through the years, Celia grew more and more protective,
standing between Mara and their father's coldness, as well
as the chastisements of Aunt Felice, who was not averse to
slapping the child.

And while Mara matured, the cauldron of emotion that
seethed in her was carefully curbed. She was volatile, impetuous, quick to anger, quicker to forgive and starved for

her father's love. Yet she was forced to hide it all in the
presence of her father, his sisters and brothers-in-law and
Aunt Felice. Or, at least, to hide it as well as she could.

Her heart ached increasingly as the years passed for she
loved and admired everything about her father, his bluff,
hearty ways, his burnished hair and sidewhiskers, the lux-
uriant bright mustache, his twinkling blue eyes and his
ability to win everyone's friendship. And Mara yearned for
the attention he gave so freely to Celia.

Sometimes, when Mara caught him staring at her, she
imagined she saw unwilling love creeping through the obvious animosity. He always swiftly averted his head when
she looked at him searchingly. Once, she chanced to see
him in a parlor mirror watching her intently for some moments, but she could not define the strange and powerful
emotions that coursed across his handsome face.

And while he ignored Mara, Ashworth was inordinately
proud of Celia's accomplishments, particularly her degree
from the finest finishing school in Richmond—and from
which only this spring Mara had also graduated with honors. But Ashworth was almost vain regarding Celia's
great musical talent that manifested itself exquisitely on
the huge, polished Steinway which stood beside tall windows in a special room set aside especially for Celia's practice.

The piano had been their mama's and Mara longed to
play it, too. Even Aunt Maggie and Aunt Julia grudgingly
conceded that Celeste Bonheur Ashworth had been a genius at the piano. But Ashworth and Aunt Felice had said
no to Mara; only Celia had inherited her mama's talent. So
Mara took up the needle and set her burning creative instincts to designing clothing. She began with doll dresses
and had taught Sudie, her playmate, to sew. By the time
she was twelve, Mara was making baby clothes as gifts
for family friends. She was grimly pleased when they
beseiged her for more.

Now she looked at Celia in her pale blue silk dress with
the handmade pink silk roses along the side and the delicate shirring over the small, piquant bustle. Mara had
made that elegant dress, and designed it, too. Sudie's dark

nimble fingers had worked with her on the many delicate pleats and the dozens of tiny tucks.

Thus Mara had proved she could now design and make even women's dresses. She had a thick portfolio of designs which she kept tucked secretly away at the bottom of a bureau drawer.

And her father had no idea that Mara had designed and made Celia's dress. Earlier he had complimented Celia on its loveliness, and Celia and Mara had exchanged triumphant glances. Celia was going to tell him at dinner tonight of Mara's sorcery. Then he would look at Mara, his eyes shining and . . .

Mara was suddenly aware that the ceremony was drawing to a climax, and as she listened to the beautiful words her heart sank slightly. *Papa loved Mother too much—too much to ever forgive her death. But somehow, someway, I must make him love me for myself. I swear it!* She had sworn it a thousand times before. After all, she was half her mother's child, and surely, surely he would come to realize it.

Mara was torn from her dreaming by the sight of the smiling couple coming arm in arm up the aisle between the chairs that filled the Ames salon. She flashed a look at Celia to find her older sister smiling fixedly.

Then, in a hubbub of activity, the chairs were folded and dispersed by a swarm of servants and the reception began in the great dining room, spilling over into the now cleared salon once more. A crystal bowl of iced champagne sat at either end of the long dining room sideboard, and on the vast, gleaming mahogany table towered a white cake decorated with hundreds of pastry rosebuds. Lucinda and David cut their cake by candlelight.

Lucinda's father, standing flushed and prideful nearby, had been a widower for several years, with only his daughter to lavish his love upon. He chose to live in the city to give his daughter all the social advantages Richmond afforded. And Richmond afforded young men like David Donellan, whose impeccable family also owned a great deal of farmland and rental properties in the city. The Donellans were old-line Virginians, as old as the Ashworths, proud of their lineage and seeking to add to it. Robert Ames was very pleased by his daughter's marriage.

The young couple would leave after the reception to board the luxurious train for New York, where they would enjoy their honeymoon.

Now Mara turned and saw Frances Bradford, who though no older was much more sophisticated, with her hair up and wearing an adult long dress, complete with bustle and bow in back. A boy was hanging over her hopefully. Mara reached back and surreptitiously felt her own firm but unobtrusive backside. Oh, she could tear the big taffeta bow out of her long, curling dark hair and stamp on it! The dress itself was bad enough. A white muslin skirt came only to the calf of her legs. The big bertha collar was childish and the big sash tied in a bow in back was just like a toddler's. Here she was, nearly seventeen and still wearing a bow and a short dress because Aunt Felice had arbitrarily decided she was still too young! Mara looked over at her papa, but there was no resentment against him in her heart, even though he could have abolished all of Aunt Felice's edicts at any time.

Just looking at him she felt a thrill of pride. He stood so straight, shoulders squared, head high. He would not bow to the so-called shame of bankruptcy. Aunt Maggie had said Papa was a poor businessman, an inept merchant, and to his great annoyance, she had said it more than once in his presence. Recently she and Papa had quarreled about it at Aunt Maggie's house until Uncle Bob had soothed his wife down and turned the conversation elsewhere. Uncle Bob had a receding hairline and mild manners, and his gray eyes twinkled in contrast to his fiery, red-haired wife. Mara almost liked Uncle Bob.

Now Papa was talking with two younger men. Again Mara recognized Will MacAdam, who had been sitting beside Papa. He was the son of Archer Ashworth's old commander in Lee's Army of Virginia in 1863 and 1864. Through the years, Ashworth talked often of Colonel William Hunter MacAdam, Senior. He was one of his idols and Ashworth could never praise him enough. Mara remembered now that the Colonel had died only three months ago, and her father had sorrowfully told the girls that the doctor had called it heart failure. He had lingered a day after he was struck, but nothing the doctors did could save him. When he finally received the news of his friend's death Ashworth was despondent for several days.

Mara noted the Colonel's son and his friend both had thick black hair and their faces were burned brown by the sun. On their feet, and Mara registered the fact with incredulity, were highly polished boots. Boots with high, narrow insteps and heels at a formal wedding!

Then she realized her father was obviously deeply interested in what the two were saying. As Mara watched, Aunt Maggie and Aunt Julia and their husbands joined them. The conversation grew more animated, and Mara saw with relief that her father was laughing, the tension so long in his face having vanished.

Her eyes swung to Celia, who was now sipping champagne and bantering with the men who swarmed about her. Her eyes met Mara's and there was anguish in them. Mara walked slowly to her sister, holding a crystal plate with some of the feathery white cake on it. Two young men viewed her intrusion with disfavor but Celia greeted her warmly.

"Mara, darling, you know Ray Kenley and Britton Campbell?"

Ignoring their coolness, Mara smiled at them with wide-eyed naiveté, trading smoothly on the little girl image that Aunt Felice encouraged.

Celia did not mask her agony when her eyes touched her sister, for Mara was where old secrets went to die. For her father's and the aunts' aversion to her through the years had made her extremely close-mouthed, which was an odd contradiction in an impulsive nature.

So she stuck by Celia's side until Archer Ashworth and his two companions left the aunts and came toward the two girls. Celia continued to sip her champagne, smiling and hiding her heartbreak.

Ashworth nodded to Campbell and Kenley and said jovially, "Celia, you recall William Hunter MacAdam, the son of Colonel Will, my commander during the war? Remember when he came to dinner during his holidays from the University of Virginia? He's in business now in Houston and doing very well. This is his associate, John Halloran."

"Of course," Celia smiled and automatically extended her hand. Kenley and Campbell excused themselves after introductions and left the five of them together. Mara noticed that Aunt Julia and Aunt Maggie were looking at Halloran and MacAdam from across the room, with what could only be described as smug satisfaction and pride.

Mara remembered Will MacAdam more clearly now, though it had been over eight years. A tall, tanned boy with penetrating eyes the color of ice, he had paid the eleven-year-old Celia much attention, treating her as though she were a grown-up lady. It was behavior that had pleased her inordinately and caused her to put on airs for a time.

Then, as she was introduced by name, Mara glanced up at his companion and sudden shock coursed through her. His eyes were gleaming black and fastened on her face boldly, with appraisal. He was more than six feet two, for her father and Will were a fraction shorter, and his finely tailored suit showed a body latently powerful and beautifully proportioned. John Halloran was handsome in a rough sort of way. His narrow nose had a slight hump in the middle and there was a thin scar, pale against his heavy tan, that ran from the outer corner of his right eye almost to his upper lip. It gave his face a rakish, yet somehow sinister look, accenting the cynicism in the polished, alert eyes. As Mara stared, unable to tear her eyes away, a slight smile tipped the corners of his mouth and the scar vanished in a crease.

She realized suddenly that she had met with a man who saw her as a woman, not a child. Further, she had the uncomfortable feeling that her short dress revealed too much of her slender legs, that the tumble of long thick hair down her back was better suited to the boudoir and that her thin lace and silk blouse was much too tight across her uptilted breasts.

"Will and John are to be guests of your Aunt Maggie and Uncle Bob," Ashworth was saying. Then to MacAdam, "It's a real pleasure to see you again, son, and I'm glad to know you're prospering."

Mara looked studiously at Will MacAdam to avoid John Halloran's amused eyes. She had often heard Papa regretting that the big, darkly handsome Colonel William MacAdam had been ruined during reconstruction and had left Richmond with his three children the year Mara was born, his wife having died two years before. And the Colonel had recouped his fortunes several times over in a variety of enterprises in Houston, long before his death three months ago. The son was evidently following in the father's footsteps.

Ashworth seemed in unusually high spirits as he went on, "The boys have come to Richmond on a buying trip. You know, Celia, Will and John have two large stores in Houston that carry every type of merchandise. Besides that, they have interests in lumber and own two sawmills. They deal in real estate and development as well." He was frankly admiring as he said to Will, "You're a chip off the Colonel—not even reconstruction could defeat your father, Will."

"No. The Colonel was one of a kind," Will replied, and Mara was aware that his eyes had gone from Celia to her, betraying a strange look that she could not define. She only knew it warmed her inexplicably. He added, "The Colonel was a gentleman of the old school and a rare individual." Mara was to learn that all the MacAdams called their father "the Colonel."

"I'm sure he was. Papa sings his praises still," Celia said perfunctorily as Mara maintained an innocent stare.

John Halloran's big hand closed suddenly over her elbow and she could feel its hard warmness through the lace that covered her arm as he firmly propelled her forward.

"May I get you a glass of champagne, Miss Ashworth?" Then once they were out of hearing from the others, " 'Call me Mara, for the Lord hath dealt bitterly with me,' eh?" She was amazed. He certainly didn't look like a Bible scholar. "Those eyes of yours confirm it, but your smooth face and that fraudulent little-girl dress make liars of them." He looked pointedly at her piquant breasts under the innocent young silk.

Her eyes flew to his tanned face and she rode her sudden flare of anger tightly. "My Aunt Felice insists I'm too young for callers and until I'm seventeen—"

"That can't be far away."

"August, not that it's any of your business, Mr. Halloran."

He laughed deeply and quietly. "Oh, yes it is, Mara. You

attract me mightily. I think you're a tiger in a lamb's
clothing."

She attempted to jerk her arm away, but his fingers bit
through the lace in an iron grip and she was steered forcibly to the polished dining room table where guests were
thronging about the bridal couple.

"Furthermore, I must confess you're the most desirable
child I've ever seen," he continued. The rumbling drawl
was disarming despite the cynicism in his wary eyes. As
she looked into them, her anger rising steadily, he winked
broadly at her and said to the servant, "Two glasses of
champagne, please."

"I'm not allowed to drink champ—"

"Shhh. Aunt Felice, the lynx, is back in the salon with
your society aunts. She'll never know. And your papa
doesn't seem to pay you any attention at all."

This apt observation turned her anger to fury and she
seized the glass, spilling a drop or two before she could
steady her hand. She gulped half a glass without stopping.
The wine stung all the way down and she stifled a cough,
aware that her face was flushing. Turning slightly, she
downed the rest in three rapid swallows. His laugh was
low and a little rough as he took another glass from the
waiter and handed it to her after she put the empty one on
the table. She took it and stared at him defiantly, chin up.

"And so, on the magic day in August, you put up your
hair, let down your skirts and cinch your waist to the
width—," he paused and his voice warmed, "of my hand,
eh?" The scar disappeared in the crease of his smile.

"I certainly shall!" She spoke with restrained violence.
There was a momentary silence between them while the
champagne, the first in her life, found its way to her
tongue. With sudden and honest humility, she blurted, "I
hate wearing these stupid, childish dresses and a damned
bow in my hair." There! She had cursed, like a common
streetwalker! But on ran the words. "Aunt Felice should
have let me put up my hair at fifteen. She let Celia do it
then."

She slanted a sooty look at him from under her thick
lashes as she took a slower, more sedate sip from the fresh
crystal glass. He was at least twenty-eight or perhaps even
thirty, much older than she and very sure of himself. In-

deed, he looked as though he had seen much—too much—
and none of it had surprised or shocked him. His eyes held
a knowing look, an intensely wary expression, and there
was something else in their black depths—deep and hurtful—that stirred her sympathy unwillingly. How could
that be when he so enraged her? Her only certainty was
that this man was different from any she had ever met before.

He looked down at her and smiled again. "Perhaps your
Aunt Felice is jealous of you. She may even fear you.
You're very beautiful, Mara, and for beautiful women, the
world holds special dangers, some worse than vindictive
aunts."

Mara was astonished at the sudden kindness in his voice
as he lifted the narrow-stemmed crystal glass. His eyes
twinkled now.

"But I'm not," she said quickly, disarmed. "Celia's the
beautiful one."

He turned and looked back across the room to where
Celia was now talking with only Will MacAdam. Halloran's gaze was speculative. Celia looked white and
strained, and it seemed to Mara there was a hint of shock
in her face.

"Yes," Halloran said slowly, "she's beautiful, too—but
not as beautiful as you. She lacks your fire." He finished
his champagne and shrugged. "Though, even so, I imagine
your sister has encountered dangers that could hurt her,
too."

David, Mara thought and was suddenly silenced. She
looked down into the gold liquid in her glass, with bubbles
rising like glitter.

"Then you have an idea of the dangers that await you,
eh?" he asked shrewdly. "Ah, well, perhaps by August
you'll develop claws, a fine defense against the world."

At a loss, Mara looked across at David and his bride
where they were laughing with an admiring circle of
young people. "They're beautiful people," she said rebelliously, "and I'll warrant the world holds nothing but pleasure for them."

"They're married, aren't they?" he asked, mockery in
the question.

"Of course. That's why—"

"They'll be miserable in a short time."

Mara looked up in astonishment to find those gleaming black eyes hard as obsidian. His lip curled in contempt. What had lurked in his eyes was now masked by something kin to hate and certainly disgust.

"But they'll probably live happily—"

"Ever after?" He laughed with genuine amusement. "You are indeed a child if you think that. Marriage is for fools. And after you've lived a little longer, you'll see some miserable ones. God knows, I have."

"I assume you're married and speak from experience?" Mara asked recklessly. The champagne was potent. It was disappointing to her somehow, to think John Halloran was married and unhappily so.

He laughed again, a laugh compounded of contempt and cynicism. "Indeed I am not, Mara. I've managed to avoid some of the most remarkable snares set out for the unwary male. I find life very satisfactory without having to chain myself to one woman and be forced to watch her change into a shrew and a termagant and perhaps worse—a drunk, while she drives me to drink."

"I think you're a—a—"

"Cynic? You bet your life I am. Marriage is not for me. I've seen what marriage does to people."

"You're denying all the good things—tenderness and loving responsibility, sharing and kindness—" She broke off. He was a spoiler and for a moment she had almost liked him!

He looked at her sharply. "Well, don't cry about it. Just take my advice and enjoy life without tying yourself to a man. I've told you, you're beautiful, enough so to make your own rules. And when you live life by your own rules, instead of society's, you can find a remarkable lot of tenderness and kindness outside of matrimony. Here, waiter, may we have another glass of champagne, please?"

"Oh, I shouldn't! I can't—," she began, but he put her slender fingers around the narrow stem.

"You're getting only a slight jump on August, Mara. And this is by way of celebrating more than one event. Since you and your family will be coming to Houston soon—"

"*What?*"

"You didn't know?" His brows lifted and his smile hid the thin scar. "Your Uncle Bob Robertson wrote Will and me several weeks ago, shortly after the Colonel's death. We knew Robertson because of his lumber interests in East Texas. He asked us to look around for a store for your father since he would be going into business in Houston. He further said your Aunt Maggie and Aunt Julia would appreciate our introducing Mr. Ashworth to the business community and . . . ah, the better people in our city. Perhaps we'll even have the pleasure of escorting all of you to your new home."

So this was the plan Aunt Maggie and Aunt Julia had in mind! Yet her father had looked alert and interested when she'd observed him talking with these young men. More than that, he had looked hopeful, a look that had been missing from his face for nearly a year.

"No, I didn't know, Mr. Halloran. And you both came to Richmond in the belief you would escort us to—to Houston?"

"Not quite," his smile grew sardonic, "though that would be an additional pleasure. Actually, we came here on a buying trip for our own stores in Houston. It happened to coincide with the sale of *Ashworth's.*" He set his empty glass on the gleaming mahogany table. "Strange, too," he mused, "for Will and I usually buy in New York, but he was quite determined about purchasing in Richmond this time. He has a lot of relatives here, you know. Cousins by the dozens and some aunts and uncles, all of whom are making a great to-do over us, with suppers and socials planned for the next two weeks."

"My father's bankrupt," Mara said flatly. "Everything we have is to be sold at auction the end of this month, and Papa won't have enough money to go to Houston, or anywhere else for that matter—much less buy a new store there." She set her untasted third glass of champagne carefully on the table.

"Bob Robertson and Abel Quayne and their wives plan to invest in your father's new venture, they informed us. Will and I found a store in Houston that Quayne and Robertson purchased very reasonably for your father, including all the stock in it. It's on Travis Street, one of our main thoroughfares."

Mara's head was spinning from both the champagne and the frightening news. She knew Aunt Maggie and Aunt Julia were mortified over their brother's failure and now she realized how sorely. They were making plans to rid Richmond of all traces of their embarrassment. Weeks ago Aunt Julia had said, *I cannot and will not stand seeing you, our brother—and your daughters and that sister-in-law—hat in hand, in worn-out clothing, subsisting on us or on the charity of our friends for the rest of your lives.*

"Does Papa know about this?"

"Of course. We were talking of it—and very pleasantly—before we joined you and your sister. I assumed you both knew about it as well." Then with a touch of mockery, "You'll like Houston. It's growing and there's a lot of social life there, too. Though it's all somewhat johnny-come-lately compared to Richmond's."

Still stunned, Mara said, "This sounds like the aunts—and the uncles," and she looked at her companion with ill-concealed bitterness. "No, Celia and I didn't know about it. I suppose Papa will tell us in his own good time, but I appreciate your informing me."

"You're welcome," he said solemnly, but amusement again colored the alert black eyes. "I should think you'd be delighted to know that your father is going to get a new start." He laughed aloud then, adding, "And when he makes a success of his store, he can buy your aunts and uncles out and thumb his nose at them."

Mara managed a wan smile at the picture Halloran had conjured up. But then she thought worriedly, her father would have to change his ways if he were to succeed. Aunt Julia said he had bought too much merchandise and sold it too cheaply. Then she silently scolded herself. What did Aunt Julia know of merchandising? She recalled Aunt Maggie's remarks that he wasn't innovative and was slow to modernize his merchandise, but what did *she* know? Oh, she ached for her father afresh; loving and admiring him as she did, it was hard for her to see where he could have failed in anything. *Besides, she had her own rich dream of success.*

"I'm going back to Celia," she said abruptly. Then as an afterthought, "Thank you for the champagne. If Aunt Felice had seen me—"

"But she didn't and don't tell her. And when you're seventeen, I'll come calling and bring you a whole bottle of fine French champagne and we'll celebrate—in Houston." He bowed slightly, his tanned face with the rakish scar now quite sober.

As she walked away she realized he was a little frightening, and a bit too wise and cynical. Worse, he could see right through her, and she had the feeling he saw through others, too. He knew she was neither naive nor childish and that her heart burned with so many nameless desires. Compelled to look back, she turned to see him bowing gracefully over Lucinda Donellan's hand.

As she looked ahead at Celia, the realization that their life in Richmond would soon be over struck her like a blow and her breath shortened. Her sympathies were mostly for her father; he loved Richmond so—how would he ever manage in a strange city like Houston? But the champagne glow lingered and in the secret reaches of her restless heart there was a dim spark of relief. *For now the dream was taking form.*

Chapter 2.

◇ MARA was quiet during the buggy ride home. She wanted to confide in Celia, but she sensed that their father had not yet told either her or Aunt Felice, and Mara knew he wanted to do so in his own way. She had forgotten Celia's plan to tell him of her dress and thereby achieve his admiring approval of Mara.

And that night, over supper, he did tell them. First he had talked of the wedding. "Celia, you never played better in your life, nor looked more beautiful. The piano music was the most memorable thing about the wedding, my dear." He paused, then his deep voice fell lower. "You know, I think I can stand to see everything go at auction but your mother's beautiful piano. It can never be replaced—not even if I make a million dollars in—" He broke off, looked at Celia searchingly, then slowly, "I must tell all of you something. We are moving to Houston in about two weeks."

Aunt Felice gave a small cry, but Celia only stared at him uncomprehendingly. Mara looked at her plate intently. Pleasance's fresh hot rolls were being served by her husband, Julius, with his customary dignity, but he, too, stopped at her father's words, his eyes widening.

"I have put off telling you until everything was completed. Your Aunt Maggie and Aunt Julia and their husbands have kindly decided to invest in another store for me, provided we go to Houston where I can get a fresh start, just as the Colonel did so long ago. And who knows? I may duplicate his success."

"And where we won't be an embarrassment to them!"

Celia burst out angrily. "So this is what they had planned, Papa, to make us leave town! I think it's despicable!"

"No, my dear. They're very generous. And what they say is true. Everyone in Richmond knows I've failed here, and even if they set me up in another store, the town would expect me to fail again." He paused, his eyes appealing to his older daughter. "So you see, Celia, dear, it's much better than staying here with everyone knowing and feeling sorry for us and looking down on us with—God help me!—pity." His face was more florid than usual and his eyes were red.

Mara knew he had been drinking heavily before dinner. It took courage to tell them that they must leave their beloved home, stripped of the luxury they had known all their lives. She grieved silently, thinking of her mother's piano. What would Celia do without it? It was part of all their lives, even Mara's, who had never been allowed to learn to play it.

There ought to be some way to save *that*, she thought as the others talked. Just that one piece could make a faraway new place more welcoming, more like home. The desire to save that piano tore at her, an almost physical pain. It was big and gleaming, and the tone was rich beyond measure, striking deep reverberating chords in the heart of any listener. But what could she do with no money of her own?

"I hope you'll be brave, Celia, about leaving all your friends," Papa was saying slowly. "And Felice, I know it will disrupt your life." Then with a brief glance at Mara, "It won't matter so to Mara. She's too young to care."

Mara looked at him, her heart in her eyes, and thought, *Oh, Papa, I care. I care!* But she knew she was merely an appendage, to be taken along not because she was loved but because she was of the family. It was Celia who had so many friends in Richmond. So many suitors. Not that their father ever thought one of them worthy of Celia. *If he could only come to love me just half as much as he loves Celia*, Mara thought with silent intensity.

That night in their high, broad bed, Celia and Mara talked of the move, and neither of them was reconciled to it. In little more than a week the auctioneers would come to the house, and all the exquisite pieces of fine French furniture their mother had brought from New Orleans and that had been in the family for generations would go to the highest bidder, to strangers, and the profit would go to *Ashworth's* creditors. Aunt Maggie and Aunt Julia had said virtuously that it was only fitting that Ashworth should pay for his mistakes.

"Mara, I'm sorry I didn't tell Papa at dinner you made my beautiful dress. But I was so shocked and the news so upsetting, I'm afraid it wouldn't have had the proper effect on him."

"It doesn't matter anymore. I don't care whether you ever tell him or not. I'll make more and one day he'll see that I'm not so young and useless, that I have some talent. Then maybe he'll really see me as a person of some worth."

Then Celia told her a strange thing. "Will MacAdam asked me to marry him."

Mara was dumbfounded. "How—precipitate!" was all she could say.

"He said he had a palatial new home in Houston and he needed a Virginia aristocrat to preside over it. Love wasn't even mentioned. But worse than that, he watched me during the ceremony and afterward—he knew I was—he sensed I was in love with David. He even said so. He said, 'Why not marry me and enjoy wealth and social position as an antidote for a broken heart.' "

"What did you say to him?"

"No, of course. He's an arrogant, headlong man. The idea of proposing on the spur of the moment! Why, I scarcely know him, except for those holidays at our house so long ago."

"And you were a little girl then," Mara murmured. "But I remember he said you were a beautiful young lady. He treated you as if you were grown up."

"And I wasn't," Celia said heatedly, "and I let it go to my head like a silly goose."

"But not for long," Mara said comfortingly. Then tentatively, "He seems like a nice enough man and goodness knows he's handsome. Papa says he looks just like his pa, the Colonel."

"Yes, he never said a word about us going to Houston while we talked. But now Papa says he and that sharp-eyed John Halloran have even found a store for him in Houston.''

"Oh, yes," Mara cut in sarcastically. "John Halloran told me that Uncle Bob had written them about it weeks ago! That Aunt Julia and Aunt Maggie told MacAdam and him they'd appreciate it so much," her voice went up an octave as she mimicked Aunt Julia's affected speech, "if they'd introduce Papa to the business community and the best people."

"Oh, my God," Celia muttered, "is there no end to the humiliation our aunts will subject us to? As if Papa couldn't even do *that* on his own."

"They'll be paying for our train tickets," Mara said bitterly, "and likely they'll finance any new home we wind up in. They might as well take it on themselves to dictate all the terms."

"So, Mara, that man Halloran told you all that at the wedding and you didn't say a word about it to me?"

"I never had the chance," she replied defensively. "Besides, it was Papa's prerogative to tell you and Aunt Felice, not mine."

Celia sighed deeply. "I shouldn't feel so hateful about Aunt Maggie and Aunt Julia. They've always been so good to me, but not to you. I guess I've always held that against them, Mara."

"Don't," Mara said dispassionately. "It doesn't matter in the least to me that they think I'm a biological mistake on Papa's part."

Celia reached her hand across the broad bed to catch her sister's tightly. "Don't say that! Never say that, for what would I have done without you?"

Mara was suddenly awakened by a low moan and she roused fully to see Celia sitting up, her face in her hands. She reached out to touch her shoulder and found she was sweating profusely.

She whispered, "Celia, what is it?"

"Nothing," the reply was muffled. "I was dreaming and it woke me."

"Why are you crying? What did you dream?"

"Of David, of course," Celia whispered hopelessly. "He

was kissing me, caressing me. Then suddenly Lucinda was there and he turned away from me." Her voice broke.

Mara caught her hand. "Oh, Celia, he isn't worth it!"

"He and Lucinda are sharing those moments *I* dreamed of—," she cried, sounding strangled. "What an idiot I am. I was so hopeful he would want me again!"

Mara brushed her tumbling hair back and murmured, "You're going to forget about David, once we're—"

"I'll *never* forget about David," Celia interrupted passionately, then shivered as she added, "And I feel I shall never sleep again."

The younger sister swung her feet over the edge of the bed. "I'm going to get you a glass of milk with a teaspoon of honey in it," she said decisively and made her way through the moonlit room to the hall.

She had been prepared for total darkness in the narrow hallway, for she knew every nook, every step, in the big old house. But far down the hall, from Ashworth's room there emanated a glow.

He was up! So he was having trouble sleeping, too. As she neared the stairs she could dimly hear the rumble of his deep voice. Who was Papa with at this hour? It was so late! Daringly, she took a few steps toward the door. Was that Aunt Felice's thickened voice? Surely not! She tiptoed forward and peered into the room from the blackness of the hall.

Aunt Felice, her long dark hair swinging in tumbled profusion about her shoulders, was facing Mara's father. Her face was contorted with tears. "And I tell you, Archer, *I don't know.* Why must you accuse me and torment me with questions after all these years? I swear, if I knew I would have told you years ago," her voice broke and Mara drew back swiftly.

The young girl's instinct to keep her presence secret was strong. She should have made her way downstairs to the kitchen, but her bare feet were anchored to the warm, smooth floor of the hall. Aunt Felice was wearing a thin, revealing nightgown with no peignoir! And now she was sobbing noisily.

"Felice, don't carry on so. You'll wake the house." There was frustration and more than a little anger in his voice. He was fully clothed still, and an open book on the lamplit table attested to his occupation when Felice had come in on him.

Mara peeked quickly around the corner again to see her father gather Felice to him, her arms flying about him.

"Forget about *her*. Think of *me!*" she was gabbling as she pulled his head down to her tear-wet face, kissing him feverishly. As Mara watched, hypnotized, Felice pulled him to the bed that stood in the center of the room. For a moment she thought he would break away, then he followed her to the bed, and Felice began frantically pulling up her nightgown as she fell beneath him.

At the sight of Felice's naked thighs and her father's hand reaching for the dark V of curling hair between them, Mara turned and fled silently down the hall.

Her breast heaving with exertion, she paused at her bedroom door, remembering her errand. She looked back down the hall where the lamplight spilled faintly into the hall and shivered. Disgust and shock mingled with repugnance, her only coherent thought *Poor Papa!* Inexperienced as she was, she recognized that her Aunt Felice was rapacious. She would devour Archer Ashworth if she could. Mara had the distinct feeling that this was a circumstance that had often happened before.

She stepped quietly into the bedroom, closing the door softly. Celia sat in a rocking chair beside the moonlit window, looking out across the south gardens. She turned around to face Mara.

"I didn't get your milk," Mara blurted. "I saw a light in Papa's room, heard voices. Papa and Aunt Felice were there and—and—they were about to—Aunt Felice pulled up her gown and he— They were on the bed."

Celia laughed with a trace of mockery. "So they've been caught in the act at last." She did not bother to whisper as Mara had.

"You knew?" Mara was staggered.

"No, but I've suspected for over a year. I'm just thankful he doesn't want to marry her."

"Why didn't you tell me?" Mara asked accusingly.

"Because *I've* never caught them at it. I only suspected. Did they see you?"

"Of course not, thank God. And I'm not going back down

to get the milk. I'll get you a handkerchief and dampen it with cologne. Sometimes that helps."

"Never mind. Your experience has taken the edge off my nightmare," she said with a sardonic laugh. "So Papa and Aunt Felice are mating in his bedroom. How anticlimactic."

"I don't think it's anticlimactic," Mara said, slipping back into bed. "I think it's—awful."

"That's because you're so young."

"No, I'm not!" Mara retorted fiercely. "I can understand the act itself. You know that. I've even dreamed it, too. And I could understand Papa with someone lovely. But Aunt Felice was so wild. Like an animal. Worse than an animal in heat!"

"You must have seen a good bit," Celia remarked dryly.

"Enough." Mara glanced at the clock on the table beside her. In reflected moonlight she could see it was ten past two in the morning. "Come, Celia. You need sleep as badly as I do."

But she kept seeing Aunt Felice's naked, writhing body, and it was a long time before she slept again.

The days slipped by swiftly and the night before the auction was to take place, everything was in order. Aunt Maggie and Aunt Julia and their husbands had dinner in the Ashworth home for the last time. They were served with the fine china and gleaming sterling that would soon be gone. The aunts were, as usual, outspoken about the failure of *Ashworth's.*

"Archer, you know we could have bought everything in this house and given it back to you," Aunt Julia said severely, "but then we might as well have paid off all your creditors and set *Ashworth's* up in business again. Except that everyone in Richmond knows you failed. You'd never live it down." It was Aunt Julia who had said they would all stay at her house after the auction, until they took the train to Houston.

Now Ashworth's face reddened and his coppery mustache and muttonchop whiskers bristled. He started to speak but Aunt Maggie cut him off. Her ruddy pompadour shook with vehemence as she spoke.

"No, Archer, I know what you're going to say. But with

new associates and a whole new community to serve, you hopefully won't run up such bills. The store is already stocked, Will says, but when time comes to buy more, for heaven's sake don't buy such expensive merchandise."

"And for goodness's sake," Aunt Julia put in, "don't be afraid to try something new. You never would put cosmetics in *Ashworth's* and a lot of perfectly respectable women use them now," she finished virtuously. Her cheeks were an unusually healthy pink and so were her curved lips.

Uncle Bob looked at Ashworth with something near sympathy and remarked mildly, "I think you'll make a great success of it in Houston, Arch. Then you can pay us all off and laugh in our faces."

Aunt Julia and Uncle Abel looked at Bob sharply, but Robertson's face was bland. Of the four of them, Mara had long suspected Uncle Bob of being the only one with an ounce of compassion or humor.

She knew Papa wanted them to save the piano, but he was too proud to ask for anything. She was sure he hadn't asked for their help at all. Reluctant as their charity was, they had proffered it only to rid themselves of the specter of failure Ashworth had become.

Just as the aunts and uncles were leaving, a buggy rattled up the drive. John Halloran and Will MacAdam got out and headed for the porch. There were greetings all around, with Aunt Julia simpering about "Will's dear father" and how pleased she was that they had come to Richmond to buy for their own large stores.

The Colonel had enjoyed tremendous popularity in Richmond and his family was an old and honored one. When he was widowed and the carpetbaggers had taken over his cotton gins, the city as a body moved to help him. He had refused them all and took his children far away to Houston. The aunts knew he had become fabulously rich and now his son was rich and growing richer, so their respect knew no bounds.

"Our home is yours," Aunt Maggie was saying archly, "but don't you two stay out in that rented buggy too long. You'll need your sleep so you'll be rested when you go out to buy in the mornings. Not to mention all the parties at night that your charming relatives are having for you, Will."

"You're a most charming hostess, Miss Maggie," Will said, bowing graciously.

"We do appreciate your hospitality," John Halloran added, his smile white in the sunburned face.

"It's a pleasure to have you—," Aunt Maggie began, but Uncle Bob took her arm and steered her deftly down the porch steps to a chorus of good-byes. After they had left, Ashworth invited the two men in for a drink. Once inside they refused courteously.

"We really came by," John Halloran said with his rakish smile, "to take the ladies out for an ice cream at the parlor. It's a hot night."

Ashworth looked puzzled and Celia and Mara exchanged glances, while Aunt Felice smiled hopefully.

"You mean—Celia and Felice?" Ashworth asked.

"No," Halloran said, still smiling engagingly, "we mean Miss Celia and Miss Mara. No offense, Miss Bonheur, but we didn't think you'd care to go."

Felice, taken aback, said sharply, "But Mara's only a child. She can't go out at night with a man."

Mara looked at Aunt Felice with a wariness born the night she had witnessed her frantic seduction of Ashworth. Her feelings had since taken on another dimension, disgust combined with the fear that Felice could eventually become her stepmother if her father succumbed to her wiles. That would give her even more power over Mara's life.

"It's true you're still a child," her father said, swinging on the silent Mara accusingly. "You can't have callers until you're seventeen and even then, I—"

"Then perhaps you'll insist on going as chaperone, Miss Bonheur?" There was a cutting edge to John Halloran's words, and the distinct insinuation that she was forcing herself on him was inescapable. Mara had the pleasure of seeing color mantle her aunt's ivory face as the impression hit home.

"I—why, no. It's just that . . . ." She put a hand to her heavy coils of hair in a characteristic gesture of confusion.

"In heaven's name," Celia cut her off angrily. "It's only an invitation for ice cream, Aunt Felice!"

"And all children love ice cream," John Halloran said

mockingly. "You wouldn't deny this—*child*—an ice cream? I swear I'll treat her with all the care of an aged uncle."

Aunt Felice paled now under his icy stare and Papa said gruffly, "Go on, go on, you young things. But be back by ten."

Celia said somewhat coldly, "I ate a good bit of Pleasance's chocolate mousse."

"Ah, Miss Celia, a little lemon sherbet on top of the mousse," Will MacAdam smiled, "will make you sleep better. John and I want to tell you ladies something of your new home."

"Celia, it might be well for you to listen to these two. They have a way of making that faraway city look most attractive," Ashworth said, his smile returning.

"Very well," Celia said, but without enthusiasm.

"And we'll have them back well before ten, I assure you, Mr. Ashworth," Will MacAdam said solemnly.

"Call me Archer, Will," Ashworth said with his ebullient smile. "Maybe it will keep me from feeling so old."

As they started to leave, Aunt Felice hissed at Mara, "You sly creature. I'll bet you put him up to this at the wedding. I'll see you suffer for it."

John Halloran's hearing was acute. "Why, Miss Bonheur, you *do* wish to accompany us! We can't have you taking your disappointment out on a mere child. I insist you come along."

For the first time in her life, Mara saw Aunt Felice completely flustered and it was a heady feeling. But Felice gathered up her customary dignity.

"Uh, I didn't mean—no, no, Mr. Halloran, I'm really very tired. It's been a long day. I must retire." And under the merciless cynicism in Halloran's black eyes Aunt Felice fled.

Papa shrugged and bade them good night.

Mara hadn't said a word, but Halloran took her arm with an assurance that assumed her enthusiastic agreement. But in her silence Mara had been thinking furiously. This man was older than she and there was something about him that affected her powerfully. She was not so young that she did not recognize the heat that rose in her each time he was near and its sharp increase in intensity whenever he touched her. It blazed in her now, with his hand on her arm. She had been powerless, because of that heat, to demur when the invitation was issued. She recognized that she wanted, passionately so, to go with him, even for something as innocuous as ice cream. She was ashamed of her thoughts, and when he spoke again, she took refuge behind her alleged youth.

"What's your favorite ice cream, Miss Mara?"

In her calf-length white eyelet dress and the inevitable large taffeta bow tying back the mane of dark curly hair, she looked at him with the naiveté that was a caricature of innocence. "You choose, Mr. Halloran," she said, wide eyed and solemn. His answering laughter told her he was well aware of her charade.

There was a waning moon hanging languidly over the pine tops and stars were brilliant in the sky. In the buggy, MacAdam clicked to the horse, and the cooling breeze came as welcome relief.

As they rode toward the George Washington Ice Cream Parlor on Catalpa Street, the two men talked freely of Houston. The city was growing by leaps and bounds. Electricity was just being introduced. They had electric trolleys, and carbide lights lit the downtown streets at night. Telephones were rapidly being installed everywhere. Business was booming. Further, Galveston and the seashore were only an hour's train ride over a high trestle bridge to the island.

When they entered the ice cream parlor, Mara looked with already nostalgic eyes at the tall, gilt-framed mirrors that lined the walls, making the room appear endless. Little round marble-topped tables with heart-shaped wire chairs and wooden seats invited them to sit down and order. There was a familiar sweet smell in the room, and the electric lights were soft and welcoming. When would she ever see it again?

Behind the marble bar, a young man in a starched white uniform looked at them expectantly. When they had seated themselves, Celia and MacAdam at one small table, Halloran and Mara at another, a young girl in a long white dress with a frilled apron arrived to serve them.

Later, as they spooned up orange sherbet, Halloran asked, "Are you going to be at the auction tomorrow?"

"Yes. Mainly because I want to say good-bye to part of my life."

"I've been to auctions and they are not pleasant for the owners of the furniture. I should think you'd go stay with one of your aunts."

"My aunts are not very pleasant either," she said briefly. "And I want to see who gets our piano." Then with sudden passion, "That's the only thing I really, *really* care deeply about. It was Mama's, and Celia plays it so beautifully."

"Why don't your aunts and their husbands buy it for your sister?"

"The aunts have it in mind to punish Papa for his failure. And as part of that punishment everything has to go. We'll have nothing when we arrive in Houston, Mr. Halloran. Not a roof over our heads or even anything to put in any small house we might rent. But if I could cry, I would cry over the piano."

"*If* you could cry?" He looked at her and the black eyes were somber, holding that same strange wary look that seemed to hide hurt.

"I never cry, Mr. Halloran. My aunts taught me years ago that tears avail me nothing. They are childish and useless. No, I'll grieve, but I will not cry."

"You're a very adult almost-seventeen, Mara," he said reflectively. "You surprise me, which I hadn't thought possible. Not only are you beautiful, you're very intelligent."

"Thank you, sir," Mara said dryly, spooning up the last of her sherbet.

"I intend to know you better." He was laughing again and she suspected he was teasing her. "I warn you ahead that I'm a fly-by-night, and looked upon in some quarters as having a bad background—wrong side of the tracks and such. But I promise not to bore you."

"There'll be so many at my door, I'm sure you'll have to get in line, anyway," she said derisively. "Celia's the beauty in our family. Why aren't you seeking her favors?"

"Will's staked his claim on her," he drawled, "and besides you're far more provocative. Much more *my* type."

She flushed. This man was an impudent devil and she wondered briefly why she felt a reluctant admiration for him. *Perhaps*, she thought, *it's because he's a realist, like me, and knows that happy endings aren't inevitable for everyone.*

Later in their bedroom, Celia and Mara talked of them.

"That Will MacAdam may think he's going to court me in Houston, but he's wrong. He's domineering and arrogant, and he's far too observant."

"You mean because he knows about your feelings for David?"

"Yes. He spoke of it again tonight and practically told me I was a fool. And he had the nerve to say we'd be married the moment I changed my mind."

They fell silent, then Mara turned restlessly and said, "I'll never be able to go to sleep, knowing what's going to happen to all our belongings tomorrow. I keep thinking about the piano."

"Don't let that worry you," Celia said tightly. "Papa can rent one for me in Houston."

"A *rented* piano!" Mara said scornfully.

"Don't belittle it, Mara. We'll be lucky if we can rent a house and furniture."

Mara said nothing. She buried her face in the pillow and, despite dry eyes, smothered a sob.

By ten the following morning, the house was swarming with people. Celia and Mara sat in rented folding chairs near the back of the big Ashworth salon.

"Most of these men are agents," Celia whispered. "Men who have been commissioned by some of our *best* friends to buy for *them.*"

"How do you know?" Mara asked in astonishment, looking at the strange men in the crowd. There were several women among the other people they did not know, for the auction had been advertised in the papers.

"Papa said so. He says every piece, including all the furniture Mama brought from New Orleans, will be bought up by someone who knows us and who knows how priceless it all is."

"I wonder which of them will get the piano," Mara said bitterly. "The Ameses? Lucinda's often admired it and you know how she struggles to play." She thought briefly of Lucinda's spun-gold, fragile beauty and her clumsy hands on the piano.

"It's possible," Celia said unsteadily as the auction began.

They sat there for an hour, watching their beautiful possessions go, one by one, before a man in the rear spoke up loudly.

"When are you going to auction the piano?" He was a tall, thin man with a little black mustache, and he had bought up several of Celeste Ashworth's marble-topped mahogany tables and two of Archer's sculptured marble heads, one of Julius Caesar and the other of Robert E. Lee.

"The piano was sold early this morning," the auctioneer said briskly. "Now we have a four-poster cherrywood bed and all the matching pieces to go with it—"

"But we were all supposed to bid on it!" the man cut in angrily, and two or three other men echoed his words.

"Several things were purchased before the auction began," the auctioneer said coldly, "for prices well above what could be expected from any bidder. I used my own experience in judging the matter." He struck the lectern with his little gavel and said determinedly, "We now have the cherrywood four-poster, ladies and gentlemen . . ."

As the bidding began once more, Mara turned to Celia, "It's already gone."

"And I think the man with the black mustache was bidding for the Ameses," Celia said slowly. "Lucinda has admired Mama's marble-topped tables and Papa's pieces of sculpture. I thought—"

"No matter, the piano's gone," Mara said dolefully. "I wonder how much they paid for it?"

"It must have been a lot," Celia said bitterly. "That auctioneer, Mr. O'Hare, is a shrewd Irishman, Papa says. The best in the business."

The two girls left then, walking out of the house into the hot sunlight in the gardens.

"I hate to go to Aunt Julia's and Uncle Abel's and stay until we leave Monday morning. She'll harp at Papa constantly," Celia said.

The fragrance of roses came to them on the air, rich and sweet, evidence of a deep and luxurious summer.

"You hate it," Mara echoed. "She won't harp at just Papa. Half of it she'll pour on me. She *likes* you and even Aunt Felice gets along with her better than I do."

"At least it's only tonight and tomorrow night—then we'll be gone. You can stand that much."

"Just barely," Mara's laugh was hollow as they turned onto the path and walked past a flower bed that was riotous with larkspur, zinnias, nasturtiums, cornflowers and dozens more.

Late that afternoon, they all stood in the empty salon, their baggage around them, waiting for Aunt Julia's coachman to come and pick them up. Pleasance and Julius, surrounded by their own belongings, faced Ashworth, while Sudie's eyes searched out Mara's.

All their happy memories hung between them. The long hours they had played and sewn together were gone now. Sudie had become almost as deft with the needle as Mara and could keep a secret as tightly as Mara. Oh, how she would miss Sudie, Mara thought with an aching throat.

Julius's chin was thrust out at a stubborn angle and he burst out in an argument that had been going on for days.

"Mister Arch, I been workin' for you since before the war, boy an' man, an' I ain't lettin' you leave us behind."

Mara knew he had a cousin in Norfolk, but he had refused to contact him and the current understanding was that Aunt Julia's coachman would drop the three of them off downtown. Julius had refused to say where he was going or what he would do.

"But Julius, I've told you over and over—I'm broke! I can't *pay* you and Pleasance! I'll be living on the charity of my sisters and their husbands until the new store starts paying."

"I know that an' so do Pleasance. You done say it and so did Miss Julia, when she offered to pay me an' Pleasance more to come work for her."

"Mister Arch," Pleasance said hotly, "we ain't care about that. You can pay us when your new store gets you back on your feet."

Ashworth sat down on one of three large brass-bound trunks which the dray men were to pick up and haul to the railroad station for shipping.

"Pleasance," he said wearily, "I don't think Julia or Maggie will buy you three a ticket on the train. They hold all the pursestrings now."

"I'll talk to Miss Julia," Pleasance said, her voice shaking with anger. "She give me trouble, I'll pay her back myself. If there's work in Richmond, there's got to be work in that Houston place. Our Sudie feels the same as we do."

"Yes, ma'am, Mama! Yes, sir, Mister Archer." She said it to Ashworth, but her big dark eyes were still on her playmate.

Mara swallowed over the lump in her throat. It would be difficult for them without those three. Just last night Celia and Mara had agreed that they had no better friends in all the world than Pleasance, Julius and Sudie.

Aunt Felice moved restlessly and said, "Listen! I think I hear the carriage." She had long known that Pleasance, her daughter and her husband were sympathetic to Mara, who had heard her tell Ashworth not to aggravate Aunt Julia by interceding further on behalf of the servants. *Really, Archer, if Julia fancies having them as her servants, it might be wise to let them go.*

The knocker sounded and Julius went to the door. In a moment, three burly men came in and picked up the heavy trunks and two large packing cases. They made four trips into and out of the house, then they rattled off in their dray.

Ashworth, who had watched them load the trunks, turned to those left and said, "Well, there goes nearly everything we have in the world. So it's off to Houston." His face brightened. "I *will* make *Ashworth's* a name to reckon with in Houston. By God, I will!"

"Of course you will, Archer," Aunt Felice said warmly, smiling up at him.

"Mister Arch, if you feel that way, you oughtn't to have no worry about takin' me an' mine with you an' yours," Julius said grimly.

"You're right, Julius," Ashworth said with sudden vigor. Then with a sharp look at Felice, he added, "I'll tell Julia and Maggie I won't go unless Julius and his family go, too. After all, Julius and I were children together. And Sudie's grown up with Celia, and Mara, of course." Julius grinned broadly at his words, and Pleasance put an arm around Sudie and hugged her. "They've given me five hundred dollars to live on the first month we get there," Papa said ruefully, "with the promise of a stipend each month until I make the store pay, *and* I have to pay every penny back. You know, Julius, it could be months before I could pay you and Pleasance wages again."

"I ain't worried. Your credit's good with us, Mister Arch."

"Abel and Bob have paid for all the stock in the new store, too. So you see how little margin I have."

"We're goin' to Houston with you, Mister Arch," Pleasance said in an iron voice. "Come hell 'r high water, we're goin'."

As a result, Aunt Julia had two rooms in the attic aired out and made up for the three servants that evening. She did it with poor grace because she had hoped to secure the excellent services of Julius, Pleasance and Sudie for herself.

"I don't know how you've inspired such loyalty," she said jealously. "I've offered them twice what you've been paying them."

"Friendship means more than money, Julia," Ashworth replied.

"Humph. That's probably why you're in bankruptcy, brother. Abel will buy their tickets Monday morning. You've certainly undertaken a heavy responsibility. I just hope you can handle it." But her tone belied her expressed hope.

Aunt Maggie and Uncle Bob came for dinner that Saturday night and the whole family was together once more. Aunt Maggie told them her houseguests, John Halloran and Will MacAdam, had gone to dinner at the Jamesons', long-time friends of Colonel MacAdam and his family.

Julius, Pleasance and Sudie helped the Quayne servants in the kitchen, while many were the admonitions and much was the advice given Ashworth before the evening was over. Mara sensed that both the aunts and their husbands were anxious to rid themselves completely of the taint of failure clouding the old and respected name of Ashworth in their hometown.

And so the next two days at Aunt Julia's were miserable, for their admonishments did not stop after the first night. On the second, Aunt Maggie and Uncle Bob returned. This time their houseguests had gone out to dine at the Olympic Hotel with some old classmates of Mac-Adam from the University of Virginia.

The sisters and brothers-in-law were free again to discuss their brother's move, what they expected of him—and since the figures had just come in that Sunday afternoon—how little the auction brought.

All the furniture, Ashworth's four horses, the surrey and the carriage had brought only twenty thousand eight hundred dollars. The sale of the house, which Uncle Bob would handle for Ashworth after their departure, was estimated at being worth eighty thousand dollars, including the two acres on which it stood. The piano, which the auctioneer said had been purchased by a certain Mr. Smith, had brought a thousand dollars, more than any other piece of furniture. The Ashworths hadn't ever heard of Smith, but he had paid cash to the auctioneer and had the piano taken away immediately.

"All of it, even if the house sells as we hope, won't cover all your indebtedness, Archer," Aunt Julia said coldly as they settled themselves in her exquisitely appointed salon.

"Now, Julia," Uncle Bob spoke up, putting his pipe in his mouth, "I've told you—and Archer—I'm going to cover the rest of it. Bankruptcy won't be on his record. Archer can pay us back when times are better for him."

"He's going to have to pay back quite a bit when times are better for him," Julia said cuttingly. "Since we're financing his new venture entirely."

"Don't worry, Julia," her brother said bitterly. "I shall pay you all back with interest, you may be sure."

"Of course we will," Celia said swiftly. "I plan to teach music to augment our income."

The aunts laughed indulgently and Maggie said, "What a darling you are, Celia. Archer has a priceless treasure in you, dear. Thank God you received your education before the debacle."

Mara silently reflected once again on the fact that she, too, had received her education, graduating with even higher honors than her sister. She was grateful for that. She had her own secret plans for augmenting their income, too. The idea was so daring she hadn't the temerity to confide it even to Sudie or Celia.

"You know, of course," Abel Quayne said, puffing on his

expensive cigar, "we bought out the stock of the former owner of your new store. But I can tell you now we shipped a good bit of *Ashworth's* merchandise to it." Uncle Abel was portly and short and his thick hair was frosted with gray.

"And I took the liberty of adding a few items," Aunt Julia said smugly. "A few things ladies of real *quality* might buy. I duly put it on the bill you owe us."

"You're all so helpful," Archer Ashworth said with a crooked smile. "You have my immeasurable gratitude."

"You needn't be so sarcastic, Archer," Aunt Maggie said reprovingly. "After all, you're our dear brother. We *want* to help."

"Your dear brother has disgraced you," Ashworth said heavily. "And by this time tomorrow, I'll be gone and you can tell everyone I'm starting anew in Houston. That should take some of the curse off my failure."

"It will indeed," Aunt Julia said forthrightly. "You know well and good, Archer, it would never do for you and the girls to stay on here, down at the heel, and working for your old friends in some low job."

"Well," Abel Quayne said pedantically, "at least you're saved from having bankruptcy on your record. Bob has seen to that. You'll be starting anew without that black mark against you. And by the way, I've made reservations at the Houston Heights Hotel for you. You can stay there until you find a suitable house to rent."

"I repeat," Ashworth replied, "I'm deeply grateful."

"You'll be leaving at ten in the morning on the Santa Fe Rose. You may even enjoy it," Aunt Julia said with a slight frown at Uncle Abel. "After all, Abel insisted that we buy you first-class tickets on the Pullman car."

"Again," Ashworth said without expression, "I'm deeply grateful."

"And thank you for letting Pleasance, Julius and Sudie go with us," Celia said softly. Mara knew her sister was writhing even as she was, under these patronizing relatives.

"I really regret that," Aunt Julia said sharply. "Julius is a perfect butler and a good carriage man, too. He'd be of much better use here than in Houston." Then with a slight shudder, "Such an uncivilized place. I was reading only

yesterday in the *Richmond Inquirer,* two men actually engaged in a gunfight on one of the main streets downtown."
Then as an afterthought, "I do hope you and the girls can
find a house to rent that's far from the rougher element
that must make up most of the city, Archer."

"We'll be very careful, Julia," Ashworth said dryly.

"You must write us every week, Celia, and let us know
how things are progressing. And when your dear papa is
prospering, we may come to Houston to see you," Aunt
Maggie remarked.

Julia gave her a disdainful glance. "Go to that godfor-
saken part of the country? Never! You may, Maggie, but
not Abel and I."

"Speak for yourself, dear," Abel said with a dry chuckle.
"I'd like to see the city and that beautiful younger sister of
yours again, Bonnie, who everyone so carefully ignores
now."

Aunt Julia turned an ugly red. "Bonnie was a wild and
willful girl. We've never contacted her, nor she us. She's
forfeited her right to be a sister."

"But they say she's prospering, Julia," Abel persisted
with a grin, "and prospering is very important to you, isn't
it? You can overlook a lot of willful hell-raising for prosperity, can't you, my dear?"

"I heard only that once about her, Abel," Aunt Julia
said icily. "And besides, if she's prospering, no doubt she
met some unsuspecting man and married wealth." Then
in an undertone, "At least I *hope* she married him."

Mara's curiosity was again piqued. The aunt she and
Celia had in Houston would no longer be known as Ashworth, if this long-ago rumor was true. Whatever Bonnie
had done in Richmond, it had been awful enough to cause
Grandpa Ashworth to strike her from his will; even her sisters would not claim her. Mara felt certain she would like
Aunt Bonnie very much.

"John Halloran and Will MacAdam will be leaving at
the same time as you on the Santa Fe Rose, Archer. They'll
be an invaluable entrée into Houston society and the business world for you. I suggest you cultivate them," Julia
said.

Ashworth was annoyed. "It won't be necessary to 'cultivate' them," he replied with a touch of anger. "I like them

very much. They are friends of mine. You forget the Colonel and I were the best of comrades during the war. I expect to see a great deal of Will in Houston."

"And you might let him help you restock your new store when the time comes," Aunt Julia said spitefully, "since he seems to have the magic touch that insures success."

The following morning, Celia and Mara woke long before dawn, tossing for hours in the darkness before they finally agreed to get up and get dressed. Celia lit the two gas jets beside the dressing table and Mara noted blue smudges under her sister's big dark eyes. Though she had said nothing, Mara knew she thought constantly of David.

Celia carefully brushed her face with rice powder after putting on her underwear and tying the small, neat bustle about her. Then she donned her pearl gray dress suit after cinching her corselet as tightly as possible. Mara knew she hated the corselet, but it did give her an infinitesimal waist, which the pearly, light-weight suit set off perfectly. She laid her jacket over the back of a chair.

Mara was clad in one of her childish dresses, much above her ankles, with a superfluous amount of lace on the blouse. Only the large, leg-o'-mutton sleeves had any style about them.

With sudden defiance, she said, "Celia, I'm going to put up my hair and the devil take Aunt Felice. I'll be seventeen on August second."

"I agree," Celia replied. "Let me help." And between the two of them, they twisted up the thick mass of curling dark hair into a passable pompadour with small tendrils about the ears and at the back of her neck. Then even in the calf-length dress, Mara felt respectably older as they made their way quietly down to the kitchen, where Aunt Julia's cook and maid, as well as Pleasance, Sudie and Julius, were having a predawn cup of coffee.

"Looks like the day finally come," Pleasance said, smiling fondly at the two girls.

"We all goin' to leave today," Julius added with satisfaction.

They poured and served the girls a cup of coffee, and as Sudie handed it to them she said, "I ain't never been on a railroad car in my whole life. I can't hardly wait!"

"I hope we'll be happy when we get there," Celia said wistfully. "I can't quite believe I'm leaving all my friends and—," she broke off.

And David, Mara thought resentfully, finishing Celia's thought. Surely time would blur David's memory. Surely, with their life-style pared down to the bone, Celia would be so busy she wouldn't have time to think of him too much.

Abruptly, Aunt Felice came into the kitchen and demanded a cup of coffee immediately.

"I couldn't sleep a wink last night," she said angrily. "In a strange bed and with all this staring us in the face today." Then her dark eyes fell on her younger niece and narrowed, her brows drawing together. "Mara, take down your hair at once. You look ridiculous and your father will be furious!" Her voice was cold. "You know your papa has said that you may put your hair up when you are seventeen and not a day before!"

Mara gave Celia a glance of repressed fury and reached up to remove the pins.

"After breakfast, you will go upstairs and tie it back with a bow," Aunt Felice said curtly.

Mara was boiling. Aunt Felice was a shrew and a fornicator, and Mara's disgust for her was boundless. But knowing that arguing would prove useless, she did as bid, and soon the gleaming dark mass tumbled down her back again.

The house was stirring now, above and below, and breakfast would soon be served. After that, Aunt Maggie and Uncle Bob would come to the Quayne mansion and they would all drive to the station together. For appearance's sake, the sisters and their husbands would see them off. Then all Richmond would talk over their tables about the Ashworth store to be set up in Houston. After all, Colonel William Hunter MacAdam had done the same years ago and made a fortune in that distant city. No doubt, the talk would run, Archer Ashworth would do the same.

Chapter 3.

ᐯ LIKE Sudie, Mara had never been on a train before, and despite her sorrow at leaving Richmond, she was aware of the excitement that surrounded their final leave-taking. Two of Celia's friends and their mothers wept openly, but most were determinedly cheerful and full of optimism regarding the Ashworths' departure. By the time the train pulled out of the station, with much hissing of steam and stowing of baggage, Mara knew a strong wave of pleasure.

John Halloran and Will MacAdam had boarded with them and they all had seats together in the plush Pullman. The windows were open and the July day was hot. The wind pouring in carried myriad odors, and Mara noticed as the train gathered speed outside Richmond that cinders blew in through the openings. She had a feeling that they would soon be dusty and perspiring despite the wind, and she had been told by a complaining Aunt Felice that they could take only bowl baths in the small, cramped bathroom at the end of the Pullman during the five long days it took to reach Houston from Richmond. No doubt the newness would wear off and Mara would be devoutly thankful by the time they reached their destination, but for now, she was wide eyed and impressed.

Sudie, Pleasance and Julius were behind in the coach cars, which were comfortable but not so luxurious and expensive as the Pullmans. Mara had gone back to see them before settling in her seat and was relieved to find they were in a state of open-mouthed delight as the train swayed through the countryside outside of Richmond.

"This is going to be a dreadful journey," Aunt Felice

moaned, taking out a scented handkerchief and patting her moist forehead when Mara returned to her seat. "Five whole days—and all this smoke and dust blowing in on us."

"But if we close the windows, we'll suffocate," Celia replied.

"It's all very well for your father to go with those two young men to the smoker and bar car, while we brave these blowing cinders," Aunt Felice said with a melancholy sigh. "There is no car suitable at all for ladies and their activities."

"They have a lovely dining car, I've heard," Mara said cheerfully. "We'll get to have dinner there this evening." She leaned back against the thick, velvety seat that would fold out into a berth tonight. She wondered how that was done, curiosity occupying her as she looked out the open window at the scenes rolling by: tall stands of pine, lonely little roads wandering through them, an occasional farm house or a wagon pulled by a team of horses as the train passed by, picking up speed.

The day wore on and the clickety-clack of iron wheels on the roadbed of steel rails was a soporific, but Mara could not doze. Celia was quiet and Mara knew her mind was on David Donellan. Oh, if only her sister could see him for what he was, an opportunist, an acquisitive opportunist!

The week before the Ashworths left, David and Lucinda had returned from New York but the family had not glimpsed the couple as they bade farewells to old friends and relations at the station. For that, Mara was thankful. In parting, Aunt Julia and Aunt Maggie had informed them that the older Mrs. Donellan had boasted a week ago that Robert Ames was taking David into his investment firm.

Now Aunt Felice kept up a running litany about the discomfort of the open windows. She could not complain about the seats for they were luxurious and exceedingly comfortable, but she was unhappy to be leaving Richmond and nothing pleased her. They passed small towns as they rolled along, and Aunt Felice made disparaging remarks about each of them.

"I just don't see how I can sit here, doing nothing, seeing nothing for five long days. I shall be wild with boredom," she said at last as the sun was lowering in the west. The men had not returned from the smoker and that also irritated her. "Your papa is so easily taken in by such people as this Halloran and MacAdam."

"Aunt Felice, they're helping Papa—not taking him in," Celia remonstrated.

"I have little use for them. I think they have their eye on you girls. Mara's just ripe enough for seduction by either of them." She gave the younger girl a vindictive stare. "You mind yourself around them, young lady." The sharp, ugly statement angered Mara but she said nothing.

Celia, who had enough of her complaints and accusations said coldly, "Papa will take a dim view of you thinking the son of his old commander would have seduction of Mara in mind. And John Halloran is certainly a gentlemen. I shall tell Papa of your suspicions."

That stopped Aunt Felice. She patted her forehead with the handkerchief again and said, "Well, I didn't mean Will MacAdam. But that other man, I wouldn't put much past him. I've seen him look at you, Mara." She turned her anger on Mara sharply. "You're not safe. None of us is safe in his presence. I know it instinctively."

"His manners are impeccable," Celia said, still cold.

"And I tell you there's something about him. That look in those black eyes. I don't trust him around Mara."

"I'll tell Papa you said so."

"No, Celia," Felice said, slightly agitated. "Don't bother him with it. He has so much on his mind. I'll keep an eye on this Halloran and see that he doesn't take any liberties."

The men returned at the dinner hour, to escort the ladies to the dining car. The women rose at their greeting and followed Ashworth and the two younger men through two noisy, lurching entrances until they reached the diner.

Mara stopped in the entrance, awed by the opulence of it. The floor was covered with a thick, velvety wine-red rug. Wine velvet curtains at each window were tied by gold-fringed velvet bands. Tables were spread with spotless linen and oil lamps sent a luxurious glow over fine china and glittering crystal. The faint fragrance of coffee and roasting meat hung in the air. On each table, in a crystal bud vase was a single perfect dark red rose. The car breathed quiet elegance and luxury.

A larger table had been set up at the rear and the five of them made their way to it, where the women were seated first. Mara felt fresh excitement at the beauty around her. The darkening landscape slipping by beyond the windows lent a delightful coziness to the extravagance and beauty surrounding the diners.

When John Halloran seated Mara, he said, "No one can fault the cuisine on the Santa Fe Rose, as you'll soon see."

And he was right. There were crystal compotes of fresh cantaloupe, browned quail, hot French bread, vegetables straight from the garden and tall frosted glasses of mint-flavored tea. There were crisp, sweet Napoleons and delicate custard-filled eclairs for dessert, finished off with cups of rich coffee.

As they ate the men talked, and for the first time, Mara sensed that the city they were moving to was not the blurred frontier town she had envisioned, but a living, pulsing entity.

MacAdam, over his after-dinner liqueur laughed at his friend Halloran, and to Ashworth he said, "John's got a new bone to worry with. He's into something now that's keeping him away from the store, the lumber mills and even from his construction gang."

"Mark my words, Will," Halloran said seriously, "it's the key to a greater Houston. A deep-water ship channel will bring ships from every nation carrying all the produce of the world. Not to mention the export business we'd handle."

"Too bad the government doesn't see the potential," MacAdam said dryly, lighting a small dark cheroot.

"The government?" Ashworth's brows lifted. "What could the government do about it?"

"Some years ago," Halloran said, accepting a cheroot from MacAdam, "Congress authorized the spending of over six million dollars for the completion of the Galveston Jetties to deepen their port waters to twenty-five feet." He struck a match, lighting the cigar and blew out a stream of fragrant smoke. "The United States is laboring under the delusion that an island city can become a deep-sea port. Nothing is further from the truth."

"I'll go along with you, John, having weathered a few hurricanes there myself," MacAdam put in. "If Houston had the money to put into dredging the bayou, the nation would have a *protected* deep-sea port."

"That's right," Halloran drawled, "a port that's expandable in all directions. You see, Archer, Houston is on a flat, heavily forested plain that spreads for miles. And unlike Galveston, it's all well above sea level." He shrugged eloquently, adding, "In the end, Houston will get its channel. I've bought frontage along Buffalo Bayou where wharves and warehouses will be thick one day. We'll all live to see it."

"How can you be so sure?" Mara burst out, deeply interested, then flushed as Aunt Felice and Papa looked at her in astonishment.

"Because a group of businessmen like myself, William Marsh, Tom Rice, John Delaney, have organized the Buffalo Bayou Ship Channel Company," Halloran said, looking at the young girl seriously. "And even conservative Will has joined the Committee for Deep Water. We've ordered two big dredges and plans are in progress even now to get federal help in widening and deepening the bayou."

"Doesn't that make for ill-will between two cities so close together?" Ashworth asked, still frowning at Mara for her interruption.

"It does. And it's serious, make no mistake. But Galveston is unprotected from the sea," Halloran said, still looking at Mara thoughtfully, "and one day the sea will try to reclaim it. In the meantime, our congressman, Joseph Hutcheson, is going to introduce a bill requesting a government survey for a twenty-five-foot deep channel to Houston."

Mara glanced at Aunt Felice to find her eyes, veiled by the long, thick tangle of Bonheur lashes, secretly fastened on Ashworth, who was now enjoying a cigar himself as he finished the last of his benedictine and brandy.

"Houston is fast becoming the rail center for the Southwest," Will put in, "as you'll see when we get there. But right now our barge traffic on the bayou is all we have in the way of seaborne merchandise for export or import."

"But the future is unlimited," Halloran drawled, smiling at Ashworth, "once we get the channel deepened."

He and MacAdam went on at length about the pine forests around Houston and the fact that thousands of feet of lumber were turned out per day. The forests were inexhaustible, and lumber traveled directly over the railroads from East Texas sawmills to the eastern and western coasts.

"Houston's putting out more than two hundred million feet of lumber a year now," Halloran said, finishing his liqueur.

Ashworth whistled softly. "Lumber and real estate! Sounds like your stores may just be a sideline."

"Our stores aren't like *Ashworth's*, for besides cloth and soft goods, we sell lumber, feed, steel and all kinds of building supplies. No fine furniture such as you handle," Will said. Then as he looked up from his cigar his eyes narrowed on the back of the car. He said softly, "Well, well, it appears another Richmond resident is aboard the Santa Fe Rose."

Mara turned and caught her breath. David Donellan was entering the diner. He did not see them and he was smiling at the white-jacketed waiter who showed him to a table. He was alone.

Mara looked swiftly at her sister to see that every vestige of color had drained from her face. She looked down as she twirled the crystal stem of her empty liqueur glass. Mara knew her sister's mind was racing as fast as her own! Where was Lucinda and what was he doing on this train? They had been married less than a month.

Will MacAdam and John Halloran reached for the check simultaneously and Ashworth said quickly, "No, no, boys. I will pay for the girls and myself."

But Will had possession of it now and he said, "Certainly not. You've been my guests this evening. John, you can have the pleasure tomorrow."

"And then *I* shall have the pleasure," Ashworth said firmly as Will laid out a handful of greenbacks including a generous tip, and they all rose from the table.

Mara caught Celia's eye and she shook her head imperceptibly as they found their way behind the men into the narrow aisle between tables. When Ashworth reached the one where Donellan sat, he stopped abruptly.

"David!" he said heartily. "How good to see you, my boy!

What are you doing on the Santa Fe Rose?" Her father had
no idea of Celia's heartbreak. He knew only that this
young man had courted his beloved daughter for a time;
then like all the others, she had let him go. And now his
feelings for the Donellan family were unchanged, feelings
of warm friendship. "Look here, Celia, Felice, it's James
Donellan's son!"

David rose to his feet gracefully and bowed to the ladies,
his broad smile exposing too many teeth, Mara thought.
His eyes on Celia were especially warm.

"This is a real surprise and pleasure, Mr. Ashworth—
ladies. And you, Will, we haven't really talked since we
graduated from the university together. Good to see you
again, too, Mr. Halloran." Donellan stood easily at the
table, his slate eyes clinging to Celia, while her color returned brilliantly. He added casually, "I'm on business for
my new father-in-law."

"Where is Lucinda?" Mara asked forthrightly.

"She isn't well," he said regretfully, "and didn't feel up
to the trip. I hated to leave her so soon after our honeymoon, but she insisted that I do as her father wished." He
paused, then added, "And I thought it wise to do so since
I've gone to work for the Ames Enterprises."

"So it's business that takes you to Houston, my boy,"
Ashworth said jovially. "I didn't know Robert Ames had
interests in Houston."

Mara noted the sudden alertness in Will MacAdam's
and John Halloran's expressions at this development.

"Not in Houston, sir," David said, "in Galveston. He's
bought into the Galveston Wharf Company and has several large warehouses there and I'm to oversee his investment. Lucinda will join me later. We plan to build in
Galveston."

Mara saw Halloran's eyes go flat and cold. Will's face
was expressionless, too. She sensed a sudden chill, so subtle that none of the others seemed aware of it.

"You must have dinner with us when we get settled,"
Aunt Felice said archly. "I'm sure Mr. Ashworth will find
a house soon. Meantime, we will be staying at the Houston
Heights Hotel. Perhaps you can come by to dine with us
there."

MacAdam and Halloran said nothing, their bland faces and cold eyes unchanged.

"Ah, we shall dine together on this trip," David said cordially. "It will be so pleasant to be among friends." Then broadening his toothy smile, he added, "Celia, I haven't thanked you for the exquisite music you played at our wedding. Everyone complimented it."

"I'm glad," Celia said simply and Mara was relieved that she didn't say it was a pleasure. It had been no pleasure. It had been agonizing. But Mara was disturbed by the warmth in Celia's eyes and as the two exchanged amenities, she found her role of the naive youngster hard to play before this man she so distrusted.

At last they left Donellan at his table and made their way out of the luxurious opulence of the diner and through the other cars. When they reached their car, they found the porters had made their Pullman seats into berths. The thick, heavy carpet on the narrow aisle floor was green and the heavy curtains that enclosed the berths were made of a green, stiffly brocaded material. Uncle Abel had seen to it that they all had lower berths, and Mara's heart warmed briefly toward him as she noted the slender little ladders leading up to the dark, claustrophobic upper berths near the polished wooden ceiling of the partitions.

She and Celia pushed the curtains aside and entered their berth. They saw that the porter had lighted an oil lamp at the head of the broad bed. A narrow net hammock swung against the windows to hold their clothing. It was cramped but surprisingly comfortable inside as they adjusted the curtains back together, completing their privacy.

"I can't believe David's on this train," Celia whispered, half to herself. "And without Lucinda—" She broke off as she pulled the stiff, heavy green shades down over the open windows, shutting out most of the night wind.

"I'll bet she's feeling perfectly all right and just didn't want to miss the summer social season in Richmond," Mara said, without a trace of naiveté. She reached through the curtains and under the berth to pull out her small suitcase, then Celia's. "I'll bet she's a cold fish, too," she continued, thumping the suitcases down in front of them where they sat, one at each end of the berth, their legs crossed under their skirts.

"Mara! You don't know whether she's cold or not."

"I've read lots of books, some on what they call psychology. And she fits perfectly the description of a frigid woman."

"What do you mean, frigid?" Celia looked at her younger sister with genuine curiosity. She did not like to read, and only read the books necessary to finish her courses.

"Sexually unresponsive. Spoiled and thinking only of herself and her own pleasures—which are not physical ones with a man."

"Mara!" Celia was sincerely shocked. "I had no idea you read such things. Where did you get them?"

"The library," Mara replied tersely. Then added, "Anyway, I think Lucinda's frigid and I think it's just what David Donellan deserved." She began taking off her clothes and laying them carefully in the net hammock.

"I'm astonished at your drawing such conclusions about Lucinda," Celia said, diverted momentarily from the shock and stimulation of seeing David. It was growing hot in the berth with the window shades drawn and they hurried to undress, donning their nightgowns.

"We were all in school together for one year, remember, and I've watched her at parties. I never saw her do one unselfish thing, or say anything good about another girl, for that matter either," Mara said.

"That's true. But her papa spoiled her dreadfully. It's not really her fault. Maybe David can bring her out of it."

Mara laughed. "Don't be so kind and optimistic, Celia. You know we never liked her. I'll bet old David is *glad* to be on this trip without her." Then in sudden alarm, "You keep treating him coolly, Celia! Remember, even if it is a bad marriage, it's a marriage just the same."

By now they were in their long, white nightgowns and had turned down the oil lamp. They each raised a shade. The night wind coming in the open windows was cool and carried the pungent scents of the open country beyond, mixed with the salty, ever-present cinders from the smokestack on the engine ahead. The train, rushing through the darkness, made the berth a cozy haven, with its fresh linen cool to the touch and lamplight casting a soft glow on the girls. The clicking of steel against steel as the cars passed over the rails combined with the slight rocking motion of the Pullman felt soothing.

"I want to sleep by the windows," Mara said, slipping between the sheets. "It makes me feel I can reach out and touch the night and still feel safe inside."

"I'll have to be nice to him," Celia said, her thoughts still on David. "I can't be obviously cool. Papa would notice and so would that sharp-eyed MacAdam."

"And John Halloran would notice too," Mara said, remembering his shrewd and caustic observations at the wedding reception. She thought suddenly of the sudden hostility of MacAdam and Halloran. They had been cordial enough to David at first, but David had said something that had engendered their animosity. What? She finished, "Celia, if only you could be just natural—"

Celia's hollow laugh broke her sentence. "Loving him to distraction, regretting I didn't have the courage to let him—that night—how I can be natural? If he'd—if we'd—he would have married me, I'm certain. It would have bound us together."

"Celia, Celia, how can you be so wise in some ways and so foolish in this? David Donellan was out to marry money. He was fascinated by you and, I don't doubt, loved you in his way. But he never would have married you after Papa's store was failing. We were *poor* and no matter how beautiful and talented and loving you are, you *are* poor, too. No, you'd have risked disgrace if you'd done anything like that."

The sway of the car and the soothing click of wheels vibrated through their bodies, relaxing Mara. Celia was silent for a long time. Then in a smothered voice, she said, "I know he would have married me if I had been carrying his child."

"Oh, Celia!" was all Mara could find to say.

The following morning, the two girls bathed in the narrow confines of the small train restroom. The lavatory was miniscule, and the water in it sloshed untidily as the train racketed over the rails. Aunt Felice's complaints were steady, unbroken throughout the entire journey, except in Ashworth's presence.

The men, having eaten earlier, found the three women having breakfast alone, and they did not see David Donellan in the dining car. The morning meal was very nearly as lavish as the evening's. Mara had poached oysters with a delicious cream lemon sauce, a baked apple in heavy cream and crusty French bread. Aunt Felice, between complaints, ordered eggs Benedict and so did Celia.

Later, when they had settled themselves in the Pullman, the train ground to a stop outside a small Alabama town. Looking out the window, they saw a hose dropping down from a tall, spindle-legged watertower. The train was taking on fresh water. Far down the curve of the tracks, the coal car was being refueled by three brawny railroad men with shovels. This became an everyday routine as they rolled across the country, once in the morning and once in the late evening.

While they were stopped Mara went back to the coach car where Pleasance, Sudie and Julius were riding and found them watching with fascination as the men shoveled coal from a huge wooden bin beside the tracks into the large open car behind the engine.

She sat down beside Pleasance and they talked of the trip. The three servants had enjoyed every minute of it. At night, their seats leaned back in an almost reclining position, and Julius declared they had slept as well as if they were in their own beds.

But Sudie whispered, "Mara, I'm too excited to sleep. I been awake most of the time."

Mara squeezed her hand and murmured, "Oh, Sudie, I have the most wonderful plan for us when we get to Houston! It'll mean money and *independence* for both of us."

"What? What?" Sudie asked excitedly, and Pleasance smiled at them indulgently, while Julius continued to look out the train window. He had stuck his head out to get a better view of the watertower and the workman filling the coal car.

"I'll tell you when we get settled," Mara said mysteriously, not yet ready to unveil the dream she had spun so carefully since her father's bankruptcy.

The train had built up a head of steam and was pulling out by the time Mara returned to Aunt Felice and Celia in the Pullman.

"David stopped by to see us while you were gone," Celia said, her eyes shining. "We're going to dine with him this evening."

Mara said nothing.

"He has a compartment all to himself," Aunt Felice said longingly. "It does seem that your Uncle Abel could have gotten compartments for us, too."

"Uncle Abel has been very generous, Aunt Felice," Celia said. "We should be grateful that we have first-class accommodations in the Pullman."

"First class," she sniffed. "A compartment would be first class. David doesn't have to sit with all these people around him staring. A compartment is real luxury."

"All these people" were no more than ten others in the car who were well away from them. Celia and Mara exchanged glances and shrugged. Aunt Felice was irascible and critical with both girls now, despite her partiality to Celia. But when Ashworth was around, she became the epitome of gracious good cheer and kindliness to both girls. Her hypocrisy had long ago been recognized and accepted by both Celia and Mara.

"Anyway, Uncle Abel says the hotel where we'll be staying until we can rent a house is supposed to be the very latest and most luxurious in Houston," Celia said soothingly. "You'll enjoy that, I'm sure, Aunt Felice."

"Humph," was the only response.

And that night at dinner, conversation was very animated. Will and David recalled old times at the University of Virginia and everyone laughed a great deal as they dined on lobster and drawn butter, anecdotes flying thick and fast. The two men from Houston masked their animosity toward Donellan quite successfully, but Mara sensed it still.

"Where did you go to school, John?" David asked casually.

"I didn't," Halloran said succinctly. "I ran away from home at thirteen and I've been working ever since. But I read a book once and can spell in a pinch."

Will shook with silent laughter.

"What's the joke?" Ashworth asked.

And Will said, "John's better educated than I, by far.

He's read more, seen more, done more and he's self-educated. He can and does read Greek and Latin."

"Of course," David said condescendingly, but his tone dismissed Halloran as an uneducated man.

Mara found herself wondering why John Halloran had run away at thirteen and her curiosity became suddenly intense. He was so powerfully built, so rugged in appearance, she knew he didn't *look* like a scholar, yet Will Mac-Adam had said he was one, a most unique one at that. She found her reluctant admiration for him now laced with respect.

Celia flowered in David's presence, her face and eyes bright with animation, and Mara knew she was responding to the love she still bore him. And he encouraged her to talk, following the girls back to the Pullman after dinner, where he chatted with Celia a moment outside the made-down berths before sauntering back to his compartment in the next Pullman.

Thereafter for the rest of the trip, David Donellan dined with them on every occasion, and during the days he always sat beside Celia for hours in the plush Pullman seats, talking of Richmond and the people they had left behind.

To Mara, David seemed supercilious and snobbish, but he and Celia never seemed to lack conversation. Mara's uneasiness for her sister grew as the two of them spoke of the future in Texas and laughed over small jokes. David never spoke of his bride. Indeed, it was as if she had never existed, but no one seemed to think anything of it except Mara.

Celia took care to be casual to their father about David, remarking often that it was nice to be with old *friends* from Richmond. And if David did not mention his wife, Celia did to her father and Aunt Felice on every occasion when she was not with David.

Each day, Celia and Mara visited with Pleasance, Julius and Sudie to make sure they had everything they needed. Sometimes their father went with them and sometimes Aunt Felice came along. They learned that food was sold in the coach cars by vendors on the train for that purpose. It was mostly sandwiches and cold milk, with cookies wrapped in heavy white paper.

"They buy them san'wiches an' such when the train

stops in these little towns. The porter says there's special restaurants just for the train passengers," Julius told them.

"They sure are good an' fresh," Pleasance added.

"I like this travelin'," Sudie grinned at Mara around her mother's shoulder.

"No matter how good they try to make it, I'll be glad to get into Houston in two more days," Aunt Felice, who had come with them, spoke fretfully. "I vow I feel every bone in my body will vibrate for weeks after I get off this thing."

She continued to complain all the way back to their Pullman, where Ashworth met them, saying he was off to the smoker and bar with Will and John Halloran.

The fourth night, on the eve of their arrival in Houston, John Halloran and Will MacAdam had dinner once more with the Ashworths, and afterward, Halloran followed Mara out of the dining car. They were the last two, the others having gone on ahead.

His voice low, Halloran asked, "Would you like to see the observation platform, Mara?" She noted with a twinge of resentment that he never prefaced her name with a "Miss" when they were alone.

"I didn't know there was one."

"I've been remiss. I should have told you it's at the rear of the last car and your trip's not complete without seeing it."

By now they were in the Pullman, and Mara noted that Celia and David were standing before the girls' made-down berth, their father entering his and Aunt Felice in front of her own.

"Aunt Felice, I'd like to go see the observation platform with Mr. Halloran," Mara said with more confidence than she felt. Seventeen! It was less than two weeks away now.

"Certainly not," Felice said with a frown directed at Halloran, who loomed up beside her. "You're too young to go with Mr. Halloran—anywhere."

"Are you implying," Halloran asked coldly, "that I would treat Miss Mara other than the lady she is?"

"She's not a lady. She's a *child.*"

"I disagree, madam," he said and this time there was amusement in his voice. "And I think your opposition lies in your own imagination, which must be exceedingly lurid for a maiden lady." The statement was hard, flat and irrefutable, and Aunt Felice reddened as she had done before.

"You're an impertinent ruffian," Aunt Felice said, "and I don't think any woman would be safe with you."

"There's some truth in what you say, madam," he replied imperturbably, "but I promise to bring Miss Mara back undamaged—this time."

Felice turned and entered her curtained berth with a touch of violence. She disliked John Halloran intensely and had done so since the evening he and MacAdam had taken Celia and Mara to the ice cream parlor.

Mara hesitated. "She didn't really give me permission," she said uncertainly.

"Are you going to let a frustrated old maid tell you what to do?" he mocked.

Mara looked at him. Frustrated, yes. Old maid, no. Of that she was certain. Now she said thoughtfully, "Well, you've always been a perfect gentleman with me."

"Don't get used to it. I don't promise anything. You're very desirable."

"You make me afraid to go with you!"

He laughed. "And I had hoped instead to challenge you. No matter. The observation car is at the end of the car containing the bar and smoker. And I promise I'll do nothing that wouldn't be mutually enjoyable."

With an excited and guilty look at Aunt Felice's closed curtains Mara turned and followed him through the swaying, rattling openings where car was joined to car, past the dining compartment and into the last car, the bar and smoker for men. There were several men about the small tables, enjoying their brandy and cigars in the thick, tufted velvet chairs. They looked at Mara admiringly as she and Halloran passed through, walking toward the end of the car. Halloran opened the heavy door, which had a clear, thick glass top and the two stepped out onto a little metal platform with a waist-high iron railing around it.

The July night was hot, but a cooling wind rushed away from them, some of it swirling back to curl about them and flutter the lace on her blouse.

Mara looked down the twin tracks, gleaming in the early moonlight. They dwindled to a point that renewed itself as the train sped along. The faint scent of smoke from the engine came to them where they stood leaning against the rail. It was wildly exhilarating to Mara. Out here, she felt at peace with the rushing night and the moon rising slowly in the east as the train sped away from it.

They stood silently, enjoying a sense of freedom, the nearness of the virgin forests, receding then looming again beside them. She was suddenly conscious of John Halloran's closeness. His big hand touched hers where they held to the railing and suddenly all her senses were concentrated in her hand. She drew it away hastily and he did not seem to notice.

Instead, he reached into his vest pocket and took out a cheroot, the match flaring in the wind as he cupped his hands about the flame. They did not speak in the speeding darkness. The moon, in the east, was losing its orange cast as it lifted above tall trees that now stretched as far as they could see.

"Oh," Mara said at last, drawing a deep, quivering breath. "It's so beautiful! I wish this moment could last forever . . ."

She could feel his eyes on her and suddenly, in his husky drawl, he quoted, "The flower that smiles today tomorrow dies; all that we wish to stay tempts and then flies. What is this world's delight? Lightning that mocks the night, brief even as bright."

Mara stared up at him in amazement. "Why, Aunt Felice says you're uneducated—a ruffian—yet you quote Shelley!"

"Your aunt's right, of course," he said lightly. "I quoted it only to make a point—that nothing lasts forever. Take your pleasures where you can, Mara. Seize every opportunity." He drew on the cigar and the tip glowed red heat, revealing the somber lines of his face, including the fine white scar on his tanned cheek.

Mara was disconcerted by a powerful urge to reach up and bring that hard face down to her trembling lips. The desire was so urgent she had to force her hands to cling to the railing.

Looking away in swift confusion, she blurted, "Tomorrow we reach Houston. I—Aunt Felice says it will be full of barbarians. People who left the East because of some sort of scandal in their lives."

"Some of us are barbarians," he said, amused. "And didn't the Ashworths leave Richmond because of a type of scandal? But never mind. Andrea, Will's sister, can introduce you to all the civilized life in Houston. The Ladies' Music Auxiliary, the Ladies' Lyceum Committee and, if you're inclined, there are charity groups who work with orphaned—"

"I won't be doing any of those things," Mara broke in, angry that he had so accurately pointed out their reason for leaving Richmond. "We're poor." She said it caustically. "Papa's in terrible debt. He'll be starting over, but Celia and I plan to help him!"

"That so? And will you take in laundry or hire out as a housemaid?" His skeptical smile was clearly visible in the brightening moonlight.

"I plan to put up a department in Papa's store," she burst out furiously before she could stop herself, "and design layettes, baby clothes and women's high fashion gowns. And I'll make money at it, too, lots of money, you wait and see!" Immediately she was sorry she had revealed her secret plan. She should have waited! She didn't want anyone to know until she could approach her father and get his approval. Why, she hadn't even told Celia or Sudie!

John Halloran whistled softly and was silent a moment. Then, "By heaven you're even more a woman than I thought." He laughed suddenly. "When I told you to seize opportunity, it seems I was giving advice you didn't need. But do you think your papa will let you do that? He seems unusually oblivious to you and, I would imagine, to your talent, if you will forgive my being personal."

"I plan to *make* him see my talent. I'll find a way. I've proof of my success, minor though it is. Our friends in Richmond clamored for my layettes and baby clothes, and I designed and made the gown Celia wore when she played for the Donellan wedding."

He bowed slightly. "I remember it and I remember thinking it was quite the most charming gown at the wedding. I apologize for offering you the social side of Houston, when you'll be on the productive side."

Her anger was evaporating and anxiety was taking its place. Impulsively she put her hand on his arm and said, "Please, Mr. Halloran . . ."

"John," he said, his big hard hand covering hers swiftly.

"Please, Mr. Halloran," she said firmly and pulled her hand away, "don't tell anyone about this. I didn't mean to tell you, but you were so . . . so . . ."

"Know-it-all? One of my many failings." He laughed ruefully.

"It will really complicate things for me if you say anything before I can make my plans with Papa. Please?"

"I shall be as silent as the tomb, *if* you let me call on you when you put your beautiful hair up. It is beautiful, you know. So thick and shining. And *if* you call me John."

"I can't call you John," she said low. "Aunt Felice would—"

"Have a rigor," he finished cynically. "Ah, well, I can understand your reluctance. But August is the magic month and you can call me John then if you please."

"And speaking of Aunt Felice," Mara said, "I think I should go back in, no matter how much I hate to leave such exciting beauty. It's been wonderful," she added wistfully. "I'll always remember how free and happy I felt out here with the world sweeping by so fast."

"All that we wish to stay, tempts then flies," he repeated lightly, taking her elbow and opening the heavy door. Then prophetically, "But there will be other moments."

Mara was already thinking of the moment when she would face her papa with her plans. She would enlist Celia's aid to make the confrontation easier, she decided, little dreaming that her greatest ally was already at her side.

Chapter 4.

ꝏ WHEN at last the train slowed to a rumble and eased into the Houston Grand Central Station, there was a great squealing of wheels against steel rails, with clouds of hissing steam rolling out beside the engine. All of the passengers crowded into the narrow aisle to the door, each of them anxious to take the steep narrow steps to the station platform.

In passing the windows earlier, Mara had glimpsed dozens of Pullmans, freight cars and engines lining the many tracks as they pulled into the station. Some engines were spewing steam preparatory to pulling out, some were quiet, and she was reminded again of John Halloran's casual remark. *Over seventy thousand people live in Houston now and twelve railroad companies use the station. There are at least two hundred and fifty trains pulling in and out of there every day, Sundays and Saturdays alike.*

Now she could believe him as she stood in the semigloom between the baggage compartments and the train vestibule to the steps, well behind her papa, Aunt Felice and Celia. The others, Halloran, MacAdam, Julius and his entourage were behind Mara and she could hear the hubbub outside and the distant whooo-ee as another train approached the station.

Ashworth stepped back, allowing Celia, Aunt Felice and Mara to descend first to the dusty wooden platform. Then he stepped down, followed by the others. The porters grouped their luggage about them as David Donellan swung down the steps, carrying his two expensive leather suitcases himself. The lock of thick, shining brown hair fell winningly over his high forehead as usual. Mara often thought he permitted and encouraged this because it increased his attractiveness.

Now he stepped up beside Celia and her father. "I must go over to track three and board the train for Galveston, Mr. Ashworth. The porter has pointed it out for me and it leaves in less than ten minutes." Then with a warm smile at Celia, "You can't know what a pleasure you all have made a long dusty trip for me." He dropped one suitcase and clasped Ashworth's hand, then Celia's, Mara's and Aunt Felice's. "I'll be in Houston often and I'll look forward to seeing all of you again soon."

He waved to them all, and amid a chorus of good-byes, he caught up his suitcase and strode down the plank platform under the narrow separated roofs between tracks, crossing the shining steel rails to where he would board the Galveston Special. Mara could see it now, glistening darkly and sending forth clouds of steam.

As they stood on the platform Mara noticed that Aunt Felice looked especially handsome, her voluptuous figure well corseted and her creamy face rosy with the heat and joy of deboarding the train. Her lustrous eyes sparkled. At this moment Mara could understand her father's desire for Felice, for at times she could be charming and she would certainly do anything to please Archer Ashworth.

A group of four redcaps approached them, smiles broad in their dark faces. They picked up the luggage, and a squat, powerfully built man asked cheerfully, "Where to this time, Mista' Halloran, Mista' MacAdam?"

"To the Washington Street side, Jim." John Halloran grinned back at the redcap. "I'll be taking a hack."

"And I expect my brother and sister will be meeting us there," Will MacAdam added, "with our attorney, Stuart Kennedy." He turned to Ashworth. "You'll like Stu. We all grew up together, Archer, only his people came from Virginia in 1868. They had to recoup their fortune, too, and Stu was born here. He takes care of our legal problems."

The group moved forward, following redcaps and crossing tracks gingerly from one platform to another until they reached the main station. The fleet, sure-footed redcaps were well ahead of them and stood holding open the tall, brass and glass doors.

It was a big, brand-new redbrick station, but it was already redolent with the flavors of tobacco and food and thick with people arriving and departing. An air of cheerful but preoccupied haste and purpose permeated the vast lobby, with its smoothly polished granite floor. The July air was hot and humid, and Mara's thick hair clung in moist tendrils about her face and neck. It had done so ever since Aunt Felice made her put it down thousands of miles ago in Richmond.

"I feel cindery and dusty in spite of our scrubbings this mornings," Celia murmured to Mara.

"And hot and hungry," Mara whispered back.

There were dozens of stands in the lobby where everything from magazines to popcorn and souveniers could be bought. There were vendors selling hot coffee, and a steaming cart pushed by an olive-skinned man gave off a delicious aroma. The latter, Will informed the girls, came from tamales, a Mexican delicacy. It made them sharply conscious of hunger for it was midday.

The place was bright with new electrical lighting. There was no gas light to be seen in any of the offices off the lobby, nor in the restaurant beyond. Through glass doors at the front, omnibuses, hacks and carriages could be seen lining the sidewalk on Washington Street, the drivers drawing close to the curb on the south side of the depot. The endless activity was stimulating and Mara's elation grew, along with hunger as they followed the redcaps out the doors to stand under a broad metal roof which extended from the brick station.

"Oh, Will! And John!" cried a pretty girl, running forward. With her were two tall young men, one of them as darkly brunette as the girl. Both the girl and the dark-haired man had the crystal blue eyes of Will MacAdam. The other man had bright red-brown hair and twinkling hazel eyes, and his smile was as broad as those of his companions. This man's eyes brushed Celia, then swung back swiftly and fastened so intently on Mara's face that she felt even hotter in the July day.

"Welcome to Houston, Ashworths! Howdy, Will, John." The glacier-eyed stranger, who had to be Will MacAdam's brother, thrust his hand out to Ashworth, who shook it vigorously.

After a swift embrace, Will introduced the girl as his sister, Andrea, and his brother, Branch. The second man proved to be Stuart Kennedy, the young attorney, who made a point of shaking Mara's hand.

"We've come in our two biggest carriages," Andrea said warmly. "Branch drove the buggy and I came in the Victoria with Sam driving." She looked no more than nineteen or twenty. "And there's plenty of room for all. You, too, John." She smiled at them, including Julius and his family, who stood staring in fascination at the boiling mass of humanity surging about them. "We've prepared luncheon for you," she went on and her eyes swung at last to Mara.

Mara was stunned by the cold malice that flashed out at her before those crystal eyes went to Will in swift warning and she saw his jaw set.

"And you must stay with us," Andrea went on, her voice still welcoming. "There's plenty of room."

"We are too many," Aunt Felice interrupted loftily before Ashworth could speak. "We would be an imposition on you."

"Nonsense. Will has built this enormous new house in the Heights. We aren't used to it yet. We even have fine servants' quarters on the third floor."

"You are too kind, Miss Andrea," Ashworth boomed gallantly, "but my brother-in-law has already reserved rooms for us at the Houston Heights Hotel." Then with the easy, endearing smile that always melted Mara's heart and made of others his instant friend, Ashworth added, "And, my dear, I would really very much like to see my new store before luncheon, if I may."

"Of course, Mr. Ashworth," Stuart Kennedy spoke for the first time and the intense hazel eyes moved at last from Mara to her father. "I handled all the legal details of the sale for your brothers-in-law, Mr. Quayne and Mr. Robertson—"

"And we'd be delighted to show you the place," Will cut in, "and before luncheon, too." Then to his sister, "Andy, you'll just have to wait on us. Mr. Ashworth is naturally anxious to see his new store."

Excitement filled Mara. Oh, how *she* wanted to see that store, and find a corner where she might set up a small *haute couture* shop! *Ashworth Originals.* She considered the name for the thousandth time. That would be the label on everything she and Sudie made from layettes to fine gowns and lingerie.

Andrea sighed, then catching sight of John Halloran as he commandeered his baggage to a hired hack, she cried, "But John," her dismay evident, "we'll take your luggage to the hotel for you. You must come to lunch, too!"

Ashworth and Stuart Kennedy were talking with Will now and John Halloran said, "I can't, Andrea. I've got to get out to my ditch right away and see if the dredges have arrived. I'll be in to see all of you later."

"Supper tonight?" she urged, her hand on his arm. Her lovely turned-up face revealed only friendliness, but Mara sensed a deeper emotion. She was torn between watching them and listening to her father discuss the new store with MacAdam and Stuart Kennedy.

"Maybe," John Halloran said carelessly, "but don't count on me. I have a couple of deals I left hanging and I've been gone too long." He wheeled about and shook Ashworth's hand, and after clapping Will on the shoulder in farewell, he turned to Mara.

"August," he said, low voiced. "Hair up, skirts down and French champagne on ice. Right?"

She nodded, cheeks hot. She was acutely aware of Andrea's suddenly intense blue gaze. Mara did not look up into the man's penetrating black eyes. There was a touch of quicksilver about John Halloran, along with his brooding cynicism. He was a man without illusions, and Mara knew instinctively she would be a fool to take him seriously. He left in the hired hack in a cloud of dust.

Branch MacAdam had been generous with silver dollars and the redcaps had carried their baggage to the large buggy at the curb and stowed it neatly inside. There was a fringed top on the prosaic buggy, but the larger, fancier Victoria was open to the merciless sun shining in a cobalt sky without a shred of cloud.

"We ladies shall ride in the Victoria—the seats are so much more comfortable—and I have parasols for all of us," Andrea announced quickly, her smile bright at the bewildered Aunt Felice. "The men and your servants can ride in the buggy. That way we will soon be in the house with a cool drink, while the men go downtown to the store."

"Oh," Mara cried out involuntarily, speaking for the first

time, "I *so* want to see the new store!" She was immediately abashed for her voice had penetrated the conversation of the three men, her father, Stuart Kennedy and Will MacAdam.

"What?" Ashworth looked at her incredulously.

"I—I'm just—so anxious to see your new store, Papa," she said humbly. All of them were looking at her in astonishment now.

"You're ridiculous, as always, Mara," Ashworth said cuttingly and Will MacAdam's eyes flashed with swiftly hidden anger. "You will go with the ladies as you should. There'll be time enough for you to see the store."

"Come, ladies," Andrea said again. "We shall ride together—"

"Not on your life, Andy," interrupted Branch with a rollicking laugh. His laughter was infectious, and though he was not quite so tall as his older brother, he was equally attractive, with something so merry in his face that a warmth of affection flooded Mara. She began to doubt her instincts about his sister. Now he was saying, "I wouldn't miss the chance of riding in the company of four beautiful women for anything."

"Oh, *you!*" Andrea laughed, too, and added. "Come on, then. You can sit up with Sam."

"Wrong again, sis. I'll squeeze in between Miss Celia and Miss Mara." His eyes on Celia were frankly flirtatious. Then he sent Mara a conspiring wink, as if to enlist her approval and aid in prospective pursuit of her sister. Celia was smiling at his audacity in spite of herself.

Andrea's saddle-colored coachman, Sam, had gotten down from the Victoria and was engaged in conversation with Julius and his family. All four servants were talking rapidly and with obvious pleasure.

"I'll drive the buggy," Will said as the men walked toward it, with Julius and his family following. Then, "Sam, you and the ladies follow us through town so Miss Mara can at least see the store from the outside and then take them on home. We'll be along shortly. Julius, there's plenty of room in the buggy for you and your family." His eyes met Mara's and she was surprised at the compassion in them.

The Victoria was drawn by two fine bays and the buggy was hitched to a powerful roan gelding. Branch carefully assisted Aunt Felice to a seat beside Andrea, then took first Celia's elbow, then Mara's, assisting them up the carriage step. When the young man had settled himself comfortably, if closely, between the two girls, Sam snapped the whip above the bays. The vehicle pulled away from the curb, following the buggy down the busy, dusty street.

Sam followed the buggy at some little distance in an effort to keep the dust from rolling back on the ladies. Andrea remarked that the weather had been dry too long and Houston was due a hard rain to lay the dust.

As they entered the downtown area Andrea noted the points of interest for her guests, the many large office buildings, the Cotton Exchange, an auditorium. Mara noticed that saloons and bars were frequent and men were going in and out of them. Some saloons had signs advertising Dutch lunches for ten cents. Most boasted imported liquors and wines and thick slices of fine beef. She was to learn that these bars never closed.

Branch pointed out the Lyceum and an imposing downtown hotel, The Houston. "John used to live there," he volunteered, "until they built the new Houston Heights Hotel."

"He lives there now—off and on—," Andrea said coolly, "no doubt you will see him often now that you will be staying there, too."

"Only until we can find a home," Celia said quietly. "We must rent, of course, until Father's store becomes the success we hope it will be."

"Of course it will be a success," Andrea said quickly, her blue eyes warm on Celia. "Houston is absolutely bursting its seams. Your father's store will be an *enormous* success."

Branch took up the conversation, reeling off the innovations, the progress and luxuries the town afforded. "We even have electric trolleys now. And the wheels send off real sparks on rainy days. All of our more progressive citizens have electric lights, too." He laughed suddenly, adding, "And they say their lights in the houses dim every time the trolley goes by."

"But electricity is so much cooler," Andrea put in, "and goodness knows, less dangerous than gas lights. We still have lots of fires in gaslit homes, some of the loveliest homes, too. People are so slow to accept change. You may be sure Will saw to it that electricity was put in our new house—and we have two telephones!" she finished triumphantly.

"And boy, oh, boy, does Andy use 'em," Branch said, not taking his eyes from Celia. Then loudly, "Slow down, Sam, we're coming up on the new *Ashworth's* now. See there, Miss Mara?"

The buggy had stopped before a broad, impressive storefront. There was a wide metal roof over the wooden porch that headed a flight of three steps. Mara's eyes grew wide at the sight of a brand-new, freshly painted sign above the roof that read *Ashworth's*. "Ashworth's Fine Merchandise" was painted in gold in a delicate arched tracery, on the four front glass windows. A wide cardboard sign at the corner of a window read "Opening to be announced soon." Even the window displays looked elegant with bolts of brocade spread about and a mannikin wearing a white ruffled blouse and long white eyelet skirt, stylishly narrow with just the hint of a bustle under the wide bow at the back.

"Well!" There was a wealth of relief in Aunt Felice's voice. "At least it's not a hole in the wall."

"Indeed not. It's one of the finer stores in the city," Andrea said.

"The man who sold it," Branch added, "had to move to Arizona for his health. He was consumptive and couldn't tolerate the humidity down here. He was very successful as long as he could run it, but customers fell away because he was unable to look after it."

"I wish I could see how it looks inside," Mara murmured.

"Andy," Branch began, "let's stop so Miss Mara can have a look around—"

"Branch, we're late enough as it is," was the quick response. Andrea's eyes followed the men as they went through the broad glass doors as Kennedy unlocked them. "I really must get home and tell Rosita and Maria that the men will be late and to put the salads in the icebox." But her sharp glance at Mara was chilly and the girl knew Andrea had no intention of indulging her desire.

The big carriage rolled on down the exceedingly wide, dusty road. Just beyond, the road was paved with broad, square blocks, and the Victoria, which was equipped with springs, rode with surprising ease over them. But the paving blocks gave way to shell, which made for even softer riding until they came to the end of the downtown area.

"It looks to be a big, fine town, Andrea," Celia murmured, somewhat embarrassed by Branch's continued unabashed admiration. Aunt Felice remained silent, her determination not to like anything about their new home quite apparent.

"I know you've left a far more beautiful city than our Houston," Andrea spoke without a trace of apology. "I was too young when we left to remember it, but the Colonel used to talk about Richmond until I felt I knew and loved it, too."

Mara realized anew that all three MacAdams always referred to their father as the Colonel, even as her father did, and she could not help but wonder about the man who had left such a mark on so many lives.

"Perhaps," Andrea added, still cool, "in time you will come to love our Houston, too, Miss Felice."

"Hmmm. I doubt *that,*" Aunt Felice said remotely, "but we must make the best of it, I suppose, until Archer makes enough money for us to return to our home."

Branch's eyes swung to her, turning glacial, as hard as ice. He started to speak, then clamped his flexible mouth tightly.

"I know I shall love it, Andrea," Mara said rapidly, hoping to counteract her aunt's rudeness. "Papa thinks Houston will be a center of progress and take its place among the great cities of the world one day. I—I hope to be a part of it."

But Andrea was not looking at her and she cried out in alarm, "Oh, Sam, look out! There's a black cat about to cross the road! Hurry—oh, you're too late—he's crossed right in front of us." Andrea's face was white and her eyes quite wide with genuine fear.

Branch laughed aloud, "Ah, Andy's so superstitious, she's worse than any Irish ancestor of ours who feared the banshee. And her conscience would do credit to a priest."

"It's not just superstition," Andrea said furiously. "You know yourself that bad luck comes home to roost. I'll wager something bad will happen as a result of this. You'll see."

"What a mixed metaphor, sister mine. If it comes home to roost, maybe it'll roost on me instead of you this time." Branch chuckled.

By now, Sam had driven into an older residential section. Suddenly there loomed up an enormous house, constructed of what must have been native red stone cut into squares. Two elegant Victorias were drawn up before it, and the coachmen sat waiting for their passengers to emerge any minute.

The house, as large as an English castle, reared up three stories, with a wide veranda around the lower floor. The multilevel roof had numerous cupolas and turrets, and the overall look was venerable and elegant. Mara was caught by its beauty, ruling at least three acres of sweeping lawn fenced by delicate black wrought iron. Spreading oaks put cool green shade out beneath them. Everyone's eyes were upon the impressive homestead as Mara spoke impulsively.

"What a beautiful house. It looks lived in and loved."

"It's loved all right," Andrea said, her voice mocking. The incident of the black cat was apparently forgotten. "Branch, or Will, or John Halloran can tell you all about the old Clive Fairweather house. His widow lives there."

"Mrs. Fairweather is a fine woman," Branch said defensively, red showing faintly beneath his heavy tan.

"Oh, indeed she is!" Andrea said derisively. "She owns so much property, too. Most of the stock in the Houston Hotel downtown. Gives to all the charities, it's said—anonymously. You can't get any finer than that."

"Clive Fairweather was one of the first Houston settlers of any wealth. He was a merchant engaged in shipping," Branch said, ignoring his sister's jeering glance. "He fell on bad times when Galveston became a major shipping port and died ten years ago. But Mrs. Fairweather's a shrewd businesswoman. She hung onto the old house and made some very wise investments."

"Had they any children?" Aunt Felice asked, curious in spite of her pretense at hauteur.

"A daughter. She's in school abroad," Branch said shortly. Then dismissing the subject, "We're coming to White Oak Bayou, ladies, and beyond it are the newer houses."

The carriage rattled across the plank bridge over a darkly shining and slow-moving stream. Along its banks towered magnolia trees bearing enormous white blossoms. Their piercing sweetness filtered into the carriage, mingling with the spicier fragrance of oleanders in the hot July air.

The houses they now passed were increasing in grandeur and size. They were great, rambling turreted homes with cupolas and ornate fretwork known as "gingerbread." Some of them were decorated with lacy ironwork, either black or painted white. Imposing gabled roofs topped off the spacious lawns exquisitely landscaped, boasting iron dogs or deer as hitching posts. Some of the big iron animals were merely set on the sweeping lawns as decorations.

As the carriage passed one estate Branch chuckled infectiously. "I'll tell you a bit of interesting gossip about this one. It's old William J. Hutchins's home, one of our pioneer merchants. His daughter, Ella, married Lord Stewart of England and that worthy nobleman brought silver plate and fabulous jewels from London for her. He even gave the beauteous Ella the 'black diamond' once owned by Mary, Queen of Scots."

Aunt Felice turned and looked hard at the mansion and Mara knew she was impressed. "Do Lord and Lady Stewart live there now?" she asked.

"Not often," Branch said dryly. "Like you, he thinks Houston too primitive and he and Ella spend most of their time in London."

There was a momentary silence before Andrea remarked evenly, "I'm sure you left many good friends in Richmond and you will miss them terribly, Celia, Miss Felice." She did not glance at Mara. "But we will do our best to make new ones for you, even though our city is still, as Branch says, a bit primitive."

Mara was at a loss to understand Andrea's subtle animosity toward her. It was incomprehensible for they had never laid eyes on each other before. She was diverted from it by the intuitive knowledge that Celia found herself in the peculiar circumstances of wanting to defend Houston, even if she had already decided she would not like it.

She was right, for Celia said slowly, "I—the city appears—quite beautiful and I am sure the advantages of living here are many."

Good for you, Celia, Mara thought silently as Andrea, encouraged by Celia's remark, began telling of the social life to be had. There was the Ladies' Music Auxiliary. "And Will told me you play the piano beautifully! Your talents will make you doubly welcome and much in demand."

"I'm afraid my sister and aunt and I will have little time for social life," Celia said abruptly. "We mustn't deceive you, Andrea. We are very poor now and we shall have to help Papa regain his fortune."

Branch asked soberly, "And how will you three lovely ladies do that?"

"I shall teach music," Celia said quietly.

"And I suppose Mara and I shall clerk in his store," Aunt Felice said with dignity. Then with a touch of hauteur in her ivory French face, "However, after the War between the States, my mama sewed for money and she was no less an aristocrat."

Mara was boiling with her own plans and longed wildly to throw them at the others, but she knew she must first get her father's permission. Still, she knew she could make money with her designs, her delicate needlework. She *knew* it! But she said nothing.

She caught Andrea exchanging a quick glance with her brother Branch. It seemed to hold the same warning look she had earlier bent on her older brother, Will. It gave Mara a queasiness in her stomach.

"Money's no measure of true worth," Branch said roughly, frowning at his sister.

"Of course not," Andrea agreed smoothly. "And I'm sure you ladies will find time to socialize with other Virginians in Houston. I know *my* friends will be glad to have you join their clubs and committees, no matter what your circumstances."

They passed another carriage coming toward them. As they had done to several which had passed earlier, Branch and Andrea called out a cheerful greeting. All the occupants of these passing carriages and buggies had viewed the passengers with avid curiosity and Mara's feeling grew that their coming had been widely broadcast in Houston.

"You've been in Houston Heights the last few blocks," Andrea said, returning to her role of guide and hostess. "It was started only five years ago by Oscar Martin Carter so nearly all the homes are quite new."

Mara noted abstractly that the ubiquitous saloons had

followed them relentlessly, right to the edge of the new residential area, where they abruptly disappeared. The road
was now broad, with an esplanade down the center. Back
at the beginning of the double roadway, the electric trolley
lines made a turn to go back into town, and nearby were
the Houston Central Rail lines as well as the M.K.T.
railroad tracks. All these new houses, despite their newness, looked settled and permanent with lawns and
flowerbeds laid out to set them off, just as did the mansion they now approached, which had at least four acres
of lawn about it.

The red brick of the house contrasted with the long,
white-columned veranda that looked cool and shady under
the groves of tall, black green pines and spreading live
oaks. There were full-foliaged pecan trees looming up in
the rear, taller even than the great house with its chim-
neys piercing the hot blue sky. Broad, two-storied wings
spread out on each side of the main, three-storied edifice.

Sam clicked to the horses and tugged at a rein. The Victoria turned and swept into an arching drive deeply paved
with shell. It was laid out in a half circle before the front of
the house and divided at the side where a branch ran to the
rear. Mara had a fleeting glimpse of a large carriage house
and stables with living quarters above, at some distance
behind the main house. As they drew up before it she realized the MacAdam's home was a more magnificent version
of the Richmond plantations, gracious and hospitable in
its beauty.

"We're home," Andrea said. "Now you can see why I
hoped you would all stay with us." She laughed adding,
"Will built it and he tried to outdo himself. Even the Colonel said it was too big, but Will says he built it so we could
live in it after marriage. Three families of MacAdams in
one big house." Her laugh was cynical. "It's perfectly monstrous."

"I think it's lovely," Mara said to end the silence that
followed Andrea's words. She knew her sister must be remembering Will MacAdam's abrupt proposal and his desire to have a "Virginian preside over my new home,"
even if he hadn't mentioned love.

A tall, well-dressed black man came out the front door

smiling. "Welcome home, Miss Andrea, Mist' Branch. You
need help with the baggage?"

"No, thanks, Amos," Branch replied. "It's coming with
the buggy and the others later." He and Sam had dis-
mounted and were handing the ladies down the carriage
step to the shell drive, which crunched pleasantly under
Mara's slippers.

Amos stood holding the door as Aunt Felice and Celia
stepped up on a flagstoned walk. As Mara followed she
heard a sudden, sharp quarrel spring up between Andrea
and Branch. She hadn't been listening to their low voices
behind her, but now they were slightly raised and she
caught part of their words.

"If you had an ounce of understanding or of forgiveness
in you, you might be a real woman, Andrea!"

"Forgiveness—understanding!" Andrea tried to lower
her voice and involuntarily Mara slowed. Aunt Felice and
Celia were well ahead of her now.

"You and Will are gullible fools, but that's men for you."
Andrea's voice was husky, low, yet clear. "Acceptance,
spineless acceptance is what you want of me and you'll
never get it. *Never!* Remember that. How you, in good conscience, can forgive it—why, I put it in the same class as a
visit to the Fairweather house and I'll never accept it, or
forgive it."

"You talk of bad luck coming home to roost, Andy. I
should think you'd worry about future punishment for
your thoughts, and for your stupid overwhelming pride
that makes you think them."

"Punishment for being right?" Andrea said angrily, but
her voice wavered slightly. "You *know* I'm right and you
better mind your own step with—"

"Shut up!" he said tightly and Mara was careful not to
glance around, pretending she had not heard as she moved
toward her sister and aunt, who were now taking the steps
up the broad veranda.

But Mara wondered as she slowly took the walkway.
What did Andrea mean, punishment for being right about
what? And Branch, talking of understanding and forgiveness—for whom? Mara tried to link their meaning with
herself. *As most eavesdroppers do,* she told herself guiltily.

You're a fool, Mara Ashworth! and she put it determinedly
from her mind as she stepped up on the porch.

As they entered the house, the coolness of the big rooms
and high ceilings met them gently as Amos took their
hats, gloves and purses in the foyer. Andrea swept up beside them.

"Amos, you may serve the chilled white wine in the parlor. And tell Rosita we must wait luncheon until Will and
Mr. Ashworth and the others arrive. They've stopped to
see the new Ashworth store." She ushered them into a spacious and beautifully decorated parlor.

The furniture was not the ornately carved Victorian
that was so popular now. Instead, each exquisite gleaming
piece was of the lighter woods, such as those in the prewar
Richmond homes. Indeed, it was so like what the Ashworths had auctioned off in Richmond that dreadful day
that Mara's heart ached at the sight of it. There was a
broad fireplace, now screened by a bank of lush green Boston fern.

Above the fireplace and its scrolled mantel hung a gold-
framed, life-sized portrait of a tall, straight-shouldered
man in the pearly gray and gold of a Confederate officer.
His chiseled features were the handsomest Mara had ever
seen. Character and courage flashed in the pale crystal
eyes, in the set of his jaw, but there was kindness and sensitivity in the tender curve of his lips. Mara was fascinated
and stood staring.

"That's Father," Andrea said arrogantly. "Colonel William Hunter MacAdam of the Army of Virginia."

"It was painted twelve years ago by the French artist
Louis Ferenc, while he was in Houston," Branch said
quietly. "It's been over three months ago we lost him. We
still can't quite believe the Colonel's gone."

The three of them, Aunt Felice, Celia and Mara, were
still standing, their eyes riveted on the arresting face
above the mantel.

"It's a remarkable likeness—as I remember him," Aunt
Felice said slowly. "Archer thought the world of Colonel
MacAdam, as indeed did *all* of Richmond. Such a pity,"
she went on, hating to give Houston credit as the eventual
home of so illustrious a man, "that he ever left home."

"This is home, Miss Felice," Branch drawled.

"As it will be for us," Celia spoke firmly. "And I'm sure we'll come to love it as the Colonel did."

Aunt Felice gave her a derisive glance and said, "I'm sorry. I'm not one to make pretenses, Andrea, Branch. I hope Archer is successful enough for us to return to Richmond one day."

Mara thought her aunt a fool, for the doors of Richmond were closed to them forever now. For better or worse, this city would be their home.

"In the meantime, we shall make it as pleasant for you as possible, Miss Felice," Andrea said quietly. Her eyes flashed to Mara and this time there was no mistaking the icy hostility in them. But she said graciously, "Do sit down, all of you. Amos will soon be here with the chilled wine."

Mara seated herself carefully in a damask chair with delicately carved wooden arms. Andrea had taken a violent dislike to her, she knew, yet they had never met before. Why? And what was the quarrel between Branch and his younger sister? Mara did not want to think about it. She wanted to think of her own plans and that beautiful store with the shining glass windows in the heart of this city. And once more she forced the MacAdams from her thoughts.

"Make mine a bourbon over ice, Sis," Branch said, going to a fine leather humidor on a big cherrywood desk. It was not the only piece of French furniture in the room, but it was the most impressive. He took out a cigar, put it in his mouth and struck a match to it.

"You have ice?" Aunt Felice asked, still looking about the room.

"Yes. There are three ice plants in the city and the ice wagon comes by each morning," Andrea smiled. "We're never without ice."

"That's a blessing," Aunt Felice said, seating herself on one of two rose velvet Duncan Phyfe sofas facing each other before the fireplace. "I wouldn't have thought the convenience had come this far so soon."

"So soon?" Branch said, eyes twinkling as Celia sat down across from her aunt. "Why, Miss Felice, even our great-great grandfather had ice all year round. In eighteen-hundred his servants used to cut it out of the James

River on his plantation in Virginia during winter and store it in the underground icehouse. The ice wagon sure beats that."

Aunt Felice's ivory face pinked up, and Amos entered bearing a tray before she had time to acknowledge Branch's faintly contemptuous smile. "Mara!" She spoke angrily to her niece to distract attention from herself. "Don't you take that! You know very well you're too young for wine."

"It's very mild—," Andrea began, but Aunt Felice cut her off.

"Mara's but sixteen. Her papa would not allow it."

"She'll be seventeen the second of August," Celia said coldly. "Less than two weeks, Aunt Felice. As I recall, Papa permitted me—"

"You're much more level-headed and restrained than Mara, Celia. You know very well what a headlong child she is." Aunt Felice lifted a crystal glass from the tray.

There was an awkward silence before Andrea said, "Amos, please bring Branch a bourbon over ice," and she took a glass of wine, leaving the last two glasses. Amos nodded and went through the door into the foyer.

"Headlong?" Branch drawled. "The Colonel once told us General Lee said *that* translated into courage and initiative."

Andrea shot him a look from under her dark, slanting brows, and Mara glanced involuntarily up at the portrait again. That man had known General Robert E. Lee well enough to talk about such things with him. She wanted to send Branch MacAdam a grateful glance, but instead she met Andrea's pale stare steadily, hands tightly clasped in her lap.

"I'm sure that may be so," Aunt Felice sniffed, "in males that is. In females it's most unbecoming. Most trying. Poor Archer has always had to ride a tight rein on Mara." She looked at her younger niece accusingly but Mara was looking at Branch.

She was astonished to see a dull red climb into his tanned cheeks once more and the muscles in his jaw harden. He was furious and he was controlling his temper with effort.

Andrea was smiling faintly as she asked politely, "Tell

me, Miss Felice, did you and your nieces enjoy your trip across the country?"

And so they talked while Branch silently drank his bourbon on ice. Aunt Felice complained while Celia extolled the beauties of the scenery and Mara shifted restlessly, corroborating Celia's cheerful comments. It seemed an eternity before the sound of the buggy could be heard crushing against the shell driveway. In a few moments the men came in followed by Julius, his family and Amos, who carried Will MacAdam's two suitcases.

The servants vanished down the wide foyer and Ashworth came into the parlor, exclaiming his satisfaction with the store and complimenting Will on the beauty of his new house. He stopped midsentence as his eyes fell on the oil portrait above the mantel. There was a moment of complete silence.

"By God," Ashworth said softly. "Except for the gray at his temples, he looks exactly as he did that day at Appomattox."

"It's a good likeness," Andrea cut in proudly. "Ferenc is a great artist."

"Ferenc did it?" Ashworth asked.

"When he was in Houston about twelve years ago," Will said.

"No wonder it's so remarkable," Ashworth sighed. "I always hoped to take Celeste to Paris and have him paint her. The only one I have, Damon Chandler did in Richmond and it doesn't nearly do her credit."

It developed that the men had stopped at the Heights Hotel and delivered the Ashworth luggage there. Now, as Ashworth, Will and Kennedy finished their ponies of bourbon, they rose and followed Andrea into the great, cool dining room, where they were served a sumptuous luncheon. It was a cold meal, delicious crabmeat salad, big pink and tender shrimp, lobster tails with drawn butter, slices of avocado, tomatoes and lettuce, and tall glasses of iced tea. Only the feather-light rolls were hot.

Afterward, while everyone except Mara had a small crystal glass of peach liqueur, Ashworth remarked expansively that he would take Celia, Aunt Felice and Mara to see the store tomorrow.

"We'll rent a buggy and drive into town, girls," he said, lighting the cigar Will had given him. "You can look over the merchandise and the layout. It's almost as elegant as *Ashworth's* in Richmond, though not quite so large. There's a department at the side of the center that's empty yet, but it will give me a chance to put in some of my own ideas."

Mara's heart leaped. An empty department! Oh, she must make her move tonight after they reached the hotel! She couldn't afford to wait. Her papa might decide between now and tomorrow what he meant to put into it.

"And afterward," he went on, blowing out a cloud of fragrant smoke, "we'll go look at the house Halloran has offered to rent to us." He sounded more cheerful than at any time since his Richmond failure. Mara's spirits rose with fresh hope as she looked into the ruddy handsome face so dear to her.

"I'm sure John will want to drive you out to see the house to explain all the features and possibly show you others to choose from," Will said smiling. "Besides, he has his own rig."

"That will be fine," Ashworth said heartily, "but we'll meet him back at the hotel. I want to show Celia the store first. Celia and Felice and Mara, of course," he amended hastily and Aunt Felice's lids fell swiftly to hide her hurt. Felice longed to be *first* with Ashworth always.

"Then I'd like to drive you all to the store in the morning, Mr. Ashworth," Stuart Kennedy said. He crossed his legs negligently and Mara could see the high arch of his embroidered boots gleaming richly. His suit, his manner, his look all spoke money, old money. She wondered swiftly about his parents and hoped suddenly that her father would refuse; she needed the private time to convince him to let Sudie and her take the empty area of the store. *Ashworth Originals.* It burned in her along with the myriad designs and luxurious materials that filled her imagination.

"That's kind of you, Stuart," Ashworth replied, "but we'll want to dawdle a bit and you would be giving up too much of your business day to us."

Thank God! It would be just the four of them.

"Not at all," Kennedy shrugged slightly, hazel eyes

brushing Mara's, his admiration inescapable. "But I can understand that you might prefer to do it with only your family along." He smiled suddenly, again more at Mara than at anyone else, and finished, "But I certainly hope you'll allow me to escort you en masse or even singly in the future." Aunt Felice bridled for his eyes had met hers in passing.

The future! Each minute was fleeting and the future was an eternity away! Unable to contain her eagerness a moment longer, Mara turned pleading eyes to her father.

"Oh, Papa, I have something important to tell you—," she blurted, then hesitated an instant before rushing on, "when we reach the hotel. But I—I can't wait." She knew it was a mistake the moment the words were spoken.

Ashworth's eyes narrowed. "Mara, I hope this doesn't mean another one of your harebrained ideas—"

"Oh, no, no!" she said hastily, aware of the sudden silence about her. She spoke so seldom because of Aunt Felice's and Papa's disapproval. "This one will mean money, lots of money and all for *Ashworth's.*"

"Oh, my God." Ashworth's sigh was almost a groan as he scowled at his younger daughter. "It *is* more of your foolishness. Well, get it over with so I can tell you why it's impossible."

"No," Mara said miserably, her eyes going around the room. "It can wait. I—I didn't really mean to bring it up. I just thought, maybe I should mention it before you made up your mind about the empty space in the store."

"Mara," he said heavily, "you're sixteen and all your life you've been a trial to me. God knows I should be used to it by now. Why can't you realize a featherbrained child can be more of a hindrance than a help where business is concerned?"

"I—I'll wait and tell you later."

He laughed sardonically. "That's a good child. You'll have forgotten it later."

Celia looked at her sister with sorrowful compassion, Aunt Felice's eyes flashing with ill-concealed triumph. Andrea's wore cynical amusement.

But Will and Branch MacAdam were looking at Ashworth and their eyes, under their black, slanting brows, were murderous.

Chapter 5.

༄ THE Houston Heights Hotel proved to be an enormous, three-storied, steep-roofed and multigabled structure of gleaming, white frame, and it was new. Luxuriously appointed, with a bell in every room for summoning service, it was lighted by gas jets. That comparatively new miracle, electricity, was not yet available in all cases, or not yet accepted in some. In the third story, where the gables jutted out, were quarters for the guests' servants, and Julius and his family were comfortably ensconced in these rooms.

Uncle Abel Quayne and Uncle Rob Robertson had arranged for the Ashworths to have a suite of rooms, since it would be cheaper than four separate rooms. Mara and Celia shared a room which opened onto Aunt Felice's, which in turn opened onto a small sitting room; beyond that was their father's room. The uncles, protecting their interests, had paid for but one week in this luxury, certain that Ashworth would find a house to rent before the week was up. In which case, they expected their money back from the unused time and had said as much before Ashworth left Richmond.

After they had unpacked their luggage and Ashworth saw that the brass-bound trunks were stored in the baggage room, all of them felt tired. All but Mara, whose feverish desire to set up a shop in *Ashworth's* filled her with a seething restlessness. As they went down to supper in the big dining room of the hotel, she knew that she was going to have to face her father with her idea and soon.

But after dinner there was no opportunity to mention it to him. So she had to content herself with pouring it all

84

into Celia's sympathetic ear after they retired for the night.

"And when we go to see the store tomorrow, Celia, and that empty space is there, I'm going to tell Papa what Sudie and I can do."

"And I'll wear the blue dress you made me for the wedding," Celia said excitedly. "It's too dressy for such, but I want him to see it again. Let him see what you can do!"

"Oh, Celia," Mara squeezed her hand, "help me persuade him! He listens to you. He knows you're smart about everything."

"I'll be more than smart," she replied grimly. "I'll lose my temper if he doesn't listen to reason."

Mara murmured, "An *Ashworth Original.*" She savored the words not knowing her help was to come from a completely unexpected quarter.

But Mara was taken aback as the family sat down for breakfast in the spacious dining room downstairs, for John Halloran joined them. Ashworth smiled warmly and gestured.

"Sit down, sit down, John. Join us in breakfast."

"Thanks, Mr. Ashworth. Will tells me you're going to see the store again and then look at houses to rent. I've my buggy outside and thought I'd make it easy for you, be your coachman and guide for the day." The faint scar vanished in a white smile. His black eyes went to Mara and the smile broadened.

Oh, thought Mara frantically, *how can I approach Papa with him along?* Halloran was so outspoken, so . . . Well, there was nothing she could do about it, she thought glumly.

"This is mighty courteous of you, young man," Ashworth beamed, helping himself to the steaming platter of scrambled eggs before them. "I was going to hire a buggy and horse. However, I'm certain you can much better show us the advantages of any house you've built."

"We're not very experienced in looking for a house," Aunt Felice inserted earnestly. "You see, Archer's family lived in the house he just sold, for over a hundred years."

"Time you all made a change, then," Halloran replied irreverently. "I've built three just outside the Heights. All good hard pine, and quite spacious. We'll look at what the competition has put up while we're about it, if you like." He spooned up eggs on his plate and began to butter toast. "I wouldn't want you to take mine as a favor. I plan to sell them eventually anyway. There's a great demand for inexpensive housing in Houston right now." He smiled again and his eyes gleamed at Mara, as he added lightly, "And when *Ashworth's* prospers, I'm sure you'll want to build your own mansion in the Heights."

Thus, after breakfast, all of them descended the smooth granite steps of the hotel and mounted Halloran's buggy. Aunt Felice wore a broad-brimmed hat with a veil swathing her face.

Seating herself beside Celia, she said in a low worried voice, "This dust is dreadful. I'm sure it and the hot sun will ruin our complexion, girls. Do keep your hats and veils in place."

Celia and Mara, in their small straw sailors with light malines tied beneath their chins, said nothing as Halloran, with Ashworth beside him in the front seat, clicked to the horses and they were off down the road, soon reaching the end of the paved portion. The dust puffed upward, sifting over them as they passed other carriages and buggies. Mara's tension rose as they neared the downtown area.

By the time they drew up before the imposing front of *Ashworth's,* Mara's excitement was almost unbearable. Entering the store after the others, her legs were weak and she paused to draw a deep, trembling breath. Why, it was almost as big and nearly as elegant as her father's store in Richmond! No wonder he had been so pleased when he had joined them at the big MacAdam home yesterday.

Her swift eyes found the empty area, nearer the back than the front, but centrally located. There were even waist-high partitions about it. It must have been a special department for the man who owned it previously. There was room for sewing machines and a cutting and designing room, too! Her elation grew as she obediently followed the others while her father extolled the virtues of the store.

She fell slightly behind, her eyes returning to the empty section, swiftly adding changes she would make to it. Suddenly Halloran's big warm hand was on her bare elbow.

Immediately the sensual pleasure of his touch found its way into her blood and her heartbeat stepped up. She drew a deep breath.

"And have you talked to your papa about your plans?"

"Oh, no!" At her startled movement, the big hand closed more firmly about her soft flesh. "Wait! Don't *you* say anything. *I'll* do it at the right time."

"That could be years from now—or never," he mocked her timidity.

"No," she said firmly, "I'm going to do it when they come back this way. Before—before Papa passes the space again." And she hurried to follow the other three. Halloran, laughing quietly, lengthened his stride and did not let go of her arm.

Ashworth and Aunt Felice, with Celia beside them, were admiring the several racks of suits and dresses, then moving on, exclaimed over the large furniture department, filled with the popular Victorian, polished, dark and new.

"Your sister's rather overdressed for the occasion, isn't she?" Halloran whispered, his eyes on the elaborate drapes and tucks of the highly fashionable silk.

"Yes," Mara whispered angrily, "and for good reason. Papa doesn't know *I* designed and made it."

"Good strategy," Halloran nodded approvingly. "That's a shot that should certainly hit home."

They passed a series of dressing rooms beyond the racks of clothing and lingerie. Further to the rear was a section of fine china, where sterling silver pieces were displayed in glass counters. Ashworth laughed grimly as he recognized the merchandise the uncles had sent from his Richmond store, the more expensive items which would least likely sell in a city were most of the inhabitants had inherited many such things.

But most of what the uncles had sent, Mara noted dryly, was that which cost the least but made the most profit. One glass counter in the center brought a scowl to her father's face, for in the shelves were Aunt Julia's contribution to the new store. It was a complete cosmetics counter, and while the items had merely been unloaded and were not placed properly, it was easy to see there were rouges, lip salves, rice powders, pomades, creams, scented lotions and expensive perfumes along with other beauty preparations.

"My sisters!" he muttered under his breath.

Felice, though her eyes touched the items longingly, sniffed, "Shocking," anxious always to be in accord with Ashworth.

"But salable," Celia said with a little laugh. "Papa, you may as well come along with us. After all, it's 1897, not 1860."

"And I might add," Halloran remarked cynically, "history tells us that even five thousand years ago this was used by not only indiscreet Egyptian ladies, but by the most respectable ones, too."

Ashworth snorted, then his winning smile was turned on Celia and Halloran. "You'll have to drag me into the next century, kicking all the way. I still don't approve."

"Nor do I," Aunt Felice said virtuously.

"Papa," Celia said slowly, "did you know that Mara designed and made this dress I'm wearing?"

There was an instant of shocked silence and Halloran's hand tightened on Mara's arm as disbelief, astonishment and anger crossed Ashworth's face swiftly. Aunt Felice's mouth was agape and her deep brown eyes, so like those of her two nieces, were wide with disbelief.

"You told me this morning," Celia went on smoothly, "that you thought it quite the loveliest dress I had ever worn. I'm surprised you didn't ask me then where I got it."

"I thought you bought it from that Madame Flammarion on Duke Street in Richmond, that Frenchwoman who imports from Paris."

"It *is* quite as good as any of hers. Better, I think," Celia said blandly, giving Mara a meaningful glance.

"Papa," his younger daughter began hurriedly, "I think I could help the store. Help it be a big success, I mean. Make a lot of money." She drew a deep breath. "I—if you'd let me have that empty space here in the store for a dressmaking department. Papa, we could call the garments I make—baby clothes, layettes, lingerie and designer dresses—we could call them all 'Ashworth Originals.'"

Archer Ashworth seemed to swell visibly, his face growing redder and redder, blue eyes flashing fire. "Are you

mad?" he asked low. "Have you taken leave of your senses,
Mara? Surely you can't be serious?" He made a valiant effort to contain his fury. "You're only fifteen—"

"I'll be seventeen in a week, Papa."

"All right, seventeen. And a very ignorant seventeen at
that. You still gallop wherever you go—you can't even
walk like a lady, yet you are fool enough to think you can
sew for ladies!" There was a long silence. *"You certainly
cannot!"* And he took out a handkerchief and mopped his
face, which was wet with the intensity of his rage.

"Mr. Ashworth, you've been to Paris, of course?" Halloran's drawl was deceptively casual and smooth.

"Of course," Ashworth retorted shortly, his eyes fastened on his younger daughter's still white face.

"You've seen the famous dress designers' shops along
the Rue de Tilsit, the Rue de la Paix, the Champs-Elysées?"

"I never paid much attention to them."

"There's not one of them that isn't taking in over a million a year."

Ashworth stared at him. "A million? You can't be
right."

"But I am. I made it my business to look into their operations while I was there on two occasions. If I could have
bought an interest in one, I would have, but," he shrugged,
"the French are very shrewd. No sale." He paused, then
soberly, "There's not a single *haute couture* house in Houston. There is money here, yes, millions, but most of the
ladies must go abroad, or at least to New York to find designer dresses."

"Haute couture. The finest," Ashworth said, his color
receding and his eyes moving reluctantly to Celia who
stood gracefully, hand on hip, her dress flowing and
rippling over her beautiful figure like crystal blue water.

"This dress is *haute couture,* Papa. I've had numberless
compliments on it, but it's one of a kind. It can't be had by
everyone," Celia said coolly.

Mara's face was ashen. She was sure that if the others
hadn't been present her father would have struck her for
her temerity. She was shattered. Her plans were shattered
and she had such a passionate desire to help her papa that
it ached in her breast.

"And you know, Papa," Celia went on reasonably, "Aunt Julia always criticized you for not trying anything new in your store. She implied it was the reason for its failure."

"The women in Houston are starved for high fashion. If they could get it here," Halloran said pleasantly, "they'd spend all that money here instead of in New York or Paris." He pulled at his chin thoughtfully and added, "You know, Mr. Ashworth, although Mara's but seventeen, she has a genius for design and creation. What could you lose by letting her try?"

Even in her agitation, Mara realized this tall young man with the enigmatic eyes was exerting a strong influence over her father. Ashworth's color was normal now and his eyes swung to Mara once more and narrowed. Aunt Felice took his arm and said low, "Archer, dear, don't be a fool. The child will disgrace the store. She's too young and you don't know how impetuous and uncontrollable she is."

Ashworth looked down into the face that was lifted to his. Jealousy and frustrated passion were barely hidden in her forced smile. He slowly put his hand over hers which was resting on his arm. "Felice, I'm tired of being called an old mossback, resisting the new." He shrugged and his eyes flickered back to Mara. "As John says, there's money to be made in *haute couture.*" Then like a striking hawk, "Mara, I simply don't think you can do this alone."

Hope flooded her breast and she said breathlessly, "I don't propose to do it alone. Sudie is as good with a needle as I am. And after we get started, I will hire more expert seamstresses."

"You could enclose the area to the ceiling, hiding the sewing room as well as the cutting and designing rooms, too," Halloran remarked with surprising knowledge. He must have looked at the Paris fashion houses very closely indeed, Mara thought. "And she could have a fitting room with several tall mirrors in front. It would cost very little to run the partitions up to the top and install a sign in fancy gold over the door—*Ashworth Originals.*" He had released Mara's arm at last and was gesturing to the empty space beyond them.

Ashworth was following his gestures and his eyes were reflective. "It could be done . . . " he muttered, then irritably, "but I simply cannot imagine Mara turning out such as Celia's dress. All those baby clothes she made in Richmond, yes. But she's so inept, so awkward and all she has is her mother's beauty." This last tasted bitter and Mara cringed inwardly, knowing well he was remembering Celeste Bonheur's death and the reason for it.

"Papa," she said softly, putting her hand on his arm, "I'll try ever so hard to be graceful and gracious, if you'll only let me try. And think, Papa, of all the people it would draw to the store if we're successful."

He shook her hand off and said brusquely, "You'll try, but only over my better judgment. I'm as big a fool as you, allowing such an idea to go into the new store."

"Then you'll let me do it?" Mara asked with tremulous disbelief. "You'll buy the materials and—and—two new sewing machines?"

"My sisters, Maggie and Julia would surely say I'm crazy," he replied sourly, "but I'll give it a try. We can certainly sell any equipment if the idea fails." He scowled at Mara and she drew away. " 'Ashworth Originals,' indeed!" His lip turned down derisively.

"I think Aunt Julia would say you were smart, Papa," Celia remarked warmly.

Aunt Felice bit her lip in angry disappointment.

"She'd applaud the *idea*, no doubt," Ashworth said. "But to put it into Mara's hands! She'd say that's the height of folly."

"But my dress—," Celia began.

"Your dress could be a fluke, my dear," and he started slowly toward the broad front doors, "and probably is."

He had not smiled once at Mara, not even as Halloran and her sister's dress won him to her idea. It was bitter victory. She had been so sure he would smile at last and praise her for her design and her needlework.

On the way out, Halloran caught her arm in a warm, comforting grasp. "Don't be downhearted," he murmured. "I'll lay you odds, you'll soon be the biggest draw at *Ashworth's*, Papa notwithstanding."

Mara shook her head glumly. "If I can just bring in a *little*, help the store achieve prestige." She knew Halloran had done more to convince her father than any of them and

he was the last one in the world from whom she had expected help.

"You'll be the most prestigious part of *Ashworth's.*
Mark my words," he said, grinning, which made Mara
smile too. "And now we'll go and put that imperious, arrogant and unloving father of yours into a new house."

The house was white-painted frame and modest enough
on its acre of land. It had the prescribed white jigsaw trim,
a narrow front porch supported by slim wooden columns,
and even a belligerent little cupola at the corner of the second story. Inside, it appeared surprisingly spacious. The
floors were oak, sanded, stained and shellacked to a temporary but bright finish. They cried out for a coat of wax and
the dull sheen that came from handpolishing.

The single bathroom on the second floor had the latest in
plumbing fixtures, including one huge claw-footed bath-
tub, which, like the kitchen sink and the commode, emptied into a covered septic tank at the rear. The attic had
been finished out into four rooms on which the four spare
gables gave light and air. Halloran, a man of the future,
had wired the light fixtures for electricity, which he had to
bring some distance from the trolley line on spindly, but ef-
fective poles. The lower floor was complete with a parlor, a
dining room, a kitchen across the entire rear and a spacious room obviously meant to be a library with its dozens
of empty shelves.

The frame dwelling had none of the grandeur the Ashworths had left behind in Richmond, and there were to the
west of them two such similar houses, already occupied according to Halloran. Still, as it was so much better than
they had expected, they swallowed their disappointment
at their lowered standard of living.

Hiding his chagrin with a wry smile, Ashworth rented it
on the spot.

When John Halloran drove his buggy up before the
Houston Heights Hotel once more, Archer Ashworth was
restrained but sincere in his appreciation of the house,
which was to be had unfurnished for fifty dollars a month.
This was in line with other less expensive frame house
rentals in Houston. The larger, finer brick homes were

never put up for rent but occupied by their wealthy owners
and kept open by servants when those owners were absent
for any length of time.

"It's only for a little while, Mr. Ashworth." Halloran
smiled as he helped the ladies dismount the buggy, and
looped the reins over the hitching rail. "You'll soon be in
the market to build one of the mansions in the Heights.
Then MacAdam & Halloran Construction Company will
put you up in a beauty."

"That will take time, my boy, time. Meantime, do you
know where I could purchase—reasonably, of course—a
good mare and buggy?"

"The public stables on Fannin Street can furnish you
both at various prices," Halloran replied as they took the
broad steps to the hotel veranda. "They do business on
credit as well, if you wish to establish yours."

"Good, I'll go this afternoon."

"And you've probably noticed the hotel stables down the
block that are kept for the convenience of the guests? You
can keep both horse and buggy there until you've moved."

"Fine, fine!"

"Your daughter Mara has a birthday coming up next
week," Halloran said abruptly as they entered the lobby.
He swept off his broad panama, holding it in one big hand
as a strand of dark, slightly curling hair slipped down his
tanned forehead. "August second, I believe. With your permission, sir, I'd like to take her out and celebrate her coming of age."

"Why, she's still a child," Aunt Felice cut in swiftly.
"Much too young to go out with a man your age."

"Ma'am, I'm twenty-eight—"

"Eleven years between you," Aunt Felice interrupted
agitatedly. "Mara isn't ready for that. Archer, you know
she isn't. And we really know nothing about Mr. Halloran,
only what he's told us. About his education, his parents,
we know nothing."

"Aunt Felice," Celia said swiftly, "how rude you are!
And after all Mr. Halloran has done for us today. I'm
shocked!"

Mara's face stung and words of accusation boiled to her
lips, but she bit her lip and, as always, held her tongue.
Someday, she told herself, *someday . . .*

"John," Ashworth said slowly, "you must understand that Felice has raised her nieces and her concern should be understandable."

Raised them! Mara knew fresh rage. Pleasance and Julius had raised them. And further, Felice had only encouraged Ashworth's coldness to Mara, all in an effort to ingratiate herself to him.

"I can scarcely believe that Mara will be seventeen next week," Ashworth went on, running a hand over his crisp burnished hair. "But I guess it's so," he said, looking down at his younger daughter in her calf-length dress, her tumbling cloud of dark hair with the big taffeta bow in back. "She doesn't look a day over fifteen," he said irresolutely.

"But, Papa," Mara burst out impetuously, unable to stem her emotions, "I'm a woman! I'll be seventeen next Saturday—I'm *not* fifteen!"

"You might think Miss Celia fifteen," Halloran inserted, smiling easily, "if she wore child's clothing."

"Your outburst, Mara, sounds as if you were fifteen," Ashworth said coldly. Then warming slightly, "Yes, John, I guess she needs to celebrate, and I did promise she could put her hair up when she was seventeen."

"Archer, you'll regret this," Aunt Felice said, her lovely dark brows drawn. "Mara's an irresponsible child and we both know it."

"Aunt Felice, you—," Mara broke off, drawing a deep breath. All her life, Aunt Felice had tried to, and mostly succeeded in, circumventing any pleasures that might have come Mara's way. Now all eyes were on Mara and she swallowed her wild rebellion. "You are entirely mistaken," she said with forced calm. "I'm very responsible."

"And further, Archer," Aunt Felice went on, ignoring Mara, "I think you'll regret this foolishness of a dress shop in the middle of your new store." Her eyes on Ashworth were a mixture of love and warning, as if there were some cherished and dark secret between them. Then slowly she turned and left, her beautiful, voluptuous figure swaying as she made her way up the thickly carpeted stairs leading to the second floor of the hotel.

Ashworth's blue eyes followed her and he sighed. "You must forgive her sharpness, John. She's very concerned about the girls."

Halloran's tanned face was inscrutable as he nodded imperceptibly. Then bowing over Mara's hand, "I'll call for you next Saturday evening at six, Miss Mara."

Mara nodded wordlessly as his warm lips touched the back of her hand. Their feel was electric and it swept from the pit of her stomach to her knees. She pulled her hand away swiftly, but the touch of his mouth on it clung like fire and she resisted a passionate desire to press it to her own lips. He bowed again, their eyes clinging, before he went out the hotel doors.

When he had disappeared, Ashworth turned on his younger daughter, scowling. "This doesn't mean you have carte blanche to do as you please, Mara. I actually do not approve of this, in fact I would have refused, but Halloran has been so hospitable, so courteous, I couldn't very well turn him down." He wheeled about, then turned back. "And I expect you to behave like a lady. No galloping or gabbling like a magpie as I've heard you do with Celia." His eyes narrowed and his voice was cold and bitter. "And certainly I hope you'll have enough sense not to allow the man any liberties."

Mara stood still in the lobby, looking after her father's retreating back. None of them had asked her if she *wanted* to go. Halloran had assumed her acceptance. So had her father, and they were right. She repressed a grin for her heart was soaring. Two triumphs in one day—the dress shop and her first caller!

"I have nothing to wear," she said to Celia after their father took the stairs and her smile broke through in spite of herself. "Only these short dresses and flat shoes."

"If only you were my size, or I yours," Celia said thoughtfully. "Can you make a dress in the next week?"

"With Sudie's help I could." Then in a rush, "But we'll be moving all next week. Papa will have to pick out furniture and all the rest. I'll have to help and I want to get him to fix up that empty space if I'm to be a couturiere. Why, I've no business going out to celebrate my birthday!"

"Yes, you have," Celia said quickly. "If we have to buy you a ready-made dress and shoes with heels, we'll do it. Oh," her voice grew more excited, "Papa has said I can pick out the portiers for the windows and the rugs. God knows, we'll have to take the cheapest we can find in his store."

"Papa won't be in the mood to spend money on a new dress now that he knows I can sew," Mara said as the two girls mounted the stairs to their room in the big luxurious hotel. But after that final comment, silence prevailed between the two sisters, each immersed in her own tumbling thoughts. The move to their rented home would not be pleasant, for it and the furniture would be tawdry compared to the beauty that had been their home in Richmond.

The following Monday, while expressing more disapproval, Ashworth grudgingly allowed his younger daughter to pick a simple dress off the rack at Ashworth's and gave her a pair of beautiful white kid shoes with slender heels. Aunt Felice, as always, was cold and critical, and on every possible occasion, she repeated that Mara was too young for Halloran. She reiterated her contempt for his lack of formal education, his lack of family and his attitude toward herself. *No respect, no real courtesy to me. He's a boor.*

During that first week, Ashworth bought his mare and buggy on credit and Andrea and the MacAdam brothers had them to dinner every night. Sometimes John Halloran was at the table, and sometimes he and Will MacAdam left immediately after dining to handle a business matter that was demanding their attention. Andrea always smiled graciously as they made their apologies and left.

And afterward, when the women would sit in the spacious parlor beneath the strikingly lifelike portrait of Colonel MacAdam, Andrea would supervise Amos's serving of the after-dinner liqueurs. She always insisted that Mara have a glass of lemonade.

On these first hot summer evenings, Mara tried to analyze Andrea. What possible reason could she have for disliking Mara with such intensity? Was she in love with John Halloran, who made no secret of his attraction to Mara? Possibly, yet before John had made his feelings for Mara plain, she had been aware of Andrea's hostility.

No, she concluded, it was none of these things. Andrea had teased John Halloran about his aversion to marriage and his affinity for women, which implied that Mara was only one of many. It ran much deeper than that, so deep indeed, that a mere look across the short distance to the rose velvet sofa into Andrea's inimical eyes sent an involuntary shiver up Mara's spine.

And the week went by with Celia, Aunt Felice and Ashworth choosing from the new *Ashworth's* the big, dark and ornate Victorian furniture which would fill their modest frame house. Though the furniture itself was new, it was heavy and gloomy, and both sisters hated it. Aunt Felice, to comfort their father, exclaimed it was beautiful once it was settled in place.

Celia herself chose the dark red plush rug and matching portiers that went into their father's empty library. All the Ashworth volumes, priceless to their father, had gone at auction, bringing very little money.

But the new Victorian desk and a sofa with two great wingback chairs with deep red floral patterns made the room look rich and elegant, particularly when the two girls tried hard to forget the opulence of the Ashworth mansion in Richmond. Meanwhile, their father supervised preparations for the grand opening of his new store and composed advertisments which he ran each day in the *Houston Post.*

Though they missed the luxury of the large cherrywood bed they had shared since childhood, Celia and Mara each now had her own room, full of the crouching dark furniture. The drawers to their highboys stuck and they were forced to rub the sides with soap in order to make them slide easily. Then they filled the drawers with their stockings, gowns, corselets and other personal garments.

Sudie came down to Mara's room shortly before dinner two nights before the grand opening of Ashworth's.

"Ma an' Pa an' me got all that fine new furniture in our two rooms 'twixt the gables, Mara. We got everything put in place since you seen it an' it sure is nice. I can look out the windows an' see the stable out back an' on up to the Heights where all them elegant homes are. Ain't you proud of your new room, all to yourself now?"

Mara was folding the clean laundry Pleasance had

brought to her and she laughed as she laid another folded chemise on top of the little stack beside her.

"Yes, Sudie," she said, "come over here and sit on the bed beside me. I've a secret I've been saving to tell you."

Eyes round and sparkling, Sudie seated herself and began folding petticoats. "What secret?" she asked alertly.

"Papa says you and I can have a shop in his store where we can design and make dresses."

"Aw! No!"

"Oh, yes! And baby clothes and layettes and we can call them *Ashworth Originals*. Oh, Sudie, we'll make a mint of money! John Halloran says there are rich women in Houston who have to travel clear to New York and Paris to find original dresses." She broke off and both girls sat staring into each other's eyes in wonder. Then Sudie broke into a high giggle.

Then she leaped to her feet and danced a dervish beside the four-poster, singing, "Camptown ladies sing this song, doo da, doo da!"

Mara leaped up and joined her, spilling the folded chemises to the floor as she seized Sudie's hands and they swung round and round, singing together at the top of their voices.

"What in the world are you two doing?" The door swung inward and Aunt Felice appeared.

Mara, flushed apricot and sparkling with excitement, cried, "Oh, Aunt Felice, Sudie and I are celebrating—" It burst out before she thought, and seeing the chilled dark eyes, she closed her mouth with a pop.

"Acting like a pair of wild animals is what you're doing. Look at your clothing, scattered on the floor. You're stepping on it you little fool! Look, you've soiled it!" She swept forward and picked up the dainty silk underthings as Mara moved her foot aside.

For a moment, Mara thought her infuriated aunt would strike her, though it had been years since she had done so. Now Sudie glided between the girl and her aunt.

"It's my fault, Miss Felice," she said. "I pulled Miss Mara up while she was foldin' her clothes—"

"Sudie, you need not lie. I know only too well how careless Mara is, how completely irresponsible. I shall have to tell your father about this, Mara. It should change his mind about permitting you to go out with that boorish Mr. Halloran on your birthday *and* having a shop in his store."

She dropped the soiled chemise on the bed and stalked out of the room, slamming the door behind her.

"She's so mean, she could break daylight with her fist!" Sudie whispered. "Ol' cat!"

"Papa won't change his mind," Mara said, picking up the fallen underthings. She spoke with more confidence than she felt. She knew from the way her father had looked at her recently, it wouldn't take much to make him change his mind.

And that evening before Julius and Sudie served dinner, Archer Ashworth reprimanded his young daughter. As they all went into the dining room, which had no rug over the slickly shellacked floor, he frowned at Mara.

"Your aunt tells me you were cavorting around in your room this afternoon like a maniac, scattering your clothes and soiling them."

"It was an accident," she replied.

"It's never an accident with you, Mara. It's the result of thoughtless, careless behavior."

"A built-in lack of restraint," inserted Aunt Felice. "I certainly wouldn't trust her to restrain herself with a man. Especially a man of such obvious appetites as Mr. Halloran."

"Aunt Felice!" Celia burst out as they reached the table. "Mr. Halloran's a perfect gentleman and Mara's very trustworthy!"

"Your loyalty does you credit, dear," Aunt Felice smiled fondly at her older niece. "But you know from long experience that I speak the truth."

"It was an accident," Mara reiterated, low voiced.

"You're being stubborn, Mara," her father said. "Another unlovely trait you have."

"Mist' Arch," the quiet voice came from behind him. Sudie had appeared out of nowhere, holding a bowl of mashed potatoes in her hands. "It wasn't an accident. Miss Mara's tryin' to cover for me. I knocked them chemises off the bed. I grabbed her and spun her round an' round. Miss Felice caught me at it." She reached over and placed the potatoes on the white linen table cloth.

"I give up," he said, throwing his hands wide and

pulling out a chair for Aunt Felice. "With the grand opening of my new store in two days and here Mara gives me
this kind of trouble. I don't know that you're responsible
enough for a shop in the new store, Mara."

Sudie sent Mara an anguished glance before she turned
and went back into the kitchen. Julius set the rolls on the
table and turned with dignity to Ashworth.

"Mist' Arch, I'll take care of my Sudie. I'll see she's punished for gettin' Miss Mara into trouble. Sudie's just full of
high spirits. She don't mean nothin' by it."

When he had disappeared behind the swinging door to
the kitchen, Aunt Felice said reprovingly, "I told you Sudie would try to take the blame and Julius would back her
up. They've been doing it for years, Archer."

"I know it," he said heavily. Then with a lightning
glance at Mara, "If any *accidents* happen, as your aunt
suggested, with your caller or at the store, seventeen or
not, by God, I'll take my razor strap to you!"

He had done that twice, once when Mara was eight and
once when she was twelve. She hid a wince, for at the spoken words, her legs and thighs stung with painful memory.

The next day, the entire family went to the store to see
that the last-minute preparations had been made. The
MacAdams and Halloran had sent enormous bouquets of
hothouse roses and gladioli. Ashworth set the towering arrangement of gladioli on the jewelry counter and the rich,
red roses on the cosmetics counter. This latter merchandise he looked at with disfavor, remarking that perhaps
the roses would lend a touch of respectable beauty to it.

A mass of peonies had come from Stuart Kennedy, the
attorney, and Ashworth permitted Mara to place them on
a small table in the anteroom of her shop.

The carpenters had sealed off Mara's rooms with ivory-
painted partitions that rose to the high ceilings. A big
glass door opened into it, and on the door in fine gold scroll
read *Ashworth Originals* and below that *Haute Couture.*
When the door was painted, Mara had expressed her long-
ing to have her and Sudie's names inscribed as well, but
Ashworth had balked.

"I'll probably have to tear this out in a couple of months.

That's a vanity I'll not permit you, Mara," he said and
turned to the head clerk he had hired, a thin ascetic young
man named Percy Mason, who was balding early. "Percy,
do you think you can manage with the two girls I've hired
to help you?"

"Oh, indeed, sir," answered the young man and he
smiled brightly at the two clerks as Ashworth turned to instruct them regarding the clothing. They were Gwen
Traynor and Grace Black, both bosomy young girls and
timidly friendly with Mara, who, for the first time in her
life, found herself regarded with something akin to respect.

Then Mara took Sudie's hand and showed her about the
narrow confines of the fitting room, in which Ashworth
had permitted her to instruct the carpenters to build a
small dais before the tall, triple mirrors. As they went
through the sewing, cutting and designing partitions she
squeezed Sudie's hand.

"In two months we'll have so many orders, Sudie, and
such an income from them, Papa will be thinking how he
can enlarge this space for us!"

"Now where do our sewin' machines go?" Sudie asked
with some trepidation.

"We'll put them here, in the sewing room. Mr. Ricci, the
sewing machine man, says he can deliver them by the end
of next week. And I'll show you how to use it. Remember, I
had a course in school? Yours will be right here and mine
over there, and see, there's even room for two more, if we
expand."

"What's that, expand?"

"If we get more orders than we can fill and need helpers."

"Law me, Mara, you are one more for lookin' on the pure
bright side."

"That I am, Sudie," but Mara spoke with grim determination.

And so, on Friday, August first, the day of the grand
opening, Mara, with her hair up and new skirts down at
last, stood unobtrusively beside the glass door of *Ashworth
Originals*. Her new dress was a modest navy blue crepe
with a high collar and short, white cuffed sleeves and a

wide waistband. The skirt flared at the bottom, with the
faintest hint of a bustle, and it gave her the perfect hourglass figure that was so popular.

She had agreed with her father that Sudie, properly
clad, would come in Monday, the first day of the week, if
things worked out for Mara today.

Celia and Aunt Felice stood near the broad front doors
with Ashworth beside them, welcoming the customers and
smiling broadly. Thanks to the week-long advertisements
in the *Post,* customers were thronging through the double
doors. Women drifted by on waves of perfume and clustered about the new cosmetics counter, keeping Gwen
Traynor busy writing sales slips. Grace Black was busy
with the racks of dresses and even Percy Mason was running back and forth between the furniture and silver department and men's clothing.

At last, Archer Ashworth had to join him and leave the
greetings to Celia and Aunt Felice, for the customers not
only looked interested and prosperous, they were also
madly purchasing. Mara, busy in her own nook, realized
that word-of-mouth had played its part in drawing the
crowds.

Several women stopped early on, fascinated by the gilt
sign on Mara's door, *Ashworth Originals—Haute Couture.*

"Oh, yes," Mara smiled in answer to a question. "And
we specialize in exquisite handmade baby clothes and layettes as well." She had brought with her the thick portfolio
of her own designs, beautifully sketched and tinted with
water colors, and she spread it out for all to see.

"How wonderful! I'd like to put in an order right now,
Mama," said the young woman beside the older matron.
"After all, my baby will be here in seven months."

The mother smiled indulgently. "Are you taking orders,
Miss—?"

"Ashworth," replied Mara. "We won't be fully equipped
until a week from today. By then we should have our machines. But I can take your orders now." She went into her
office and brought forth a small notebook and took down
the young woman's name, address and telephone number.
Then she listed the items that were wanted.

"And you make ladies high-fashioned dresses as well?"

"Yes, madam." Mara gestured to Celia's blue dress on the mannequin just inside the door.

"How gorgeous! How marvelous!"

"Yes, madam. They will be specifically designed and fitted to each client, and for every occasion from ball gowns to dresses, blouses and dress suits."

"I must tell Betty! We shall be in to order next week, my dear Miss Ashworth. What a blessing to have an original house in Houston at last!"

After giving her name and making an appointment for a ballgown next week, the two women bade Mara good-bye and strolled to the far side of the broad store where one of the young clerks began showing them the ready-made dresses.

Mara drew a deep breath. It was going to be all right. It was going to be even better than she dreamed. Her old certainty returned. She *knew* it! And when she turned all that money over to her papa, he would see she was not irresponsible, nor willful and headlong. He would perceive her talent, her perseverance and her determination. And most of all, her success. Her father admired success. *And he would love her at last!*

Between customers, Mara thought furiously. On Monday morning, she and Sudie would come in together, for the cutting tables and chairs and the fitting room were all in readiness. They could cut, paste, and sew by hand until the machines came in. Already she had sent to New York and Paris, subscribing to four glossy fashion magazines. And she had her own portfolio, which seemed to impress the ladies most, even more than Celia's fabulous blue silk on the mannikin just inside the anteroom.

As the day wore on she showed the portfolio over and over to the delighted women who crowded into her small shop. Mara told them there was no style that she could not copy or improve upon. By simple measuring, she could cut a pattern for any client and make a unique and even more attractive style.

And so she took order after order, filling her notebook half full before the day was over. Ashworth had reluctantly told her that if she got a bonafide order she might dip into the bolts of silks, muslins, taffetas, rich velvets, tulle, and satins that were in the large dry goods department at the rear of the store. Her mouth watered at the pleasure she would find in creating fashions. Why, she would even have access to the Mousseline de Soie!

When the last customer left at six-thirty, Ashworth bade his three clerks good-bye and called his family to leave, locking the broad glass doors behind them. They were all tired and Mara knew from looking at Aunt Felice's lovely face that her feet hurt unbearably and she would probably take it out on her before they reached home.

But most of all, she was aware of her father's curious glances at her. Had he been impressed? Yes, she thought triumphantly, for his face betrayed it in the evening's pale light. Still, it was a curious expression, not love or affection yet, she thought. But she knew it was mingled with respect. The love would come, she told herself silently and joyfully.

They walked the half block to the public stables where Ashworth had left his horse and buggy. When at last they were inside, it was nearly seven-thirty as they rambled down the darkening streets.

Ashworth let out a gusty sigh. "If every day goes so well, Halloran just may be right," he said jovially. The carbide lights winked on as they passed each street corner, casting a bright glare over the store fronts and the sidewalks which alternated first wood, then cement. "Tomorrow we'll stay open until six-thirty again, even though it's Saturday. Young Percy Mason gave me the day's receipts, over fifteen hundred dollars," Ashworth continued with satisfaction. "I put it in the safe in my office. Half of it's in personal checks."

"And Papa," Mara leaned forward from the back seat of the buggy, "I took orders for fittings from six ladies plus two layettes. I figured that comes to near thirteen hundred right there." Beside her were packaged lengths of batiste, lawn and flannel so she and Sudie could start the layettes over the weekend.

There was a long silence. Then Aunt Felice said with a smile, "It was probably just talk, Mara. The ladies won't come back to be fitted."

"Aunt Felice," Mara said quietly but firmly, "they signed their orders. They are coming in on Monday to choose their designs. Six more are coming back to order tomorrow. We closed before I could sign them up. Sudie will come to work with me Monday and help take their measurements." She held the small notebook toward her aunt, who turned away indifferently.

"You didn't get any *money,"* Felice said, refusing to look at the names. "I'll believe it when I see the money in Archer's safe."

"I've invested a goodly sum in your enterprise, Mara, all on credit, the latest being those very nice dresses you're carrying home for Sudie and yourself," her father said slowly. "Not to mention the two machines and all that carpentry, painting and mirrors."

"Papa, just the orders I got today will more than pay that back."

"Not, as your Aunt Felice has pointed out, if your ladies don't come back. This may be just an opening-day flash in the pan, Mara, though I admit you did far better than I expected. I'm very surprised by it, but we will wait and see."

Mara was silent the rest of the way home while her aunt, father and sister talked of the people they had met during the long day. But Mara was thinking.

Though I admit you did far better than I expected. Those words were balm to her sore heart. Papa was impressed! Love for her was bound to follow. Oh, what a joyous moment! This was no "flash in the pan" and she knew it. Intuition told her that she had set her small feet on the broad road to success and, further, that Papa knew it, too.

When at last they drew up before their home, dusk was becoming evening and shadows flung themselves long and purple, about the house and under the pine trees. Mourning doves in the tallest pines, the small stable and the carriage house sent out their sad cry, accentuating the coming night. Streetlights had been left far behind.

Now Julius could be seen hurrying from the back of the house, where he had switched on a light illuminating the small back porch. Behind him followed an excited Sudie. Pleasance could be glimpsed standing in the lighted doorway.

"How'd it go, Mist' Arch?" Julius asked eagerly, reaching up to catch the reins as Ashworth drew the horses to a halt before the stable.

"Fine, fine, Julius! We made a little over fifteen hundred dollars."

"Law me, Mist' Arch! Reckon it's goin' to go like that every day?" He began to unharness the horse as the buggy's occupants stepped to the ground.

"It might, Julius, for a while anyway. Be sure you rub the mare down well. She's come quite a way at a spanking trot."

Sudie caught Mara's hand, taking some of the packages from her and pulling her toward the house. When they had moved some distance from the slower-moving Felice and Celia, she whispered hoarsely, "Mara, did the ladies like your shop? Was there many come? What'd they say?"

"Yes, yes, Sudie! We have six coming in tomorrow to choose from my portfolio and six already signed up." She paused to catch her breath. Then, "And you'll come with me tomorrow instead of Monday. Papa has let me pick out three dresses apiece for us to work in until we can fashion some sort of uniform for ourselves."

By now they had reached the back door, which Pleasance held open for them. Mara thrust her other packages into Sudie's hands and caught Pleasance in a wild hug, crying, "I've brought home batiste, lawn and flannel so Sudie and I can start two layettes over the weekend."

Pleasance's grin faded and she asked Sudie anxiously, "You tell Miss Mara about them strange men comin' an' what they brung?"

"No'm," Sudie said quickly, putting the packages on the broad kitchen table and catching Mara's hand. She pulled her through the kitchen, fragrant with baking rolls and a cinnamon apple pie in the big iron wood-stove in the far corner.

Mara heard Pleasance greeting the others as she followed Sudie hastily into the hall. Sudie kept tight hold of her, half running into the parlor where she pulled a light switch.

Mara blinked. Then her eyes narrowed on the great, gleaming mahogany Steinway that stood proudly in the corner, dwarfing the sitting room and the brave new Victorian chairs and little tables. *Mother's piano!* No, Celia's piano now. But a man named Smith had bought it . . .

"An' that ain't all," Sudie said breathlessly, pulling her

again into the hall, then to Ashworth's library with its empty shelves. She pulled the dangling cord to the light and four broad wooden boxes were revealed. On one box, the top had been pried loose. Mara stooped to see *Plutarch's Lives,* the volumes containing Shakespeare's plays, *The Dialogues of Plato*—all from her father's Richmond mansion. Why, the other two boxes must contain the balance of her father's prized collection of books!

Sudie caught her hand again and pulled her across the hall to the sitting room. They could hear Pleasance dimly now, taking Felice, Celia and Ashworth into the parlor. But in the sitting room, Sudie pulled the other switch and the mellow, shaded light gleamed on the highly polished fruitwood of the delicate French tables, the finest, the most treasured pieces! There were two gold-leafed pedestals, topped by the marble busts of Robert E. Lee and William Shakespeare. All, well, nearly all, of her mother's tables, the ones she had brought with her from New Orleans as a bride. Pleasance and Julius had made no attempt to arrange them and they stood clustered in the center of the room.

"Who were these men, Sudie?"

"Paw asked them an' they said they're just from the depo. Then Paw asked who sent this from Richmond? An' the men scratched their heads and say, 'Mister, we don't know. We just deliver. You all supposed to know!' "

Now Pleasance and the others entered the sitting room and she had evidently repeated what Sudie had just told Mara, for Archer Ashworth was swearing under his breath with relief at the sight of his treasures.

"Pleasance," his rich voice was full of laughing triumph, "I'll wager my rascally sisters did this, and after all their threats and remarks that losing them would teach me a lesson."

"Oh, Papa, we must write and thank them this very day," Celia cried.

"And tell them what a successful first day you've had, too, Archer," Aunt Felice put in happily. "I just knew Julia and Maggie couldn't bear to see you lose them."

But Mara stood silently, her eyes on the softly glowing marble-topped tables with their finely carved legs. She was remembering her conversation about her mother's pi-

ano with John Halloran, and Will MacAdam's wholly unexpected proposal of marriage to her sister, Celia. As incredible as the thought was, perhaps Julia Quayne and
Maggie Robertson had relented and sent these cherished
possessions out of the generosity of their hearts. But the
aunts were neither generous nor forgiving. Worse than
that, they were stingy, even with Celia, whom they loved
because she looked a little like them.

No, it was much more likely that Halloran had told Mac-
Adam, and MacAdam, moved by his hidden feeling for
Celia, had made this anonymous gesture.

Mara looked into Sudie's dark eyes and met a cynicism
as strong as her own. She smiled suddenly and whispered,
"Come on, Sudie. Let's go up to my room before dinner
with our dresses and materials and plan for tomorrow."

"Yes, ma'am!"

And the two of them slipped from the sitting room, taking stairs two at a time.

Chapter 6.

 THE following day, Mara took six more orders for dresses chosen from her portfolio and had to refuse three other women because she didn't want to be booked too far ahead. She had over three thousand dollars worth of orders.

Celia's borrowed blue silk dress remained draped on a figure just inside the shop. The women waxed ecstatic about it and two placed an order for it, one in flowered silk and the other in a solid rose silk.

Sudie, clad in one of the navy blue dresses Mara had chosen for her, spent Saturday industriously fitting customers and cutting materials to pattern on the broad table in the cutting room. Mara had promised the slender dark girl that she would pay her ten percent of everything they sold and the prospect of such riches had gone to Sudie's head like wine. Her eyes sparkled and her smile was almost constant. Further, she was making a studied effort to speak more like Mara.

As her father finally closed the store that Saturday Mara knew she had never had such an exhilarating birthday in her life. Though only Julius and his family and Celia had congratulated her that morning, she knew her papa had far too much on his mind to remember. As for Aunt Felice, she bore her niece no good wishes, and though Mara had expected it, the hurt still stung.

Since the arrival of the piano the previous day, Celia had stayed home. She told Mara that she was going to spend the entire Saturday playing her treasured Steinway. And she had Julius paint a modest sign saying *Piano Lessons Taught Here*. He had driven it into the ground in

front of the house and Mara saw it when they returned
home that evening.

Though Ashworth had put in an order for one, there was
not yet a telephone in the house, so Celia would have to depend on her sign and word-of-mouth until she could put a
small advertisement in the *Post.*

And last night, when the excitement of seeing all their
precious belongings was hot upon them, Aunt Felice, Ashworth and Celia had written effusive and lavishly grateful
letters to Aunt Maggie and Aunt Julia for their unexpected generosity. Ashworth had mailed them only this
morning on the way to the store.

But Mara had not written. She felt the aunts had nothing to do with it and her suspicions still fastened on Will
MacAdam as the unknown benefactor. She based her conclusions on the fact that he wanted to marry her sister,
suspecting he might love Celia in an inarticulate way. Besides, he was the only one with money enough to indulge
in such philanthropy. Except Halloran, of course, who
would have no reason to make such an expensive and
anonymous gesture.

Mara thought about this as she bathed that Saturday
evening, later donning the white silk and lace-covered
dress with the lace band trimmed with black velvet that
circled her slender throat. Then she thought about Halloran, who would come soon and take her to celebrate her
birthday. Her skirt swept the floor, and the taffeta petticoat beneath it held the gored skirt out slightly. Her corse-
leted waist was satisfyingly narrow, she thought, looking
in the mirror at the single pink rose at her waist.

Halloran had come into the store earlier that Saturday
and told her briefly he was going to take her to dinner at
the Grand Central Hotel Dining Hall. Mara had been impressed by just the name of the place.

Now she enlisted the aid of her sister in putting her hair
up, and Celia talked as she worked with the thick shining
mass.

"Andrea told me that the Grand Central Hotel is the
most elegant place in Houston, Mara. They serve ten-
course dinners!" Celia said teasingly as she tucked pins
into Mara's curling pompadour. "And furthermore she
says that *everyone,* all of Houston's rich and socially promi-

nent citizens dine there on Saturday nights. You'll be with all the best people."

Mara looked down at the simple white silk with the fine lace outlining her delicately pointed breasts. She was wearing the corselet for only the third time in her life, and her waist was, in truth, no bigger than the span of John Halloran's tanned hands. Now she wondered if the simple, fluid lines of the dress would be appropriate. She put it from her mind, for she decided that the little peplum at the rear gave the dress a very elegant look.

"I forgot to get a hat at the store," she said regretfully.

"Oh, I'm sure a white net scarf over your coiffure and loosely trailing about your shoulders will be quite appropriate, at least we know it would be in Richmond and I have one in my drawer. I'll get it."

When she returned with the scarf, Mara asked, "Why wouldn't you go out with Branch MacAdam tonight? I heard him ask you three days ago."

"Ah, I will, one of these days," Celia answered evasively, working to get the pompadour just right. "I like him and his sister well enough, but their older *brother!*"

"Both MacAdams are quite smitten with you, *I* think," Mara laughed. "Much more so than John Halloran is with me. I think the man's merely curious about me for some reason and he's certainly a cynic." She paused, then, "Did you know he doesn't believe in marriage? Says it makes people miserable."

"I guess there's some truth in what he says. David told me—" She broke off, her ivory face flushing.

Mara stared at her. "You mean David Donellan told you on the train his marriage wasn't happy?"

"Not in so many words, but he implied he had an unhappy experience with Lucinda on their honeymoon. He says she's not strong. They cut it short, you know. They were supposed to stay three weeks but they stayed less than one."

"He *told* you he was unhappy?"

"No, no! He's too much of a gentleman for that, but I could *feel* his unhappiness."

"Celia, you stay away from David Donellan!"

"I'll do no such thing! I had a note from him the other

day, and he's coming over next week to dinner. After all, he's an old friend."

"Old friend, indeed! I don't think he's above playing on your sympathies, Celia, and I *know* he could hurt you again in some irreparable way if you gave him the chance."

Celia put down the comb and brush silently and went to her own room, leaving Mara fearful she had offended her sister. It was the first time Mara had spoken so sharply about Donellan, and her immediate inclination was to run after Celia and hug her impulsively, murmuring, *I'm sorry. I didn't mean it.* But that was the rub. She was sorry if she had hurt Celia, but she had meant every word of it.

Julius admitted John Halloran, and Aunt Felice was the only one who greeted him with Mara in the parlor. Her father remained in the library, caught up with his books, and her sister remained in her room. Mara was certain now that she had offended Celia or else she would have joined them in the parlor, making the moment easier for Mara. Instead, Aunt Felice greeted him coldly.

"You'll have her in by twelve, you understand?" she said icily and without smiling.

"Yes, madam." Halloran was equally chilly. "You will give my regards to Archer?" Holding his fine panama hat with its slightly curled brim, he was wearing the inevitable polished boots, but his gray suit had the luxurious sheen of the finest gabardine and it was tailormade to his lean, muscular body. There was a thin string bow tie, black against his snowy shirt. "How are you this evening, Miss Mara?" he asked gravely.

"Very well, thank you," Mara replied evenly. "Shall we go, Mr. Halloran?"

And as they stepped out the door on the short veranda Aunt Felice called, "Mind what your father said, Mara Ashworth." Her voice was just short of shrill and she let the screen door close with a sharp bang.

"And just what did your father say, Mara?" Halloran asked, dropping the "Miss" before her name as he half-lifted her to the buggy seat. It was thickly upholstered and very comfortable, and not at all as spartan as the three-seated buggy in which he had driven them about in the city when they had first arrived in town. She had no intention of passing on to him her father's warning that she was not to let her escort take liberties with her.

"This is a very fine rig, Mr. Halloran. I didn't know you had two."

"I have three, counting the Victoria. However, I preferred to drive us alone tonight." He chuckled and with sudden insight added, "And your father probably cautioned you against my overtures." He paused, then, "I *am* going to make overtures to you, Mara."

She took hold of the metal arm beside the seat. None of the books she had read in the Richmond library had covered conversations with an older man on anything as nebulous as overtures or liberties.

"Besides, I thought we had an agreement that when you were seventeen you would call me John," he added teasingly.

"That would only make it easier—for overtures," she said cautiously and was disconcerted when he burst into laughter.

"If you call me John, I promise to tell you before I make an overture," he said and sobered slightly.

They were coming to Houston Heights now, and the huge, imposing houses had gas lamps on either side of their front doors. Three of them had gas piped to the edge of their drives, where tall lanterns cast their pale tracery on nearby shrubs and lawn.

"You are destined to live in one of these someday, Mara. Probably married and miserable with some wealthy philanderer," he said, turning to look at her. His smile shone whitely in the pale moonlight.

She lifted her chin. "I probably will, but it will be because Papa is a huge success, and he'll build us one like our home in Richmond, only lovelier!"

"You think a great deal of your papa, don't you, Mara?"

"I love him with all my heart," she said simply. Halloran was silent, and the long silence implied criticism of her father. She said defensively, "He's not really cold to me. It's that he's never been able to rise above my mother's death." She paused, then plunged on, "I was the cause of her death, you see, when I was born. Can you blame him for the turn his grief has taken? I can't! But someday he'll

come to love me for what I am, and forget what I did by
being born."

"I'm sure of that," he said easily. "And everyone likes
your papa—"

"Oh, they do, they do! Why, only a few days ago, some
kind persons who had bought some of our most treasured
pieces at the auction in Richmond sent them to him anonymously. All of Papa's fine library, the piano, some of
Mother's loveliest tables and chairs."

"That was uncommonly thoughtful of someone. Who?"

"Papa and Celia and Aunt Felice are sure it's the aunts
and uncles in Richmond. I'm not so sure."

"You suspect others?"

"I think it's Will MacAdam. I think he's in love with
Celia. And I know he thinks a great deal of Papa, because
his father, the Colonel, did, too." She slanted a look up at
him from beneath her sooty lashes. "Come now, Mr.
Hallor—John. He did do it, didn't he?"

"I don't know. I wasn't with him all the time we were in
Richmond. He doesn't tell me all his secrets. In fact, I
didn't know he was in love with Celia." His deep voice was
full of amusement.

"Well," Mara said uncomfortably, feeling she had spoken unwisely, "it's just an idea I have. And Celia doesn't
love him. That I know."

"Then his efforts are wasted. Too bad."

They had traveled across the rattling wooden bridge
over White Oak Bayou, and the piercing sweetness of hon-
eysuckle and magnolias came to them on the cool night air
as they passed the big Fairweather home and drove into
downtown Houston.

"I don't *really* know," Mara temporized. "I think Celia
will fall in love again, and Will MacAdam is a fine man."

"Again?"

"Oh, she's had a romance or two," Mara said hastily,
catching her slip, "but she's over them by now."

"I think you're a bit of a liar and a matchmaker, too,
Mara."

"Of course," she said flippantly. "I intend to prove
you're a misogamist, a cynic and entirely wrong about living happily ever after."

His laughter rang out unrestrainedly, causing a couple passing by in a Victoria to look at them half-smiling.

"And did they teach you about misogamy in that fine finishing school in Richmond?"

"No," she said, glad that the carbide streetlights did not reveal her reddening face. "I—um—was ever a one to read, and I went to the library often."

"And learned from a book what to call people who hate marriage, eh? Well, my dear Mara, we'll wait a few years and see if you don't, after a proper time spent in observation of wedlock, agree to join the ranks of misogamists."

He pulled the buggy up beside several others before the imposing facade of the Grand Central Hotel and handed the reins to a young boy who looped them over the rail in front of the building. He flipped the boy a quarter and turned, taking Mara's arm to assist her to the ground.

Then as they crossed the planked floor of the hotel veranda and stepped through the broad doors onto the lobby floor inlaid with white marble, he bent down to her and whispered, "Besides, we might as well be as honest as possible tonight. You see, I know your sister is still in love with the elegant Mr. Donellan."

"You know no such thing!"

"But I do. I'm curious about people, and I watched your lovely sister when she chanced to look at Donellan." His eyes twinkled with mischief.

"That's not curiosity. That's impertinence!" But she had to smile as she said it.

Her eyes took in the enormous potted palms in glazed containers that stood foursquare around the broad marble columns in the lobby. The rich dark green velvet couches and wingback chairs, the polished occasional tables and mahogany Victorian chairs that were placed comfortably about gave her a feeling of opulence. She was glad that her white silk and lace dress with its single pink rose at her throat was simple, beautiful and very avant-garde in its sweeping lines.

She was entering the adult world for the first time and she felt confidence flowing into her, tingling at her fingertips and sending a rippling little thrill through her stomach. She glanced up at her escort to find him looking at her speculatively, and she gave him a brilliant smile as she drew off the misty white net from her abundant coiffure. She saw reflected in his eyes that she was beautiful and she let the realization seep into her. Others were looking at the tall man and the slender girl as they made their way into the impressive dining room, and Mara could feel the approval as well as admiration, in their glances.

The black-suited maître-d' met them at the threshold and said, "Good evening Mr. Halloran, Miss Ashworth. Your table is right this way."

Mara followed, marveling that Halloran had the power to command such personalized service. There was a three-piece orchestra on a small dais at the far end of the room, and the music was muted softly, as were the lights spangling through the crystal prisms of the dozens of elaborate chandeliers above the tables.

There were many guests in the great room, and the curtains at the long windows fluttered inward as a breeze from the nearby gulf blew coolly in. As she was seated Mara glimpsed Andrea at a far table, but she could not see her escort.

She and Halloran had scarcely taken their seats when a waiter drew up with a bucket of ice from which the neck of a bottle of champagne extended.

"After all," Halloran said, as the waiter put a cloth over the top and expertly popped the cork, "I did promise you buckets of champagne on your birthday."

The waiter poured a few drops into Halloran's glass. Halloran sipped it and then nodded to the waiter's evident pleasure. The man then proceeded to pour a crystal glass full for Mara, then filled Halloran's.

"Shall we toast your new business venture?" Halloran asked.

"Oh, yes! Yes, let's do!"

And they lifted their glasses, touched them tinkling together and took a first sip.

"And a second toast," Halloran said soberly, "to your *continued* success, no matter what the future holds."

"That sounds ominous," Mara said uneasily, sipping the champagne.

"Just playing it safe," he smiled. "I've taken the pleasure of ordering our dinner ahead. I hope you like it."

"Celia told me this place serves the most wonderful food

and that everyone who is anyone comes to dine here," Mara said, looking about as casually as she could. Some of the men wore frock coats and striped pants and diamond tie studs. The women were beautifully clothed, some elaborately and some in exquisitely good taste. Among the latter was a woman seated at some distance, with a crown of red-gold hair piled high upon her head. Even from across the room, Mara could tell she was as flamboyantly beautiful as her low-cut green chiffon dress. Over her magnolia white shoulders was flung a gossamer net, much like the one Mara had used to cover her head and which was now draped over her own lace-covered shoulders.

"I've ordered two entrées, suckling pig and larded quail, served with calve's foot jelly. We shall have English plum pudding and fresh strawberries, too. And any other viand that suits your fancy. I'll have the maître d' bring you a menu when he starts to serve."

The champagne was crisp and cold and it gave Mara even more confidence. Her extroverted nature triumphed over tutored reticence, and she began to talk.

"Do you know that I've already orders for dresses and two layettes that amount to three thousand dollars?" She looked at Halloran solemnly over her glass.

"Good lord!" he spoke with satisfying astonishment. "You're going to be the making of *Ashworth's.*"

Across the room, she glimpsed Andrea's companion and as he caught her eye she saw it was Stuart Kennedy. He nodded and smiled, and when he did so, Andrea also turned and gestured.

In the meantime, the champagne loosened Mara's tongue further and she launched into a description of all the furniture their anonymous benefactor had sent them from Richmond. Then she talked enthusiastically of the many materials she had assembled for her dressmaking orders.

"And you design them yourself," Halloran said with proper respect, half-smiling at the flushed and earnest face before him.

Mara noted that he had inclined his head to several men and women in the room, including the blonde beauty that had first caught her eye. And every time her glass neared empty, he quickly refilled it from the apparently bottomless bottle.

Mara looked down into the golden liquid and at the minute globes of air that rose like diamonds to burst at the top. Then as she looked at the man across from her the most curious and vulnerable tenderness rose in her, seemingly dangerous, for suddenly the hard-faced man before her looked softened, too. Their eyes met and clung, for a brief moment.

"Now what are you thinking, beautiful Mara, to make your eyes so luminous."

She looked down at the champagne again and realized she had drunk a great deal of it before their main course, or even the turtle soup, had arrived. On an empty stomach, champagne could play odd tricks, she was learning.

"I was thinking," she replied. "I have told you a great deal about myself when I really wanted to talk about you."

"I'm not nearly so interesting," he said leaning back with a half-smile.

"To me you are." With her champagne courage, she asked, "Why did you run away from home at thirteen? And how did you come by that little scar?"

"All that's too far back to remember," he said evasively. "Let me tell you about the future instead. You're part of it, and, like you, it's much more interesting. You see, I happen to be one of those fools who think Houston and its surroundings sit on a sea of oil. And I've bought into a salt dome ninety miles away, in Beaumont, though most experts laugh at me. I think there's oil under it. So does an old friend of mine, Patillo Higgins. It's called Spindletop."

"Oil? Lumber, construction, the boat channel in Buffalo Bayou—what *is* your main business?"

"They're all my main business. With Will, I deal in cotton, too."

"I can see you're a man of varied interests," Mara said, realizing a faint tendency to slur her words. She looked down at the glass of sparkling wine and pushed it further from her. "But oil's only good for lanterns and stoves and to sprinkle on streets to lay the dust. I can't understand your enthusiasm about it."

His eyes gleamed, and as he leaned toward her, his face lit with an inner fire. "The future of oil is unlimited. They run engines on it already. There's a man I've heard about, a man named Ford, who is working on a horseless carriage that will run on it. Why, the by-products and chemicals that can be derived from oil are limitless." His brilliant eyes looked beyond Mara, beyond the spacious dining room at a vision of his own.

For one transcendent moment, Mara shared the feeling that boiled within him. It was wildly exhilarating and she was suddenly conscious of the powerful sexual pull between them. She lowered her lashes swiftly, but not swiftly enough, for she sensed his alertness to her every feeling.

"So you feel it, too, Mara." His voice was low and caressing, and her blood pounded up to her cheeks. She was spared a response by the waiter, who drew up with the soup.

After the first course the effect of the champagne had lessened and Mara talked less of herself and more of Halloran's many business interests.

Midway in their meal, two men, having finished dining, came by their table and spoke to Halloran. He introduced them to Mara and she learned that the first, a tall broad man of indeterminate age, with character in every crag of his face, was William Marsh, a man of vast wealth and power in Houston. The other, shorter and portly, was Henry Seagram, a cotton broker. Both men were on the Committee for Deep Water, which had financed the dredges now working to deepen Buffalo Bayou into a ship channel.

"They're laughing at us and our dredges, John boy, the Galveston Wharf Company," Marsh said, his face growing craggier with a smile.

"They're still the Octopus of the Gulf," Seagram put in sourly. "I lost a hundred thousand in storage fees to them last year. By God, those dredges of ours better do the job, John."

Halloran shook his head. "They're a start and they'll help, but they won't do it. We need federal help, and you know well enough that Hutchinson has already introduced a bill requesting a survey for a twenty-five-foot channel to Houston. And when he retires next year, we can run Tom

Ball for Congress in the fall. He'll see it through, mark my words."

"Yes, yes," Marsh said impatiently. "We know that, but in the meantime there are those damned Galveston jetties. Hell—pardon, Miss Ashworth—Congress authorized over six million for them and they're completed now. Yet not a penny for the channel to a real port."

Halloran's laugh was cold. "A lot of good those jetties will do them when the bad storms roll in."

"That's so." Marsh pulled at his chin. "Though God knows I wish them no harm from that quarter."

"You might as well be practical about it." Halloran's voice was hard. "It *will* blow in there one day. It's only a matter of time."

"So history tells us," Seagram said, then bowing to Mara. "I'm very glad to meet you, Miss Ashworth. My wife is already singing the praises of your shop and has ordered a dress from you."

Mara smiled and acknowledged that she knew Mrs. Seagram. "We are making her a beautiful dress!"

When the two had left, Mara asked, "Why do you call David Donellan's company the Octopus of the Gulf?"

"It's been called that a long time and for many reasons. Their tentacles reach out and strangle the competition. They take advantage of their position to collect unreasonable rates for shipping. The high cost of imports has been laid at their door for years. Now with these jetties complete—well, you see, so long as deep-draft ships had to anchor outside the Galveston bar to load and unload, barges could carry cargo to Houston up the Bayou almost as easily as to Galveston. But since ocean vessels can load and unload directly at the wharves in Galveston, the barges will become obsolete. Moreover, deep water at Galveston threatens Houston's position as a railroad center. As it becomes more and more imminent various railroads at Houston will begin considering spurs to Galveston. You understand?"

Mara nodded slowly. "It's all a quarrel over money—"

"Over how money is made, their way or ours and for whom. Houston men or Galveston men."

"I guess you hate Galveston—"

"Indeed not!" he replied, apparently shocked. "It's a city

of such beauty in spots as to take your breath away. I fully intend to build a summer home for myself there soon." He smiled at her and the scar vanished in its winning crease. "I'd like to show you Galveston—and these blasted jetties. Would you care to spend next Saturday afternoon with me? We'll take the train over the trestle and dine on a pier out in the gulf. I'll show you the jetties and the beauties that wonderful little city offers."

"That sounds delightful, but I have so many orders. If this were not a birthday treat, I would be home sewing right now with Sudie."

"You'll be working very hard all week, I'm sure," he said gravely, "and I think a treat a week is in order. I prescribe it."

She was thinking. Sudie could run the shop Saturday afternoon. She'd be pleased to take charge of it. The new sewing machines would be in by then, too.

The waiter arrived with strawberries on light, flaky cakes piled high with rich, whipped cream. A fresh bottle of champagne was opened and placed in the silver bucket of ice.

"I dare not take another glass," Mara said with a small grimace. "I'm already light-headed as a goose."

"Ah, but you haven't giggled. Every seventeen-year-old girl must drink champagne on her birthday until she giggles deliciously."

"I should hate to *giggle.*" Mara frowned at him as he refilled her glass.

"Forgive me. Until she laughs without restraint."

"I've talked without restraint. Won't that do?"

He shook his head. "Drink one more glass—a full one."

She took a large sip, then took a spoonful of the strawberry confection. The two went well together and she polished them off, regretting that she couldn't ask for a second serving.

His eyes on her were teasing. "Now if you had on that short dress, with your hair spilling about your shoulders, it would be perfectly proper to ask for another dessert. Aren't you sorry you're an adult?"

She burst into laughter at his sharpness, then put her fingers to her rosy lips. "There. I laughed and it wasn't a giggle, either."

"It was pretty close. I'll settle for it. Ah, here comes Mrs. Fairweather."

Mara turned and saw the beautiful woman in green chiffon floating toward them on the arm of a tall, handsome man. Her red-blonde hair gleamed in thick profusion atop her high-held head.

"Ah, Johnnie Halloran!" She spoke in the gentlest of voices, well bred and cool. "It's been far too long since you've come calling. I had Juanita make your favorite *buenelos* twice and we've had to eat them all ourselves."

John Halloran had risen to his feet and now he bowed gallantly over the woman's pale, slender hand. Looking up at her, Mara was enthralled. Her eyes were the same pale, clear green as her gown. She looked somehow familiar, yet so much more beautiful than the two women she brought to mind.

"This is Mrs. Clive Fairweather, Miss Ashworth. She is the widow of Houston's only legitimate aristocrat. Clive was English and gave up an earldom to settle here."

"Mrs. Fairweather, you—you—," Mara hesitated as she stared in rapt admiration, "you remind me of my aunts in Richmond, but you're far lovelier!"

"Thank you, my dear. I was just thinking what perfect taste Johnnie Halloran has. You're quite the most beautiful young girl I've seen in a long time." Her voice was still quiet, but full of such tenderness and warmth. Mara's hungry heart went out to her as she went on, "I have a daughter near your age. She's in school in France right now. I love her and miss her very much."

"I imagine she longs for you, too," Mara murmured. How could a woman so young have a seventeen-year-old daughter. "Will she come home this summer?"

"No, but I shall go to see her next spring. Let me introduce you to Desmond Brant, Miss Ashworth. He is my business manager. He looks after my investments for me."

The man was as tall as Halloran and his eyes were pale hazel. His flat-planed face was inscrutable despite a perfunctory smile at Mara.

"Things going well with you, Des?" Halloran asked.

"Right as rain, John." His voice was slightly raspy but not unpleasantly so, and Mara, after a moment, decided she liked him when he shook her hand, for his grip was cool and dry and quite firm.

"I've been hearing about the new *Ashworth's*." Mrs. Fairweather smiled at Mara. "And about your originals. I am coming to see you soon, for I shall need some very lovely things to take to Paris with me. And it would be great fun to astonish the blasé Parisiennes with something truly gorgeous and truly American!"

"Oh," Mara said breathlessly, "it would be an honor to design for you, Mrs. Fairweather. *You* would make any dress beautiful!"

"How nice she is, Johnnie," her smile was sunny and completely without artifice, including both Mara and Halloran. "I will see both of you soon." And with her hand on the arm of her tall escort, she drifted away from their table and out of the dining salon. The orchestra was playing "On the Banks of the Wabash Far Away," and Mara was always to think of Mrs. Clive Fairweather whenever she heard it again.

"Isn't she simply gorgeous?" she breathed to Halloran.

"Indeed she is," he said dryly.

"How long has she been a widow?"

"Ten years."

"I can't understand why she hasn't married. You know she must have dozens—"

"There you go, marriage again, Mara. Perhaps Mrs. Fairweather prefers the single life. In fact, she strikes me as being one of the most satisfied women in Houston, independent and making money in several ventures." And suddenly he laughed hard.

"I don't see what's so amusing," she said swiftly. "She must have married when she was just a baby. She doesn't look twenty-five."

"She's thirty-five. Her daughter is just your age."

"Then she *did* marry young, when *she* was but seventeen. She said she hadn't seen you in some time. Do you know her well? Are you old friends?"

"How curious you are. Every man in Houston that's worth more than half a million knows Mrs. Fairweather, for she's a businesswoman herself and worth quite a tidy sum."

"She has business dealings with them?"

"That's right. She owns more than half the stock in the old Houston Hotel."

"I hope I come to know her well. I admire her so."

"Clive Fairweather was a ne'er-do-well. All he left her was that house and in ten years she's made a fortune. Quite admirable, I'll agree. Will you have one last glass of champagne, my little inquisitor?"

Mara looked at the bottle hidden in the silver urn of ice. She was satiated completely with both food and drink, but she was loathe to leave this lovely place of soft lights and softer music. She shook her head slowly.

"I've had quite enough champagne for one night."

"I was hoping you'd have a little more. You see, I intend to make overtures and it might make you a little more receptive." He laughed quietly as he saw her back stiffen and her chin go up.

"I—" She broke off as Stuart Kennedy and Andrea Mac-Adam drew up to their table, both greeting them with pleasure.

"Miss Mara, when I asked her, your aunt told me you were not yet allowed to have callers." Kennedy smiled, his light brown eyes shining. "I'm glad to see it isn't so."

"As of today, Miss Mara Ashworth had joined the adult world," Halloran said, grinning at Mara. "She's seventeen."

"I wish you'd quit harping on my age," Mara spoke sharply.

"I agree with Mara." Andrea smiled. "It's rude of you, John. And she seems much older than that."

Mara looked at her quickly, gratefully, but when their eyes met, Andrea's were a smokey, spiteful blue, and Mara looked away.

"Sorry about that," Halloran said easily. "At any rate, now Stuart can pay you a call as he so obviously wants to."

"Obviously," Kennedy echoed. "Andrea and I grew up together, and she came with me tonight out of sheer courtesy and kindness."

"That's true enough, old dear," Andrea said lightly. "Now if John had asked me, or one of the Marsh brothers, I'd have ditched you happily. But as we see, John chose instead to initiate Miss Ashworth into what he blithely refers to as the 'adult world,' which seems to me to be full of grown-up children most of the time."

"Now you're wading into philosophy, Andrea," Halloran said, his voice still light. "And this is not an evening for the esoterics."

"We must be off," Kennedy said cheerfully. "The real reason Andrea honored me was because I had tickets to hear Riesel, the violinist, at the Lyceum tonight and we must hurry to make it by curtain time."

When they had gone, Mara said quietly, "Andrea dislikes me and now I know why. She's interested in you."

He laughed shortly, laying the damask napkin carelessly by his empty dessert plate. "Andrea's proprietary interest in me is that of an old friend. Don't you realize Andrea's love and admiration for her father make it impossible for any other man to measure up to her standards?" He rose and came to pull Mara's chair out for her. He signaled the waiter who nodded and smiled but did not bring the bill before the two of them left.

So, Mara thought wryly, *his credit seems to be good here.* And everywhere else, murmured a still voice in the back of her head. What's more, he was probably right about Andrea. Why, then, did the girl dislike her so intensely? It was a riddle to which there was no answer and she put it from her mind.

Halloran caught her arm. "It's only nine-thirty, Mara. Are you of a mind to hear Riesel at the Lyceum, or would you prefer the bawdier, much more entertaining Miss Aziza Hassan and her dancing troup at the Orpheum?"

"Have you tickets?" She looked up at him in surprise.

"I have a box at both," he replied.

At Halloran's suggestion, they went to see Aziza Hassan. Mara was both fascinated and slightly embarrassed by the gyrations of the half-nude male and female dancers as they writhed sinuously, weaving in and out of contact with each other. They performed sensuous dances of the Mideast with obvious pleasure and abandon.

Mara stole a glance at her companion during one particularly erotic sequence to find that he was studying her intently, and his smile flashed in the dark as her eyes met his.

"Like it?"

"It's—certainly different," she whispered, wishing she

had a fan. Despite the huge dome of the Orpheum Theatre and the open windows at the sides and top, it was very warm.

"I'm hoping this will do what that last glass of champagne might have done for me," he murmured. And in the warm tide of darkness, he reached over and took Mara's slender hand in his big one.

He turned it slowly so that his hard thumb was directly pressing the middle of her soft palm. He moved it slowly in a gentle circular motion that was more potently sensual than any aphrodisiac.

Slowly her palm opened wider under the caressing movement of his thumb. Mara watched breathlessly the thighs of the male dancers as they closed about the slender legs of the females on the stage, and her own thighs felt weak with pounding desire—she was fluid with desire—and all for a man who had sworn he would never marry.

Still the slow, intimate caress of his thumb continued and she could not bring herself to break the hypnotic charm of it. Ah, she was a fool! A fool yearning after something she could never have and powerless to fight against. She realized with a touch of panic that she was captive of her own burning desire for John Halloran.

She made a half-hearted effort to pull away but the warmth was like a narcotic, spreading through her body and creeping up to shorten her breath.

"I forgot to tell you," he whispered, "I'm making an overture. Or, as your papa would say, 'taking a liberty.'" Then laughing softly, he added, "But a very small liberty."

But it wasn't a small liberty, Mara thought feverishly, for it was having a very large effect on her. She tried once more to pull her hand from his, which tightened correspondingly with that slow, insistent and now rougher caressing of her palm.

The show was over shortly afterward, but Mara could not have told anyone about the last sequence of dancing, for she had been aware only of Halloran's big body so close to her own slender one, of his hand over hers, moving, warming the soft and tender palm of her hand.

She dragged in a deep breath of the cooling night air as they walked silently down the three blocks to where the young boy was guarding Halloran's rig. The man lifted her into the seat, his hands clinging to her waist, lingering to slide past her hips. She had the curious unclothed sensation that he had put his hands on her most private parts, and in the darkness she blushed furiously. Then he came around and got in, taking the reins from the boy and turning the horse deftly.

"It's eleven, Mara. Plenty of time to get you home before that ogress aunt of yours can set up a howl."

She said nothing. The palm of her hand still stung with remembered feeling, and with her present fierce desire to have his hands caress her elsewhere.

As the horse cantered past other late-night carriages under the star-studded sky they passed through town and into the suburbs without speaking. It seemed to Mara that the unspoken desire between their two bodies was swelling to enormous proportions, shutting them into the night and drowning them in its soft warmth.

At last they drew up before the Ashworths' modest frame house, where a small electric lamp in the window glowed on Celeste Bonheur Ashworth's marble-topped table.

As Halloran looped the reins over the buggy rail he turned to her smoothly and caught her in his arms. She flung off the gauzy veil that covered her hair and began struggling silently against his grip.

"I've thought about this, for days." He laughed huskily, seeking her lips as she twisted violently. "I've thought about you fighting—and about you not fighting." He held her head against his hard shoulder and his lips came down on hers with such stunning sweetness that the breath went out of her and she ceased struggling. For a timeless moment she allowed the hot tide to engulf her.

Then as his lips grew more demanding, parting her trembling mouth, his hands moved over her unresisting body, one of them catching an uptilted breast. He lifted his lips from hers and bent his head to put them hotly against the silk and lace covering her nipple. The sheet of flame that swept her galvanized her to action.

Groaning, she began beating her freed hands against the broad shoulders, lashing at the dark face above her now, her body tightening like a steel band against him.

She had been unaware there could be so much strength in her slim frame.

"You let me go!" she gasped thickly. "You must think me a child indeed. You—you've probably done this with dozens of women . . ." To her horror, she began to cry and she fought against that, too. "I hate you, John Halloran! I'll not go to Galveston next Saturday with you—or ever anywhere again." She swallowed a large sob and gulped, "You do this to me, and call marriage miserable, and all the time you—you're a dishonorable, contemptible man."

He leaned back in the pale gloom and scrutinized her thoughtfully as she struggled to straighten her dress. The pink rose at her waist had come loose and lay in her lap, where she picked it up and put it with trembling fingers into her small purse. She started to get down from the buggy.

Swiftly he swung around and was beneath her in time to put his hands up and help her.

"Don't touch me—ever again!" she hissed, flinging away from him. He followed her up the wooden steps and across the porch where he caught her arm, swinging her about to face him.

"What a little hypocrite you are," he said quietly, "all wounded virtue and tears, too, from one who boasts she never cries."

"Hypocrite! How dare you call *me* a hypocrite, when it's you who makes all the advances that are supposed to pre-cede marriage—"

"Precede marriage?" His smile was frightening. "I told you in the beginning I'd never marry you. Yet your eyes, your lips, your every movement told me you wanted me as much as I wanted you. Not even a seventeen-year-old can be that ignorant."

"I'd never let you take me without marriage. Never!"

He swept off his panama, made a little bow and said sardonically, "I'm a patient man. I can wait."

He was in the buggy, clicking to the horse as she slammed the door hard.

Chapter 7.

᭟ SHE turned to face her Aunt Felice in the hallway. The woman stood straight and her eyes were triumphant as she observed her niece, whose hair was tumbling now about her shoulders and whose lovely, slim dress was still slightly awry.

"I knew you'd be bedded by that uneducated barbarian!" She drew up before Mara and peered into her flushed, tear-wet face. "You're not going to stand there with your skirts looking like they'd been above your hips all evening and try to tell me he didn't bed you?"

Suddenly, spontaneously all the volatile nature Mara had kept bottled up for years, erupted.

"What a filthy-minded creature you are," Mara spoke low and furiously. "You, who bed my father every chance you get!"

Aunt Felice's face blanched and her hand flashed out, cracking hard against Mara's cheek. "Don't you dare speak to me like that, you little bitch!"

"You don't deny it," Mara's voice was cold with contempt. "You *can't* deny it, but I deny John Halloran has bedded me, nor will he ever."

"What's come over you?" Aunt Felice wore a stunned look.

"I'm seventeen now, Aunt Felice, and I'm making money for Papa, and you'll never intimidate me again. And I warn you, if you ever strike me again, I shall return the favor." She turned and moved to the stairs without glancing back.

Halfway up, she was halted by Felice's clutching hand on her arm. "You whey-faced little liar! You'd better never

say anything to Archer. I just might tell something on you
that could destroy you!"

Mara's eyes narrowed. "What could you tell on me?"

"Just you mind me still, my *dear* little niece, or I'll see
that your world comes apart." She released Mara's arm
and took the stairs.

Mara stood on the fourth step from the landing and
watched her disappear into the dark hall. She stood there a
long time, waiting for her racing heart to slow. What lie
could Felice tell about her that would ruin her? It would
have to be a lie, or did she know some dark, awful secret
about her?

Mara shook her head positively. Her memory of the past
was too clear. Her aunt, though, was perfectly capable of
manufacturing some terrible untruth that could harm her.
It was another of Aunt Felice's threats that had woven a
cage about her for years. Now that she had burst from that
cage, Felice was ready to stop her again with poison.

Suddenly she was very tired and she walked slowly to
her room. She looked at Celia's closed door and wished
fleetingly that they shared their room still. No. It was better this way. David Donellan had somehow come between
the two sisters. Mara knew she could not confide John Halloran's lovemaking, or his biting accusations. Worse still,
she could not explain her hot desire for the lean, sunburned man while his cynicism repelled her so violently;
through all her emotions about him ran a contradictory
thread of sympathy.

*It's because he had to run away from home at thirteen
and make his own way in an unfriendly world,* she told herself. *It's because of that cursed appealing scar on his cheek
and my certainty that the pain of it had somehow been
much deeper and more permanent in his heart than that
thin white thread on his brown cheek.*

Sleep took her at last.

The following week slipped by faster than Mara could
believe, for the machines arrived three days early. For
three nights she and Sudie stayed at the store until eleven
o'clock, when Julius would drive in and take them home.

Three times the hazel-eyed Stuart Kennedy had stopped
at the house, to find that Mara had not returned, so he

came twice to the shop to ask if she would go out with him. This pleased her, but she was so obsessed with making her new venture a success that it was easy to put him off.

Her father and sister received two curt letters from his sisters in Richmond denying that they had sent them their beautiful furniture, the books or the piano. Furthermore, they implied a certain disappointment that anyone else had done so.

Ashworth and Felice were stunned. They tried to think of some friend in Richmond who would have done them such a kindness but could not. Ashworth finally resolved it by telling the girls it must have been the uncles, for it would be like them to keep such a sign of weakness from their bronze-haired, strong-willed wives and from anyone else.

This merely confirmed the busy Mara's suspicions that it was Will MacAdam who was their unknown benefactor.

As for John Halloran, she neither saw nor heard from him, but she thought about him, which annoyed her. Still as the days went by and the exquisite dresses were turned out, each one with special and expert care, the money began to come in. Sudie proved to be amazingly quick to learn the use of the sewing machine, and Mara found herself wishing she had two more just like her, for orders were stacking up. She had enough now to keep her busy for three months. But her great disappointment came the night she handed over to her father nearly three thousand dollars.

They were in the parlor and Julius had just brought the girls in from working late at the store. David Donellan was in the process of bidding the others good-night, for he had dined with Felice, Celia and Archer Ashworth.

"Now you're sure you don't mind my borrowing Celia's excellent taste in planning the Galveston house for Lucinda, Archer? Felice?" he was asking as Mara came into the hall and greeted them.

"Indeed not, David," Ashworth said heartily. "She needs the diversion, even though she's been going out with that young Branch MacAdam some. She's been too much at home as it is."

"My hope of teaching children hasn't worked out too well," Celia said regretfully. "We haven't the telephone yet and I think perhaps we live a little too far out for the children to walk to lessons."

"Ah, I'm sure you'll have more than you can handle later, when the phone is installed and word gets around about your extraordinary talent." Donellan smiled broadly, showing his fine white teeth. He nodded to Mara, adding, "And word has already gotten out about your talent, Miss Mara, even as far away as Galveston." Then with a courtly little bow to Mara, "Congratulations."

"Thank you, David," Mara replied without smiling as Pleasance appeared behind her.

"You come on into the dinin' room, Miss Mara. I done kept a piece of fried chicken an' hot biscuits with honey for you an' Sudie. I'll bring your plate for you."

It was after Donellan had departed and she had eaten and joined her father in the parlor that she handed the pouch of money to Archer Ashworth. She hadn't expected immediate warmth or congratulations, but she had hoped he would at least smile at her with that wonderful charm he possessed, when she put it into his hands.

Celia put down her book and Felice's brilliant expectant eyes were on his face as Ashworth slowly counted out the bills and checks, laying them in small stacks on the mahogany table that had been his wife's in New Orleans.

When he finished counting, he said slowly, "There's only two thousand seven hundred and fifty-four here. Didn't you just say you cleared a little over three thousand?"

Felice could wait no longer. "I told you, Archer! I told you she'd promised Sudie ten percent. *Ten percent,* when it's *you* financing the whole operation!"

Ashworth scowled at his daughter. "I don't intend that you shall handle the money, Mara. You are a minor still and I will take the payments from your customers." He paused, then added heavily, "And I will decide how much Sudie is entitled to receive."

Mara felt the blood leave her face. It had been her hope that *she* would handle the money, no—*give* the money she earned to her father each week. More than that, she had determined that Sudie should have ten percent. The girl worked just as hard as Mara did, even if she did not design the gowns and baby clothes.

"After all," Ashworth continued, "I have invested money in this shop and I have invested more in your machines and the materials you use. It will take some time to amortize my investment in your so-called *haute couture* shop."

"I know that, Papa," Mara said, looking down at her hands. "But I have figured materials and costs and I believe that the profit margin will be greater than we hoped. In less than a month more, I will have more than paid for the materials and the machines. And I thought I would have the authority to pay my help, for I shall need to hire more if the orders continue coming in."

"And I suppose you intend to pay them all ten percent?" He lifted one thick coppery eyebrow. "You'd soon be making nothing, I assure you." He stroked his fingers across his bright mustache and added, "Sudie may keep the three hundred you gave her, for I have not yet been able to pay Julius and Pleasance. But hereafter, I will put her on a straight salary."

Mara hesitated, then plunged in, "But you *are* pleased with the success of my designs, aren't you, Papa? You do think I'll be able to add to your income?"

He waved a hand carelessly. "Oh, yes, as long as the fad for originals lasts, we might as well capitalize on it. But I doubt it will prosper in the long run." He was brusque and did not look at her as he took out his wallet and began folding the bills and checks into it. "I'll take this with the other and deposit it all at the Houston National tomorrow."

"How much will you give Sudie?" Mara asked boldly. "She's very good. In fact, I couldn't produce nearly as much as I do without her help."

"I'll determine that later. And you will tell your customers to come to my office for payment of their bills hereafter." He got to his feet. "I'm going to the library and read, my dears. I'll be up to bed much later."

Celia began, "Mara, I think you're positively—," but Aunt Felice interrupted her.

"You're such a night owl, Archer," she said, putting a nervous hand to her thick coil of black hair. "You stay up reading much too long. You have circles under your eyes when you leave for the store in the mornings. Please go to bed before eleven tonight."

"You're sweet to worry, my dear," he said absently, going into the hall and down to the library. Celia had decorated the library as much like the one at home as she could. The heavy red velvet curtains, the red velour chairs, big and inviting, and a more expensive rug than they really could afford, covered the garishly shellacked floor, blending its deep vermillion with the rest of the decor. Archer Ashworth had told them all he felt at home in it, that it was the only place in which he *did* feel at home.

Mara was wearily disrobing when Celia tapped on her door and entered.

"I'm really proud of you, Mara," she said immediately, sitting down in the one chair the room boasted. There was no rancor in her voice, no implication that she remembered any of Mara's criticisms of David.

"Thank you, Celia," Mara said with a rush of relief. "I hope Papa was pleased."

"He was, I'm sure. It's old Aunt Felice who's pea-green about your success, but she'll be glad to help Papa spend the money, you may be sure. And it means she doesn't have to clerk in his store."

"I hope it will all go to pay off the aunts and uncles," Mara said uneasily. "I wonder just how much we *do* owe them?"

"Not quite ten thousand dollars, Papa said, after Uncle Bob sold the house. And Papa says we can pay it off by the month very slowly."

"I want to pay it off *fast,*" Mara replied with tired fierceness. "I hate owing them money. It's much worse than if it were a bank." She slipped her nightgown over her bare slender body and donned a wrapper much too short. Her wardrobe was still sadly lacking in adult apparel.

"Did you hear? I'm to help David with the decor in the new house he's building for Lucinda in Galveston."

"I heard," Mara said shortly, "and I notice your sign for teaching piano lessons is down."

"Well, I never got a single pupil, Mara!" she said defensively. "And Papa says that things are going so well at the store that I need not teach. Besides, he wants me to join

Andrea's club, that is, the Ladies' Music Auxiliary. He says I can bring goodwill for *Ashworth's* that way."

Mara looked into her sister's beautiful, earnest face under the tumbling red-gold mass of hair with a loving smile. "He's right, you know, Celia. You can be a model for my dresses, too. Why, you'd be our best advertisement!"

Celia blushed. "I don't know about that, but even David says I wouldn't make enough teaching piano. I couldn't charge more than a dollar and a half an hour."

"Besides," Mara said coolly, "it gives you more time to help David decorate his house in Galveston. Which reminds me, when is the pale and frail Lucinda going to join him?"

"He isn't sure," Celia said, even more defensively, "only that she's written she isn't well yet. Mara, working at the store has changed you somehow."

"Maybe she's going to have a baby," Mara said, ignoring the last of her sister's comment.

"Oh, no, it's a nervous thing she has. When she gets the least bit excited her heart—"

"Well?"

"Her heart seems to fail. She has sharp pains in it and has to lie down a lot."

"It would seem that with all that money her father has, he'd have taken her to the great specialists."

"Oh, he has! But they say it's not exactly organic—it's—it's in her mind, Mara. But the doctors say that's just as bad, maybe worse than having a *real* failing heart."

"It appears that you and David have pretty well covered Lucinda's ills. Why is he building her a house down here when she can play sick and stay in Richmond forever?"

Celia gave her a shocked look. *"Play* sick! She doesn't play sick. She hates what's the matter with her. It keeps her from doing all sorts of things. You certainly are unsympathetic, even cynical."

Mara was reminded sharply of John Halloran's mocking voice: *Marriage is for fools. And after you've lived a little longer, you'll see some miserable ones. God knows I have.*

"Maybe I am a little cynical, Celia. Lucinda seemed well enough until she married."

"Yes, she did," Celia said thoughtfully.

"Maybe marriage makes her sick—part of it, anyway."

Mara flung herself across the bed. "Did David say *anything* about when she'd join him here?"

"As soon as he gets the house finished and decorated, he hopes."

"He hopes. Well, I hope so, too, but I doubt it. Seems to me Robert Ames could have found a better place for him in Richmond, where Lucinda would be happier."

"I said as much to David, but he told me her father had thought Lucinda needed to be away from home, to learn to fend for herself, live in a new environment."

Mara was silent as she looked at her beautiful sister's troubled face. Fend for herself indeed. With a loving husband to stand between her and every misery, and a doting father to stand behind both of them? No. It was more than that. Mara suspected Lucinda wanted all the trappings of a society marriage and the safety of her wedding ring. And Robert Ames, for all his talk of her needing to leave home, wanted his daughter near him.

"The reason I know Lucinda isn't pregnant," Celia said in a low, tremulous voice, "is because David told me that—that—she wept every night and wouldn't—couldn't—"

"Celia!" Mara was aghast. "You didn't *talk* about that?"

"It just slipped out of him," Celia said defiantly. "He's very lonely. Oh, I should have known you wouldn't understand." She flung herself out of the chair and left the room. She left Mara's door open but closed her own with a subdued bang.

Again Mara was struck by the desire to follow her, put her arms about the beloved sister who had stood between her and harsh punishment so many times. But that would put her stamp of approval on this thing that was growing insidiously between David and Celia. And that, she could not condone. In her heart, she knew her sister was standing on the brink of a nameless abyss.

From that moment on, the rift between Mara and Celia widened. It grew because Mara was so busy with her high fashion shop that she scarcely thought of anything else.

Even so, she was aware that Celia went to Galveston on the train and met with David nearly every day. When she came back from these sorties, she was pink cheeked and beautiful, full of enthusiasm about the house. She would remark how much Lucinda would like this or that, and how beautiful Galveston was and what pleasure Lucinda would find there. Lucinda, it was always of Lucinda that Celia spoke, but in her eyes and her smiles, Mara read the name *David*.

So the Indian summer days swept by, warm as midsummer, with tropic winds from the Gulf cooling the hot afternoons. And Mara persuaded her father, with Celia's unexpected cooperation, to put two of the new ceiling fans in her little shop. With the skylight open high above at the rear, the rooms were airy, light and cool as the ladies came for their fittings, sitting in the two velvet chairs in the anteroom and poring over Mara's books of designs.

It was October when Mrs. Clive Fairweather came to *Ashworth's*. Archer Ashworth was in his office and did not see her arrival with her maid accompanying her. Her black driver parked her Victoria at the front of the store and sat comfortably in the lowering sunlight while she occupied herself with shopping.

She went directly to *Ashworth Originals* and opened the glass door on Mara, who was watering a hanging Boston fern. Mara turned at her entry and it was as if a cool, green breeze had come into the room, exhaling a nameless, delicate and entrancing perfume. She wore the shade of green that set off her burnished hair beautifully.

"Ah, Mrs. Fairweather! I am so glad to see you! I feared you might have changed your mind about coming."

"Changed my mind? When I see Mrs. Marsh and Mrs. Seagram, not to mention several others out at dinner, at the Lyceum and the Orpheum, in dresses that are the envy of all Houston? Not likely, my dear Mara! I've come to choose several dresses, all for spring wearing in Paris as well as in Houston. I expect to stun my darling daughter Fleurette, with my divine fashionableness."

"It will be such a pleasure to design and fit you, Mrs. Fairweather. You are so lovely," Mara smiled.

"And you are so kind. This is my maid, Dominique. She is from Haiti where her father was a French general."

The beautiful girl with the patrician features of a French aristocrat and the ebony skin of a Haitian, grinned proudly and bowed imperceptibly to the smiling Mara.

She seated the maid and her mistress at a polished table and gave them two thick folders of sketches to look through, saying, "And if there is nothing there that strikes your fancy, I will design a new one, just as you visualize it, Mrs. Fairweather."

The beautiful woman glanced upward, and with her large green eyes focused intently on Mara's dark ones, she said, "Do call me Bonnie, Mara. For when you call me by my name, I can forget that I am growing older each day."

"Oh, but you are so young!" Mara cried, the name not registering. "You are one of those wonderful women who *never* grow old, only more and more beautiful."

Still those pale, sparkling green eyes held hers and Mara felt a curious yearning to put her arms about the woman.

"I had an aunt named Bonnie," she said slowly, her voice distant in her ears, like a voice in a dream. "She ran away to Houston when she was no older than I. The aunts in Richmond won't speak of her." Then realization engulfed her in a tidal wave. It washed over her and she struggled to breathe, for Bonnie Fairweather had not taken her eyes from Mara's. In the silence the whirr of Sudie's machine came to them from the rear of the shop. Sudie was back of the fitting room and far from hearing.

Mara whispered, "You are—are you Bonnie Ashworth?"

"Indeed I am, my dear. I am your father's youngest sister, the outcast. Your mother was the best friend I ever had. She gave me the money to come to Houston when I was pregnant with my Fleurette, and more than that. She gave me the *courage.* Celeste was a very courageous woman and you look very much like her."

"Oh, you are *my aunt,* and you are so elegant, so beautiful and so respected!"

Bonnie Fairweather made a wry face and Dominique smiled obliquely. "By a few, but not by many for I am a businesswoman. But I can tell you this much, Mara, you will have a staunch friend in me." She hesitated, then stretched a delicate, rosy-tipped hand to her niece and said quickly, "I must ask you to keep our relationship a secret, for your own sake."

"Oh, but Papa will—"

"I have no love for my brother and sisters, nor they for

me." At Mara's look of bewildered disappointment, she said quickly, "I see I must tell you the truth of the matter. My daughter's father was a Richmond man and he was killed in a hunting accident. Not that it made any difference, for he was married. My brother and sisters and father turned their backs on me. Only Celeste understood, so I came to Houston, knowing that Colonel MacAdam had found his fortune here. I thought I might also. And I met Clive. He married me, adopted my daughter, and I—" She laughed shortly, a weary, unhappy little laugh. "No one in Houston knows I was an Ashworth. I took the name of Bonnie Moore. I have made my own way and I have succeeded in finding financial security."

Mara was silent, her eyes liquid with sympathy and love for this newfound and wonderful relative.

"So you see, Mara, Archer will not acknowledge me as his sister and we shall be as strangers. But I do not think he would dare forbid you to design for me. It might lead to revelations he would rather keep secret."

"And I shall design the most fabulous, the most beautiful clothes for you, Bonnie! You shall be my most treasured client!"

"Then you and I will share the most pleasant relationship—a secret from your papa, Aunt Felice and even Celia, eh?"

"Even from Celia," Mara said slowly.

"And you may be sure your beloved papa will look through me each time we meet. Yes, I can safely say that."

"I don't care," Mara replied defiantly. "You and I shall be the dearest of friends."

And after that, Dominique, who seemed to have an astonishing flair for designs, and Bonnie Fairweather pored over Mara's folders, chosing dresses and suggesting modifications.

When they had finished, they left the excited Mara and Sudie, who had been called in to observe Mrs. Fairweather's choices, with ten dresses to make and fifteen sets of chemises and dainty underclothing. Bonnie Fairweather agreed to pay five thousand dollars for the work, and she insisted that she pay it in advance.

Mara then confessed that her father insisted the money be paid direct to him.

"This is only one of many future moments when the imperious Archer will be defied. I will pay you now, or I will pay you when you deliver the other gowns, but I will pay *you,* my dear Mara." Bonnie had smiled cryptically when she handed Mara a five-thousand-dollar check made out to her.

As the two went out the door Mara thought she saw her father look up from his desk at the back office in the store. She was right for he came into the fashion salon shortly afterward.

"Who was that woman who just left your shop, Mara?"

"Mrs. Clive Fairweather. She ordered five thousand dollars' worth of gowns and lingerie and insisted on paying me directly and in advance. Here is her check. I'll endorse it to you."

"Hmmm. Five thousand, eh? I've heard of Mrs. Fairweather. Something unsavory, I believe, and I don't like you working for her."

"But five thousand dollars, Papa." Mara shrugged with elaborate carelessness as she endorsed the check to him. "And gossip is a chancy thing, isn't it?"

He looked at her coldly. "Sometimes you sound so much like your mother," he said, turning sharply to leave her.

It was then the shop began to possess Mara body and soul. And the two times—once in September and once in October—that she went out with the hazel-eyed Stuart Kennedy, she was absent in her replies and he was frustrated by her coolness.

She was able to cajole her father into allowing her to hire two more seamstresses, pretty little women whose husbands were streetcar conductors and who needed the extra money at home. Their names were Bella Flaherty and Anna Beckman.

The fame of *Ashworth Originals* was growing and spreading. Women from as far away as Beaumont and Galveston and even three from distant Dallas came to choose from Mara's designs.

She saw John Halloran at dinner at the MacAdams' three times and he was pleasant to her, as to any friend, warm but not excessively so. She missed the wicked look in his eyes when they rested on hers. Indeed, they were cool and appraising, with a *waiting* look in them. Why this latter expression should cheer her, she did not know, but whenever she had seen him at the MacAdams' she came away buoyant and more sure of her success with *Ashworth Originals.*

So he was a patient man, she thought dryly. Well, so was she a patient woman. And when she was successful enough, had achieved what she had set out to achieve, pay off the aunts and uncles and see her father highly prosperous again, she would show John Halloran. She would marry—and happily, too. And the attentive and courteous Stuart Kennedy came to mind most readily at these times. Now there was a man for a good solid marriage. Then John Halloran would know she cared not a whit about him.

The store itself was doing so well by the end of the year that Archer Ashworth was able to send a ten-thousand-dollar cashier's check to his sisters and brothers-in-law, wiping out his debt to them. That Mara was responsible for over half of it was a source of great satisfaction to her.

Another satisfaction during this busy time was the fact that Aunt Felice had become somewhat subdued in Mara's presence. She was not so quick to criticize, and Mara knew that several times she had bitten her tongue on sharp comments. Aunt Felice was fully aware that Mara was making a great deal of money for the store and thereby making life much easier for herself. She smiled at Mara occasionally now, when the girl came home tired but excited from a busy day in the shop. But Mara noted the smile did not extend to the beautiful dark eyes with their tangle of black lashes. And she knew intuitively that Aunt Felice nursed a secret grudge against her, a grudge that Mara could never overcome. For that reason, she put it from her mind and thought of her aunt only when she was forced to do so.

Celia came out of her dreams of Lucinda's house and husband long enough to congratulate her sister on her growing success. But the approbation Mara longed for most—that from a loving father—was not forthcoming.

It was only Mara's secret bookkeeping ledger that told her how much she was contributing to the success of *Ashworth's,* for her father gave her none of her earnings. All the money from *Ashworth Originals* went directly into his account. His one allowance was to permit her to make her own dresses and to choose accessories from the store.

Even so, her contribution to the store could not be accounted accurately, for many of the monied women who came solely for the high fashion and personally tailored gowns stayed to buy some of the better merchandise in the store.

It was this that sent Ashworth off on one of his buying trips to New York, where in November he purchased more of the better furniture, china and silver that was the despair of his sisters in Richmond. This was because in Richmond most of those items had been handed down from generation to generation. In Houston, however, many of the newcomers had only recently made their fortunes and were anxious to acquire the accoutrements that bespoke their rise in society.

During these months, when Mara had time to think of it, Celia's long days in Galveston, working on the decor of Lucinda Donellan's house, worried her. But Celia talked in a very businesslike manner about chairs, drapes, rugs and linens. It was all for Lucinda and she mentioned her at every breath. This eased Mara's deep-seated fears and her memory of Celia crying, *Oh, I should have let him, I was a fool not to.* No, this was a different Celia, a controlled Celia who would stop short of irreparable folly, Mara assured herself.

In early November, Mara had swallowed hard and accepted Archer Ashworth's edict that all those working for Mara would receive twenty dollars a month.

"That's an enormous sum for the work they do!" he said accusingly. "Even now, I'm to pay Julius and Pleasance only twenty dollars a month, when I was paying them thirty dollars in Richmond. That's forty a month between the three of them. Really, Mara, you're for giving away all our profit. I can't run a business that way. And you have absolutely no head for any of this, Mara."

She was depressed, but then he had said an unusual thing, which lifted her to the skies. "Really, Mara, I would never have thought you could do such a thing as this. It appears that you inherited some of your mother's talents after all."

She stood expectantly, waiting for him to brush her

cheek with his lips, but, instead, he strode from the parlor to library without further words. Still, she cherished his comment to her heart. She was making headway! As her business grew, and she would see that it grew, he would eventually admit his love and pride in his younger daughter.

The entire Ashworth household was to spend Christmas day and evening with the MacAdams, who had an enormous blue spruce tree sent down from Colorado which they had set proudly in their parlor. It was elaborately decorated with every bauble imaginable and it took Mara's breath away when she chanced to see it a week before Christmas, when they added their presents to those stacks already beneath it.

The MacAdams, in their hospitality, had included the lonely David Donellan and the not-so-lonely John Halloran in their invitation. Stuart Kennedy was to be there as well. Members of the Committee for Deep Water and their wives, with whom Will and John were involved, would also call in the afternoon for eggnog and fruitcake, and the day would be finished with a buffet and dancing in the evening.

Mara had been looking forward to it for weeks. She had even taken time to create a stunning red velvet dress for herself, with long tight sleeves and a draped décolletage that suggested poignantly what it did not reveal. Further, she had hand-fashioned an exquisite red silk rose to be pinned in her dark, shining hair.

To add to Mara's pleasure, Julius, Sudie and Pleasance had been invited to share Christmas at the MacAdam mansion with all the MacAdam servants and the occupants of the house that day.

Christmas day dawned bright and clear, warm as April, for roses still lifted their opulence from bushes in the yards along Heights Boulevard. Mara had kept her dress a secret and she donned it now with something of misgiving. What if Papa thought it too extravagant?

Surely not, for she had shirred and tucked where ruffles might have flaunted. She had pulled one drape over her left hip, with a touch of fullness across the back, the rich folds of velvet making her slim figure a perfect though small hourglass. The whole effect was that of a luscious crimson flower, with Mara's ivory oval face, crowned with masses of gleaming hair rising from the center of it.

Andrea had told Celia she had hired a three-piece orchestra for the dancing Christmas evening. They would roll back the imported rugs and dance on the smooth parquet floors of the main salon. Thinking of it made Mara's heart beat even faster.

She held her breath with excitement and a touch of fear as she took the stairs to join the others waiting in the parlor. As she stepped into the room a hush fell on Aunt Felice, Ashworth and Celia. Even Julius, who was brushing Ashworth's coat, and Pleasance, who was putting last-minute touches to Aunt Felice's skirt, fell silent.

Only Sudie spoke, "Oh, Mara, your Christmas dress is perfect!"

"She looks like we ought to hang her on the tree." Ashworth sounded strangled.

"She looks like Celeste the Christmas before she died," Aunt Felice blurted shrilly.

"What in God's name is wrong with the navy blue you usually wear Sundays? You look like—like a woman of the streets!"

"But Papa, it's Christmas and I wanted to be in the spirit."

"Believe me, you're conspicuous enough. I'm ashamed to show up at the MacAdams. Look at your sister. That pale gold is beautiful and *modest.*"

It *was* beautiful. Mara had made it herself with painstaking care, chosen the color because it highlighted Celia's glistening red-gold hair, and the décolletage was much more daring than Mara's.

"If you wanted to be the center of all eyes," Aunt Felice said spitefully, "I think you've succeeded marvelously. A truly scarlet woman." Mara looked at her steadily until her aunt looked away.

"You go put on that new navy blue I let you have off the rack some time ago," Ashworth blustered.

"No, Papa, that's an everyday dress," Celia said sharply. "It's Christmas. We should all dress for it. Besides, it's too late for Mara to change now." She shot her sister a quick look of conspiracy, then smiled persuasively at Ashworth. "We must all be there by noon for opening the presents."

With Ashworth still grumbling and Felice still spiteful, they donned their light wraps, the servants included. Julius, who had missed the exchange about the dress, having left quickly to bring the carriage to the front of the house, opened the front door, a happy grin on his face, "All ready, Mist' Arch?"

"I guess so, Julius—"

"You *do* realize that some of your best customers will be there for the dancing this evening, Mara?" Aunt Felice asked as they clambered into the buggy. Sudie and her mother sat behind Mara, Celia and Felice, who occupied the seat behind Julius and Ashworth, with Julius driving.

"Yes, she does," Celia said coldly, "and likely they'll all be clamoring for a dress just like hers before the evening is over, Aunt Felice."

There were too many presents beneath the giant spruce to be handed out and opened one by one. Instead, with servants, family and friends gathered around him, Will MacAdam acted as Saint Nicholas. Andrea had made him a red cap with white fur around the crown and he wore it slightly askew, which made the ready laughter all the greater.

There were gifts for everyone, from nearly everyone there. Most were baubles and trinkets, but Donellan gave Celia a gold chain with an obviously real diamond pendant. When she opened it, he was quick to speak.

"A thank-you for all your time and work on Lucinda's behalf. She suggested it, Celia."

His remark took the intimate and personal nature of the gift and made it quite respectable.

Mara gave Celia a handmade peignoir of the finest silk and her father gave her a diamond ring. Ashworth was finding his new prosperity quite comfortable. Celia's gifts were quite the handsomest of all, for Will and Andrea had given her season tickets for two to all the spring musicals to be held at the Lyceum, and Branch had given her a leather-bound, velvet-lined jewelry box. Aunt Felice had given her a down comfort for her bed and Celia was aglow with happiness.

"What in blazes is *that?*" Branch asked Mara as she sat to one side opening her small gifts.

"That's a length of navy blue wool from Aunt Felice. I'm to make another dress to wear in the shop, I suppose."

"Hmmm. Deuced practical woman, isn't she?"

"You might call her that," Mara said absently, opening a very small box with a tag that read only, "To Mara from an admirer." She glanced at Stuart Kennedy and he was smiling at her. But she still held the gift plainly marked from him unopened in her lap.

"And what is *that?*" Branch reiterated as she lifted the lid.

"Have you opened all yours?" Mara asked, laughing at his curiosity.

"Of course, like lightning. I can never stand to wait. No patience at all. Now what is it?"

Mara lifted the tissue to find a round-trip ticket to Galveston for two, lying on top of a small bottle of *Dr. Weston's Repellent. Keeps all pests at bay,* read the smaller print. It was a well-known preventive of chiggers, mosquitoes and other flying insects.

Mara couldn't keep from laughing aloud. It had to be from John Halloran. Who could stay angry with a man whose sense of humor was so endearing? Too, she told herself swiftly, she had gained so much confidence during the months at *Ashworth Originals,* she was certain she could handle the magnetism between them now.

Branch handled the bottle inquisitively. "Strange—now who'd give you stuff like this and two round-trip tickets to Galveston? What does the tag say?"

"It doesn't say who it's from."

"Have you no idea?"

"No idea whatsóever," she lied, smiling, but her eyes swept the room and found the tall, lean John Halloran, elbow against the mantel, observing the room impartially. His eyes met hers in the flick of a second, and without changing his bland expression he gave her a swift wink before stooping to poke at the unnecessary, but festive fire beside him. All the doors were open and so were the windows, but a fire at Christmas was mandatory, so Andrea had said.

Slowly the hubbub, the oh's and ah's, the showing of gifts fell to a hum of conversation. The servants retired to the rear kitchens to prepare the late and large Christmas dinner. Amos returned shortly with wine for the ladies and bourbon for the men.

Another half hour passed as they laughed and talked, finishing their drinks. Mara's dress had received a compliment from every man in the room. Even Andrea had remarked coolly that she was going to come into *Ashworth Originals* for a new fitting, but Mara discounted the comment, feeling it was made for the benefit of her brothers and Celia, who were standing near at the time.

Suddenly, Amos appeared in the door and announced dinner would be served in the main dining room. As they all rose and streamed forward, Mara counted those invited.

There was Stuart, John Halloran, the Ashworths and Felice, two younger men friends of the MacAdam brothers and Andrea, whose names she had not caught, though they had been introduced earlier during all the excitement. And there was David Donellan.

Mara left her small gifts, among them a box of handkerchiefs from her father and a gold lavalier from Celia, in the big wingback chair she had occupied in the salon. The others had left theirs in various places to be put into the buggy later.

There were place cards at the dining table and Mara seated herself alone. She was not surprised when Halloran took the seat next to her. One of the new young men introduced himself again to her as Brett Patterson, seating himself at her left.

"And the other one you can't remember is sitting near the foot of the table by Andrea. He's Richard Buyers," he grinned amiably at Mara and began to talk to her aunt, who was seated at his other side.

Andrea looked down the table with a slight shrug and said, "John, you switched place cards, you rascal. I had planned for you to sit next to Will, knowing you all usually talk business through every meal." Her light eyes were cool and they swept Mara, disparagement clear in them.

"I like it here, Andrea," Halloran replied casually, his black eyes flicking about the table idly. Then *sotto voce* to Mara, "Unless you care to use the pest repellent now."

Mara smothered her laughter. "No. But you're an unregenerate rake and I don't trust you any further than . . . than as far as you are from me now."

"And well you might not. Just keep Dr. Weston's handy if I get out of hand. Now how about that trip to Galveston?

You shouldn't let an unregenerate rake do you out of a tour of that fair city. It's beautiful and you should see it."

"I've been wanting to, but I've been so busy."

"I know how busy you've been. Several thousand dollars worth of busy. Your ticket's good anytime. How about next Saturday?"

"New Year's Eve?"

"Have you other plans?"

"You know I haven't," she replied, little dreaming the disaster that waited her.

"Stuart Kennedy would argue that point. He has that look in his eye even now."

"Stuart is a dear and if he asked me out, I'd go, I'm sure."

"Even if I ask you first?"

"Well—"

"I promise no talk about marriage."

"There never has been any talk about *marriage!*"

"All right. Then nonmarriage, or antimarriage."

"Now *that's* what you've talked about."

"Then we'll just ignore it and talk about the jetties and look at the beautiful houses and flowers. I'll show you a slice of paradise that has nothing to do with marriage."

"That's just fine!" she said, still angry without being sure why. It had to do with the effect he had on her. Just looking at him made her palms moist and her heart jump. And when he touched her—no more than taking her hand or elbow—she felt that touch in every part of her body. She straightened her shoulders involuntarily, her newfound confidence asserting itself once more. Anger wouldn't do. Cool detachment would.

"Then you'll go with me next week?"

"Well, I guess so," she said cautiously.

"I've never had such a halfhearted acceptance in my life."

"I'm not sure I should accept at all."

"Even with Dr. Weston's? I assure you my hands are tied and my lustful nature completely under control."

"That's hard to believe."

"Give me a chance to show you how reformed a character I am. Not as far as marriage, of course. But every inch a gentleman with a lady who's so inclined to marriage."

"I'm not so inclined," she said, angry again. "Not to marriage. And certainly not to you."

"I'm glad to hear it. We should get along famously. I can see that you're going to be a businesswoman, a woman of independent means and very self-sufficient. Marriage will be the last thing you'll ever need."

She looked at him silently as the food was served. Independent means? When her father took every penny she made? Even her helpers made more than she did. All she ever got out of her shop was a few very sober dresses, the exception being the elegant one she wore now. She had nothing really fetching to wear to the meager entertainments she allowed herself with Stuart Kennedy. And only her father and Halloran had not complimented her rich velvet dress this evening.

In the silence, she became aware of other conversations going on about them. Stuart Kennedy was saying, "And the old man made a deathbed confession and said he had taken every penny from his ward and squandered it. He even left a letter explaining why he did it—the love of women and gambling—and saying he was sorry. But a lot of good that did his penniless ward."

Andrea's brows were drawn and she said sharply, "Deathbed confessions should never be made. And old letters should always be destroyed when they contain ugly secrets. Your poor ward would have been better off if her guardian had kept his mouth shut. At least she would have thought her penniless state a natural consequence of unwise investments. Instead, she lost all faith in someone she loved dearly, her guardian."

Will was scowling at his sister. He was seated beside Celia and had been trying to engage her in conversation, but she was more interested in what Donellan, on the other side of her, had to say.

"Andrea," Will said sardonically, "pride and a hard heart are worse than most other human weaknesses. I expect his ward forgave him and loved him anyway."

"I expect she didn't," Andrea flared.

"As a matter of fact," Stuart said mildly, "she did. And kissed the old man and told him so before he died. And surprisingly enough, some of the investments he made so unwisely are proving to have some, if only a little, worth. Oil lands, you know."

"Oil," Andrea said contemptuously. "It's good for lamps and laying dust. Why you and John are interested in it is a mystery to—"

"And running engines," put in Halloran. "We all saw that horseless carriage that was brought to town for a run down Travis Street last month."

"*Some* engines," Andrea said stubbornly. "Most are steam, I understand."

"Steam can be and is generated by oil," Branch put in.

"Oh, Branch, you've always got some silly answer." Andrea tossed her head.

"That's not silly, it's so."

"So it's true. But you certainly don't hear much about it. Anyway, I think the world would be better off without deathbed confessions and old letters."

"You sound like you've had some personal experience, Andrea," Halloran said, lifting an eyebrow.

"Indeed not! Stuart's cases are always interesting even though he won't tell who they are. Sometimes I think he makes them up."

"Some of them are stories Pa told me years ago, when Houston was young and legal disputes were often settled with a gun." Stuart grinned. "And no lawyer violates the confidence of his clients, Andrea. That's why I can't tell you who they are."

"Anyway, Andy," Branch put in, "the people Stuart has to try in open court are no mystery to you. You're just curious about a man who loved women and gambling."

"And that could be any of us." Halloran grinned, lighting a cigar.

Amos moved quietly about the table, removing dishes. Rosita came in from the kitchen with a tray of sterling finger bowls, followed by Maria, also with a tray. They placed one before each diner about the table.

Mara dipped her fingers into the lemon-scented water and wiped them on the damp cloth beside the silver bowl, her mind skipping back to Richmond, where such pleasant conveniences were an everyday occurrence. It was the first time she'd seen a sterling fingerbowl since the last dinner party at home, unless she counted the silver-plated bowls on the Santa Fe Rose. She knew it was no everyday thing with any of the Houston residents. As if to corroborate her thought, Andrea spoke.

"I bought these bowls from your silver department, Mr. Ashworth, and this is their initiation. It's good that you are bringing such civilizing touches to our city. I'm sure the Hutchins, who have a lord in the family, use them, but I expect they are the only ones."

"Not quite," Branch drawled. "Mrs. Fairweather's dinner guests are so honored."

"You would know, of course." Andrea's voice was cutting. "It's a wonder she doesn't give them pitchers and bowls—or use of her bathtubs. They probably need it."

In the immediate silence that fell, Mara's voice was clear and concise. "I've met Mrs. Fairweather and she is a delightful and intelligent person. Her taste is impeccable and I found her most charming."

In the dead silence that followed this remarkable outburst—remarkable because Mara had always held her tongue during dinner conversations—her father's face flushed until it almost matched his hair. Mara felt her own face pale slightly, but her chin was lifted at a defiant angle.

"My sentiments exactly," Halloran said, laughing.

"Mara's met the woman only once," Ashworth said to Andrea, "when she came into her shop to look at her designs."

"And frequently during the following weeks as we fitted and completed her wardrobe for her trip to Paris to visit her daughter," Mara added firmly. "I like her very much."

She was aware that all the men were smiling now, except her father. He cleared his throat twice. But it was Felice, with Julius always driving her about to town, who knew the gossip of Houston and she spoke up.

"Mara's just a child really. Archer let her go into business against his better judgment. She's always been a poor judge of people." Felice's eyes sought Andrea's cold contemptuous ones.

"Miss Felice," Halloran said courteously, "I must take issue with you. I think Mara's a remarkably good judge of people and her business seems to be flourishing unbelievably. You have no idea how many times I've heard the words *It's an Ashworth Original.*" He paused, then smiled persuasively. "Actually, Miss Felice, Mara has become something of a legend, a magician in the short span of five months."

Andrea rose and pushed back her chair. "I think we should all retire to the salon for after-dinner liqueurs. And besides, Celia has promised to play for us before the others arrive. I've been looking forward to it for days!" Her smile at Celia was warm, and she studiously avoided looking at Mara at all as she chatted with Felice and Celia.

There followed an hour, while the liqueurs were served and the men smoked cigars and pipes, talking among themselves about their various enterprises. After that, Celia sat down to the grand piano and began to play. As always, her expertise, the feeling and emotion she put into the chords, made gooseflesh rise on the backs of Mara's arms. Celia's music released all of Mara's pent-up, volatile emotions, and the softer compositions soothed and charmed her.

Now she leaned back against the couch and closed her eyes as the silvered richness of Mozart, Chopin, Liszt's *Liebestraum* and Brahms rippled through the warm, scented air of the room.

Then Celia turned, her fingers trailing on the keys. "Let's all sing carols. I haven't played them since last Christmas." Celia's little smile was pensive and Mara knew she was remembering how happy she had been last Christmas, for David had been courting her then and word had not yet broken that Archer Ashworth's store was failing. She began with "It Came Upon a Midnight Clear."

The piano was a Steinway, like Celeste Ashworth's, but it lacked the resonance and tone that Celia could bring forth from her mother's older, more often played Steinway. Mara knew that Andrea also played. Her father, the Colonel, had bought this piano hoping she would take to music. But she got no further than the latest songs and her knowledge of the classics was, to quote her, "Terrible!"

Mara rose with the others who clustered about Celia as she played and all the voices, bass and soprano, rose high with the old sweet songs. Celia played several and closed with a rousing chorus of "Adeste Fidelis."

By five in the evening, those invited to the buffet and dancing began to arrive. Celia and Mara had gone up to Andrea's room to repair their toilette, and when they came down the stairs, the big foyer was filled with guests. Mara again met Mr. Marsh and Mr. Henry Seagram. Their wives were with them and each woman wore one of Mara's creations, shimmering in the candlelight and the reflection from crystal lamps.

Mrs. Seagram, short and plump with a beautiful smile, said, "Ah, Mara, you look like a gorgeous flower! I suspect you designed and made that dress, didn't you?"

Mrs. Marsh chimed in, "Oh, if only I were young enough to wear that."

"But you are!" Mara smiled. "You look lovely tonight, Mrs. Marsh. That pale blue silk is ravishing on you."

"What a little diplomat you are, Mara!" cried Mrs. Seagram and turning to Mrs. Marsh, she said, "Elizabeth, we must go in as soon as the holidays are over and get Mara to design our spring wardrobes."

The two women stood talking further with Mara before they all drifted in about the great crystal bowl of eggnog, where Andrea, with Rosita, was serving the guests.

The air grew thick with laughter and animated conversation, threaded with the scent of expensive cigar smoke and even more expensive perfumes. Mara found herself talking with women who had already been to her shop, two more who were wearing ball dresses she had designed. The compliments Mara received on her own gown were myriad, and once she saw Aunt Felice looking at her with bitter frustration and rage. There was a dark promise in her eyes, of something unpleasant to come.

After the buffet, which consisted of roast wild turkey, dove in wine sauce, mounds of crabmeat on ice and every side dish Houston climate produced, the orchestra began playing softly, unobtrusively. The guests drifted into the main salon where all the rugs had been taken up by the servants and the furniture pushed back for dancing.

Mara was to remember that this was the first time she had ever had the feeling of being popular and wanted, the first entirely carefree good time she had in her life, for the two attractive young men, Brett Patterson and Richard Buyers, sought her favors constantly. So did Stuart Kennedy. But she found herself often seeking Halloran's tall form in the crowd, usually with a group of older men, engaged in intent conversation. He did not dance with her, which piqued her. Still, the evening ended in a glorious

round of pleasure for her. She had no inkling of the blow
Felice was waiting to deliver.

It came long after the party was over and they had all returned home and retired for the night. Mara was lying in
her bed, hands clasped behind her head, remembering
with a little smile all the compliments and the three young
men who had begged to call. She had promised them all
with reckless abandon, without thinking how she could
work their attentions into her ever-increasing schedule at
Ashworth Originals.

Then suddenly her bedroom door swung open, silently,
without a warning rap, but Mara, wide awake, heard a
hinge creak. She rose up on her elbow and switched on the
electric lamp beside her bed to see Aunt Felice tiptoeing
in. Her face was set and angry and Mara thought swiftly
that she was going to berate her as she always did, probably ending with a hard slap on her face. She rose up higher.
If that happened, she was fully prepared to slap Aunt Felice with all the force in her arm. She had promised herself
that, the last time her aunt had slapped her.

Instead, Felice crept to the bed and pushed Mara down,
hissing, "It's time you knew a few things, you ignorant
child!" She seated herself on the edge of the bed. "You embarrassed your father unforgivably this evening, even
though he and I are apparently the only two who know the
truth of the matter, that is, your complete ignorance."

"I don't know what you're talking about, Aunt Felice,
and I don't care. Get out of my bedroom!"

"Gladly, as soon as I enlighten you. That woman you so
impertinently defended at the table—that Mrs. Clive Fairweather—operates a brothel!" At Mara's swift drawn
breath, she went on, "That's what I said. *A brothel.* Oh, it's
a high-class brothel and she's a high-class madam—doesn't
take in any but the wealthiest clients—but it's their guid-
ance and business tips that have made *her* wealthy."

"I don't believe it—"

"And worse. Your father thinks she is his baby sister,
Bonnie, though he's investigated discreetly and everyone
says her name was Moore before Clive Fairweather married her, but that is obviously an alias. Archer says she
looks so much like Bonnie did eighteen years ago, he can't
get it out of his head that it's anybody but her. At least her

alias covers him, protects him from having to claim a relationship to her."

"I don't believe she operates a brothel."

"Well, she does, you little fool and you may as well face it. You have a whore for a client. You'll turn her away next time!"

"I will not."

The air went out of Felice explosively. "You will!"

"I will not."

"Then your father will take away your shop."

"No, he won't. I'm making too much money. I'll take any client I choose." Mara was amazed at her own cool determination.

For a long moment, Felice looked as if she would strike her, but she did not. She rose from the side of the bed and stood looking down. "You're more a fool than I ever thought, and I've always hated you for reminding Archer of Celeste. Now this. I'll never forgive you for catering to that woman Archer hates and despises."

Mara lay there for a long time, turning the astonishing fact that Felice had revealed over and over in her mind. Bonnie had been turned out by her family. Pregnant by a married man, a dead man, with no one to turn to, only Celeste had understood and helped. It was true she was repelled by the thought of a brothel, but behind her eyes, she saw the infinitely kind and tender smile of Bonnie Fairweather and she knew there were extenuating circumstances. Bonnie had been driven to her profession, by finances, by the desire to protect and rear her daughter properly, and she *had* protected Fleurette. Evidently the daughter knew nothing of her mother's profession in Houston.

Mara sighed and made up her mind. She would continue to design and create for Bonnie Fairweather as long as she wanted her creations. And she would be a friend to her. As she drifted off to sleep she remembered Bonnie's softly spoken words, *But I can tell you this much, Mara, you will have a staunch friend in me.*

Chapter 8.

〰 MARA was not to see Galveston on New Year's Eve
with John Halloran. Instead, there began the chain of
events, as Aunt Felice had promised, that was to blow Mara's world apart.

Thursday, she had let Bella Flaherty and Anna Beckman off at their customary five o'clock, so they could go
home and prepare supper for their husbands. But Sudie
and Mara had stayed until eleven, finishing a ballgown for
a young customer who wished to wear it to a holiday celebration. When Julius arrived in the buggy to take them
home, both girls were weary and more than a little hungry. In the kitchen, Pleasance fed them cold sliced beef and
some of her rolls which were still faintly warm. The parlor
was dark, everyone having gone up to bed long before.

Mara had finished undressing and had donned her long
white nightgown when Celia slipped into her room, silently and smoothly as a wraith. By the light of the one
small lamp by Mara's bed, her face looked white and the
dark eyes wide, pinned back by the thick fringe of black
lashes. Mara's heart took a great leap of fear at the expression on her sister's

"What is it, Celia?" she whispered.

"Come," Celia said low as she sat on the edge of the bed.
"Sit beside me, Mara."

She did as Celia bade, instinctively putting out her hand
to take one of her sister's. It was cold as ice. "Why, you're
freezing. Where is your robe?"

Celia shook her head. "It's only—nerves. Mara, all these
months David's let me think he was going to divorce Lucinda and marry me. I'm—I'm pregnant."

"My God!" Mara's breath went out of her in a gasp.

"He told me today he can't divorce her, that he loves her. He—he offered me money to get an abortion—offered to find an abortionist for me."

Mara flung her arms about her sister. "No! No! You could be killed or become desperately ill from such an operation. You mustn't even think of it!"

"I didn't and I won't," Celia replied grimly. "I told him as much."

"How can you love such a man?" Mara asked passionately. "How can you?" She looked at Celia's pale face and saw that perspiration glistened on her forehead and upper lip. "Are you all right, Celia?" she asked anxiously, catching her sister's other cold hand and holding them both warmly in her own.

"I'm a little nauseated, but I've had that for nearly a month now. It comes and goes. I'm about two months along."

"And yet you love him." All Mara's hatred and contempt for Donellan was packed into the words.

Celia was silent a moment, then in an odd, detached voice, "I didn't know the deep love I bore David could vanish in so short a time. I thought I would love him all my life. I was wrong."

"Thank God," Mara breathed.

"But there's a great hollow in my heart. An emptiness that can never be filled."

Mara thought she was wrong about this, but she did not say it. Instead her thoughts flew to her adored father. "What will Papa do? You know how much he loves you."

"Papa will never know. I have a plan. I shall marry." Her colorless face was resolute.

"Branch?" Mara asked. Celia had gone out with Branch a number of times and he seemed in his rollicking way very taken by her.

Celia's smile was chill. "By the time I'd get Branch to propose, it would be much too late. I haven't time. Besides, I could never tell Branch the truth."

"Then who?"

"Will MacAdam asked again to marry me, Christmas Day at his house. I plan to tell him everything and I have a feeling he'll marry me anyway." Her voice altered strangely. "I think he *wants* me—and he loves children."

"But you don't love him, either. That's cruel!"

"No. I'll be honest with him when I tell him. He can make up his own mind." She laughed hollowly. "I'll be a dutiful wife to him, and I don't recall him mentioning love when he asked me to marry him, not even the second time."

"You'll tell him David Donellan's the father?"

"Certainly. I'm staking my future on his understanding and acceptance—and his silence." She lifted her chin and looked into Mara's eyes. "I want *you* to be with me when I have to go through this thing with Will. I—I don't think I have the courage to do it alone."

Mara was silent. She had seen Will's eyes when he looked at Celia and she concluded that he had loved her sister for years. Probably since those long ago days when he came to the house in Richmond on his holidays from the University, but she did not say this to her distraught sister. Celia had enough to worry about.

"When do you plan to tell—to ask him, Celia?"

"Tomorrow afternoon, at his office at the Exchange Building. I know he's there usually at that time of day. Can you take off and go with me?"

"I will, but what excuse can we give to Papa?"

"I'll tell him you promised to go downtown and have lunch with me at Mrs. Primrose's Tea Shop. I've gone there with Andrea several times."

"He knows I don't usually do such things," Mara said doubtfully.

"I'll convince him somehow before you leave for the store in the morning. Then Julius can drive us downtown and I'll send him back to the store with word that Andrea will bring us home. It won't matter by then, for Will and I will be married."

"I see you've thought it all out," Mara said slowly. "But what if Will says no?"

"I'll call the store and get Papa to let us take a hack home." A touch of panic sped the next words. "Besides, Will won't refuse. Whether he wants me as an ornament or just a hostess, or even if it's physical, he wants me." Then doggedly, "Besides, he's told me about his cousin's babies in Richmond, and from the way he talks, I know he loves them. And did you know he gave a thousand dollars' worth of toys to the Houston Orphanage for Christmas? Delivered them personally, Andrea told me."

Mara thought, *Of course it was Will MacAdam who sent us the furniture and the piano. I knew it all the time.*

Julius let Mara and Celia off in front of Mrs. Primrose's Tea Shop. He had picked Mara up from the store, where Ashworth had bade the two girls good-bye with a somewhat puzzled air. It was not Celia's custom to demand her sister accompany her to lunch and to the music store to buy new sheet music that was very popular in Houston now.

The two girls walked from the Primrose Tea Shop to the Exchange Building without speaking, each lost in her own misgivings. Mara was apprehensive that Will might not be at this particular office today, for his business interests took him to as many places as did Halloran's.

When they reached his office, his secretary, a Blanche Hazlett, so read the placard on her desk, said he had gone down the hall to Mr. Rice's offices and would be back shortly. She was working over two ledgers.

"Will you wait?" she asked.

"Yes. For a short while."

"I'm sure he'll be right back. Could I help you ladies?" She was plainly curious.

"No," Celia replied, lying smoothly. "We want to talk to Mr. MacAdam about some mining stocks that were left to us by our mother." It satisfied the secretary who went back to her ledgers. Mara sent her sister an admiring glance. At least, Celia was composed and had herself well in hand.

After an interminable five minutes, Will strode into the office, bringing with him that indefinable sense of outdoors that was such a part of both him and John Halloran. For the first time, Mara thought of her New Year's Eve to be spent with Halloran, and the strange mixture of antagonism and pleasure unsettled, for a moment, the unhappiness that had depressed her ever since Celia had confided in her.

Will looked at the pale-faced Celia and then Mara with

unconcealed surprise. But Celia rose from her seat, smiling, and extended her hand.

"We need to talk to you privately, Will." She hesitated, then with firmness, "It's about that mining stock mother left us that we talked about Christmas day."

"Come in," he motioned them into the inner office. Then as he scrutinized Celia's translucent features he slowly closed the door, shutting out Blanche Hazlett and enclosing the three of them in silence.

"Stocks your mother left you two?" he asked, the light blue eyes gleaming with curiosity. "I don't recall—"

"No," Celia said flatly, plunging into the truth without preface. Will MacAdam was not a man to beat about the bush. "I've come to you with a proposition—Will."

"And it's 'Will,' twice now. That's a signal honor, to be addressed by my first name by you. It's so rare that you do. Have those two chairs, ladies." And he seated himself behind his vast desk. "I take it you both have something more urgent on your minds than fictitious mining stock."

"Yes. *I* have. Mara came along because I asked her—to lend me strength to do it." Her voice was suddenly spent and weary. She swallowed twice when he lifted his black brows. He was looking at her now with an intensity that made Mara suddenly uneasy about his reaction to Celia's request. After all, it *was* a request and not an opportunity. Silence strung out.

Then Will said, "Well? Let's have your proposition."

"Do you still want to marry me?" Celia asked, her face growing paler.

For a moment he said nothing. He was expressionless and his big body still as stone. He glanced at Mara, who had reached across and taken her sister's hand firmly in hers.

Very slowly and deliberately, he said, "Yes. I still want to marry you." He said no more.

It was as if a flood was suddenly released in Celia and words poured out, words that she had rehearsed in the dark hours since her decision. Her voice was low and tense. "I'll marry you if you still want me, after I tell you the circumstances. I owe you that. I'm two months pregnant with David Donellan's child. He led me to believe he loved me, would divorce Lucinda and marry me. He never spoke of her—but he's—now he says he loves her." Her words grew bitter. "I'll have to be honest with you, Will, I was nothing more than a diversion. He wanted me to have an abortion. Worse, he actually wanted to continue our relationship afterward. He said—he—he still loved me, too." She was silent then for a long moment and Will said nothing. He merely looked at her without expression.

Celia's voice was low as she took up again. "Now I'm caught. I'll *never* have an abortion. I *want* my baby. And I shall have it, no matter your decision." Her head lifted and her eyes flashed. "Even if I must leave Houston to bear it and bring it back to adopt it." Suddenly she was out of breath and tears filled her eyes.

Mara rose from her chair and bent to put her arm about her sister. "Celia, dear," she whispered, "don't cry. I'm here and I know Will understands." She glanced back at him and was thoroughly frightened by the man whose black brows were drawn together and whose icy eyes held cold fire.

"That son of a bitch," he said roughly. "He doesn't deserve to live after leading you on." He made a visible effort to control his rage and said, "Then confronted with the consequence of his lying, he turned you out, eh?"

Mara sank back into her chair thinking, *Dear heaven, what a pair of fools we were to come on such an errand to such a man.*

"That's it," Celia said bravely, ignoring her tears. "David's most concerned for his own reputation now—and Lucinda's innocence."

There was a long silence after this, but Will MacAdam's rugged face did not reveal what was going on behind it.

"I won't blame you, Will," Celia said with finality, drying her eyes with the back of her gloved hand, "for not wanting to marry me. Now that I'm carrying another man's child." She prepared to rise from the chair.

He swore softly and vehemently under his breath. Then harshly, "Sit down. Children don't ask to be born." He looked at Mara and his long, measuring glance caused her heart to turn over. Why did he look at her so strangely? "The baby you carry, Celia, is innocent and deserves a life of its own. I feel no anger at your child." He paused, swept the papers on his desk into a rough stack and pushed back his chair. He came to tower over Celia. "We had better do it now, Celia, since time is of the essence. A seven-month baby will be believed, but not six months or five."

A great wave of relief and gratitude washed over Mara and she saw it reflected in her sister's eyes. He was going to do it! *Celia was right,* Mara thought, *Will loves children.* She was troubled by a peculiar feeling that in some curious way Will even loved Mara, but not in the way he loved and wanted Celia. Of that, she was certain. But she knew it even as she recognized that he was that paradox, a tough man who was kind, despite the ingrained hardness that was part of his character. At that moment, Mara did not think what it would be like for Celia to live with him without loving him.

"Come, Mara, you can be your sister's maid of honor. We'll go to the courthouse and be married. We can say it was a whirlwind love that overcame us, Celia."

Celia rose to her feet, swaying slightly but stiffening against it. She clenched Mara's hand as a drowning swimmer holds to another.

"Yes," she said tremulously. "And Will, I swear I'll make you a good wife."

He turned back to a small safe, dialed the combination and reached inside. Rising, he handed a small black velvet-covered box to Celia. "I bought these before my trip to Richmond last summer. But you never gave me a chance to really court you, Celia." His smile was wintry.

Celia snapped open the box and looked at the two sparkling rings. They were big, solid diamonds, like the man himself, Mara thought as she saw two bright spots of color climb into Celia's white face.

He took the box from her and caught Mara's hand in his big, rough warm one, taking Celia's arm with the other. "And I'll make you a promise, Celia," he said gently. "I'll be a good father to your baby."

He said nothing of being a good husband, but what he said was enough for Celia and Mara, as he opened the door on the reception room where Blanche Hazlett looked up from her ledgers expectantly.

"I won't be back today, Miss Hazlett. I'm going to the courthouse with these two young ladies.

* * *

Securing the license was surprisingly easy for Will Mac-Adam. He knew everyone at the courthouse, and when his mission was known, word spread like wildfire throughout the big red-stone building. Clerks and lawyers alike were full of smiles and congratulations as the three of them finally made their way to the judge's chambers, after Will had the waiting period waived. There, the brief ceremony was performed by a white-haired and beaming Judge Phillips, with a clerk from the license office and Mara as witnesses. The rings flashed brilliantly on Celia's left hand, where Will had placed them and which she had left ungloved.

In the hall, they encountered Stuart Kennedy who smiled broadly. "What's this I hear about a wedding that's practically an elopement?"

"You know I've never been one for waiting, or a big fol-de-rol wedding, for that matter." Will laughed as the two shook hands.

"All the ladies in town are going to hate you for doing them out of a big fol-de-rol wedding, too! And you know I have designs on the Ashworth family, also," Stuart said, looking at Mara and becoming serious. "But Mara's so busy with that high fashion shop of hers, she won't give me time to persuade her."

Will's smile was easy. "When she says 'yes,' Stu, you'll take her and run, just as I have, and wedding be hanged. The important thing is to get your girl."

Celia looked up into the tanned face of her husband and smiled fixedly. With some difficulty, Mara managed to disengage her hand from Stuart Kennedy's.

"I'll see you later, Stuart," she said. "Do come by tomorrow night, but right now I must go with Will and Celia."

"I know," he said, grinning boyishly. "This is a real occasion, Will and Miss Celia getting married."

They managed to get away from him in the courthouse halls, but not from the small army of well-wishers who followed them out to Will's buggy and waved them off.

The three were quiet as Will clicked to the horse and the buggy moved away from the courthouse. *It must be well past three o'clock,* Mara was thinking. Looking up, she saw the heavy clouds and felt the cold north wind blowing across the Houston skies. It was going to rain at last, she

thought, noting that the road had been oiled to lay the dust
only recently. It had been a dry month and unusually
warm for December. People had been watering their lawns
and gardens.

As they drove down the broad expanse of Congress
Street in silence, it was so dark from the approaching bad
weather that all the stores were turning up their lights.
Everyone who lived, or did business near the streetcar
tracks, had easy access to electricity and many of the
stores were brightly lit. They were all still gaily decorated
for the Christmas season. Looking at them, Mara was
thinking how hard it was going to be on their father, this
hasty wedding, yet how good it was that people wouldn't
suspect what had driven Celia to marry Will.

Ahead of them came the clatter of an approaching streetcar and a factory whistle sounded mournfully. Other carriages passed them, some of the people calling out a hello
to Will occasionally. The sidewalks bore only a few late afternoon shoppers. It was a singularly dreary day.

Nearing the center of town, Will asked, "Shall we drive
out to your house so you can pick up your clothes and
things?"

"I—I guess so." Celia's voice was uncertain. She was
looking blindly into the decorated shop windows beside
them. Will was driving carefully to avoid the streetcar
tracks and the wind was increasing in its velocity. Mara
put a hand to her hat and saw that her sister had done the
same.

"Don't you think we should stop by the store and tell
your father first?" Will asked carefully. "I think he'd like
to know."

Mara glanced quickly at the impassive face. Had there
been a trace of grim pleasure in his cool voice? Surely not.
Archer Ashworth would be as happy as possible, for losing
his favorite daughter. More so, since it was to the wealthy
son of his long loved friend, Colonel William Hunter Mac-
Adam.

"Papa would never forgive us if we didn't," Celia said, a
touch wearily.

"He may never forgive you anyway," Mara said quietly.
"You know what a store he sets by you, Celia."

"But he's very fond of Will," her sister replied positively. "I know he'll be pleased."

She was wrong.

As the three of them walked into Ashworth's small office at the rear of the store he looked up, saw Celia first as always and broke into a smile of pleasure. Then he included Will MacAdam in it, and Mara only casually.

"It's a surprise to see you two together, Will and Celia," he said, laughing. "Did you run into these two girls during lunch, Will?"

"No. We came by with a bit of news for you, Archer," Will drawled, but he offered no elaboration.

As Ashworth continued to look inquiringly at the two of them, Celia was driven to speak. "I—Papa, Will and I—" She swallowed and finished in a rush. "We were just married. We wanted you to be the first to know. Mara was a witness, and my maid of honor."

In the bright glare of the exposed lightbulb above him, Ashworth's face went white. "You're joking, of course," he said roughly. "And it's not amusing."

"It's no joke, Archer," Will replied, taking the folded license from his pocket and holding it out to him.

It came to Mara with renewed force that her father's love for Celia was almost obsessive, that he had somehow intended she would be under his roof always, not even withstanding a husband who had as much money as Will MacAdam and was the son of his beloved friend, the Colonel. His blue eyes darkened with sharp pain as they went to Celia's ivory face.

Mara's heart swelled with love and sympathy for him. She longed to go to him and lay her cheek against his and murmur consolation. He looked so handsome, so hurt and so dear.

Celia saw his stricken look and was swift to say, "Papa, I love you, but you've always known, surely, that I would fall in love someday. You see, I love—Will—too. All this time I thought I disliked him, it was because I loved him and I was fighting against it."

"I don't believe it," he said flatly. His gaze on Will was hostile and his burnished mustache quivered angrily.

"I asked her to marry me as long ago as when I visited you in Richmond last summer, Archer. She turned me down then. But as you know, I don't give up easily. This time she finally said yes."

Ashworth expelled his breath gustily. "I'm damned sorry you didn't see fit to wait and have a decent wedding. Give me a chance to get used to the idea. Why such a goddamned hurry?" His fury was rising and he had hit upon the crucial point.

"Archer, you know I never delay when opportunity presents itself," Will said in a voice that cut like a whip through Ashworth's anger. "When Celia said *yes*, I said *now*."

"And Papa," Celia said hurriedly, "I must confess to you that some of those times I was supposed to be in Galveston, I was seeing Will instead of tending to Lucinda's and David's house." The words tumbled out more swiftly now as she sought to mend the growing rift. "I thought you'd be happy! You're so fond of Will, and his father was your best friend—"

"Friend, yes. The Colonel was an example and an inspiration, but you didn't need to marry and leave home to prove my friendship. You're too young for one thing."

"I regret we haven't your approval," Will said with sudden coldness.

Celia went to her father then and put her arms about his stiff, unyielding shoulders. Mara heard her softly murmur, "Papa, be glad for me." Then she added the lie that was needed to further seal her bargain. "I'm so very happy. I love Will so much. You must be happy with me."

His big hands with the thick, wiry gold hairs on them gripped his daughter's arms, bringing her face to his. "Are you, daughter? Are you really happy to be leaving me?"

"You wouldn't expect us to live with you now, would you, Archer?" Will asked, still cold. "She'll be no more than a couple of miles away and you've acquired a son—of sorts."

Celia's laugh had a catch in it. "That's true, Papa. You've always wished you had a son."

"Why did you see fit to keep—this thing—a secret?" he asked, going back to the heart of the matter.

Mara could almost feel the quick beating of her sister's heart as she hastened to add another lie. "Because of this, your very disapproval. I knew no matter whom I chose, you wouldn't like my marrying. And to tell the truth, I—I just couldn't face that." Suddenly, fortuitously, she began to cry. "I still can't face it."

It was more than Ashworth could bear. As Will enfolded her against his broad chest Ashworth rose from his chair and began awkwardly patting her shoulder, murmuring, "Now don't cry, my dear. Don't cry. I'll try to accept your decision. Ah, don't cry, Celia!"

Ashworth looked crushed and broken-hearted and Mara's throat ached with love and pity. She felt every pain, every frustration, each disappointment that surged through the small office. They battered against her sensibilities like waves upon a shore.

As Celia wept against her husband's shirt front, Mara knew she was weeping for the love she had wasted on David Donellan, for the warm, loving home she was leaving, for the lies she had just told and for the marriage she had entered into without love.

Will MacAdam did not soothe or pat Celia. He murmured no endearments. He simply waited until she was cried out and Ashworth was reduced to mumbled apologies and tender promises.

Then Will said, "I regret, Archer, that you don't fancy me as a member of your family."

"Ah, now Will, the truth is, I guess I wouldn't have welcomed any man Celia married. She's been my life since my wife died. I've never remarried and it's been because Celia was enough for me."

"But you still have Mara," Will said with a trace of irony. "She loves you a great deal."

"Oh, yes, Papa!" Mara burst out, catching his hands in hers. "I'll try so hard to make it up to you."

Ashworth released his hands and waved one negligently. "Mara and I have never been close. She's such a child, not like Celia."

"A child," said Will, "who's made a smashing success of your store."

"Nonsense. The store would have done as well without that high fashion shop of hers." Then grudgingly, "Still, I must give you credit for it, Mara. You've done very well for a flighty child."

Celia was wiping her eyes on the big linen square of

Will's handkerchief when Ashworth asked thoughtfully, "Will there be a honeymoon?"

"No," Celia said hastily, "I—I can't ask Will to leave his business right now. You know how many irons he has in the fire. He and John Halloran are the busiest men in Houston."

"We'll save the honeymoon for later," Will said quietly. "We're going to take Celia to pick up her things at your house, Archer. Then we'll go home and tell Andrea and Branch and the household. Would you like to come along for the excitement, Archer?"

"No," Ashworth said with curbed violence. "I'll stay here. I have invoices to go over." Then touchingly, "Kiss Papa good-bye, Celia."

"Not good-bye!" Celia cried, kissing him warmly. "Just so long for now. Why, why I'll see you tomorrow likely enough, Papa."

"Then come," Will said. "You, too, Mara. The family would never forgive me if I didn't bring the maid of honor to help break the happy news." Will's twinkling blue eyes held a special smile for Mara and again she wondered at his fondness for her.

But it was pushed from her mind by the thoughts crowding into it. This time, *she* would comfort her father. She would tell him that she would do just as he asked, always, and her love could be a buffer against this hurt he had been dealt. Tonight when she got home after the visit with the MacAdams, she would approach her father.

She began to rehearse what she would say, even as they mounted the buggy and pulled away in the lowering gloom. The north wind blew colder and it was damp, but there was still no rain. Thunder rumbled in the distance and Mara thought, *Surely, with Celia gone, Papa will turn to me for comfort at last.* She did not think of her Aunt Felice.

And thus Will sat in the Ashworth parlor, having coffee with an exceptionally cordial and pleasant Aunt Felice. There was something disturbingly triumphant in her reception of the news of the marriage, while a wildly excited Pleasance hurriedly helped Celia and Mara pack up two large portmanteaus. Julius, who would not go to the store to pick up Sudie and Ashworth for yet another hour, hovered in the background anxiously, hoping to assist in some way.

"I'll come back for the rest of my things later," Celia said, handing first one and then the other of the portmanteaus to Julius in the hallway. Pleasance carried the small valise that contained toothbrush, toothpaste and other small necessaries.

At the door, it could be seen that scudding clouds were thicker and the wind was still rising.

"You're going with them again?" Aunt Felice asked Mara with a faint touch of disapproval.

"Certainly," Will answered roughly. "She was our maid of honor and I expect her to be there."

"Of course! It's only that the weather looks very threatening." And she smiled with quick warmth. "When will she be returning home?"

"I'll see she gets home no later than ten. She'll have dinner with us, of course."

Mara looked at him in some puzzlement. Obviously Will meant to make his relationship as a brother-in-law a forceful one. But Mara was glad. She was glad because she sensed that Will was truly fond of her and she was, as always, grateful for friendship from anyone.

It was almost dark before they pulled up before the Mac-Adam mansion.

Will told Sam, who came to meet them, to take the horse and buggy to the stables and hitch up the bay mare to it, as he would be taking Mara home in a few hours. Inside, the three found that Branch had just come in from the lumberyard and Rosita and Maria were preparing supper. When Will told the two their news, both Andrea and Branch were astonished and at first disbelieving.

"Ah, go on!" Branch said with his rollicking laugh, "I don't believe it! When she could have had *me?*" Then suddenly sober, "Will, you're a cool one. How long has this been going on?"

"I've been courting Celia secretly for a long time. It had to be a secret because she was so sure she didn't like me, and then the wind began to change."

Andrea cried joyously, "Oh, Celia, you're my real sister now! I'm so glad, we'll have such fun together!" Then her face changed dismally and she lamented, "But you should have had a big fine wedding with all the trimmings. Will, don't you know a runaway marriage brings ill luck?" Then in a rush, "And it's going to rain buckets and that's a bad omen, too, on your wedding day. Don't you remember the old adage, 'Happy is the bride the sun shines on'?"

"Sis, if you think I was going to wait a minute after she finally said yes," Will said firmly, "you're a hundred percent wrong. Besides, big weddings are a deal of trouble. Celia didn't want one either."

"You know we all adore you, Celia," Andrea said hastily. "I'd rather my brother married you than anyone else in the world." But superstition haunted her voice as she added, "I just want everything to be perfect for you." Then anxiously, "You'll want to stay on in the big master bedroom, won't you, Will, where the Colonel was."

"Yes. I want Celia to have everything possible to make her happy and comfortable." He called the butler, "Amos!" and at his appearance, he said, "Take Miss Celia's things to my rooms on the south, please."

Amos's grin was broad. "We heard already 'bout the weddin'! Congratulations an' all good luck, Mrs. Mac-Adam, you, too, Mist' Will." And he vanished in the corridor with the baggage.

Andrea was staring at the big portrait of her father above the mantel. She spoke low, "The Colonel should have been here. He'd be so proud. He missed it by only a few months. I'll never get used to his being gone."

There was an awkward moment of silence which Celia covered by saying softly, "I'm sure, Andrea, that somewhere he knows and is happy with us."

Mara looked at her sister with deep affection. Celia knew so well how to comfort, to console, to say the right thing. She had done it for Mara for years. Oh, she would miss her!

Amos returned shortly with a silver tray of glasses of cold champagne. "I thought you might like to toast yo' bride, Mist' Will."

"Bless you, Amos, you're damn right I do, and after this, break out another bottle. I want us all to be a little tipsy when we sit down at the table."

Branch turned to Mara, who had not spoken since arriving and said, "So you were the lucky bridesmaid. Who married them, old Judge Phillips?"

"Yes, it was a lovely ceremony."

"He was one of the Colonel's best friends. They used to go dove hunting together in the early fall and deer hunting later on. Did you cry at the wedding, beautiful Mara?" Branch asked.

"I didn't have time to," she replied, sipping the champagne. It was cold, yet it warmed her to her toes. She noted that a small cozy brace of logs burned in the fireplace under the Colonel's imperious presence.

They all had another round of champagne before Rosita announced supper was served. And as Will had desired, everyone was just a little tipsy, enough to make jokes and laugh in celebration of the hasty wedding. They had talked honeymoon and Celia had firmly put it off, Will agreeing, the season being such a busy one. Andrea never once spoke to Mara, nor looked at her after her first cool and remote greeting. But Mara had come to accept Andrea's inexplicable aversion to her, even though it troubled her. She could not fathom a reason for it unless there were some things in her personality that simply turned Andrea against her.

Under the stimulation of champagne the conversation grew merrier, and color came into Celia's white face. She looked quite beautiful, and only Mara knew what it cost her to banter with her new relations, or to chatter about secret meetings with the man who was now her husband. Will's bland smile did not give away any of her lies, and Mara knew fresh gratitude to this handsome, hard-eyed man who had saved her sister from scandal.

The merriment lasted until well after supper and all the servants came in after dessert in response to Will's urging. They lifted small crystal glasses of wine to the newlyweds and Mara was suddenly anxious to get home. Her father must have been there alone with Aunt Felice and the servants for over two hours by now. But as she started to ask that Branch drive her home, a great crack of thunder shook the strong house and wind could be heard lashing the treetops.

"Mara, dear," Celia spoke, "do come up and help me unpack and give me a proper good-bye." Her eyes pleaded with her sister. "Do, please."

And when the two of them were in the room, Mara was amazed at the vastness of the bedroom. So was Celia. The first thing that met their eyes was the enormous bed. But then it would have to be to accommodate the six-foot-three-inch frame of its occupant. It was a typical man's room, with dark, heavy furniture and severely masculine drapes and spread. There were two big overstuffed chairs that invited a man to sprawl comfortably before the fire or to lie on the huge velour sofa between them.

Celia turned to Mara, her lustrous eyes blazing. "I'm thinking about getting into that monstrous bed with *him* tonight, Mara, and I'm so afraid!"

"Don't be," Mara said quickly, firmly. "Will's kind and gentle. I just *know* he is. He'll be good to you."

"It doesn't matter," Celia said slowly. "My baby is *safe*. That's all I care about. My baby will carry the MacAdam name and be looked on with respect in the city. That's worth everything, worth any risk or unhappiness."

The two girls then methodically unpacked Celia's dresses and underclothing. They took out her toilet articles, her silver-backed hand mirror, brush and comb, then the crystal bottles of fine perfume. Her toilette added a feminine touch to the broad dressing table, which was sternly bare of all but Will's own brush and comb. There was a large bathroom off to the left and Celia put her toothbrush and toothpaste in it.

At last, all her dresses were hanging in the closet beside Will's suits and all her nightgowns and peignoirs had been put into the tall chest of drawers.

"I must get home, Celia. Papa will be missing you so. He's been dreadfully hurt by this hasty marriage."

"Oh, Mara," Celia cried suddenly. "How did I ever come to be in this terrible circumstance?"

"David Donellan," Mara said laconically.

"Damn him, damn him!" she whispered and began to weep softly.

"Don't cry! They'll never understand if they see you've been crying when you see me off downstairs." Mara took her cold hands and chafed them together.

"I can't let you go," Celia said desperately. "Why not spend the night here? The weather's so threatening."

"What good would that do, Celia? You must face the bargain you've made and keep it."

"Oh, I know, I know!" she responded distractedly.

"And I'm thinking of Papa at home, with only the servants and Aunt Felice to comfort him. He took your marriage so hard."

"He'd take an illegitimate grandchild even harder," Celia said, pulling her cold hands from Mara's. Then with decision, "Come, I'll go back down with you. Branch should take you home before he gets any drunker."

In the buggy on the two-mile drive from the MacAdams to the Ashworth house, Branch was merry and full of song. His pleasant bass carried through the moisture-laden air and despite the thunder and lightning, engaged in a light popular tune of the day.

"Oh, her heart was fickle and she left me for a smile and a handful of flowers and a heart not half so true . . ."

"Were you really so in love with Celia?" Mara asked, smiling in the gloom. The air was oppressive for it had not yet begun to rain.

"No more than with you, beautiful Mara. May I still come a-calling at the Ashworths? I won't ask *you* to marry me, though. We're too much alike." He laughed joyously as he touched the mare with the whip and she increased her pace. "I must get you home before the rain starts, so your old man—oops, pardon—so your father won't be angry."

A silence hung between them but Branch was too tipsy to let it last. "I wonder, though, if you can find time for any man, relative or courting, with that big baby you've taken on at *Ashworth's.*" He paused, then with monumental dignity, *"Haute couture*—my God, that's impressive! And you're such a little thing to have the whole female population of Houston beseeching you for designer clothes."

"I'm a lucky girl, and I just may well make time for you, Branch. You're so complimentary and what girl can resist that?"

His jolly laugh rang out as he pulled up before the modest frame house. He reeled slightly as he helped her to the shell drive and then to the front door. "Can't really court you, you know, beautiful Mara," he said again, with a cunning glance at her.

"Branch, you must go right home. The weather's going to break any minute and you've had quite enough to drink for one evening. Promise?"

"No promises," he wagged his head in a negative. "I'm not afraid of a little weather. I'm going to the saloon on the corner of Portland and Ninth, where I plan to become much drunker. But ol' Nan here, she knows her way back to the stable at home. She'll see I get home."

She bade him good-bye and heard him whistling merrily as he made his way back to the buggy before she closed the front door against a strong wind. Her mind turned back at once to her father. Thunder grumbled from the direction of the Gulf and she heard the first faint patter of rain against the roof and windows as she tiptoed past pale light spilling through the library door and went on up to her room.

Celia was gone. Not just for the night, but forever, and the loss struck her anew. If *she* felt so lonely for Celia, how must her papa feel? Her throat thickened and she squeezed her lids against hot tears as she turned on the light. Blindly she flung off her clothes and let them fall from the chair to the floor unheeded.

In her long white nightgown she hesitated. She could hear her father's voice down the hall. What was he saying? She could not be sure, but she heard her aunt's response in a tearful voice, trailing away, then the slam of a door.

Though she had not made out his words, her father's voice had sounded hoarse and broken. Poor, distraught man! There must be something she could say. Her mind flew back over all the tender words she had framed for her beloved papa throughout this interminable evening. She went to the closet and took out the new burgundy velvet robe she had finished only the day before for herself. She belted the warmness about her slender waist. Hastening to the door, she went into the hall, leaving both lamps burning.

At her father's bedroom door she rapped softly. There was no answer. She opened it on the dim, empty room. He was not there.

She walked back to the head of the stairs and looked down into the warm foyer below. The light spilling from the library door was brighter now. He had gone back to his place of solace in the house, his library.

Creeping silently on bare feet down the uncarpeted stairs, she approached the library door and stood there peering in.

The fire Julius had built earlier, flickered in the black depths of the small fireplace. Ashworth was sitting in his big, richly red velour chair, his bright head thrown back. A nearly empty glass dangled from his hand as his arms hung over the sides of his chair. Were those tears glistening beneath his heavy red-gold lashes? A flood of tender pity filled Mara.

Oh, Celia, Celia, even knowing what drove you to it, you have broken our papa's heart! For a brief instant, Mara wondered if it would help him to know the truth, but she discarded the thought before she finished thinking it.

Without waiting, she flung herself across the room, dropping to her knees before her father, causing him to release the glass, which struck silently on the ruby rug below. He was still as death. Mara's own eyes were wet with sympathy.

Slowly, Mara raised her head, her heart lifting with hope. He was staring down at her, his lids drooping over the blue eyes and tears trembled heavily on the thick fringe of golden lashes.

"Oh, my darling Papa," Mara whispered huskily. "I love you so!" There was a sob in her voice and all the anguish she had suffered through the long years poured out in her next words. "Please let me help you! Please love me!" she begged, but she did not add *as you have always loved Celia.*

Her father half rose from the chair and she was forced back to a sitting position, still with his eyes on her.

The overpowering odor of brandy enveloped Mara as he stooped, swinging an arm back and she realized he had been drinking more heavily than she thought. There was violence in the movement, and as his arm came forward his thrust knocked the nearly empty brandy decanter from the small table beside his chair. It hit the rug with a soft thud and in some detached compartment of Mara's brain, she thought, *That's the crystal stopper rolling across the hearth,* as the faint tinkle sounded. It was drowned in a sudden, mighty crash of thunder as the lights flickered, went out and came back on. At last there came the sound of heavy rain beating on the windows under violent gusts of wind.

Her father swayed above Mara, and in the pale light of the lamp behind him, his hair was a red-gold halo about his head. His face was in shadow, but his eyes glittered under the lowered lids. Suddenly Mara realized her father was very drunk.

"Papa," she whispered, "Celia did what she *had* to do. Please forgive her, and let me comfort you."

He stooped over her, thrust his face into hers and laughed harshly. The tears shook from his lashes and fell upon his cheeks to run down into the coppery mustache.

"Comfort me?" He laughed harder, fresh tears spurting from his narrowed eyes. He reeled over Mara and his hands shot out to grip her like iron prongs. "Comfort me, then, *Celeste.*"

He slammed Mara down against the thick rug.

Struck dumb by a sudden burst of terror, she could not move as he swung his heavy frame over her. With one strong hand, he caught the neck of her lovely new robe and with a slashing swing ripped it and the batiste nightgown away from her body.

Mara could not register, let alone believe, what was happening.

"Ah, my faithless and beloved Celeste—this time it shall be *I*. . ." His brandy-hoarse voice chilled Mara to complete stillness. She did not begin to struggle until he forced her legs apart with his knees while grappling with the buttons on his trousers with his free hand. The other was already entangled in her hair, holding her head against the rug.

Then the full realization of his purpose struck her. She began writhing beneath him. "Papa, Papa!" she cried in horror, "Papa, you can't—you *can't*—" She still could not believe this was happening. How could her father do this thing to her?

But he was and she was painfully aware of the sharp thrust between her pinioned thighs, the forcing of her flesh to accommodation even as her legs jerked frantically in futile revulsion.

The great weight above her moved faster and faster despite her frenzied efforts to escape.

This is a nightmare, she told herself in frantic, despairing hope. *In a minute I'll wake up sweating and crying with relief.* This could not be her papa, this hoarsely breathing animal, reeking of brandy as he invaded and violated her slender body. But the hope of a nightmare was broken as he expelled the last of his passion within her and fell inert across her trembling flesh.

His face was in the tangle of her long dark hair and he was whispering, "Ah, Celeste, Celeste! How could you do it to me? How could you? And now, even Celia is gone, our Celia . . ."

Mara moved more fiercely now, shoving with impotent hands against the dead weight upon her. "I'm not Celeste," she sobbed, "I'm Mara, your daughter . . ."

At her words, his body became rigid, then slowly he pulled away. "Mara . . ." The word was dragged from him and it had all the virulence of an epithet. The strong fist that held her head immovable loosened, then sought his trousers. His head lifted and he looked down into her face, eyes reddened and still glittering.

"You look so goddamned much like her. I've never been able to see *him* in you, never known who he was," he muttered.

"Who are you talking about, Papa?" Mara pulled herself to a crouching position, clutching the torn pieces of her robe and gown about her. She was shaking violently.

"Don't call me 'Papa,' " he said furiously, buttoning his trousers with awkward fingers, then seeking the fallen brandy decanter on the table behind him. Not finding it, he lurched to the liquor cabinet and took out a fresh bottle, which he laboriously opened, while Mara stared up at him from the ruby rug. What did he mean? She *must* know.

He looked around the chair, found his fallen glass and filled it quickly. Tossing down the contents, he said viciously, "Get up from there, you little bastard! Get up!"

Slowly she stood. Her thighs ached and shivered. She felt torn. Worse, she felt she had been betrayed, repudiated and befouled. Never again would she know security or peace.

"What are you trying to say, Papa?" She trembled. It

was the last time in her life she was ever to call Archer
Ashworth *Papa.*

"You're the result of adultery, girl," he said with a
cruel, drunken smile. "Celeste was two months pregnant
with you when I returned from a six-month buying tour in
Europe. You're no daughter of mine." He filled the brandy
glass again and tossed it down. "She refused to tell me who
the man was right up to the moment of your birth. Right
up to the moment of her death, and you were palmed off as
being premature. God, what a joke on me. She called for
me, not him, for *me!* And you, you look just like her,
goddamn you!" He sank heavily into the chair as if unable
to stand any longer.

Mara stared down at him, filled with devastation and
horror. All she could think was, *He isn't my father. He has
never been my father in any sense, never.* And he had raped
her, with nothing of true desire, nothing of tenderness that
he must have once felt for the woman who had given her
birth at such cost. He had known only a drive to destroy, to
punish. Mara looked down at her ripped garments and
pulled them closer about her nakedness. A nauseating disgust began to rise deeply in her stomach.

"You are not my father," she said low, more in confirmation to herself than to him.

"Hell, no. Would to God I had never laid eyes on you!"

"Celia is my half sister," she murmured.

"More's the pity. But she doesn't know that and she
didn't choose her mother. *I* did that. Felice knows, Celia's
all mine."

"No, she isn't," Mara said clearly, and with the raw,
new desire to cut this man to the quick, "she's Will Mac-
Adam's."

"Ahhh!" he groaned. "Christ! And I'm left here with you
and Celeste's sister for consolation!" It was a cry of pure
agony. Mara knew then that she was right. Archer Ashworth had really thought his beloved Celia would never actually leave him, that she would stay with him forever, his
darling, the sunshine of his life. And she had chosen to
marry Will MacAdam instead, while Mara had hoped to
comfort him!

But he was wrong. He might be left with her mother's
sister, but he was not left with Mara!

She felt a mirthless laugh bubble in her throat, but it died as she swore silently to herself, he would never hear a comforting word from her as long as she lived. And someday, someway, she would pay him back. She would seek and find vengeance—for herself, and for her mother.

He looked up at her cold, still face as she stared back with increasing hatred. His narrowed drunken eyes wore the old watchfulness that was all too understandable now. He was searching for some trace of the man Mara's mother must have loved so long ago, the man who was her father.

She turned, the pain in her groin easing slightly with the movements. Holding the torn remnants of her beautiful sweeping robe about her, she made her way into the hall and up the long stairs.

Chapter 9.

∾ MARA did not lift her eyes until she reached the landing, suddenly finding Aunt Felice standing before her. Her aunt was staring at her from a tear-stained face, yet there was triumph in the long, dark eyes so like Mara's and Celia's.

"He's told you at last," she said, her voice vibrant with emotion. Mara went past her silently and the woman followed. "And more than that, he's taken you, hasn't he?" Her voice rose slightly, "Because you look so damnably much like her, he finally did what he's had in his mind for years, didn't he?" Her voice was shrill, then fell to a whisper, "He did, didn't he? He's torn your gown and robe off you." As she spoke her fingers dug clawlike into Mara's arm and the girl twisted out of her grip with a quick ferocity.

"Get away from me, Aunt Felice, or so help me God, I just may kill you!"

Felice stepped backward, smiling faintly as she ran the tip of her red tongue over her lips like a satisfied cat.

Mara suddenly remembered that night when she had seen her aunt with Ashworth in his bedroom in Richmond and Felice had cried, *I don't know!* Now she wore a frothy peignoir, and before Mara turned away, she saw her aunt reach the stairs and start to descend.

She has known all this time I was not Ashworth's child, but not whom my mother had taken as a lover. She was suddenly fiercely glad.

In her room, she looked at her fallen clothing and stooped automatically to pick them up, then stopped short. Why bother? She was leaving this house now forever. She thought of the ties that bound her to the Ashworths: Celia, whom she loved, Felice, whom she did not love, those were ties of blood. Julius, Sudie and Pleasance were ties of love. And there was her pleasure and her pride, *Ashworth Originals.* But the man she had thought to be her father all her life had severed them with one irreparable blow. The heat of fury was dying in her, and cold rage laid its burning, but frosty fingers over the whole of her.

Swiftly she took her wine woolen dress from the closet and her new embroidered underthings. A flash of lightning penetrated the window draperies, followed by a tremendous crash of thunder that caused the house to tremble slightly. Rain on the roof was drumming a chill and heavy tattoo.

It did not slow Mara's hasty preparations. She went into the hall bathroom and bathed herself swiftly in cold water. Then, quickly, she donned the clothing she had laid out. She had a right to them, she had earned them, she told herself. After all, over ninety percent of the money she had made from the *Originals* had gone into Ashworth's pocket. She packed a small valise with her personal toilet articles and a fresh nightgown.

She knew where she was going. In spite of hell and all the rain in Texas, she would walk the three miles to the Fairweather house. She could *tell* Bonnie why she had left the Ashworth house, never to return. After all, Bonnie had done it herself. And, thank God, Bonnie would not be leaving for Europe until spring.

Shrugging into her coat, she paused, glancing at her image in the mirror for the first time. The long dark eyes were enormous, framed by thick black lashes, and her face was colorless. Even her lips were pale and she had not bothered to pin up the mane of dark, curling hair.

She would be soaked before she could reach her destination. Not even the big black umbrella which stood in the closet corner would help. Indeed, from the sound of the Gulf wind lashing the house, it might well carry her off if it did not turn wrong side out immediately.

It didn't matter. Nothing mattered but that she get out of this house, away from the lustful, vengeful man who was not her father, away from her lewd and hateful aunt. She put on her heavy coat. Then pulling on her felt hat and kid gloves, she caught up the valise and stepped into the hall, walking silently to the stairs. Looking down, she hesitated. Light still spilled from the open library door.

She eased herself down the steps, her small black patent shoes, with the gray kid, buttoned tops were mute as she set foot on the hall runner. At the edge of the library door, she paused. Ashworth's voice was a low rumble and Aunt Felice's answers were tender, but invigorated by that strange wild triumph she had shown earlier on seeing Mara's torn robe and gown.

Mara slid like a ghost past the library and made her way swiftly to the front door. Opening it narrowly, she slipped out into the wild darkness, then closed it carefully behind her.

The wind took her breath away, and even beneath the porch roof, rain pelted in, the fine droplets stinging her face. Yes, she would be soaked but she had set foot in the Ashworth house for the last time. How her sudden absence would be explained to their friends did not matter either. Putting her head down against the wind, she stepped off the porch into the maelstrom.

The gale caught her angrily, and before she had reached the road, it sent her hat flying away in the darkness, flaring her long hair about her face and tearing at her coat and trailing skirts. But her rage was colder, more furious than the wind, and she did not yield to the storm that boiled about her, but instead walked steadily forward. Her shoes sank in the sandy shell road, and her skirts dragged wetly behind. Her grip on the valise did not lessen, and in a little while, as if the elements admired her courage, they seemed to lessen.

Her hair was thoroughly soaked, hanging now down her back in a thick sodden mass. The tops of the live oaks on either side of the long road lashed each other in the wind, and the few houses she passed were unlit, for it was well past midnight.

Mara walked down the darkened streets as swiftly as she could. Carbide lights that lit the corners of every downtown street had yet to make an appearance in the outskirts. All was dark as she hurried past the sleeping MacAdam mansion. She could not stop there! Celia must never know the confrontation that had taken place between her father and her half sister.

Mara's mind cooled further in the wild night. She would tell Celia that she and her father had quarreled, an irreconcilable rift that could never be bridged, driving her to leave her home, abandon the business she had started in his store and swear she would never see him again. What reason could she give for their quarrel? In the black night, her shoulders squared and her tender mouth set. He had again accused her of her mother's death and *this* time Mara had lashed back. In the ensuing altercation, words had been spoken that could never be forgotten or forgiven. But she knew it was all her fault; she would take the blame. She had reached the end of her patience and all her love had turned to hatred. Why not? She thought harshly, it was part of the bitter truth anyway.

This settled in her mind, she increased her stride, but her soaked garments hindered her speed, dragging at her in slithering swishing movements around her hips and legs, holding her back.

But the rain was definitely lessening, and she looked up at the boiling sky above her as she turned the corner on Hutcheson Avenue and into Fairweather Boulevard. She could see breaks in the clouds. Far, far down Fairweather Boulevard she could see the faint twinkle of carriage lamps that illuminated each side of the door to Fairweather mansion. The tall streetlight that Bonnie had installed at her own expense beckoned from the distant mansion.

Was that a horse and rider coming toward her at this hour?

She put her head down and trudged forward. Less than a mile to go now, she thought with relief. And the worst of the winter storm was over. But now she realized how bitterly cold it was and suddenly a vast weariness overcame her. She staggered and almost fell. Her teeth began to chatter and she clenched them tightly.

Suddenly her shoe caught on a protruding rock in the leaf-covered pathway. She went down to her knee, the valise flying off to one side as she put her hands out to break the fall. It was too late and she went down in a miserable wet heap on the leafy walk beside the roadway.

The sound of hooves sounded near, and before she could drag herself upright, a man's voice rumbled. "Who is it? Are you all right?"

As she attempted to struggle to her feet, the ragged clouds suddenly broke, a thin sliver of light caught her, then vanished as the moon was again covered by swiftly moving clouds.

"By God, it's a woman!" He was off the horse in an instant and at her side, hands gripping her shoulders, pulling her to her feet. He had not yet recognized her, but she would have known that voice anywhere. The last person in the world she wanted to see her in this pitiable condition. John Halloran.

"I'm—I'm all right. I simply tripped."

"Mara! What in the name of God are you doing here in this storm? You're soaked through."

"I'm on my way to Bonnie Fairweather's," she said, lifting her chin and trying to quell her chattering teeth.

"Bonnie's? The devil you say!"

She stooped and grabbed her valise. "Would it satisfy you if I told you I'm delivering a—a dress to her?"

"At two in the morning and on a night like this? Why in hell *are* you going to Bonnie's?"

"What are you doing riding around in a storm at two in the morning?" she flashed.

"I've just come from—dinner—at Bonnie's." The moon broke through again briefly, but long enough to reveal his mocking grin. With a sudden swift movement he lifted her to his saddle and vaulted up behind her. "Whatever your reason, it must be urgent," he said with a touch of grimness. "I'll take you there." He turned the horse deftly and they started toward the distant house. "Now you'd better tell me why you're abroad on the devil's own night."

She began to tremble with cold and fatigue and he must have felt it. He put an arm about her and pulled her tightly against his oiled-cloth raincoat. In an instant, the warmth of his big hard body penetrated her wet garments, and she drew a long breath as it seeped into her chilled back and hips. Her shaking limbs eased, but her long wet hair was cold as death on her face and neck. He took off the broad felt hat with its curled brim and jammed it on her head.

under her. Exhaustion rushed into her like a tide. How had she come so far after such a day? Only a few hours ago, she stood beside Celia while she took her vows with Will MacAdam, and from that moment on, she had been tense, hopeful, vengefully raped, and bruised by a winter storm. She leaned against Halloran weakly as he knocked loudly with the big, gleaming brass knocker.

The door was opened by Desmond Brant. Mara had glimpsed him with Bonnie several times. He stood tall and lithe in a dark green dressing gown, impassive as always, but his pale eyes widened a trifle as they fell on Mara.

"Miss Ashworth," he said in his flat voice but there was an undertone of astonishment. "And Halloran—back again? Thought you had gone for the night."

"Miss Ashworth wants to see Bonnie. She needs help," Halloran said bluntly.

"I'll get her," Brant said as Mara looked about the sumptuous foyer. Gold-framed mirrors, statuary on pedestals, fresh flowers on a gleaming mahogany table. It exuded luxury and money. She thought, *Why, it's beautiful!*

Brant took the long curving stairs two steps at a time, disappearing into the darkness above.

"You must get out of those wet clothes or you'll have pneumonia from exposure, Mara," Halloran said roughly.

When Bonnie came hurrying down, clad in one of the filmy peignoirs of which Mara herself supervised the making, she said not a word but gathered the bedraggled girl into her arms. Mara, too, found herself without words, so full was her throat. Gratitude was drowning her. The beautiful woman asked no questions, merely took her in with a welcome that needed no speech.

Brant retired discreetly, but Halloran stood his ground, and when still the two women did not speak, he said grimly, "She needs dry clothes, Bonnie. She's walked nearly three miles in a December blue norther."

"Of course, Johnnie," she responded. "Thank you for seeing her in." Bonnie looked up at Halloran with a warm smile. "Would you like for me to have Dominique serve you coffee before you leave again? She's gone to bed, but for you she'll do it."

"No thanks, my dear. I'll call tomorrow morning to see how she's doing."

"D-don't tell anyone you saw me, or where I am until I—," Mara broke off.

"Not a word, not a soul," he said firmly.

As soon as the door closed behind him Mara began to shake again, more violently, and her head throbbed with pain.

"My poor darling," Bonnie said softly, "you're soaked through and cold as ice!" Her warm hands caught one of Mara's and she called over her shoulder, "Desmond, get Dominique up and tell her to meet me in my suite." Then to Mara, "Can you make it up the stairs and down a long hall?"

Mara nodded. She wondered if all the things in her valise were soaked through. Bonnie looked down at it and picked it up, saying, "Come along, dear," and together the two climbed the long curving staircase.

Mara was aware of oil paintings on the walls of the long hall they took, and small tables with marble heads and silver vases on them. All the furnishings suggested opulence. They passed many closed doors and Mara felt only the faintest stirring of curiosity. So this was a brothel. The big, luxurious house was singularly quiet. At the end of the long hall, Bonnie opened a door into a suite of rooms that surpassed in beauty any that Mara had ever seen.

Creamy cloudlike draperies hung from each window, delicately ruffled at the edges. All the furniture was French, carved and upholstered in satins and velvets. The fruitwood four-poster gleamed in the pale glow of shaded lamps.

Bonnie took Mara directly across the thick plush carpet to an enormous bathroom, where she said firmly, "Take off all those wet clothes. Here's a wrapper." She handed Mara a robe made entirely of white toweling and started the water running in the tub. Steam immediately began rising from it as Mara's trembling fingers unbuttoned first her coat, then dress and, last of all, her ruined patent and kid shoes.

"You'll be all right?" Bonnie asked anxiously as she hesitated in the doorway.

"Y-y-yes—and thanks—Mrs. Fairweather."

"Bonnie, please, dear," she said closing the door firmly.

* * *

Warm again at last, with a cup of hot chocolate in her hand, Mara sat up in a bed in the second room of Bonnie's private suite. She felt curiously light-headed despite her throbbing temples. In fact, she was more than warm, she thought, pushing the eiderdown back a little. Bonnie sat on the edge of the bed.

"I feel I owe you an explanation—Bonnie," she said slowly, placing the empty cup on the round fruitwood table beside the bed.

"You don't owe me anything," Bonnie replied with gentle emphasis. "You forget. I know my brother and the cruelties of which he is capable."

"He told me—he told me—"

"That he is not your father," Bonnie supplied. Then with bitter irony, "He *would!* In fact, I don't know why he waited so long. I guess fear held him back. Fear of scandal marring the precious Ashworth name. I suppose Celeste held her tongue to the end, God bless her."

"Yes, she did," Mara said, her great dark eyes on Bonnie were haunted, puzzled. "Bonnie, do you know who my father is?"

Slowly Bonnie shook her head. "Celeste never told me *that.*"

"What *did* she tell you?" Mara asked hungrily.

"When I went to her," Bonnie began, dredging the words out of a memory long put away, "to tell her that I was going to have Fleurette, she told me that she, too, was going to have a baby. I was astounded because I knew Archer had been gone six months and Celeste didn't show, hadn't told my older sisters."

"Why would she have told *them*, even if I were Ashworth's?" Mara interrupted bitterly.

"I said the same thing, but she laughed and said, 'Oh, I would have told them if the timing had been right, but you see, I can't tell them. It isn't Archer's and if he won't back me up when he returns this next week, I may be doing even as you are with my babies, Celia and the one I carry.'"

"Oh," Mara's face crumpled, "my poor mother!"

"I told her that if she didn't love Archer, if she felt as I did about him, she should run away with me." Bonnie paused and her big green eyes filled with tears. "She looked at me so sadly and said, 'You forget that Celia is his. And I do love Archer in a way, though not as I love this baby's father, madly, wildly. Still I must stay if he will let me, for Celia's sake.' She said a lot more, about how she was sure Archer would come to love you, that the man she loved had gone away in order, he said, to save her good name. He thought she could claim you were a seven-month baby."

"And so Ashworth did," Mara said angrily. Her head was really pounding painfully now and even her bones were beginning to ache. "He claimed me to save his face, and because Mother had died, he blamed that on me, too. But now I know it was purely to save scandal."

"Dear, your face is very flushed. Do you feel well?"

Mara had flung off the eiderdown minutes before and suddenly she pulled it up around her ears, feeling a violent chill sweep her. "No, Bonnie, I—I don't feel well. I'm so c-c-cold all of a sudden."

"Dominique!" Bonnie called and the beautiful dark girl came swiftly from the other bedroom where she had been readying Mara's wet clothing to be cleaned. "Dominique, get my thermometer and my small bag of medicines."

"Ees she seek, *madame?*"

"I'm afraid so."

"I breeng eet, *vite.*" She disappeared and was gone but a short time. When she returned, Bonnie sent her for a glass of water and immediately thrust the thermometer between Mara's chattering teeth. Her temperature was 102 degrees and climbing.

It was three-thirty in the morning and Bonnie did not leave her bedside the rest of the night. She dosed her with powders the doctor had given her and put her cool soft hands on Mara's brow when the fever rose, pulled the covers about her when the chills struck, which was less and less as the fever rose steadily.

It was a pale girl with dark circles around her big brown eyes who sat in the sunny parlor of Bonnie's suite on the morning of Tuesday, January third. The new year of 1898 had come in while Mara was ill. She occupied a chaise lounge of flowered taffeta and was drinking a cup of tea when Bonnie ushered in John Halloran.

"Thank God you're well enough to see me," he said soberly. "You scared the hell out of Bonnie and me and her whole house."

"I know," Mara said repentantly, glad that Bonnie had loaned her the pale blue ruffled dressing gown. "I'm sorry."

"Now Johnnie can tell you how the town's taking your disappearance," Bonnie twinkled.

"In a nutshell, it's a great mystery and is causing Ashworth no end of trouble. Your sister is the one who is truly distraught and I'd like your permission to tell her where you are." He cocked a quizzical black brow at Mara.

"Heavens! If you tell anyone where she is, it will cause an even worse hurrah, Johnnie. Better wait until she can find a place of her own," Bonnie said hastily, gesturing to Dominique, who vanished at her low whisper.

John Halloran pulled out a cigar, then looked at Bonnie. "May I smoke?"

She wrinkled her pert nose and winked at Mara. "It smells very pure in here, Johnnie. You might as well ruin it as not."

He grinned, lighting the cigar and blowing out a thin stream of blue smoke across the sunny room. "Your pa, that is, Ashworth, is telling everyone you two quarreled, but that he let you leave to buy materials and you'll be back in the shop as soon as you stop pouting. Sudie is sore because you didn't tell her you were leaving; your Aunt Felice looks relieved and uneasy at the same time. But Celia and Julius and his wife are genuinely worried. What *are* your plans, Mara?" The last words were sober and concerned.

Mara's shoulder lifted and she set the empty teacup down on the French table beside the chaise. "I haven't any plans. As soon as I can get about, I'll be looking for a job. I ought to be able to get a job as a seamstress somewhere."

"You really won't go back to the business you've built, *Ashworth Originals?*" he asked.

"No," she said flatly. "I don't intend to see Ashworth again."

"Seems like cutting off your nose to spite your face," Halloran said idly, examining the tip of his cigar.

Dominique came in with a small silver tray and on it was a tall, mint-garnished glass of bourbon over ice. She bent to Halloran, who took it and lifted it to Bonnie in a silent toast and took the first sip. The room was still, and with mixed feelings, Mara looked away from his darkly handsome face, glad that he did not know the indignity she had suffered at Ashworth's hands, glad that she had not told Bonnie after all, glad that Felice could only guess. The rape was a bitter secret that would lie forever in a cold pool of hate deep in her heart.

Breaking the silence, Halloran said, "Then I'd like to make you a business proposition." He squinted at her judiciously over the glass.

"A business proposition?" She stared at him blankly.

"I'd like to buy into the original dressmaking business. I own two vacant buildings on Travis Street and one on Congress. I'd like to rent one to you, invest in machines and materials for an interest in your genius for making clothes."

"You're joking." Mara looked at him suspiciously, all his cynicisms, his obvious disillusions regarding life sweeping through her mind. If he were making such an offer there must be strings, probably some very sticky ones attached to it.

"I never joke about money," he retorted coldly.

"Then what would I have to do for it?"

"I should think," he smiled cryptically, "that Ashworth's revelations to you about his marriage would have convinced you that my creed is the correct one. Marriage is a miserable affair. So you may be sure I have no desire to make you marry me."

Mara flushed to the roots of her hair. "Of course not. But you've made it plain enough there are other things you want of me."

Bonnie hid a smile and he laughed heartily. "Of course I have, but not in this case. I told you once sometime ago that I had tried to buy into a couple of Paris designer houses but they wouldn't sell. And I think it's a money-making business. Hell, I *know* it's a gold mine, women being how they are about clothes."

Mara stared at him silently, lips parted, while Bonnie laughed merrily. "Johnnie, you are the *most* acquisitive man. You're one of the few I know who can turn a disaster into dollars and cents."

"Mara's Originals," he said thoughtfully, drawing on the cigar. "Why, Mara, I'll bet Sudie and the other ladies will come to work for you immediately. That'd really be getting back at your—at Ashworth."

"That would be wonderful," Mara admitted uneasily, "except I hate becoming obligated to you, and it would take an awful lot of money."

"Are you still marriage minded?" he asked bluntly, his narrowed black eyes on hers.

"Absolutely not!" she burst out. "I think you're a hundred percent right about it and I *never* intend to marry. I intend to be completely independent of every man. That's why I hate the prospect of owing you."

"You won't owe me if I buy part of the business. We'll be partners and I'll be the silent partner."

"But you'll still feel like you can—"

"My God, Mara, did that one kiss we shared scar you so irreparably?"

Again she flushed. "I won't do it, unless you swear it will be a strictly business proposition, nothing personal."

He tossed off the last of his bourbon and smiled at her, "Strictly business—in the shop. Outside of it, I make no promises."

"You're looking very healthy now," Bonnie said with a motherly pat. "All that color in your face, when you've been so pale."

"Is it a deal, Miss Mara?" he asked mockingly.

"It's a deal," Mara said slowly, but her eyes were beginning to sparkle in spite of her misgivings. Halloran was a dangerous man, but that was part of his excitement, too. And she now heartily agreed with him regarding marriage. The final blow had been her mother's marriage to a man to whom she had obviously been unfaithful. Theirs must have been an unhappy marriage. There was David and Lucinda Donellan—and now Will and Celia. None of them were really happy. Yes, John Halloran was right. Marriage was something to stay clear of.

She leaned forward on the chaise, a cynical smile on her soft mouth. "How can I—I mean, when do you want to start?"

"We'll start as soon as you're able to be up and around," Halloran said briskly. "I'll deposit—no, I'll have the bank deposit ten thousand to your account at the Houston National. I want to be a silent and an unknown partner. I'll tell Will only. No use in stirring up any more animosity. You can use the building you choose rent-free for the first year and you can *really* go to New York for materials, if you like. We'll tally up my investment at the end of the year and that'll be my percentage of the ownership."

"And you can get a room at the old Houston Hotel downtown, Mara," Bonnie said softly. "I own most of the stock in it and you can tell everyone that's where you stayed when you came back from New York. I don't want it known you've been *here* a week." Her little laugh was rueful. "After all, I'm afraid my clientele might wonder about it and the good ladies of Houston might never speak to you again, high fashion or not."

"I'm proud to have stayed with you, Bonnie," Mara said swiftly. "And I don't care who knows it. I feel you are much more my aunt than Felice ever was. Thank God you took me in, for I had no one to turn to."

"Dear, Celia would have—," Bonnie began.

"It was Celia's wedding night and she must never, *never* know Ashworth isn't my father. It would break her heart to tell her the things—the awful things he said about our mother."

"That's true," Bonnie acceded thoughtfully. "And you did the only thing you could do by leaving."

"And I'll always be grateful to you," Mara said passionately. "And I'll always let everyone know I think you are one of the finest women in the world." Then slowly, reluctantly, "And I'm grateful to you, John, for the opportunity to go into business for myself."

"Don't worry. I always get my money's worth." His lip turned down in a half-smile. "I expect you to be a tremendous success. And an independent woman of means, now that you've got the silly notion of eventual marriage out of your mind."

An independent woman of means. She savored the words silently. All her life she had craved a father's love, suffered for it, knuckled under and even toadied, hoping to get it. And in the dim future, there had been the thought of a husband's love, warm and comforting. Well, thank God her goals had changed, she thought grimly. What John Halloran was offering her was what she wanted most in the world. He might give her trouble. In fact, she *knew* he would by the look in his clear, biting glances, but she could handle that, no matter how often he incited that strange vibrating quiver that went from her stomach to her thighs. She was knowledgeable now and would not be caught unawares again. She would pick up her shattered life, her finished dreams, and build new ones.

"I'll pay you back every cent, John," she said coolly, "every cent. And half the profits shall be yours, too."

"Fifty percent ownership, eh? That's more than I figured I'd get." His eyes twinkled but there was a faint jeer in his words. "But if you want to be so generous, far be it from me to turn you down."

"Can you think of anyone else, bank included, willing to lend me ten thousand dollars on just the little talent I've shown in less than six months?" she asked dryly.

"Nope," he shook his head. "And if I didn't have a powerful block of stock in the Houston National, I know you wouldn't get it from them."

"Very well. I think fifty percent of the business is only fair."

"So young and so honorable." He laughed. "Would that everyone I do business with were so ethical. Later on, you may learn to haggle."

"I shall learn to haggle when the business is firmly settled, you may be sure." She grinned at both Bonnie and Halloran. "But right now, I'm not in a position to be anything but grateful and honorable."

He looked at her sharply. "You've aged about five years in the last few days, Mara. You've lost that little girl wonder that used to fill those beautiful eyes."

"And high time," she said shortly.

"And furthermore, John," Bonnie began determinedly, "she didn't take a thing with her when she left Ashworth's and the rain has ruined what she wore. Getting her a wardrobe before I let her go will be a challenge but necessarily a secret one."

"Ah, Bonnie, you can do that with a snap of your fingers. I never knew a woman as astute about figures—all kinds, including 36-21-36."

"Mara's smaller than that," Bonnie said knowingly, "but I can do it."

"If I had time, I could make myself a wardrobe right here."

"No," Bonnie said pensively. "You mustn't stay so long with me, my dear. Word would get around eventually, and since people love the worst, they'll probably think you've gone into business with *me.*"

John Halloran rose, hat in hand. He came to the chaise and leaned down. "Shall we shake on our deal, partner?"

Mara's smile was only faintly skeptical as she put her small hand into his large brown one. "It's a deal," she said with conviction.

"We'll make a mint of money and you'll find vengeance is sweet after a lifetime under Ashworth's mistreatment. A very satisfactory arrangement because he'll never be able to replace your talent." His low chuckle was infectious. "Shall I drop by and put a rumor in Sudie's—and the other two ladies'—ears?"

"Yes, in about a week," Mara said eagerly. "You can tell them I'm going to have a *haute couture* shop that will put Ashworth's to shame." Then with angry certainty, "I'll decorate it lavishly. It will be a showplace."

"That's what I wanted to hear," Halloran grinned as Bonnie saw him to the door of her suite.

When she returned and sat in one of the tufted blue velvet chairs near Mara, she sighed and said, "Johnnie is a wonderful man, an unpredictable, generous *and* disillusioned man."

"So I've found. He refuses to talk about his past or anything that would lead me to understand anything about him," Mara said, careful to keep a twinge of jealousy out of her voice. "Only that he left home at thirteen and has educated himself—*and* hates marriage."

"He's had a very hard life. And he didn't run away from home. He was driven from home."

Mara turned fascinated eyes to her friend. "Bonnie, do you know how he got that scar on his cheek?"

"Yes, but not from him. Will MacAdam told me and I think he's the only man Johnnie ever confided in."

"Would you tell me? I would so like to understand him, a little, anyway."

Bonnie looked down at the skirt of her pale green crepe dress and smoothed a nonexistent fold in it. "I don't suppose it would matter, if you just don't say anything to him about it."

"Oh, I won't. I promise!" Mara's curiosity was tinctured with that faint and indefinable tenderness that only John Halloran's secretive yet vulnerable eyes could evoke in her breast.

"His mother and father were drunks," Bonnie said flatly. "The worst sort of drunks and they beat Johnnie unmercifully. His father left his mother after one of their violent, brutal quarrels and Johnnie stayed on with a mother who cared nothing whatsoever for him."

"Dear God," Mara whispered. This was much worse than her own miserable childhood.

"He got the scar the day his mother left for parts unknown. She took after him with a butcher knife after beating him nearly senseless. He barely got away with his life, and if Colonel MacAdam hadn't taken the boy to a doctor, he would have been disfigured for life. His mother left town and was never heard from again, nor was old Halloran. Johnnie lived out of old packing crates and trash heaps until he was fifteen. That was when the Colonel finally persuaded him to take a job in the lumber mill. After that, the scars seemed to heal, and at eighteen, Johnnie went to sea out of Galveston harbor. Somewhere in between, he traveled the world over, educated himself and came back at twenty-two to form his own construction gang. After that, his rise was meteoric. Will and the Colonel finally prevailed on him to go into partnership with them in several enterprises, which he did. But mostly, he's his own man and worth a moderate fortune already. The Buffalo Bayou prospective ship channel is his newest crusade. He owns half the frontage along the irresponsible little stream."

A long silence followed Bonnie's revelations. Then Mara said in a thickened voice, "He's had a much worse time of it than I. Though I was whipped and sometimes slapped, no one ever took a butcher knife to my face."

"Now perhaps you can understand his antipathy to marriage. He witnessed at first hand how terrible it can be." Bonnie's voice softened. "Yet I know he seeks understanding. There's still that boy inside that hard man and he keeps searching for tenderness."

"I guess he's found it—occasionally anyway—with you, Bonnie," Mara said humbly.

Bonnie's laughter was light and her eyes on Mara were inscrutable as she replied, "Ah, no, darling. I've never slept with him, if that's what you mean. Will, yes, and Marsh, and two or three others in town who have helped with my investments, but Johnnie never asked, the rascal! With some of my girls, yes. The man's not a monk." She rose purposefully and added, "I'm going down and have Gertrude prepare a good supper for us and I'll dine with you tonight, my dear."

Mara watched her departure, the swaying, graceful hips, the high-held head. Bonnie was a kind and generous woman, no matter what was said of her and her business, Mara thought rebelliously.

During the following days while she remained in Bonnie Fairweather's mansion, Mara wrote to the great merchandisers in New York for sample materials. She had decided against going to that fabulous city in the interest of speeding up her new operation in Houston.

During her stay at Bonnie's, she had met but one of "her girls," a golden-haired beauty, not yet twenty, she told Mara as they chanced to meet on one of Mara's infrequent sorties to the kitchen regions.

"I'm Tosca," she told Mara. "Of course that isn't my real name, dearie. I came to Bonnie from New Orleans and I must say I like Houston better."

To Mara's inexperienced eyes, she looked a perfect lady, talked like one, too, before they parted on the stairs with Mara little dreaming she would ever see her again. Mara was curious about the others, but at Bonnie's request, she spent her time in Bonnie's private suite of rooms, was served her meals there by Dominique and ate alone except when Bonnie was free to dine with her.

Bonnie was noncommittal about the girls who lived in her house. She did not seem to want to discuss any of her businesses, and Mara, sensitive to her wishes, did not ask.

* * *

As he had contracted, Halloran made reservations for her at the old Houston Hotel downtown and she was to go there after a pretended trip to New York. And the day before she left the Fairweather mansion, Bonnie had a final supper with her.

"I'm getting out of this business," Bonnie told her slowly and deliberately, "before my Fleurette comes home from France. I have other, more respectable interests that keep me quite busy and I'm having a new home built for us in Galveston." Then briskly, "I've bought you seven sets of underthings, a peignoir, seven dresses and four pairs of shoes. You shall see them tonight when they are delivered. They are all quite lovely." Her laughter rang out suddenly like little bells. "I even went to *Ashworth's* and bought two dresses from Sudie, who is agog over the rumors of your expected arrival from the big city of New York and the further prospects of your new business venture." Then as an afterthought, "And don't worry over what they cost. Johnnie says he'll put it all on your bill."

"When you went to *Ashworth's,* did you see—"

"Archer? Oh, yes. He was back there in that little glassed-in office of his. It was about noon and your aunt was hovering about him. I think they were going to lunch together and I must say they looked somewhat worried, but not so much that they could not glare when they saw me coming out of the *Originals* shop."

"Did Sudie mention anything about me or—or Ashworth?"

"Indeed she did. It seems Will MacAdam was the bearer of the rumors of your trip to New York and the financial backing you had somehow managed. And the other two, who are they? Bella and Anna, they've been quite openly unhappy since your abrupt departure. They're threatening to leave, rumors of your new enterprise or not. Of course, Archer's story of a real row between the two of you has been a great scandal among the ladies of the city."

"The only one I care about worrying is Celia."

"Ah. Celia. Now there was a whirlwind marriage." Her green eyes narrowed on Mara, but they twinkled with humor. "I have a feeling there's more to that than meets the eye, but we don't ask each other questions that might embarrass us, do we, Mara? You've been a lovely, uninquisitive guest. I appreciate that."

"Have you heard whether Celia's very worried about her father and me?"

"Yes," Bonnie said bluntly. "Will says she's taken to her bed and weeps entirely too much. She refuses to believe you are all right since she's had no word. Will says she keeps saying, 'I simply will not believe that my darling sister would leave town without seeing me first, and I know she loves Father enough to forgive him any kind of row.' Sad, isn't it?"

"Forgive him any kind of row, eh?" Mara's large dark eyes with their inky lashes were hard. "Not quite, Bonnie, not quite."

On Tuesday, the seventeenth of January, after dark, when Bonnie saw Mara to the door, Desmond Brant followed them with the two rich leather suitcases of clothes Mara was to take with her. At the door, Mara paused and Bonnie handed her a thick envelope.

"That's a thousand dollars, Mara. Johnnie says that should be enough to cover any bills until you go to the Houston National Bank and draw up to ten thousand as you go along. He'll see you occasionally, and if you need more, he'll arrange for it."

Mara took it slowly and put it in the new, beige leather purse Bonnie had selected for her. It was a capacious purse with room for many things from cosmetics to receipts.

Outside there waited a hired hack, ordered by Brant. Mara wore a broad-brimmed dark hat, and a veil swathed her face against the chilly wind that sounded in the eaves of the great house.

"Bonnie," Mara said, "you've been wonderful to me. I'll never forget it. Never!" And impulsively she caught the older woman in a fierce hug.

"Just keep making these fabulous dresses for me. When I go to see Fleurette in the spring, she'll be so proud of her mother."

"She should be. You're a wonderful mother."

The door opened and wind swirled in as Desmond Brant carried the suitcases to the hack. His dark face wore only a faint smile as he bade her good-bye. The hack driver jumped to the ground and assisted Mara into the rear of the buggy, where the cold wind swept around her. She was grateful for the warm beige wool coat with the soft mink collar that Bonnie had bought for her. She clasped her kid-gloved hands over the purse and the hack pulled away from the broad steps, circling the curved drive and into Fairweather Boulevard.

Thus it was that Mara Ashworth left Houston's most elegant house of ill-repute without ever really discovering anything about its operation. She had learned only that Fleurette Fairweather was safely ensconced in a French school without the slightest idea of her mother's many professions. And she had learned, too, that Bonnie was one of the kindest women she had ever met.

Chapter 10.

☙ THE following morning, before Mara could dress, one of the desk clerks rang her room and told her that Mrs. Will MacAdam was below and wished to see her.

Hastily Mara flung on the soft apricot woolen robe Bonnie had purchased and met her pale-faced sister at the door. Celia flung herself at her sister, her arms closing convulsively about Mara's shoulders.

"I've thought everything in the world," she said thickly, choking back a sob. "I've even thought you were dead! Oh, Mara, you *must* see Papa! He's become so thin since you left over two weeks ago. It's aged him—I know you still love him." Words spilled forth unrestrainedly, even after Celia released her sister and was led to the divan near a window. "I know you two can make it up. You *must.*"

Mara sat beside her silently, as Celia went on, "Old Aunt Felice has tried to simply take over the last two weeks. She goes to the store with Papa every day. And since Will's had a telephone put in Papa's house—he has influence with the company, you know—Aunt Felice answers the telephone all the time herself. Why, once she had the nerve to tell me Papa was napping and she would have him call when he wakened. Mara, I'm so afraid she's going to get him to marry her at last! You must go home and comfort him, even if the store is doing well enough, except the *Originals,* so Sudie tells me."

Celia's white, strained face held eyes filled with fresh tears. Mara's throat tightened as she took Celia's hand in hers. She felt suddenly years older than her sister.

"Celia, I'm so sorry you've been worried, but when I left

202

home in December, I'm afraid I wasn't thinking of anything but getting out and away from—him."

"You mean *Papa?*"

"That's right. You see, the quarrel we had cannot be reconciled. Not ever, Celia. I'm never going back."

"But what shall you do?" Celia's utter bewilderment was touching. "Whatever shall Papa do?"

"He's glad to be rid of me, Celia. You must believe that. The things he said to me cannot be unsaid." *Nor the thing done, be undone.* "You *must* believe me. As for me, I'm going to set up *Mara Originals.* I've secured financing from the Houston National Bank and I shall go into business for myself."

A long silence fell between the two girls and their eyes held. At last Celia said, "You've changed, Mara. Something's changed you—you're so—so *hard.*"

Mara longed to tell her sister the truth. *Wouldn't it change you to discover the man you thought your father wasn't? To be raped by him, called a bastard by him, hear your mother cursed by him?* But she bit her lip instead and steadied her voice.

"No. Not hard, Celia. Just finally convinced that he never has loved me and he never will. So I'm through trying. I never want to see him again."

Silence fell again while Celia searched her sister's face. And Mara saw conviction finally struggle through her sorrow and dismay.

"But you're so young," Celia protested. "How will you manage a shop by yourself?"

"I managed the one at *Ashworth's* by myself. The only thing he did was take the money." Then with an anxiety that matched Celia's, "Tell me. How are things with you and Will? And how are you feeling?"

"I'm feeling better now that I know you're all right," Celia replied slowly. "As for Will," she hesitated, "he's very kind and thoughtful." She flushed suddenly and painfully. "He doesn't—sleep with me. He says he knows I don't love him, and his voice was sort of mocking when he said he wouldn't want to inflict *that* on me." Then irrelevantly, "He's building us a summer home in Galveston."

"So he hasn't forced you. He *is* kind, then," Mara said in her new, firm voice. But she tempered it with humor as she added, "Most men, I'm sure, wouldn't be so forbearing. Especially with the woman he's evidently wanted so long. As for building you a summer home, that's very thoughtful, too."

"But he's never said a word about loving me!" Celia protested with disbelief.

"Oh, come, Celia, how do *you* feel about *him?*" But an answer was not forthcoming, and Mara continued. "Still, I think he does love you. I think someday he'll tell you he does."

"I doubt that," Celia replied, her voice suddenly cold. "What he wanted was a pretty ornament for the big new house, a hostess for his dinner parties."

"And a mother for his children, or have you forgotten he plans to claim your child? Furthermore, you say yourself he's kind and thoughtful of you. What else does love consist of?"

Celia looked down at her gloved fingers. "I don't know. Love can be so many things," she said uncertainly, then lifted her chin. "But I've made my bargain and I'll stick by it. We sleep in the same bed, back to back, and it's his choosing." Then swiftly, "Mara, you must forgive Papa. You *always* have. If you two could just *see* each other . . ."

"No. I don't ever want to see him again," Mara replied tonelessly. "It's better not to talk of it, Celia." There was a warning note of finality in her last words and Celia bowed her head. "Come now, big sister." Mara caught her hand again. "Maybe he and Aunt Felice will make a good pair. You know she loves him."

"But he doesn't love her," Celia said sorrowfully. "Not that way, I'm sure."

"Perhaps he'll come to love her now that we're both gone."

"Perhaps," Celia responded doubtfully.

"Now let me order some breakfast tea for us and I'll tell you about my plans for *Mara Originals.*"

When Celia left at last and the bellboy came and took away the breakfast dishes, Mara began to dress. She congratulated herself on having convinced her sister that it was a quarrel of such ruinous depth that she could never return to Celia's father's house.

And she had told Celia everything about her project except that Halloran was backing her. By the time she had seen Celia out the door, Mara knew she had persuaded her sister to accept the situation and look with some cheer on the opening of a new shop. She had skipped lightly over her fictional trip to New York and she had even told Celia she was sure her new shop would have no effect on *Ashworth's Originals,* because Aunt Felice would certainly find a way to keep the haute couture shop operating.

Mara knew better than this, however, and as she readied herself to go look at the buildings on Congress and Travis streets, she put a touch of lip rouge to her mouth and smiled grimly.

Bonnie had given her the cosmetics, carefully instructing her in their skillful use so that no one could really be sure she was wearing such an artifice. Her appearance was important, now that she was going into business for herself, even as Bonnie had, she thought wryly, and perhaps the gulf that divided her from Bonnie's "girls" was not so wide as she would have wished. After all, she was actually being backed by a patron of those "girls." Then her smile tightened. She did not like to think of John Halloran in bed with that lovely little blonde called "Tosca," the one who had for a short time talked with her in the hall of the Fairweather mansion.

Resolutely she pulled on the lovely soft beige wool coat, drew the mink collar about her throat and picked up her purse.

Earlier she had called Halloran's office and asked for one of his real estate men to meet her at the Travis Street location. As she mounted a hired hack with the assistance of the driver, she tried to recall the two main blocks and the location of the empty shops, but they eluded her. She knew that Houston's first asphalt street paving was laid between Franklin Avenue and Buffalo Bayou only last month, and it would not be long before more was laid. Halloran himself had said that Travis and Congress were early on the list and it would transform all the stores along those streets into prime locations.

She alighted at the Travis Street location first, where she was met by Richard Buyers, the young man she had met with Brett Patterson at the MacAdam house at Christmas. He greeted her warmly and told her that he had been with Mr. Halloran's organization for over two years and enjoyed the real estate end of it greatly.

"These two stores are rather large and look very dusty and dirty right now. The former tenant here was a feed merchant, and over yonder a leather tannery was housed. But Mr. Halloran said to tell you if you like either of them he'll have them cleaned thoroughly before you rent them."

From the balance of his conversation, Mara gathered that word had been thoroughly spread through Houston that she was well financed by the bank, despite her youth, because of her tremendous success with *Ashworth Originals*. And Buyers's face was so artless that Mara was reassured that no one knew of her secret partner in the business. The young man was certain she was the sole owner of the projected shop.

"Mr. Halloran himself wants to show you the location on Congress, Miss Ashworth, so I'll see you there in the buggy and leave you."

As he trotted off down the street on his big roan and the hack driver clucked to his bay she frowned slightly. She wasn't certain she and Halloran should be seen talking together too much. The more she thought of it, the less she wanted it known that he was part owner of *Mara Originals*. Bonnie had unwittingly implied that his reputation with women in town was as colorful as his enterprises. It was not beyond the realm of possibility that people would whisper that the partnership no doubt extended to the bed as well.

Halloran must be aware of this himself since he had suggested their association be a silent one. She shrugged her shoulders. If she were going to rent from him, they would have to meet occasionally, and rumors be damned.

Halloran's buggy was drawn up before the Congress Street location and he was inside waiting for her. The minute she walked in and saw the wide and fairly deep store, she decided it was best for her purposes. The other two had been long and narrow.

"Hello, John," she said extending her gloved hand.

"Good morning, Mara. I'll dismiss your hack and take you back to the hotel myself after you look at this one. Unless, of course, you're going elsewhere?"

"No. I'm hoping the afternoon mail will bring the

samples and magazines I ordered from New York. I gave the hotel as my new address."

He stepped outside, paid the driver and was back before she had a chance to look at the few partitions already in the building.

"I wanted to show you this one myself because I think it's the best location. Congress will be the first to be paved. And the stores in the general neighborhood are good."

"Yes, I saw Mrs. Primrose's Tea Room is only three doors down."

"And *MacAdam & Halloran, Merchants* is at the end of the block near the courthouse. Of course, we don't sell merchandise that's quite as elegant as Ashworth, but a lot of it is exceptional." He grinned at the last, a conspiring grin and she couldn't help responding in like. "And anything we don't have," he added, "we can order."

"Hmmmm. I visualize this front section as the area where ladies can browse over the design folders and look at the latest fashion magazines," she said firmly. "And I want to hang gold-framed beveled mirrors all around the room. I want richly luxurious velvet drapes and a matching plush carpet. We'll have a few pieces of discreet and beautiful marble statuary about, with potted ferns and palms to give an airy atmosphere."

"Sounds a lot like Bonnie's place," he grinned again.

"That's right. Bonnie has created the ideal atmosphere for pleasure and I want to create that atmosphere in my shop—our shop."

"How practical you've become. It doesn't daunt you that you want a shop as opulent as a Madam's?"

She was silent for a moment. Then lifting her chin, "I refuse to think of Bonnie's house as a brothel. I saw nothing to indicate it was, the entire time I was there."

He shook his head admiringly. "None so blind as they who will not see, but so be it. I think you'll draw customers like a honey jug draws ants."

"Do you think I should hire a decorator?" she asked worriedly.

"I think you are eminently qualified to decorate your shop yourself."

"I'll need carpenters. I want partitions put in to make this the first parlor, then the fitting rooms, then my own office with a table for drawing designs, and last, the cutting and sewing rooms. I want mirrors everywhere, they give such a lovely illusion of spaciousness. I'll want potted ferns and palms in all except the cutting and sewing rooms. Only mirrors will go in there."

"You've already decorated it in your mind, my dear. I'll see that you can give the carpenters your instructions directly. If you like, Will and I can order your mirrors through our connections in New York, furniture, too, if our catalogues please you. Unless, of course, you wish to go through *Ashworth's* or some other merchant.

"Never *Ashworth's!*" Her face flushed and she added, "I can say I'm going to do it all through *MacAdam & Halloran* because Will's my brother-in-law."

"Very shrewd, and it won't add many more coals to the fire that's already burning about your break with your supposed father. Your former patrons have heard about it and I imagine every parlor in every fine home in Houston is buzzing with it."

"Let them buzz," Mara retorted, her back stiffening.

"Some of them may take sides, you know. Ladies are famous for that." The words were jeering.

"I know," Mara answered. "It's a risk I must take."

"Not too big a one, when you have all the talent."

She looked into his mocking eyes and said seriously, "There are others with greater talents. Ashworth may find one. And I haven't talked to the girls yet—Bella, Anna and Sudie."

"I've been in to see the girls. *Ashworth Originals* is living on its hump. Sudie is working over the orders you had already taken and what few orders she gets come from the design folder of designs you had left there and the patterns you had already cut. They'll soon run out of original frocks."

"Sudie could keep it going with just the baby things. She knows all my tricks and designs for them. If Ashworth can persuade her to stay, he could do very well with simply layettes and christening dresses."

He shrugged. "Sudie says she's waiting only to hear from you. Now would you like to go to the lumberyard and sketch your ideas for the carpenters?" Then hastily, "That doesn't mean you have to turn it over to them. Just give them an idea and you can stay right there and supervise."

His eyes began to twinkle. "I know this new Mara will want to supervise."

"You sound as if I've turned into a—a monster."

"A beautiful monster."

"But a monster all the same," she said thoughtfully. "I can't have that. When my patrons come in I'll be so sweet, butter won't melt in my mouth."

"Ah. A beautiful and *shrewd* monster. An unbeatable combination."

"Yes," she said a touch grimly. "Now let's go to your lumberyard and talk to the carpenters."

It developed that only one carpenter came to the office that was shared by Will and Halloran, and it slightly irritated Mara to find that Halloran had already drawn a plan of the empty building. All that was necessary was for the carpenter to draw in the lines as Mara indicated, which he did swiftly and exactly.

When he had gone and Halloran assisted her into the buggy, he said, "Will you have lunch with me at the hotel?"

Instead of answering, she said sharply, "You were mighty certain I'd take the Congress Street location."

"Well," he said judiciously, taking up the reins, "it was obviously the best and it was a block over and two blocks down from *Ashworth's*. I didn't think you'd want to be on the same street with your—ah—former partner."

He was right. She could find no argument with his reasoning. Then she said, "No, I don't think it would look good to have lunch with you after being with you this morning. People might think—"

"People are going to think you rented a building from me and I took you to lunch afterward." He looked at her through slightly lowered lids, a side glance that made her heart skip a beat. "A strictly business luncheon with a satisfied renter."

"Everything between us is going to be strictly business from now on, John Halloran."

"What a pity, I was going to show you Galveston one day soon, since our New Year's Eve plans crashed." He grinned at her, adding, "Strictly for pleasure, of course."

Disappointment streaked through her, but she said quickly, "I shall be much too busy for such as—"

"I wanted to show you the house Will's building for your

sister's summer pleasure. Especially since I'm building one a few blocks over for my own pleasure. And, too, I imagine you'd like to see the beautiful new *private* house Bonnie's building for the day her daughter comes home."

She turned her dark eyes full on him. "It seems to me you have a number of houses, John Halloran, for your *own* pleasure. Bonnie told me you have two you won't sell in Houston Heights and that you stay first in one and then the other when you're not in the hotel. Now you tell me you're going to build one in Galveston."

"I am already building one, if you please, and until you see the city, you're no judge of why I would want a place there. You can't conceive of how beautiful it is." Then mockingly, "And I intend to sell all my houses eventually."

She gave an elaborate shrug. "Of course, it doesn't matter to me how many houses you have, or what you use them for, even in Galveston."

"Or what I use them for?" His black arched brows shot upward. "Why, Miss Ashworth, are you implying I use them for immoral purposes?"

Her face heated up. "I'm sure you do," she blurted. "After all, you are a regular at Bonnie's house—for pleasure."

"Did she tell you that?" His voice was sharp and cold.

"No. I assumed it. You seemed quite at home there. Are you going to deny you frequent Bonnie's house?"

"For a girl who's just told me that she refused to think of Bonnie's house as a brothel, and furthermore saw nothing to indicate it was, you are quite audacious to indict me for paying her a call now and then."

Mara thought swiftly. Bonnie had said *she* had never slept with him, then she recalled the other woman's words, *But Johnnie never asked, the rascal! With some of my girls, yes. The man's not a monk.*

"It's nothing to me whether you pay her a call or have all her girls pay you one in your houses," she said, drawing the rich mink collar up high about her pink face. The wind was cold, but not that cold. She peeped at him above the fur. He was looking straight ahead and his jaw was set at an angle that made the white scar stand out plainly on the smooth, hard face.

As always, her heart caught at the sight of it and the

memory of Bonnie's words coursed through her brain. *He was driven from home.* And all the ghastly suffering that had been his as a little boy—at least, they had that much in common. She, too, had been a woman long before her seventeeth birthday. Her eyes softened on the hard lean jaw.

"Yes," she said quietly, "I'd love to have lunch with you, John."

He turned swiftly, his eyes seeking hers, but her thick black lashes fanned low on her cheeks. Then his voice was deep and cool. "Sure you won't feel soiled in such company?"

"Can't we lay down our swords and just be friends instead of—"

"Instead of adversaries or lovers?" His sudden laugh was hard. "I think not, Mara. We must always be adversaries or lovers and I much prefer the latter."

"Very well, then. We won't have lunch together for I certainly don't intend to be lovers."

"What do you know of love, Mara?" he asked with quick bitterness. "The love you gave an evil old man, thinking him to be your father? It was gone in a puff. I'll tell you what love is and give you a quote with it. 'Love is a familiar, love is a devil; there is no evil angel but love.' "

"I think you may be right," she replied low, with a bitterness equaling his own. "You and Shakespeare, John. So why not, since we're doing business, be friends instead? God knows I need a friend."

"You can't escape that easily, Mara. The greatest love there is, surpassing those I quoted, carries friendship with it."

"I'll risk it," she said, glancing again at his set face and the thin scar, which disappeared suddenly in an unexpected grin.

"I'll settle for that. It may lead to better things."

"Better things? Isn't that marriage?" she asked ironically, slanting a look from under her lashes to see annoyance cross his face.

"I thought we agreed that marriage is an unnecessary misery."

"So we have. I was just wondering what 'better things' might be."

He looked at her directly then, black eyes lazy and mocking, and her own fell under their force. "You know what better things there are. Give up that hotel room and move into my house with me in the Heights. You're riding out one scandal, another added to it won't matter, and I think I can more than comfort you for the lack of a father. I promise you pleasure—real pleasure."

All the tenderness she had felt in thinking of Halloran's past suffering vanished, and boiling anger took its place.

"You must think me an utter fool to risk illegitimate children and disrepute! Just take me to the hotel, John Halloran. If I can't have your friendship, I'll certainly have your respect. And don't look to see me again unless business demands it."

Their parting at the hotel was cool. His hidden laughter made itself felt in the hard, cool hand under her elbow, in the smiling bow as he bade her good-bye. As for Mara, she was too angry to go into the hotel dining room and order lunch for herself. She went straight to her room on the second floor, where she took out her key and entered swiftly, slamming it with all her force.

She turned to find Archer Ashworth staring at her from under drawn, copper brows, his ruddy face unusually pale and the weight he had lost showing in his sagging throat muscles.

All the breath went out of her in a gasp, and for a moment, the old awe of him swept over her before new rage surged up.

"How did you get into my room?" she asked between her teeth.

"I told the desk clerk I'm your father. He had the room clerk let me in to wait for you. You're a minor and I've come to take you home."

"You must be insane, Archer Ashworth. I may be a minor, but you are not my father and you cannot force me to return to your house." Panic fought its way through rage and she knew she was really frighened despite her brave words. Her breath came hard and fast. For years he had provoked fear in her, even as she had loved him so desperately. Loved him? Had it been love? Where did the anxious desire to please leave off and love begin?

"I can and I will, young lady. You will return to your

place in *Ashworth's* and conduct yourself in a ladylike way until you are twenty-one. Perhaps by that time you will have acquired enough wisdom to know your place." He rose slowly and came to tower over her.

She wanted to flinch for his face held the old look that presaged a blow struck at her face. But she stood straight and kept her face turned to his, hatred and fear burning in her eyes.

It evidently registered for he lowered his hand and said roughly, "Let's have no histrionics, Mara. You know very well the town is gossiping about your foolish dash to New York. Oh, yes, and I know the Houston National has loaned you money, plenty of it. I made inquiries and you got it all on the reputation you garnered from *my* store. You *owe* me for that! I told them you were a minor and couldn't sign for it." His face reddened as he halted and sputtered the next words. "And by God, if they didn't tell me my own son-in-law had endorsed the note. I've talked to him about it, but he's so stubborn and thick-headed he refuses to release his signature on the note."

"Then there's nothing you can do. If you touch me," she stepped back from his once more upraised hand, "I'll scream at the top of my lungs!" Then with real terror, she sought for a means to stop him. He loomed over her like some avenging god and she fought down hysteria. Suddenly the words tumbled out, dredged from the depths of fear. "And if you *ever* approach me again, I'll tell everyone you're not my father by your own admission! And worse, *I'll swear you raped me.* Are you prepared for a scandal like that, Ashworth?"

His face sagged with horror. "You wouldn't tell anyone *that!*" He seemed to crumble before her. "My God, Mara, I was so drunk that night, I thought I dreamed—I couldn't bring myself to believe *that.* You're making it up, aren't you?"

"You know I'm not," she said, her clipped words fell like ice in the silent room. She knew she had won. Terror subsided slowly. "I don't know what you told Aunt Felice for I met her on the stairs that night, with my robe and gown torn to shreds from your attack. She guessed, and if she hasn't corroborated it, she *will* eventually, you may be sure." Then cruelly, "If you really want to shut her up—*my mother's sister*—you ought to marry her. *She* loves you and you deserve each other, Ashworth."

He sank back down on the divan and put his bright head into his hands. He sagged as Mara had never seen him—an old man's slump, defeated and hopeless. All fear had flown from her now; only courage flowed hotly in her veins. Not even a pinpoint of pity stirred in her. All she wanted was to get him out of her room, out of her life.

"You *loved* me," he mumbled. "I *know* it. It can't have all gone. You must forgive me. In my drunken haze I swear I thought you were your mother. That's why it all seemed like a dream in the morning." His bright blue eyes beseeched her. "It *was* a dream! You're lying when you accuse me of—of—it's all lies, you little liar!"

"Get out of here."

"What's the matter with you, Mara?" Bewilderment was in his voice. "You're not the same girl who was so soft, so loving, so willing to please—"

"That's right. I've changed, thank God. Remember, you named me the day I was born, the day my mother died. 'Call me Mara for the Almighty hath dealt very bitterly with me. I went out full and the Lord hath brought me home again empty.' Shall I go on? I've read it many times in the Bible, because it hurt me so that you would feel that way about your daughter. Your *daughter!* What a monstrous joke on me! I'll probably never know who my father was, but I'm glad it wasn't *you*," she said passionately. "My mother must have loved him dearly and he must have been a much better man than you, kinder, handsomer, more forgiving, less selfish and bigoted."

Her words seemed to galvanize him. He straightened his back and rose once more to lean over her, the bright blue eyes narrowed and blazing. "Your father must have been a bastard, too, by God! And you're no better than your mother—a tramp! Oh yes, it's rumored around town some man besides Will is backing you through the bank's connections and I don't doubt it. You probably share this room with him in the small hours of the night!"

Without any thought, Mara's right hand flew out and struck him flush across the mouth. It was a ringing blow and accentuated the stillness that fell upon the two, who stood where the late noon sunlight streamed in through the windows like a band of gold. It glittered on his hair, haloed his mustache and echoed in Mara's dark, shining eyes, which were wide now with deep hostility as well as amazement at her own reaction.

Archer Ashworth put his hand to his whitening face slowly and whispered, "Mara, my *affliction.* No one could be better named!" He turned and picked up his hat from a nearby chair and strode to the door. Opening it, he went out silently, closing it behind him.

Mara ran to it and turned the key in the lock, leaning back against it, breathing heavily. The years of loving him, seeking his approval, praying for his smile and his appreciation, had weighed her down without her awareness. With an effort she threw them off and went to the mirror to look at the white face, the wide pain-filled eyes.

The blow she had struck him was nothing, *nothing.* It could not begin to pay for those lost years. But someday means would come to wreak her vengeance.

"God," she prayed in a whisper, "you say vengeance is yours, but please, please let retribution come to him for the cruelty he has shown through the years to me—and my mother."

Her eyes filled and she squeezed the tears back determinedly. She had fought her emotions ever since she was old enough to know what they were and she would not weep now.

She flung herself on the bed wiping her eyes resolutely and turned her mind fiercely to the bright future that was opening up for her. Minor or not, she could not be stopped by Ashworth as long as she had backing. Will MacAdam must have sworn responsibility for her loan, and in her heart she blessed the big handsome man who had rescued not only her sister, but herself as well. Halloran had arranged that, of course, she thought suddenly. Well, she was grateful to him for that, too.

What a strange, contradictory man he was, proposing seduction on one hand and protecting her reputation on the other.

No, she did not understand John Halloran but her gratitude to him was an undeniable fact.

* * *

The next few days found Mara exceedingly busy. As Halloran predicted, she couldn't stay away from the new shop. She had conferences with sign painters, she pored over catalogues in *MacAdam & Halloran,* picking and choosing furniture, rugs, mirrors, bric-a-brac and her precious marble statuary, which was to rest on two gold-leaf pedestals in the room she had come to call the Selection Parlor, where the ladies would examine her designs and sketches. Since the mirrors and other delicate furniture had to be ordered from New York, the wait would be long. Even the carpeting had to be shipped from a Boston firm.

To Celia, who constantly invited her to dinner and would have sought her company during the days, she pleaded her lack of time and her many new responsibilities.

In due time the materials and magazines came in from New York and she stored the expensive silks, satins, muslins and other choice materials in the back room of *MacAdam & Halloran.* And she marveled at the magazines. The luxuriousness of the dresses shown in *Harper's Bazaar* and the opulence of materials offered inspired her and kept her busy with her sketchpad, pencils and watercolors.

With the coming of February, spring began capriciously with a delicate pale green leafing of trees and the golden bloom of jonquils along the borders of flowerbeds all over town. While she waited for the delivery of her furnishings, Mara acceded at last to Celia's constant invitations to dine at the MacAdam mansion.

"I won't ask Pa and Aunt Felice when you come, I promise. I'll have them other evenings," she prefaced her invitation.

"I appreciate that, Celia. Seeing him, or having to be civil to him, would only make matters worse, believe me." She was not sorry for her new hardness. Indeed, she felt like some soft, scarred creature that had at last developed a protective shell.

"Ah, Mara, I feel that if I could just get you two together again under happy circumstances, this quarrel would be seen in its proper perspective."

"Celia, dear," Mara interrupted, "you must understand. He doesn't love me, he has never loved me and he will never even like me, nor I him. There's nothing that can be done about it. And I can never forgive the things he said to me, never."

Then Celia would sadly agree, but it was plain from her voice and her words that she felt the rift would be healed someday, and this worried Mara.

And it still worried her slightly that on these alternately balmy, then chilly nights of February, Andrea still greeted Mara with veiled hostility. And she was always there. Apparently she went out rarely and then mostly with old friends rather than suitors, though she and Celia led an active social life during the days. During her meager moments of conversation with Mara she spoke frequently of her deep grief over the death of her father, the Colonel. That Andrea had suffered an obsessive love of her father was becoming clearer and clearer to Mara, who would have been very sympathetic if Andrea had given even an intimation that her sympathy would be welcomed. Instead, she led Mara to understand that she was somehow shutting her out from the circle of grief she drew around herself. Mara was certain now that her overpowering worship of her father had indeed ruined other men in her eyes.

Of further worry to her was the fact that Stuart Kennedy was always invited on these nights when Mara dined with the MacAdams. Frequently, Celia would arrange for him to pick Mara up at the hotel instead of sending Sam, the MacAdam coachman, after her. It was obvious that Celia hoped their friendship would warm to something deeper.

John Halloran's presence was accepted as a matter of fact. Mara realized that he came to dine at the MacAdams' table a great deal more often than she did.

Branch MacAdam was there for dinner only occasionally, for he had many friends and played no favorites among the eligible girls in town. He had asked Mara out twice in a joking way, but when she told him she was too busy with her new business venture, he had shrugged and asked her no more.

It was during these evening meals with the MacAdams that Mara realized Andrea regarded Halloran with the proprietary attitude of an old and very trusted friend. And she did not approve of Halloran's obvious admiration for

Mara, simply because she did not approve of, nor like, Mara herself.

Mara was easy, however, at the table with them, because Branch and Will so obviously liked and wanted her there. As far as those at the table knew, Mara had received her loan to go into business from the Houston National Bank on the reputation of her own success alone, with merely an endorsement by Will MacAdam.

When she came to dinner the night of February sixteenth, Mara realized that the world and events occurring in it had escaped her notice because of her preoccupation with her new shop. The talk about the table was animated and intense as the men discussed the fact that the U.S. battleship *Maine* had been blown up in Havana Harbor the day before, killing two hundred and fifty-eight sailors and two officers.

"If you ask me, the Spanish did it," Branch said heatedly, "and there's going to be plenty of trouble as a result."

"You're right, Branch," Will drawled, lighting a cigar. They had finished with dessert and Amos was removing the last of the fingerbowls. "There'll probably be a war before long, between us and the Spanish."

"And there should be!" Branch said. "Cuba should be a free territory. I'd be willing to put on a uniform myself to see it done!"

"Don't be too hasty, Branch," Halloran said. "There'll probably be a long session of dickering back and forth before anything's settled."

"Spain will deny she had anything to do with the explosion that sank the *Maine*," Stuart put in quietly. "But I'll lay you odds, Spain engineered it. They've been hard to get along with on the Cuban question for a long time."

Mara listened to them as the talk of Spain and the United States was bantered between the men, and she realized that these faraway events were having repercussions in Houston. That it might in any way touch her new venture did not occur to her at all. Indeed, as talk of it died down, Celia brought up the French mirrors Mara had ordered and Mara began telling her of other items that were expected to come in by next month, when she hoped to have the grand opening.

"All those things shipped in from New York and Boston

and some of it, you say, came originally from Paris." Andrea's pale eyes looked into Mara's dark ones. "It seems to me that must be terribly, terribly expensive. I should think you'd have run out of money before you make your first sale." She gave a light laugh, as if she meant it as a joke, but the words hung in the air accusingly. Mara's financial affairs had been brought into the conversation for the first time and she was not surprised that it was Andrea who had done it.

"Yes"—Mara looked unwaveringly at the girl now— "these things have been terribly expensive, Andrea. And I am going to have to ask the bank for an additional loan." There it was out! She had been dreading this revelation to John Halloran for over a week, but her bank account at the Houston National was down to less than a thousand and she needed at least five thousand more.

Halloran, who had just lighted his own cigar leaned back and asked casually, "How much more do you think you'll need?"

The explosion of the *Maine* had been forgotten now, for even Branch, Will and Stuart were listening closely to the exchange regarding money.

"Why, John," Andrea said, smiling, "what a very personal question to ask a lady. I'm sure that's strictly between her and the bank." Then with a cold glance at her brother Will, "And Will, of course, who endorses her notes, so Mr. Ashworth told me."

Halloran's black eyes on her were impersonal. "Who knows, Andrea? Maybe I'll endorse this next note. It'd be good business. Because, as you remarked about her decor, *Mara Originals* will be terribly, terribly expensive."

"And Mara'll make terribly, terribly much money," Branch gibed at his sister. "And likely the bank'll get back two dollars for every one it's loaned her. Did Mr. Ashworth mention that probability?"

Mara sent him a grateful glance and he winked at her as Andrea flushed slightly but replied, "I'm sure Mr. Ashworth doesn't care one way or another. He said he was importing a fine French designer from New Orleans to take over *Ashworth Originals*. He expects to make his *haute couture* shop famous all over Texas and I'm sure he will."

"Mara's will be just as famous, I'm sure," Celia said nervously. "Do let's retire to the parlor and have Amos serve us a coffee liqueur."

Then as they all rose and filed out of the dining room, Andrea refused to let the subject die. "If John wants to endorse her loan, Will, are you going to let him? I know you fancy yourself as the paternal head of the family now, and after all, Mara *is* your sister-in-law." She addressed her brother as they all drifted to seats in the enormous parlor, but her eyes had gone to the oil portrait that hung above the fireplace and her face tightened with hidden grief.

"No," Will said, sitting beside his wife on one of the sofas that faced each other across a marble-topped coffee table. "I'll take pleasure in endorsing any amount Mara needs." His eyes on his sister were openly angry. "To be brutally frank with you, Andrea, I'm on Mara's side in the quarrel with her father. Ashworth has never appreciated her talent. And I take a dim view of your discussing her affairs, financial or otherwise, with him."

"It came about very naturally," Andrea said defensively. "He had asked me how she was doing as a concerned father would. I think you're much too hard on Mr. Ashworth, Will."

"Nonsense. You know we have my father-in-law to dinner often enough, along with his sister-in-law. But you also know that we don't discuss Mara when he's here."

"*You* don't, Will. But he asked *me* about her. And very kindly, too, I thought," she retorted angrily.

"Now, now," Stuart put in, his voice lawyer-smooth. "We don't want the quarrel between Mara and her father to spread. I know you from childhood, Andy, you were ever one to take sides in the name of justice. But sometimes justice is two-sided, there's argument for the right on both sides."

"Well put, Stuart," Halloran blew out a thin stream of smoke as Amos entered, bearing the coffee liqueurs on a silver tray. "I'd say we've all been guilty these past few minutes of mixing into something that's none of our business. I'm sure Mara will get her loan, with or without Will's or my endorsement, but simply on her own merit as a successful businesswoman."

Mara glanced swiftly at his ironic eyes and looked away, her eyes falling on her sister's burgeoning figure. The word was out now that Celia was expecting a baby—in July. But Mara knew that the baby would arrive in May. It would be a seven-month baby, just as she, herself, had been a seven-month baby—and for the same reason.

Ah, but this little one would receive a much greater welcome than Mara had, and more, for he or she would never know that Will MacAdam was not the father. Will had promised Celia. And if anyone should have the temerity to look askance at an early birth, they could only conclude that Celia and Will had been incautious and failed to wait for the marriage vows to legitimize their passion for each other.

"Your baby will have two layettes," Mara said lightly, after Halloran's pronouncement. "For surely I shall make one for you, Celia, and I know that *Ashworth Originals* will make one for you. You'll have to alternate between them." She laughed. "For *Ashworth Originals* would never forgive you if you used only mine and I should never forgive you if you used only theirs. Family feuds have a way of splitting even hairs!"

Branch rose, stretching to his tall height, and put down his empty cup on a nearby table. "If you good people will excuse us, Stu and I are going to play poker with James Phillips and his brothers."

Andrea looked at both of them affectionately as Stuart got to his feet and she said, "Don't you two stop off at any saloon on the way home, you rascals."

"We're grown men, Andy. Older than you," Branch said lightly, "and we shall stop off where we please."

"You're a headstrong, selfish, and daredevil *boy,"* she retorted. "You always did as you pleased. Even when the Colonel was still with us. You caused him grief."

"Now, Andy," Stuart's voice was soft and affectionate. "The Colonel understood Branch and he—well, he loved us all, even me."

Branch said low, "My sister, you should remember *that* when you sit in judgment."

Andrea looked back at the portrait of her father and Mara saw that her eyes glistened with tears, as Branch and Stuart took their departure.

Andrea abruptly excused herself and left the room, and Will began talking of five-hundred-thousand feet of lum-

ber that had been ordered from *MacAdam & Halloran*.
Mara and Celia found they had the rest of the evening to
talk together.

But their talk was light and neither touched on the tender nerves that were exposed by the gulf that now existed
between Mara and the man Celia thought father to them
both.

Before the evening was over, they argued once more
about Mara coming to live at the MacAdams' house.

"But Mara, you know how many empty rooms we have.
Good heavens, you'd have all the privacy in the world. You
could get lost up in the east wing."

"You know I can't do it, Celia," Mara answered patiently. "Andrea, for some inexplicable reason, can't abide
me."

"She's never said a word to me about such! And Will and
Branch love you and—"

"And I can't endure Andrea's constant disapproval. If
you needed any proof, the way the conversation tonight de-
generated into a near quarrel should be enough." Then she
reached over to hug her sister lightly. "No, darling, when
my shop gets going, I'll either rent or buy myself a little
house. It will be better all the way around and there
wouldn't be the constant chance of running into Aunt Felice and—*him,* as there would be here at your house."

"Well, that hotel's such an expense, and here you are,
going to have to borrow more."

"Dear, the hotel's no higher than a house would be and
my meals are easy to come by. When I get my own home,
I'll have to worry about cooking and I'd much rather do designing." She laughed.

The argument ended with Celia unconvinced as always,
and Halloran wound up driving Mara back to the hotel in
his buggy. They talked but little and only regarding Mara's new loan. He was more than willing to lend her more,
certain that her shop would be a great financial success.
But in the back of Mara's mind lay the bitter knowledge
that Halloran had convinced her at last of the folly of marriage. She thought of the big man who was so carefully re-
sponsive to the outward aspects of his marriage to her
sister, and could only conclude that neither Celia nor Will
was happy. The thought served only to harden her decision.

After a cool good-bye to Halloran in the lobby, she went to her room quickly. As she began to undress she visualized herself at seventy, alone, withered and thin, but at least she would still be creating the exquisitely rich gowns and accessories in which she found such satisfaction. Mara didn't know any downright spinsters, except her Aunt Felice, and she certainly didn't seem too happy about her state. And if rumors were any indication, Aunt Felice would soon give up spinsterhood for marriage.

She sighed as she slipped from her petticoat and corset cover. She regretted that she could not encourage the eligible and attractive Stuart Kennedy as her sister wished, but her course was set. It did not include having a man to whom she would have to bend.

Mara did not see Ashworth or Aunt Felice during these spring weeks, not even on the streets, and for that she was thankful. She did become more aware of the newsboys hawking their papers on street corners and found herself becoming uneasy about national events that were sweeping the country toward war.

She knew that a navy board of inquiry had been held regarding the disastrous sinking of the *Maine*. It was being rumored that the Assistant Secretary of the Navy, a man named Theodore Roosevelt, had sent secret orders to the Commander of the U.S. Asiatic Squadron to proceed to Hong Kong and to prepare for an attack on the Spanish Squadron in the Philippines in event of war. This rumor could not be verified and was discounted by members of the press.

But when mobilization of U.S. Army forces began on March 9 and Congress appropriated fifty million dollars for national defense without a single dissenting vote, Mara felt deeply apprehensive. She looked with real fear at her half-finished project, with its newly laid carpets and hung mirrors, and the lovely oil paintings that hung between them.

What would war between Spain and America do to her brainchild, the hard work and dreams that were so near fruition?

Chapter 11.

JOHN Halloran was of some comfort to Mara regarding her fears of the war. When he came by the shop as the new electric sewing machines were being delivered to the rear door, he stood with Mara in the Selection Parlor and laughed at her gloomy remarks that the war might well put her out of business. Spain was a formidable adversary.

"Nonsense, Mara. It's a bad thing, but war always stimulates an economy. It's only bad if you lose the war, and, believe me, we won't lose it. Women being the way they are about pretty clothes, you'll have more business than you can handle."

"I hope you're right," was her glum rejoinder. "Everybody's talking about sacrifices we'll have to make and now with the streetcar conductors striking and picketing, Houston already seems in a state of war."

"They're importing strike-breakers to break it up," Halloran replied soberly. "That's a mistake. The company can well afford to pay the twenty cents an hour the trainmen are demanding for a nine-hour day."

"Why don't they, then?"

"Greed, my dear, greed for money. Speaking of money, what have you used the extra five thousand for?"

Mara pointed to the oil paintings, each one depicting some aspect of the sea and giving a sense of immensity to the viewer. The mirrors added to this by reflecting the room endlessly. "And besides the oils, my drapes cost more. I got the better velvet, with real silk panels between. And I bought the new electric machines, five of them instead of four." Her brows drew together in worry. "I was so optimistic. I was sure business would demand that I hire another seamstress. Oh, I'm afraid I've been a fool!"

"Now don't start that again. You haven't talked to Sudie or the other two seamstresses since you ran away in December, have you?"

"You know I haven't. I wouldn't go into *Ashworth's* for anything!"

"Well, I did, and I can tell you Sudie's dying to talk to you. In fact, I promised I'd pick her up at the store and bring her to the hotel for a visit with you this evening. After all, she needs reassurance, too. She has only my word that you want her in your new enterprise."

"Oh, I'm glad you're bringing her! I've wanted to see her ever since I left but didn't know how to arrange it, what with her living at *his* house and working all day."

"You should have asked me before."

"But you've done so much for me. I hate to impose."

"Hogwash. I've bought into a goldmine. We're about even in the favor department."

Her laugh was a little hollow. *"If* you're right about the economy and if the shop *does* do well, despite the rumors of war."

That evening, Halloran brought Sudie up to her room, and after the two girls had fallen into each other's arms in greeting he considerately left, telling them he would return for Sudie in an hour.

When the door closed on him, Mara spun Sudie around and cried, "Ah, Sudie, *Mara Originals* is going to be so much more elegant than *Ashworth Originals.* And I've designed over thirty new ballgowns and town dresses to show the customers when we open." Then holding the slender black girl at arm's length, she looked into her eyes and said, "You *are* going to work with me, aren't you, Sudie?"

"You know I am! I can't hardly stand stayin' on at *Ashworth's* without you, Mara. When d'you think we'll be ready for business?"

"About the middle of April. I'm hurrying everyone who's connected with getting it ready, until I've made a perfect pest of myself. We're waiting for some of the furniture to come in and for the drapes to arrive from New York. After they're hung and the furniture placed—" She stopped suddenly then proceeded seriously. "I'm scared of all this war talk, but I've been staying awake nights and drawing the new designs and improvising on those in the fashion magazines from New York and Paris. I actually get a magazine from Paris every month now."

"Lord love me!" Sudie was awed. "From way over to Paris!"

"Sudie, we'll have the most elegant and beautiful clothes that can be found anywhere, just you wait! What do Bella and Anna say about coming to work with us?"

"They're comin' just as soon as you open the store an' say you want 'em. We haven't told Mist' Arch yet. We've been doin' mostly baby things the last few weeks. We've run out of orders for dresses an' we ain't—haven't—got any new designs or patterns, Mara."

"I hear he plans to continue the *haute couture* shop?"

"Yes, he sure does. Your ol' Aunt Felice sent to New Orleans for a high-class seamstress who says she designs, too. But they're goin' to have to get a whole new staff of seamstresses, because we ain't—aren't—any of us stayin'." Sudie paused and looked searchingly into Mara's eyes and whispered, "I'm so glad you left your pa, Mara. He ain't never been good to you an' I been holdin' it against him since I was no more'n four years old."

"What do Pleasance and Julius say about you leaving him?"

"Well, we all feel bad about your quarrel, but they understand why you had to get away from him. He's been mean to you since you was borned. But Paw says he's goin' to stick with Mist' Arch, because he's been his friend since they was babies. An' Maw, though she wants to come with me, she's goin' to stick by Paw. We're buyin' a little house out to the south of town, now Mist' Arch pays 'em twenty dollars a month an' me ten, an' we pay fifteen a month on the house. But you know how Maw and Paw feel about your Aunt Felice an' she's worse now that you an' Celia are gone." She paused, then portentously, "They're goin' to get married, Mara, in a couple of weeks. I think Mist' Arch done give up out'a pure tiredness of bein' chased."

"It's a matter of indifference to me. I think they deserve each other."

"I can't see 'em bein' very happy together. Seem like she

wants to gobble him up whole, an' now she's takin' a big interest in the store. She goes with him to it every mornin' an' she says this French seamstress from New Orleans goin' to be here sometime this April."

Mara smiled wryly. "Maybe she *will* be of some help to him. I really hope he makes a success of the store just to spite Aunt Julia and Aunt Maggie. They were so snobbish and know-it-all."

"Yes, ma'am! They sure was. All the time tellin' Mist' Arch how to run his business. I felt sort'a sorry for him then, but no more."

By the time Halloran knocked on the door, the girls had discussed every aspect of the new shop. Sudie was glowing when he took her from the hotel. Mara felt better than she had since the Spanish and American troubles had begun. She knew she had the nucleus of a fine organization, and the day they opened in April, they would be ready to turn out her beautiful designs. That night she slept soundly.

Early the following morning, before Mara had even dressed, Celia knocked on the door.

"Celia! What in the world—" Mara stared at her sister as she opened the door on her. Celia was clad in a full-gathered frosty white skirt, generously draped over her abdomen and a white blouse with leg-o'-mutton sleeves. The skirt minimized her condition, while her hat, white with a multitude of pink roses on the brim, emphasized her golden loveliness and her pink cheeks.

"Get dressed, lazybones! It's three days into April and it's hot as July outside. You've lived in Houston nearly ten months and you've never seen Galveston." The color in Celia's face was the first Mara had seen there in a long time, and her even white teeth gleamed in a genuine smile. "Will's going to take us over to see the city and the houses he and John are building. John's going to meet us at the station in Galveston and drive us everywhere!"

"John Halloran?" Mara frowned faintly with surprise.

"Of course! He's got a new rig in Galveston, Will says, and you know both of them are building summer homes there. This is one day you're not going to spend in that fancy shop of yours, or poring over those designs on that

desk yonder." She pointed at the Victorian desk that held
a sheaf of sketches and the folders stacked neatly beside it.

"Help! I'm being kidnapped." Mara laughed, hurrying
to the closet and pulling forth a pale blue dress. It was one
she had bought at *MacAdam & Halloran* and had spent
several hours remodeling to her liking. It was of the finest
muslin and had a little drape over the stomach and a faint
hint of a bustle, just enough to make her figure a slender
hourglass. She hastened to fit the small corselet about her
waist, drawing it tight, put on her corset cover and petticoat, then slipped the dress over her head. It had no trace
of the leg-o'-mutton sleeves, for they fitted her slender
arms smoothly, coming to a narrow lace point over her
long fingered hands.

So John Halloran was going to drive them about Galveston, she thought, an inexplicable dart of excitement going
through her. She hadn't seen him since he had brought Sudie to her room to talk, and she was surprised at how long a
time that seemed when it was only last evening. She found
herself suddenly in a state of anticipation and exhilaration.

"Ah, Mara, what a precious dress," Celia cried enviously as she watched Mara adjust the folds of the skirt
about her. "Did you make it?"

"Practically. I took it apart after I bought it, changing
its design to suit me." She adjusted the lace inserts over
her pointed little breasts and tied the narrow muslin sash
firmly about her slim waist.

"Oh, I shall be glad to have my figure back," sighed
Celia, watching Mara place her broad-brimmed hat over
high-piled hair. Like the dress, it was pale blue, and there
were little cornflowers clustered about the crown.

"Are we going in Will's buggy?" she asked Celia, as she
placed two hat pins neatly through the back and into her
thick hair.

"Only as far as the Galveston, Houston & Henderson
coach. We'll go by train. I've been over dozens of times
when I—" Her voice broke off, then began again determinedly. "When I was helping David do Lucinda's and
his house. I adore the city, and so will you, I'll wager."

With Will's hand under an elbow each, he and the two
girls boarded the train for Galveston. He seated them in

comfortable plush seats and said to Mara, "It takes ninety minutes to go from Houston to Galveston on the coach. A dual-racked long bridge connects the island with the mainland. It sure beats that sandy, sometime road that's between the two cities. Half the time it's underwater."

"Is it very large? Galveston, I mean," Mara said.

"About thirty thousand people live there year round. It's quite lovely," he replied as the whistle sounded its long, vigorous cry and the coach began to move forward in a slow series of jerks. Will wore a white linen suit with his polished tan boots and looked cool.

The open windows allowed all the hot April smells to pour in upon them. The savory scent of tamales mixed indiscriminately with oleanders and magnolias. Train smoke blew back, flavored with the fresh scent of neat green growth and Celia's delicate perfume.

When at last the train racketed onto the bridge, Mara caught her breath. As though perched upon the tall trestle, she peered out at the broad inlet of water between the island and the mainland and she felt an exhilarated sense of suspension. She could see the thin trail of the sand road far below and to the right.

"I feel like a bird," she cried, looking out the window at a pair of curious seagulls who had swung low to examine the passing train.

"Wait until you see Galveston," Celia said cheerfully. "You're going to love it."

Mara doubted it, for the city was too entangled in her thoughts with David and Lucinda Donellan. But she made the expected reply, "I'm sure I shall," even as she looked out the window at the approaching city.

At that moment a strange chill swept her, a kind of premonition for which she was totally unprepared. It formed a tight little knot of apprehension in her breast and a nameless fear crept into her as she looked up at the friendly warm, blue skies, pale from so much water and bright sun, just the color of the dress and hat she wore.

Foolishness, she told herself, *it's because you know David and his bride live here.* But a cold whisper in the back of her mind said, *No. Destiny lies in this beautiful island. Your destiny.*

One sniff of the tangy, salt air magically wiped free her mind as they stepped down from the train into the smaller brick station. John Halloran stood waiting for them, his cynical smile white in his brown face. It was only April, yet his perennially tanned countenance was already a shade darker. Mara's heart stepped up its already fast beat and she could feel the apricot flush that warmed her cheeks.

"I've a spanking new rig waiting to take you on a tour of the town, ladies," Halloran said. "Will, Celia and I intend that you shall miss nothing, Mara." He wore a beautifully fitted white linen suit much like the one Will had on, and each man carried a broad panama hat in his hand.

When they were all seated in the buggy, Halloran flicked his whip and they set off through the business section of the city.

"This is the Strand, Mara," he said, "known as the Wall Street of the Southwest. Millions and millions of dollars are exchanged here every day."

The buildings were two and three stories high and new. They gleamed in the tropic sunlight and Mara realized she had never seen a city so clean as this Galveston that glimmered in the morning light, nor one that exuded such an air of success and pleasure. The people on horseback or in buggies wore pleasant, tanned faces and even strangers smiled and nodded as they passed. Possibly they did know her companions, but they could not know Mara, yet their smiles at her were equally disarming and pleasing.

As they drove onto Broadway she was amazed at the width of the street, at least a hundred and fifty feet. Great palm-filled esplanades separated one side from the other, and in the center of it ran the twin streetcar lines with cars filled with happy passengers. An esplanade, at least thirty-six feet wide, separated the southbound traffic from the northbound.

Mara was silent, for her excitement mounted with boundless admiration. Galveston was like a dream city, with its white houses and lacy trims, like great ladies in ruffles perched upon the flat sandy soil from which sprang palms and huge oleander bushes in full bloom. Jasmine contrasted their starlike blossoms in profusion beside scarlet, fluted hibiscus. So caught up was she in the sights that she scarcely heard the light, desultory conversation of the others.

I shall call you Fair Isle, Mara thought silently, *my fair isle.*

As they progressed down Broadway toward the Gulf, her mouth parted like a child's, looking up at the awesome and fabulously expensive mansions that rose above forests of orange and lemon trees. Giant, broad-leaved fig trees were as frequent as the lemon and orange trees. Verandas were draped with blossoming vines and the whole scene was that of a veritable fairyland. The meticulously shrubbed esplanades with the streetcars rocking up the middle with bells clanging particularly fascinated her. They were far larger and more lush than even those she had known in Richmond.

"That's James Brown's Italianate villa," Halloran said, gesturing with his whip to an exquisite redbrick, white-trimmed house with lacy ironwork painted dark green. There was a fountain in the yard beside it with a long-legged bird in the center and a spray of crystal water shooting from its beak.

"Now this next one down here—there—" Halloran gestured once more. "That's Walter Gresham's house. He had most of it imported from Europe and they say it cost him nearly four hundred thousand dollars."

Mara was awed by the sheer opulence of the enormous, turreted house made of rosy pink granite blocks. It was built up high, over a lower basement section, which, Celia volunteered, was the main kitchen. One would have to climb a steep broad stair to reach the front gallery, and on each side of the gate leading to it were perched strange, mythical beasts of iron. Mara had never seen such grandeur, not even long ago in Virginia.

But the house just down from Gresham's, still under construction, took her sharply back to her home. It was of pale pink brick, with round, white marble columns across the front veranda. Unlike the Virginia masions, however, this one was built up high, like Gresham's. There was evidently a basement kitchen beneath it, too, for the white marble steps led upward at least fifteen feet to the veranda. The two wings on each side were also pink brick and many windowed, for the house was a full three stories tall.

"That's Mrs. Clive Fairweather's new home. It isn't quite finished yet—our construction company's doing it— but I'd say it runs the Gresham palace a close second," Will said quietly. Celia said nothing as she looked at the beautiful house.

"She must be building for the ages." Halloran chuckled. "I told her that, the last time she was over here looking at it, but she said, and very cheerfully, too, 'When those big blows come in from the Gulf, I want my house to still be standing.'"

"Very wise of her," Will said. "You and I should have put well-fortified basements unders ours, John."

"If I had built on Broadway, I'd have felt obliged to do so. But these won't be the last houses we build here, Will. And I expect to weather a few hurricanes in my one-story little house. At least we've got slate shingles on our roofs." He smiled at the two girls and added, "Since the terrible fire of 1885, nearly everyone has the ubiquitous slate roof."

Both men laughed and Celia looked studiously ahead until they were well past Bonnie's new house. Only Mara looked back, thinking to herself that it looked cool and gracious, inviting and welcoming like the woman for whom it was being constructed.

As they drove down Broadway, Will looked at Mara with a smile and said, "This trip is solely for your benefit, Mara. You've had your nose to the grindstone too long. You need a change of view."

"And I thought you girls might like to see Galveston's famous jetties at the far end of the island before we look at Will's and my houses. After all, the government sank a lot of money into those jetties that could have been better spent on deepening Buffalo Bayou," Halloran said. "Though it did Galveston a lot of temporary good, in the end it'll be money wasted."

They came at last to the shore where the waves came rolling in endlessly, to break foaming white on the sandy shore. Mara stared at the endless horizon beyond and saw one ship, sails spread, but she could not tell if it were coming or going. Only that it was an old-fashioned schooner in this day of more and more steam vessels.

The beach looked so inviting that Mara longed to take off her shoes and stockings and wade in the surf. The sky above was still that pale shade of blue found only in hot, bright places. The breakers to their left rolled in only to be broken where the tops of the gray granite boulders formed the first part of the jetties.

"They had only fourteen feet of water this side of the jetties before they were built. And now, after the government shelled out its millions, they have twenty-five feet. Almost any ship sailing can make safe harbor here," Halloran said dryly. "Safe harbor, that's the catch. But when we get our bayou made into a ship channel, it will be even deeper and it will really be a safe harbor. No storm can strike so far inland and destroy the ships."

They had all stepped down from the buggy and stood in the cool, moist sand, looking at the jetties. The wind was strong and both Celia and Mara held to their broad-brimmed, flower-strewn hats. Even so, the flowers and brims bobbed merrily and their long skirts whipped about their legs.

When they were all in the buggy again, Halloran said, "Will, let's show Mara the Midway and take her to lunch at the Pier Restaurant before we take them to see the houses."

"Right. If all this hasn't won her to the beauty of the city, the charm of the Midway ought to catch her."

"Honestly, Mara," Celia said, "the Midway is like one big continuous party. I love to go and just watch."

It didn't take them long to reach what was designated as the Midway at Galveston. It was like a carnival. Dozens of small wooden stands selling everything from kewpie dolls to satin pillows embroidered with the word "Galveston" on them lined the Midway. The mouth-watering smell of popcorn and cotton candy came on the strong Gulf winds.

There were big bathhouses on the beach area, and one enormous bathhouse and hotel was called the Pagoda. It was hugely ornate and bevies of people were going in and out. And the bathcarts were a kaleidoscope of color, each one painted with brightly colored scenes, and all drawn up right on the beaches for people to change into their bathing suits. The rolling breakers were dotted with intrepid bathers and squealing children, all enjoying the salty Gulf waters.

The atmosphere, as Celia said, was that of one great big party going on indefinitely, and it excited Mara further when she saw two women who had taken off their shoes and stockings among the shoreline bathers. She cried impetuously, "Oh, Celia, do let's wade in the surf!"

Will and Halloran laughed aloud and Will said, "Why not? Take off your shoes and stockings here in the buggy and join the children, ladies."

Mara could hardly wait and stripped off her stockings by reaching unobtrusively up her multiple skirts, then dropped them on the floor of the buggy beside her shoes. Meanwhile the two men stepped down, then helped the girls alight.

The hot sand felt delicious and soft, squishing up between her toes, as Mara and Celia, laughing joyously, joined the bathers playing in the shallow surf. The two girls held their skirts up as far as they dared and squealed as loudly as any of the bathers about them when a wave came in a little too high. Girls and boys were calling and splashing farther out, and Mara was entranced by the fetching, varicolored bloomers and short-ruffled skirts on the young women. She and Celia spent the better part of an hour there and were finally recalled by the impatient men.

"Aren't you hungry, Mara, Celia?" Will asked as they walked back to the buggy. "How about crab Louis, or shrimp and rice, or a seafood platter?"

The two girls sat down on the beach in their pretty frocks and dried their feet on the hot sand, then entered the buggy to wriggle modestly back into their stockings and shoes.

"I'm starved!" Celia said enthusiastically. Mara reflected that all Celia's nausea must have left her some time ago, for her arms were plump and lovely and evidently her appetite was good.

"Crab Louis sounds wonderful," Mara said, "I've never had that."

"We'll go to the Pier Restaurant and eat right over the Gulf," Halloran told her. "You can toss scraps out to the gulls and watch them squabble over them."

"Then we'll go see the houses. They're just off Broadway and back a couple of blocks from the shoreline," Will told them. "I think you'll be pleasantly surprised, Celia, since the last time you saw it. The carpenters have put the trim on ours at last. You ought to be settled in for the late summer season."

"I'm looking foward to that before the baby comes in July," Celia replied.

Mara glanced at her quickly, then away. The baby would be here in May and no doubt be a welcome resident in the new house by July. But Celia's face was serene and Mara wondered if she and Will still slept in the Colonel's great bed, back to back. If so, they gave no outward sign of it, seemingly a happily married couple. Mara wondered how much of the situation John Halloran knew. A lot more than he would ever tell and she would lay money on that!

She glanced at his face, set in pleasant lines with the scar brightly in evidence. His expression told her nothing. No doubt he fully expected Celia's baby to arrive in July, too. Or did he? Will was close-mouthed and there was no way of knowing how much he had said or not said to his friend, John Halloran.

Dining on the pier was one more wonderful experience to add to those of the day. Mara sat by the window where she could stare out across the blue water and down to where the bathers frolicked. Gulls swooped by the open windows constantly, some of them appearing to float there, almost bold enough to dart in and snatch food from the diners. They were beautiful to watch in their soaring, effortless flight, while Mara had her crab Louis, with salad and hard, crusty French rolls. She threw some of the rolls out to the birds and they were arrowlike in their precision to grasp the tidbits.

The others in their group, dining on various seafoods, were equally generous with the gulls, who now swarmed around their broad, open window. Mara noted that Celia did full justice to her seafood platter, which was composed of crab, shrimp, sole and oysters.

Mara herself felt she had overeaten as they left the airy restaurant. Even so, she was already anticipating a return to the diner to try some of the other viands so temptingly prepared.

The ride to Will's house was a very short one, for he had built near enough to the beach for Celia and the family to walk to the shore. It was a white-painted, two-story frame house, with a gabled attic for the servants quarters. Its lines were sweeping and beautiful, and the ornate trim was exquisite.

"Nick Layton designed both our houses as a favor to Will and me," Halloran said casually. "He's built most of Galveston's outstanding buildings and homes. He's become very famous and rightly so."

"Indeed he is marvelous," Mara murmured, trying to keep envy out of her voice. Already she was envisioning her own home springing up among hibiscus, cape jasmine and palms. First, though, she must pay enough of her profits to Halloran—fifteen thousand dollars' worth, before she would be free to build her own house. But she wouldn't mind commuting ninety minutes every morning to Houston, if she could live in this shimmering, diamondlike city by the sea. The foreboding she had known when she first saw the city had vanished without a trace. She realized as they rode to Halloran's house, two blocks down, that she had already lost her heart to this city, glimmering, glowing Galveston with its white-lace beaches, and lilting merriment and friendly smiles.

Halloran's house proved to be nearer to finish than the MacAdams'. They descended from his rig and walked through the rooms. It smelled deliciously of pine, for the wallboards had not yet been papered or painted. Unlike Will's, Halloran's home was a single story, but it rambled through three bedrooms, kitchen, dining room and bath.

"What made you decide on just one story, John?" MacAdam asked idly.

"Ah, it's cozier," was the light reply. "And when the sea rises during a storm, I'll know when to get out."

"You'd have a better chance if you had a second story. It'd keep you out of the water."

"Maybe a little longer. But if you haven't gotten out by the time the first story's flooded, Will, your chances of getting out at all are pretty iffy."

Celia glanced at Mara and laughed. "Are you frightened of storms?"

"As far from us as the shore is?" scoffed Mara. "It would take *some* storm to get up this far!"

"John, you aren't trying to scare the girls, are you?"

"Furtherest thing from my mind, Will." He grinned but the scar did not quite disappear and his eyes were somber. "How about stopping at the Pagoda for an iced drink, before we catch the train back to Houston?"

"I would love to see that great enormous palace!" Mara cried.

Later, inside the Pagoda, Will and Halloran had removed and carried their broad panamas. The Pagoda was huge and lavishly decorated and Mara was properly awed. There were rooms to be had as in a hotel and there were bathhouses in connection with them for the changing of clothing to bathing suits. People were milling through no less than three lobbies and beyond them were three separate dining areas.

The two men escorted Mara and Celia deftly through the sea of people and into the comparative quiet of a smaller dining room, where other ladies, elegantly clothed and in company with linen-suited men sat at tables sipping from frosty glasses. Most of the men had juleps or ponies of bourbon, but Mara knew the ladies were drinking orange crushes or lemonade.

Suddenly Mara's eyes fastened on a bright head in a far corner of the room. *Bonnie Fairweather.* She rose from their table at once, saying, "You all must excuse me. I see a good friend and client and I must say hello to her."

Halloran rose immediately, as did Will. But Halloran strode purposefully beside her as she swiftly made her way through the tables of people.

"Don't forget," he murmured as they walked toward Bonnie and Desmond Brant, "she's my friend, too—and you might say I'm *her* client." There was laughter in this last claim.

"That's not what *she* says," Mara blurted. "A client of 'her girls,' yes. But not Bonnie." But she was thinking, *Will goes to her. Oh, I should hate for Celia to know, even if Celia doesn't—won't—sleep with him.*

"Ah," Halloran sighed with mock resignation, "you ladies *do* talk of such things after all. I'm disappointed."

"You're disappointed? I found it hard to believe. Ah,

Bonnie, dear!" Mara stooped swiftly and kissed the satin cheek, breathing in the delicate, enchanting perfume. "How good to see you and Desmond." She included the saturnine man in her smile.

Bonnie's smile was beautiful and her gentle hand closed about Mara's softly. "How good of you to come speak," she murmured. "I hear all sorts of wonderful things about your new shop, *Mara Originals*. I can hardly wait."

"When did you get back from Paris?" Mara asked.

"Only two days ago. I had a wonderful visit with Fleurette. She wants to come home for her eighteenth birthday and I shall be ready for her."

"Then you're really—ah—going to—"

"Yes, dear, I'm going out of the business of comforting. I have many other investments and interests that Desmond watches over for me. I shall sell the old Fairweather house and move to Galveston and I shall be as respectable as the good people of Houston and Galveston will permit."

"Oh, Bonnie, I just saw your house and it's beautiful!"

"Ah, you liked it then? I hope you'll call on me when I'm settled in."

"Perhaps she'll let me bring her, Bonnie," Halloran said, with a grin of his own at Desmond. "I'm anxious to see the finished product, too."

"I fear my callers will be few—"

"I shall certainly be one of them," Mara cut in fervently, "and you shall be an honored guest at the grand opening of *Mara Originals.*"

"I shall not, my very dear. But I thank you for the invitation. I shall not come until you have been opened a full week and then only as a friendly and eager client."

"You are going to leave a lot of unhappy, lonely men in Houston, Bonnie, my pretty." Halloran smiled.

"Not too many. Who knows, perhaps it will wake some wives up to what they are missing." She shrugged her pale green silk shoulders and winked audaciously at Halloran, who laughed aloud. "We're having champagne," she added. "Will you join us?"

"We're with my sister and her husband, but thanks anyway." Mara smiled. "Actually I should invite the two of you to join us."

"Then I should have to refuse you and tell you what an

absurd and gallant child you are." The soft voice was a touch mocking.

"And calling me a child would hurt me as much as your refusal," Mara said low.

"Ah, me! I forget how important it is to be older, when one is younger. Now I would adore being called a child!" Then seriously, "Only I, who am very fond of you could refer to you as a child, my dear. You are the most independent young woman I ever saw."

The silent, dark Desmond smiled suddenly, and Mara realized that he was actually quite handsome. He nodded and echoed, "Very independent indeed. I shall drive Bonnie to your new shop with pleasure."

"Then I'll look forward to seeing both of you very soon."

Halloran bowed and added, "I believe Mara's opening is set for April the twenty-fourth, my dear Bonnie."

"Then by April thirtieth I shall be there."

On their way back to Will and Celia, Mara murmured, "Maybe we'll be ready by the twenty-third, if I can get the furniture arranged to suit me by then."

At the table, Celia said low, "Mara! That woman—Papa says she's—"

"I know what 'Papa' says and he's a fool. You know how I feel about 'Papa.' He doesn't *know* Bonnie Fairweather at all."

"She trades at our store a lot," Celia said angrily, "and Andrea's said enough to make me believe it. You're very foolish, sister, to have anything to do with her. You could ruin your reputation with the ladies of the city before your shop is ever opened."

"Do you know that Mrs. Fairweather has a daughter in school in Chartres, France, just my age?" Mara asked coolly. "She is coming home to live at her mother's house when she is eighteen. I think as time goes by and you hear more, you will find Bonnie Fairweather quite as respectable as your father."

Celia's face wore bewilderment. That her beloved sister should be so fierce in her defense of a reputedly "bad woman" was more than disconcerting. It shook her. Will and Halloran were unusually quiet, and at that moment the waiter drew up.

"Ah, now your party is together, Mr. MacAdam, will you order?"

"Ladies?" Will turned to his wife first, then Mara.

"I'll have a lemon soda," Celia responded.

"I shall have champagne," Mara said defiantly. "Not the domestic, please. French."

And before Celia's parted lips could issue astonishment at such a request at three in the afternoon, John Halloran said smoothly, "Make mine bourbon over ice. No water please."

"The same for me," echoed Will and the waiter left before Celia turned to her sister.

"Mara, dear! It's only three o'clock."

"I wouldn't care if it were breakfast. I'm thirsty and I *like* champagne."

There was a long silence and at last Celia remarked sadly, "Oh, Mara, how you've changed since leaving home. Papa's heart would be broken if he knew."

"Nonsense," Mara said briskly. "He's getting married in about two weeks to our tenacious Aunt Felice, I hear."

Celia turned pink. "Who told you that?"

"Sudie, no less. And she ought to know. You mean you hadn't heard?"

"None of us seems to have heard," Halloran remarked dryly.

"Ah, well. He was always close-mouthed," Mara replied, unrepentant at having broken what was doubtful news. "No doubt he'll tell you all in his own good time. Or *she* will."

Celia shook her head dolefully as the waiter drew up with a tray. "You know we always hated the thought of her as a stepmother. And I don't think Papa really loves her."

"I'm not too sure of that, Celia. They're a lot alike in many ways. They may surprise us in a very happy union." Mara lifted her glass, "Let's toast the Ashworth-Bonheur nuptials."

"No," Celia said doggedly, "Let's toast *Mara Originals.*"

"Now that's something we can all drink to," Will said smiling broadly.

"Absolutely," agreed Halloran and his eyes on Mara's were gleaming wickedly.

On April twentieth, Mara received a stiff little note from Ashworth in his own hand, inviting her to the wedding to be held on the twenty-first in his home. He was marrying her mother's own sister and he hoped she would come and wish them well.

She replied, declining but thanking him for the invitation and pleading the press of her business while wishing them both great happiness.

Celia telephoned the hotel that morning, begging her to reconsider and come, to let bygones be bygones, and Mara was forced once more to tell her sister that the quarrel was too deep, the rift too wide, ever to be bridged.

So she spent the day of his wedding at the shop supervising the hanging of the velvet drapes and silk panels and the arrangement of some of her prized statuary. She was particularly worried over the hanging of a crystal chandelier that glittered like a cascade of diamonds in the center of the Selection Parlor. It took two days to perform that one chore safely.

On the twenty-third of April, an excited trio showed up at the front door, ready to take their places in the establishment. Bella Flaherty and Anna Beckman, Irish to their toes, were red-faced with excitement. Sudie, on the contrary, was silent in admiration as Mara took them back to the room that held the latest in electric sewing machines. The shop was fully equipped with electricity, run in from the trolley lines down the middle of Congress Street and Will had personally seen to it that two telephones were installed, one in the front and one in the back rooms for Mara's convenience.

And in the middle of the excitement of the preopening day, newsboys on the street corners downtown began hawking papers, their voices hoarse with excitement. The Spanish had declared war on the United States.

Despite this, the following day, Mara held her grand opening. And when all the girls were at their places in the luxurious shop, with banners and streamers hanging outside announcing that coffee and cake would be served to each customer on this momentous occasion, the newsboys again called hoarsely from nearby street corners.

The United States had declared war on Spain.

Mara's heart sank like a stone, so heavily she felt sick to her stomach.

Chapter 12.

☙ WHEN only Mrs. Marsh and Mrs. Seagram dropped in during the entire opening day, Mara was sure her business was a failure. She served them coffee and cake and they distractedly thumbed through her carefully laid-out *haute couture* folders, chattering the whole time about the war and what effect it would have on Houston.

Halloran had sent a great sheaf of gladioli from the hothouse with a card of good wishes. It stood on the one counter that held cosmetics along with the large spray of roses Will and Celia had sent and the large vase of carnations from Stuart Kennedy. Looking at them after Mrs. Marsh and Mrs. Seagram left, Mara thought they seemed positively funereal, quite fitting for the demise of her dream.

Just before closing time, when her spirits were at the lowest ebb, Halloran drove up in his luxurious Victoria. She had let the seamstresses go home early, Julius picking up Sudie, Bella and Anna catching the streetcar.

Halloran came in the door and greeted her cheerfully, "Well, I understand the war upstaged you, Mara. You mustn't let it disappoint you. The war will be very old in a couple of days and you will be very new."

"You can say that," she retorted bitterly, "when you didn't have to stand here and watch people go by without a glance all day long. Just two people came in, just *two*. Mrs. Marsh and Mrs. Seagram and all they did was talk about this terrible war. Oh, John, I've made such a mistake! And I owe you so much beastly money!"

"That you do. But I'm surprised at your pessimism. I thought you shrewder than that. Women will be flocking to this shop in a couple of weeks and you'll be hard put to keep up with orders."

"Not if what Mrs. Marsh says is true! They're all forming committees for everything from knitting socks for the soldiers to making bandages and joining the Red Cross." She looked at him grimly. "According to them, every woman in Houston is in a patriotic fever to do something for the war effort and clothes are the last things on their minds."

"I give them a week. Surely you have *that* much patience." Then oddly, "Since you and I seem to have so much in common in our early years of growing up, you must have learned patience as well as I."

She wasn't surprised that he knew of her childhood, deprived of love, starved for love, for he had seen her father with her and John Halloran was a man of acute observation. Her father's strong antipathy to her, her aunt's cold dislike could scarcely have escaped him. But he couldn't know that she had been apprised of his growing-up years. She could only conclude that Bonnie Fairweather had revealed her confidences to Mara.

"Yes," she said slowly, "I've learned patience. It's only that war seems to demand more than patience—from everyone."

"No. You practice your patience and see if I'm not right. Now," he said firmly, "I've come at the express request of your sister and brother-in-law to bring you straight to their house for dinner tonight. Celia's arranged a sort of celebration. I brought my formal carriage in honor of the occasion."

He was dressed casually, but the fitted beige twill suit and the little black string tie on his snowy shirt gave him an air, a jaunty one to be sure, but fitting a formal occasion. Suddenly, as she looked at him, a curious burst of emotion shook her.

He was so big, too big for the feminine room in which he stood. The delicate furniture, the silk panels and velvet drapes, the glass cases of cosmetics and dainty accessories intensified his raw maleness, and she was totally unprepared for the sudden pounding of her pulses.

He stood looking around the room, satisfaction on his darkly tanned face, but Mara was shocked into stillness by the ferocity of her own desire to touch him, to have him gather her into his arms.

That she had been drawn to him through the months was a familiarity, but this sudden heated sensuality was new and its depths unplumbed. Her lips stung with remembrance of his mouth on hers. She wanted more than anything in the world to fling her arms about him and have him kiss her again until she drowned in this aching desire.

He looked at her, for she stood so still, so silent, and his black eyes were suddenly alert.

"What is it, Mara? You're pale. Are you all right?"

She nodded wordlessly. It would never do to get into the Victoria with so little control over her sudden passions. She turned and moved some of the accessories around in the case and murmured, "There, that's better." She drew a long breath and added, "Let me get my hat and we'll be on our way." But she was thinking desperately, *I must be very calm, very cool.* He must never know of this madness that coursed through her body.

When they were all in the parlor having an aperitif, Mara looked at her sister with new eyes. She was very, very pregnant. And Celia, catching her widened eyes, laughed deprecatingly.

"Doctor Samuels says it looks like twins. Won't that be lovely?" But her light voice was strained and her eyes, looking into Mara's were anxious. Next month, this baby would be born and Celia and Will would have to claim an early birth, a seven-month baby. Mara silently prayed it would be a small baby, just small enough to confirm the story.

Branch was talking of the war. His voice was excited and his older brother said, "Now wait, Branch, we can't spare you at the mill or the lumberyard. You don't need to enlist."

"But I'm going to enlist. Why, I'd feel like I was missing out on one of life's greatest adventures. Besides, we didn't start it and Spain would really make it rough on us if they win." Andrea looked at him indulgently.

"Ah, I don't know," Halloran grinned. "If I didn't have

all ten fingers, each in a different pie, I'd enlist, and I may do it yet, if it looks like they need me."

"They're setting up army camps right now, just outside of town," Branch said eagerly. "Camp Tom Ball has been established at Forest Park just east of Heights Boulevard. And the Ladies' Military Aid Society is forming and so are half a dozen others."

"That certainly is true," Mara said, thankful that the fever which had shaken her earlier when she was alone with Halloran in the intimate confines of her shop had abated. The conversation cooled her further. She continued, "Only two ladies came to my opening today and they were more interested in talking war than looking at frocks."

"It's a shame it happened on the day you opened your shop," Celia said angrily. "I told you, Andrea, that you and I should have gone to the opening."

"You know very well you're too big now to go prancing downtown, darling," Andrea said warmly. "We can't take chances with my nieces or nephews!"

"I'll admit I'd be a scandal to see at *Mara Originals*, but at least I could have stopped in for a minute."

"Mara's just too impatient," Halloran drawled. "In two weeks that shop of hers will have so many orders she won't be able to fill 'em all."

"Of course," Celia brightened. "It's just the shocking news that kept them away. You wait and see, Mara."

"I have no other choice, Celia," she replied wryly. "Indeed I shall wait and see."

Branch was still gesticulating with his pony of bourbon and talking to Will of the injustices America had suffered at the hands of the Spanish, the sinking of the *Maine* and their arbitrary rule over Cuba and the Philippines.

"By God, I *am* going to enlist, and no later than next month when things get set up!" he said loudly.

Andrea turned widening eyes on him. "You aren't really serious, are you, Branch? It's just talk. You know you're needed here to help turn out all the supplies they'll need for this war." Her voice rose as her deep love for her brother asserted itself. "Oh, you just *can't* enlist!"

A momentary silence followed her outburst, then it was broken by a harsh ripping sound that came from above the mantel. Suddenly all eyes were turned to the portrait of the Colonel as it slowly slipped to the side. To Mara it seemed interminable, but it was only seconds before the bolts which had held it so long gave way and the portrait crashed to the floor before the startled eyes of all those in the room.

Andrea gave a shrill cry. "Oh, my God! The Colonel's portrait has fallen!" She rushed to the big canvas and tried to lift it before either of her brothers or Halloran could reach her. It was unharmed, having fallen on the open space between the facing sofas and missing the marble-topped coffee table by inches.

"I've been expecting that," Will swore softly. "I should have had the fastenings looked at two years ago. The heat up the chimney and time have finally brought it down."

"No, no!" Andrea cried hysterically, still holding to the gold frame. "Don't you understand? It's the Colonel's answer to Branch! Branch, don't you see this is an omen, a sign? You mustn't, you *can't* go to this war. I *know* it's a sign."

"Now, Andy, calm down," Will said. "I'll have two men out here tomorrow and rehang it, with larger bolts this time and it will never happen again."

"That may be," Andrea said, almost weeping openly now. "But I know this was the Colonel's way of telling Branch he must not go. Oh, Branch," she wailed, "people get killed in wars! Don't you think the Colonel was trying to tell us something?"

Branch's color was coming back into his face now and his jaw set stubbornly. "Andy, you see omens in everything. You know damned well that portrait fell of its own weight, that and the fact the bolts were loose from the chimney heat."

"You're wrong," Andrea said, fresh tears welling from her eyes. "It's the Colonel's way of trying to stop you. Promise me you will think about it before you do anything. Promise?"

Tears streaming down her pale cheeks, she still clutched the edge of the frame even as Will and Halloran moved it back to lean against the empty fireplace, where the Colonel's fine features and light blue eyes looked out on all of them with what could only be described as fortitude and charm.

Branch looked at Andrea and said low, "Doesn't it occur to you that maybe the Colonel's showing his disapproval of *your* course of action?"

Andrea grew paler and swallowed hard. "No, it doesn't. I'm right and—"

"You're the one who took the letter, Andy," Will said quietly.

"I tore it up! I tore it up and threw it in the trash where it belonged!"

"But you couldn't tear up what it contained. Those words are burned in your brain—*if* you tore it up—and they must weigh on your conscience," Branch said grimly.

"I don't care! I don't care, and I know this was a warning for *you.*" Hysteria was still in her voice. "You must promise me you won't run down in the heat of this war fever and enlist, Branch!"

Branch's jaw was tight and he frowned, but he said, "All right, sis. I promise I won't do it tomorrow. I promise to wait and see how things go, before I— Well, we'll just drop this war for tonight, eh, fellows? Let's talk about Mara's prospects and the new and beautiful shop. I stopped in last week and looked it over. Very posh!"

Mara looked down into her wineglass. "That's not a very happy subject either, Branch."

"All right then." He expelled his breath in a snort. "For God's sake, let's talk about the baby and all the outlandish things Will's having done upstairs to create a nursery to end all nurseries."

They had all returned to their seats in the parlor, but Andrea's eyes kept seeking the painted eyes of her father, love and fear and something of uncertain guilt in her expression.

Mara and Celia exchanged glances quickly, and Mara realized that the secret problem between the three MacAdams was as much a mystery to her sister as it was to her.

"Well," Will began, as he put a match to his cigar, "I expect this new MacAdam to have a lot of brothers and sisters, so we need a big nursery and a schoolroom next to it, for I plan that they shall be well educated as early as possible."

Mara's eyes sought Celia's again, but her sister was looking away and her cheeks were a fiery pink. She looked quite beautiful and her features were serene. Only Mara guessed the turmoil Will's remarks had stirred in his wife. *It's his doing, this sleeping back to back each night.* Mara could hear Celia saying it now. Would it be the same after the baby was born? Evidently Will didn't think so, and Celia, without loving him, had promised to be a good wife.

"Heigh ho, heigh ho, it's the bachelor life for me." Halloran laughed, blowing out a stream of blue smoke and taking a sip of his brandy. "I'll content myself with watching yours grow, Will. Little tads are a great care."

"But they're worth it, my friend," Will replied, smiling. "As you will no doubt come around to agreeing."

Halloran shook his head positively. "Not a chance."

"Mara, I'm so glad you're making my baby's layette," Celia said softly. "Your little fingers are magic."

"Don't forget, you'll have one from *Ashworth Originals,* too," Mara replied.

"But it's yours I'll cherish most."

"And that will be one of your first sales," Will said smoothly.

"No, no. It will be my gift," Mara said firmly.

"I insist," Will said positively. "After all, my sister-in-law is going to have the most exclusive shop in Houston, with only the finest for sale. You can give our baby one small gift, but the price of the layette will be paid in full."

Mara looked into the set face and knew he meant every word. It was useless to argue. She sighed. "I only hope you're right. With Houston in such a turmoil, it may be months before my shop catches on."

Halloran put down his empty brandy glass and grinned. "Want to bet some money on that, Mara?"

"I've very little money left to bet with," she said dryly. "In fact, I must find a boarding house and leave the luxury of the hotel and soon."

"Mara, your place is here with us," Celia said quickly, her eyes brightening. "You know it is and think what a comfort to me it will be to have my own sister with me when the baby comes."

"I can't do that," Mara said. "I don't want to run the risk of seeing Aunt Felice and her husband. You have no idea how repugnant the prospect is to me."

"That must have been some quarrel," Branch said, with

a touch of his mocking laughter, "the way you speak of your—pa."

"It was what was said by *him*," Mara put in swiftly. *It was what he had done to her as well,* but she would never reveal that. "There are cruelties you wouldn't dream of, Branch, being the happy-go-lucky, friendly person you are. Archer Ashworth hates me deeply, and the feeling is mutual at last."

"Mara," Will said slowly, "you are very young to be on your own. And if I guarantee you won't meet up with your—papa—and aunt, would you consider living here with your family?"

"Will, you know you couldn't guarantee that. Besides, it would disrupt your household. I'd be bound to run into them sooner or later as they visit you so often."

"I *can* guarantee it," Will's jaw was set and the blue eyes smoldered. "The nights he comes, you can take supper in your room, or go out with Branch or John, or even poor Stuart, who's been so lovesick over you all these months."

"Living in a hotel or a boarding house is too dangerous for a young girl of seventeen," Celia pleaded. "Darling, do come here and stay."

"I'd be glad to squire you, beautiful Mara, any night you name"—Branch chuckled—"and treat you with gentlemanly restraint."

"And so would I," Halloran spoke up, "though I make no promises about restraint. A kiss or two would do you a world of good." His lips twisted in a half-smile and Mara felt her cheeks burn.

God knows, she had thought about Halloran's kiss and the quiver that went through her at those thoughts. It added to her uneasiness when she was near him. It had occurred to her that he would be easy to love, because she knew his background, and despite her efforts to put it in a cold light, her sympathy and her own childhood intruded, making him even more attractive to her.

"I'll have to think about it," she said slowly. "I *would* like to be near Celia as her time comes. Already my little niece or nephew has become very dear to me." She smiled at her sister and was rewarded with a look of intense gratitude.

"All *femmes seules* belong with their family and you're

one of the family, Mara," Will said with certainty. "You belong here in more ways than one."

Andrea was the only one who said nothing. She had fixed her eyes on Mara's lovely face and they were hostile, but acceptance was struggling behind it. With both her brothers arguing that Mara belonged, she could not brook them. But her face was cold and she spoke no word of encouragement.

"Promise me you'll do more than think about it? Promise that you'll *come.*" Celia's eyes were sparkling now. "You can have that big room on the east that overlooks the Boulevard. There's scads of room in there for a drawing table and all the little accoutrements that a designer needs. It could be a sort of office-bedroom. You know you could—"

"Celia, Celia." Mara laughed. "You are so persuasive. I'll make up my mind by the end of this week, I promise, for I must cut down on my expenses until the shop gets going—if it ever does." Her voice dropped gloomily. "I just can't borrow any more money. I feel already that I have the burdens of the world on my back in the form of the Houston National Bank." But it wasn't the Houston National that burdened her so heavily. It was Halloran, for it was his money. She owed it all to him, and he had said plainly he never joked where money was concerned.

And it was Halloran who drove her back to the hotel that night. As the horses drew the Victoria down the Boulevard, he said abruptly, "You know you can draw money from the Houston National as long as you need it, Mara."

"No!" She spoke with a touch of violence. "I've reached the end of my borrowing, without repaying any yet—"

"You could pay it all back in one night." He laughed suddenly. "Of course I'd be paying more than usual for such favors, but then I want you more than I've ever wanted a woman."

"Oh! You are *so* vulgar! When you talk like this, I hate you. I'd sell the shop, find work and pay you back every penny before I'd—"

"Let me into your bed? Come now, Mara, think of what fun we'd have on a month's trip to New York. And I know you find me attractive."

"What conceit! Attractive, indeed—you have all the instincts of a beast."

"Beast or no, your response is one no man mistakes. For instance—" He drew the horse to a halt on the dark street, with the fragrance of the April night swirling about them, the fully leafed trees making a patchwork of the moonlight.

Before she knew it, he had removed her hat and had his arms about her. She drew a sharp breath as his lips met hers with a sweet touch of fire, and before she could rally, she bent with the caress, her arms involuntarily closing about him. It was what she had craved earlier in her shop, only it was more wonderful than she had hoped. Her whole body opened up with rapture so keen she could scarcely breathe. She clung to him, her mouth parting under his. Then suddenly he let her go.

"You see?" he asked with casual softness. "We have something that's rare—and it could be beautiful and rewarding.

"Beautiful!" she exploded. "Rare? It's common, common as pig tracks and I'm stupid to succumb for even a minute. No, if the shop fails, I'll find work! You'll be repaid in dollars and cents, the same coin I borrowed!"

His warm laughter was genuine as he picked up the reins and clicked to the horses. "That shop's not going to fail, my young and despondent partner. You'll see. As soon as the war fever settles down, there'll be balls and parties given in every home for the soldiers and all the ladies will be buying *Mara Originals* to wear."

"So you say," she retorted, still angry and her heart still pounding furiously from that periously hungry kiss. She drew a deep breath. "I'll believe it when I see it and I'll thank you to keep your hands off me, John Halloran."

"Oh, no, my pretty prude. That's not in the bargain. I plan to take advantage of you on every propitious occasion and you knew that before you took my money and fixed up your shop."

"Then I'll see that there are no propitious occasions. I'll see very little of you."

"You'll see a great deal of me. I'll see to that."

As they drew up before the hotel and he halted the horses, he turned to her quizzically in the bright carbide light and spoke again. "Tell me, why do you so admire and defend Bonnie Fairweather, when she has only done as I ask of you—to capitalize on your charm? You are just so hard-nosed about doing it yourself."

She looked into his dark face and confusion spread through her. No answer came readily to mind. There was a moment of accusatory silence on his part before she burst out in a violent whisper.

"Just because I love Bonnie for being kind and understanding and admire her for doing what she *had* to do to survive, doesn't mean *I* must do it, too. I couldn't live with myself if I had to bear children without a father. I'd be disgraced in my own heart."

He stepped down from the carriage and took her hand helping her to descend. "I think you're very young and very confused, Mara." He smiled but not so deeply that the scar disappeared. "And as I've told you before, I'm a patient man. When you're an independent woman, and able to take your place in a man's world, likely you'll soften your hard set of morals."

"That's just it," she said tartly. "Morals. I shall never abandon them, no matter how long you wait or how independent I become."

"We'll see," he murmured, taking her into the lobby and removing his hat. "Do you mind if I stop in tomorrow to see how business is picking up?"

"I'd rather you'd wait a week," she said coolly.

"I'll come when I choose. Good-night, my dear."

"Good-night."

The next few days flew by and Mara was astounded and deeply gratified when the wealthy women of Houston began coming into her shop by twos and threes. Even women of more modest means sought her out and pored over the sketchbooks with the less expensive gowns in them. By the end of the first week in May, Mara had nearly five thousand dollars worth of orders and was putting more on hold.

Halloran had been, as he usually was, right, she thought with chagrin and reluctant admiration.

He stopped in just long enough to taunt her.

"I told you so." He grinned infuriatingly as he added, "Houston is boiling with soldiers, and social activities by the dozen are being planned." Then he was gone on one of the many business trips he made in connection with the construction company he and Will MacAdam owned and operated.

The days continued to speed by and the new electric sewing machines were whirring without cessation. When Mara told her girls they would receive percentages for the amount of work they did, they came early to the shop and stayed late. And fabulous gowns were created from the exquisite materials Mara had ordered from New York.

Mara herself waited on the ladies and, with Sudie's expertise, helped drape materials on the women and cut out the patterns. She was busy and she was happy, thinking but infrequently of Archer Ashworth and his bride, her Aunt Felice.

However, the knowledge pressed in on her that Celia's baby was due late this month, so on the fifteenth of May, she agreed to her sister's importuning and moved her things from the hotel to the big east room upstairs in the MacAdam mansion. With Branch MacAdam and Stuart Kennedy each helping, her newly purchased drawing table, trunks and folders were transported to her new residence in Houston Heights.

Mara was amazed at the amount of belongings she had managed to collect in the short months she had been on her own. But there was more than enough room in the east room. In fact, it was so spacious, it boasted a sofa and large wingback chair before a modest fireplace, seldom used because of the climate.

The day after she had moved into Celia's home, Sudie greeted her at the shop with some gossip.

"Miss Felice got that French seamstress now. Her name's Madame Choisse an' she's might hoity-toity. They've turned *Ashworth Originals* over to her and she brought three little gals from New Orleans with her to sew. They all come over to dinner at Mist' Arch's last night and gabbled a lot of French together. But they talk English, too, with a funny accent that Miss Felice says is goin' to really impress the customers."

"I wish them success," Mara replied, feeling slightly hypocritical.

"You can afford to," Sudie giggled. "Our place is *the* high fashion shop in this town, now."

It was shortly after this that Mara, coming home from the shop in the small surrey she had bought for transportation, had Sam put the horse away and curry him. She entered late and Felice and Archer Ashworth were there, dining with the MacAdams. They had just finished cocktails and were going into the dining room as she came upon them. She had known this was bound to happen, no matter Will's vow to prevent it, and she had steeled herself for the meeting.

"I know you're tired, Mara," Celia said hastily before anyone could speak. Will MacAdam was still out of town with Halloran, and Mara knew Celia had invited her guests on impulse earlier, for she had not prepared Mara for their presence. "I'll have a cocktail and your dinner sent upstairs as soon as you're ready. Just press the bell for Maria."

"Thank you, Celia. Hello, Aunt Felice and you, too." She gestured to Ashworth.

"It's good to see you," Ashworth said stiffly. "We hear great things about your shop and we hope you'll soon be hearing about *Ashworth Originals* again." This last had a touch of spite in it.

"I'm sure I shall," Mara said coldly. "Good-night."

And as she left she heard him ask Celia, "Does she always eat in her room? Seems pretty temperamental."

"No," Celia said baldly. "She has requested to eat there when you are dining here. She doesn't wish to see you, Papa. Oh, Papa, I just feel that if I could get you two together for any length of time, I could heal this hideous quarrel between you. I *know* I could."

"You don't know your—sister. There's a streak of meanness in her I hoped you'd never see. But now you know. She's cold and unforgiving. That's why I could never love her."

"But Papa, she wasn't always like that! She worshipped you as a child. In fact, until this awful quarrel between you—"

Mara, proceeding down the hall, heard their voices fade. Well, if it never came to more than that, she could stand seeing him on occasion in this house. But it brought back all the memories, the acts of cruelty, the galling words he had flung at her. *Bastard.* Yes, *she* was a bastard and the knowledge had changed her.

She entered her beautiful spacious room and began to disrobe. She had worn a most becoming apricot voile that day, one of the five she had made for herself. She knew it fit every slender curve of her body and was draped most effectively on the hip. She had seen Ashworth's brilliant blue eyes take her in and the flicker of interest that followed.

I hope I looked just like Mama, she thought bitterly. *I'd like to remind him of Mama since it hurts him.*

But she put him from her mind as she donned a tailored beige satin dressing gown and rang the bell for Maria. She went then to her drawing board for she had earlier had an inspiration for three new fall outfits and a fabulous peignoir.

As May swept by, Houston was caught up more and more in the patriotic fervor that moved the rest of the nation. As far back as April twenty-fifth, when President McKinley had called for Congress to declare war, Houston's fighting spirit had been well aroused. And on May fourth, the Light Guards and the Emmet Rifles of the Texas Volunteer Guard left for Austin. A recruiting station was opened at 209 Main Street, and Theodore Roosevelt, who was the Assistant Secretary of the Navy, acknowledged an offer of the services of the Houston Yacht Club. The Brunner Old Man's Club, made up of "ex–Johnny rebs" and "Johnny yanks," offered to defend the Texas coast from Spanish invasion. It seemed to Mara that things were happening so swiftly she could not keep up with the news, though she read the newpaper assiduously each evening.

Mara Originals grew with the war fever, and she ordered two more electric machines and interviewed ladies who wished to sew in the shop. She was a little awed by the money that poured through her cash register. By May twentieth, she had paid Halloran back a thousand dollars but was keeping the rest to replenish her materials, which she was having to do with increasing regularity. Things were speeding by at such a pace that she was not too surprised when two crises appeared at once.

On the same day, June first, Celia MacAdam went into labor and Branch MacAdam and Stuart Kennedy enlisted in the service.

On the way to the hospital with Will driving, Mara received firsthand word of both events.

"She's not far along yet," he said of his wife, "but since it's her first, I want every care taken. Though the baby may not come until tomorrow, Celia's asked for you."

"Will, you are so good to Celia. Now tell me about Branch and Stuart. I thought you had persuaded Branch not to go."

"Theodore Roosevelt resigned as Assistant Secretary of the Navy and is now Colonel Roosevelt. He came through here last night, pacing up and down at the train station, in a deep study and a fine impatience with the slowness of the United States war operations. Stuart and Branch went down there to see him, with some other hotheads—James Phillips and his brothers—and before you could blink, they all enlisted in what Colonel Roosevelt has dubbed his Rough Riders. As you might guess, Andrea has taken to her bed with a fine case of the vapors. I couldn't even get her to go to the hospital with us."

"When will Branch and Stuart leave?"

"They're to leave at the end of this week for San Antonio, to meet again with Colonel Roosevelt and become part of his Rough Riders. It's a cavalry group and you know no one can beat Branch or Stuart in the saddle. The Colonel and Captain Kennedy, Stuart's pa, saw to it that they both rode before they walked."

As they drew up before the broad, white-painted frame hospital Mara asked, "Is Celia in much pain?"

"It comes and goes and they tell me, rank amateur that I am, that it's to be expected. She's on the second floor and I know she'll be glad to see *you.*"

They climbed the steps and went into a big cool hallway, going to the rear where the stairs mounted to the second floor. Celia was uppermost in her mind now as Mara had left Sudie in charge of *Mara Originals.* Sudie had blossomed in the last few weeks, her language improving dramatically, and her courteous and charming behavior with the clients went far in pleasing them. Mara always introduced her as "my collaborator" and her slender, facile dark fingers proved her expertise over and over.

"Celia!" Mara cried, rushing into the sterile white room where her sister's coppery hair fanned out across the pillow and her broad white forehead was slightly dewy. Celia held her arms out to her younger sister and Mara went to her.

"Is it bad?" Mara whispered.

Celia shook her head, smiling. "They're over fifteen minutes apart. No one seems to know just when we can look for her or him." Her face tightened as another pain struck her and she drew in a sharp breath. "But I want you to stay with me until it comes, Mara. Can you—will you do it?"

"Of course," was the swift reply. "Sudie's taken over the shop and you've no idea how expert she's become. I'll stay here if it takes all night," she finished sturdily.

Celia's eyes went to her husband, who stood looking down at her. Mara was certain love and compassion were concealed behind the curtain of his stiff black lashes.

"Will's promised to stay, too," Celia said almost apologetically. "I told him he didn't have to, but it was his decision."

"I have a big stake in this, Celia," he said firmly. "A son or a daughter. And I want to be one of the first to see that little new person."

"You're good, Will," Celia said, her voice muffled.

"Not very. Mainly I'm selfish. I want our baby to love *me* from the moment it's born."

"I have a feeling you're going to spoil the baby dreadfully," Celia's smile was wan.

"You're absolutely right. I'm going to anticipate its every wish. A pony, a cart, every toy it wants, the best universities."

"You'll ruin the child!"

He shook his black head. "I'll love the child and never let it forget it. It's so important to be loved." His eyes went to Mara, who stared into them, gooseflesh curiously creeping along her arms.

"He's right," she spoke her thought as she held one of Celia's slender hands in hers.

Two nurses appeared, clad in stiff white uniforms, long

skirts swishing. As they smiled and greeted those in the
room one placed a hand on Celia's abdomen and looked at
her watch. A long silence followed, before one of them
spoke.

"Now that's a good strong contraction and they're getting closer together, Mrs. MacAdam. You may have your
baby before tomorrow." The nurse smiled and removed her
hand from Celia. The dew on Celia's brow was becoming
perspiration.

"I want my sister to stay with me until it comes," she
said to the nurse holding her wrist.

"I don't think Dr. Samuels will allow that. After all, this
baby is nearly two months premature, but she can come
back in immediately after delivery."

"But I want her here every minute—"

"We'll talk to Dr. Samuels and see if it can be arranged," soothed the second nurse. "After all, your husband wants to stay as well, and I'm sure you want him,
too."

"Yes," Will said brusquely. "I've already talked to Dr.
Samuels. I'm staying until my child is born."

"Very unusual," murmured one nurse to the other as
they went out the door together.

Unusual or not, both Will and Mara were there at the
bedside, and all through the evening and half the night until Dr. Samuels lifted up the red wriggling six-pound girl
and spanked her little curved bottom, whereupon she let
out a healthy cry. It was two minutes past midnight on
June second and the doctor was pleased that the child
should be so well developed and healthy, coming almost
two months ahead as it had. If he was surprised, he hid it
well from the proud and smiling Will MacAdam.

"After all, it sometimes happens that early babies are so
healthy, Mrs. MacAdam," he told the exhausted mother.
"She *is* small, of course, but you are one of the fortunate
seven-month mothers."

The nurses took her away to be cleaned and two other
nurses began to bathe Celia, wiping her face with warm
soapy water and tidying up the linen beneath her.

Will and Mara stood silently by, each of them greatly relieved. Mara thanked God that it was a small baby. From

Will's slightly drawn face, it was obvious that he was thanking God in his own way for his own reasons.

"Now I suggest you both go home," Dr. Samuels said, looking at them kindly. "Look. Our little new mother is drifting off right how and she'll sleep for hours. Go home, Mr. MacAdam, and get some rest. You too, my dear."

Both Will and Mara bent and kissed the drowsing Celia and together went quietly home.

When they reached the house, Will said low, "Only you and I and Celia know. As far as the world is concerned, she's *my daughter*."

"She *is* your daughter," Mara replied softly, but she was thinking. There was one other who knew. David Donellan.

It was after two o'clock in the morning when they pulled up in front of the MacAdam mansion, but the lights were still on and Will pulled the horse to a halt before the well-lit front door.

He said quietly, "No, Mara. I haven't forgotten Donellan." She gave him a startled glance. His smile was wintry. "He'll never dare open his mouth to make such a preposterous claim—or *I'll kill him*."

Chapter 13.

꩜ THE servants were pouring out the door and Mara glimpsed Sam Johnson, Bo Jones, and after both of them, excitement struggling with dignity, Amos, the butler. Rosita and her daughter, Maria, were close on their heels.

"I've got a fine and healthy daughter," Will cried, handing the reins to Sam and assisting Mara down into the circle of congratulations and laughter. She glanced up to see Andrea, clad in her peignoir, standing in the open front door of the long gallery.

Andrea greeted her brother with, "One is born and one will die." Her face was drawn and her eyes reddened.

"Is that all you can say when Celia and I have a brand new daughter?"

"A girl? Thank God for that," she said, her eyes filling afresh. "But I've had a—a premonition. I *know* Branch will die in this war."

"Andrea, don't be a fool," Will spoke sharply. "He hasn't even left yet."

"But he and Stuart have enlisted and so have those wild and reckless Phillips brothers. They are to leave the end of this week and I feel in my heart that we shall never see Branch again."

"Aren't you concerned to know how Celia is? I imagine she came closer to death than Stuart and Branch will."

By now they were in the hall and Andrea's mournful tones had sent the servants drifting away.

Will called after them, "Amos, you set 'em up in the kitchen! A brandy for each of you to celebrate the arrival of my daughter! And please bring a bottle and some glasses to us in the parlor. I think Miss Andrea could use it and I know Mara and I could."

"How—how is Celia?" Andrea asked belatedly as they made their way into the brightly lit parlor.

Will sprawled in one of the large velvet chairs. "Fine, by God. And so is the baby. That ought to put a smile on that long face of yours."

Andrea said tremulously, "Congratulations, Will. I'm happy for you both."

"Then for God's sake quit bawling and have a shot of brandy with me. You will, won't you, Mara?"

Mara smiled. "I've never had a brandy but I think I'd like to toast your daughter—and my niece."

Amos strode grinning into the room, the brandy decanter and three glasses on a tray, which he put on the polished table beside Will MacAdam. "We sure are proud for you an' Mis MacAdam, Mist' Will."

"Thanks, Amos. Now you and the rest toast her, too."

"What you all goin' to name her, Mist' Will?"

"Mrs. MacAdam wants to name her after my mother— Elizabeth."

And they did name her Elizabeth Celia MacAdam, but it was John Halloran who gave her the name that was to follow her all her life.

The day after they brought the two of them home from the hospital, Halloran came to dinner that night. After tiptoeing into the nursery, he looked down on the sleeping pink morsel and murmured, "Betsey MacAdam. Great Scot, would you look at those red-gold ringlets! I thought sure she'd be bald." Then in a tone of wonder, "Why, Betsey, you're beautiful!"

Mara, who stood back of the others, Branch, Andrea, Stuart, Will and Celia, thought to herself, *So you are susceptible to babies, after all, my cynical, unmarriageable friend.*

In further confirmation of her thought, he whispered, "When she wakes up I'd—I'd admire to hold her, Celia."

"You certainly shall. She'll wake up for her ten o'clock feeding tonight and you can hold all six squirmy pounds of her." Celia laughed softly.

And from that day on, the baby was Betsey. She was a

week old when her Uncle Branch MacAdam, with her
Aunt Andrea clinging to him and weeping, left to join Colonel Roosevelt's Rough Riders in San Antonio. Stuart
Kennedy left with him after a brief, unsatisfactory kiss
from Mara, who, with the others, saw Stuart, Branch and
the laughing Phillips brothers off on the train. On the way
back to Mara's shop where they were to drop her off, Andrea was doleful and her predictions so dire that Will grew
annoyed.

"Will you kindly stop acting as if they're dead already,
Andrea? You've always been given to anticipating the
worst."

"And I've been right, too. If you will recall," she said
coldly, "I predicted the Colonel would be lost to us."

"You certainly did. *After* he had his first seizure. Even
the doctor's prognosis was negative after that massive
heart attack."

"Just the same, I felt it in my bones. I have a sensitivity
to these things, Will, and you know it."

Mara felt smothered by Andrea's gloom and wished she
could shout, *You bring it on yourself, Andrea!*

But she remained silent, peering at the bundle in Celia's
arms. The June morning was deliciously cool and everything in Houston was in full flower. The scents that met
them as they bowled along the street toward Congress,
were sweet; even the dust carried a certain fragrance. And
Betsey looked up with those slate blue eyes of David Donellan, but they were round and fringed by thick wheaten
lashes. Mara wished briefly that her eyes could have been
brown, like her mother's. But she was grateful that her
features were exactly like Celia's, the narrow patrician
nose, the full, curved lips, and the eyes, though blue, were
long and remarkably shaped like the Ashworth sisters.

Celia exchanged glances with her sister suddenly and
Mara recognized the hidden fear in Celia's dark eyes.

When they let her off at *Mara Originals*, there were
three women waiting to see her. One of them was Bonnie
Fairweather and with her was the beautiful dark maid,
Dominique. The other was Mrs. Donald Sewall, whose husband was on the Committee for Deep Water and worked
hand in glove with Halloran on that project, though their
money came from cotton.

"This lady came before I did, Miss Ashworth," Bonnie said formally, gesturing at Mrs. Sewall, whose little rabbit nose quivered with distaste at being in the proximity of so notorious a woman as Mrs. Fairweather.

Nevertheless, she went into the fitting room with Mara and Sudie and permitted herself to be fitted in a new ballgown, which with the help of corsets marvelously slimmed the bunchy little figure to a trim and neat body. She was effusive regarding the gown.

"Oh, Mara, there's no one who can fit a lady like you and your Sudie. I had one gown made by that Madame Choisse and those little French girls of hers and I looked like a frump. It just hangs in the closet. I'll never go back to *Ashworth Originals.*"

"It might have been a one-time mistake, Mrs. Sewall. You should give them another chance, then you'd have two high fashion shops to choose from."

"You're sweet! And generous, too. I've heard that you and your father quarreled, for which I'm sorry, but I'm so glad you have your own shop!"

Mara sent her on her way with the promise that the ballgown would be ready for the giant soirée to be held at the Houston Ball Room next weekend.

Then she was free to be with Bonnie. When they were in the privacy of the fitting room, she hugged her friend enthusiastically. Dominique remained in the Selection Parlor, turning the pages of Mara's fashion sketches.

"I'm so glad you came in for another gown, Bonnie, dear. It's such a pleasure to fit a fine figure like yours!"

Bonnie looked troubled. "I came to choose a gown, it's true, but I have something rather troubling to confide in you."

Mara's heart sank. "Troubling? About what, Bonnie?"

"Remember the Donellans in Richmond, Mara? Well, David Donellan's been a client for nearly a year now. Though his wife's been in Galveston for weeks, he's still a regular. Not mine, of course, but Rosalee's, and she says when he drinks he talks."

"Oh, God," Mara whispered under her breath. "What has he said?"

Bonnie paused, lowering her voice further, "He says he can guess why you and your father quarreled, why he's been so cold to you all these years and that it runs in the family. Because, he says flatly, that Celia's little daughter is *his.*" Bonnie's pale green eyes looked directly into Mara's dark ones and she asked softly, "Is that true?"

"You *know* he's guessed right about me, you might as well know he's telling the truth about Celia," Mara replied bitterly. "So bastardy does run in the family, Bonnie."

"Will loves Celia," Bonnie said carefully. "Though he comes to me for consolation, he loves Celia. Did you know that, Mara?"

"I suspected it. And he loves Betsey now, too."

"I know it. Will is magnificent. I don't see how Celia can resist him." Bonnie's little smile was cryptic.

"I don't think she can," Mara said slowly. "Already she's saying things to me in confidence that make me wonder."

"Ah, well," Bonnie sighed, "you know as far as I'm concerned, Betsey *is* Will's child. And you, unfortunately, are *legally* Ashworth's."

"I'd rather be a bastard," Mara flashed, "so that part of David's loose talk doesn't bother me. David's claiming to be Betsey's father does!"

"I don't know what either of us can do about that, Mara," Bonnie replied thoughtfully. "Too bad we don't have information we can threaten *him* with regarding his loose tongue."

"Or better yet," Mara replied angrily, *"somebody* who can threaten him!" Then with sudden fear, "Will said he'd *kill* him if he ever dared say anything."

"That might have tragic results for Will," Bonnie said. Then with her smooth brow creasing, "I wish we could get somebody we trust to keep *his* mouth shut to threaten David."

Both fell silent for a moment and Bonnie fanned out the pages of Mara's latest bound folder of dress designs, which she had brought into the fitting room with her. She stopped at a black velvet with a square-cut neckline and thin spaghetti velvet straps. It fitted the breast closely as well as the hips, then fell in graceful folds from a gather at the rear where a single pale pink rose nestled. "Has anyone ordered this, Mara?"

in Houston before we take the train back to Gal-

, dear. Just let me finish this delicious coffee and
her peek at the beautiful Betsey." His eyes had
he pink and gold child in Celia's lap since he
r there.

uld feel Celia's frantic discomfort, sense that she
g him to leave, knew her sister's fear and appre-
hat he should have even called to see the baby.
a thought, *The man's cold nerve is outrageous!*
g must be done about it and soon. These visits, if
eased, could become dangerous, for the fatuous
avid Donellan's face was a dead giveaway to

you want to hold Betsey a minute, Lucinda,
asked ingenuously.

shifted uncomfortably. "David, you know I
anything about babies. I'd be scared to death of
er."

all right," Celia cut in hurriedly, holding her
"A lot of people feel that way with little ones,
nd since you can never have any of your own,
best."

ight," Lucinda said relievedly. "She's adorable
g and all that—but so small and—well, slip-
smiled her spun-sugar smile and looked at the
ympathy.

ker sounded and Mara glimpsed Amos going to
couldn't be Will, she thought. He wouldn't
open the door and come in.

surprised when Amos ushered John Halloran
m. She hadn't seen him in over a week. He
yone, including the Donellans, and Mara no-
nt chill in his voice as he exchanged greetings

t brings you two here?" he asked, after shak-
's hand.

iendly call. A friendly call," Donellan said
y wife is so lonesome for her old friends from
e had to pay a visit. And too, we wanted to see

ttle beauty, isn't she? A dead ringer for her

Mara smiled. "You're the only one who could wear so daring and beautiful a dress, Bonnie, or afford it. It's one of my best, and I promise you I'll make but one."

"I wear so much green, so many different shades—"

"That color does set off your remarkable eyes, Bonnie."

"So I've been told many times," she replied deprecatingly. "Do you think I could get away with black velvet?"

"Get away with it? My dear, you'll likely set a fashion if you appear at the opera or the Lyceum in this during the fall season."

"I have a lovely black-dyed mink wrap, full length, I would wear with it."

"Oh, no! You must let me make you a matching wrap, lined in ivory slipper satin."

"Ah! Of course—"

Mara took the bound designs, flipping swiftly through the pages until she came to a pale gray velvet cape, full and luxurious. "I've made this cape in gray for Mrs. Seagram, but I can assure you that yours in black velvet would look entirely different on you. Because of the difference in your figures, I would make yours fuller, bolder, more dashing."

Mara called in Sudie and together they draped the fine black velvet along Bonnie's figure, marking and cutting swiftly. She stayed until they had cut the cape as well. But when she started to leave, she went back to the problem of David Donellan.

"I'm afraid Will really would kill him," Bonnie said low. "Best that he know nothing of this."

"But he's bound to hear something if David talks more."

"Let me think about it," Bonnie said, drawing on her gloves and adjusting her beautiful wide-brimmed summer hat on high-piled copper hair. "I may come up with something we can do." And she went into the Selection Parlor, smiled at Dominique, and the two stepped out into the late June morning.

It was two weeks later on a Saturday that Mara closed the shop at noon, giving her employees and herself the half-day off, as well as Sunday. But it was when she arrived at the MacAdams' that Bonnie's warning was driven home with stunning force.

She found David Donellan and his wife, Lucinda, in the big parlor having coffee with a white-faced Celia.

David rose at once at Mara's entry, hands both extended to take hers. She withdrew from his touch as quickly as possible, but his deep musical voice made an unwelcome asault on her.

"Lucinda is anxious to pick up old friendships, Mara. She's so lonely at the house in Galveston and nothing would do but that I bring her to see Celia and the new baby. What a little beauty!"

"Lucinda, I know what a friendly person you are," Mara said quickly. "You'll have more friends in Galveston than you can count in a few more weeks."

"They're not like all of us who grew up together in Richmond," Lucinda said peevishly. "Not like old schoolmates. I've been dying to come and see you all and you *must* come and visit us—have dinner with us!"

Andrea entered, bearing a tray of freshly baked cookies and a steaming coffee pot for refills. Her face was somber and her eyes distant.

Mara noticed it immediately and she saw her sister register awareness of it as well, but she was diverted when David approached Celia and said, "Do let me hold her, Celia. She's such a beauty!"

Slowly, Celia handed the infant to Donellan, who took her easily and began walking about, talking to the child in a very fatherly manner.

"I wish I could have a dozen," Lucinda said sadly. "David loves them so. But the doctor—remember old Dr. Armstrong in Richmond?—he says I must *never* have any. I'm too small. It would kill me, he said." She gave a delicate shudder as she spoke the last words and Andrea looked at her with unseeing eyes.

"Andrea, has something happened?" Celia asked anxiously. "You look so worried!"

"The mail just came. There was a letter from Branch to all of us, with a note at the bottom from Stuart. They're together, they and the Phillips brothers, near Santiago, Cuba. It's dated June twenty-first, seven days ago, and all of them were looking forward to doing battle with the Spanish. With Colonel Roosevelt's Rough Riders!" she finished despairingly.

"Dear me," Lucinda murmured, a[s] walking with the baby and making [o] dreadful, Andrea. Does he say nothi[ng]

"He says they all left American [] teenth, singing 'There'll Be a Hot T[ime] Tonight,' " she said bitterly. "And t[] more about how 'keen' Colonel [] 'great' it is to be part of the troop.' "

"Surely your brother and his fri[ends] Lucinda said comfortingly, glancin[g] still held Betsey.

"No," replied Andrea, dredging [] den suffering. "I've dreamed of Br[anch] two nights. Something terrible wi[] it in my bones."

"Oh, Andrea, *don't* say that!" [] Donellan uneasily. "They're goin[g] home before you know it. John Ha[] last much more than three months[] did he say? Strung out the way [] haven't the firepower and men[] "David, I think you'd better give [] sets her to be handled too much[]

Andrea had been refilling cu[ps] they spoke and now she gave a [] the tray as she took two cookie[s] the saucer beside her cup.

"Andrea," she said quietly[] brave and cautious. They're g[]

"No," Andrea spoke with lo[] Colonel's portrait fell when [] going, I've known he wouldn'[t] never fails. You'll all see—Go[] containing the silver pot and [] coffee table between the two [] father's portrait with anguis[h]

"Where is Will?" Mara as[ked]

"He's still in town," Celia [] on Saturdays he doesn't co[me] him," she added uncertainl[y]

"We're sorry to have miss[ed] smiled, "but really, David, []

shoppin[g] veston."

"I kne[w] take an[d] not left placed h[]

Mara [] was *wil[l]* hension [] And Ma[] Somethi[ng] they incr[] look on [] Mara.

"Don't [] dear?" he[] Lucinda[] don't kno[w] dropping [] "That's [] baby clos[e] Lucinda, [] perhaps it [] "That's [] and darli[ng] pery!" She [] others for [] The kno[] the door. [] knock. He[] She was [] into the ro[om] greeted eve[ry] ticed the fa[] with David [] "And wh[] ing Donella[n] "Just a f[ew] heartily. "[] Richmond, [] the baby." "She's a [l] mother," John said coolly, and at the sound of his voice an idea streaked like lightning through Mara's mind.

John Halloran was close-mouthed, even secretive, and he had no liking for Donellan of the Galveston Wharf Company, who was trying his best to discourage the completion of the Houston Ship Channel, Halloran's ambitious project to make a seaport of Houston.

"I noticed you raised your wharfage and warehousing rates again this month, Donellan," Halloran said, drawing a cigar from his breast pocket and putting a match to it.

"Yes, well, with the war and all, everything's going up." He laughed deprecatingly and added, "And we all have to make a profit, you know."

"I know." Then with sudden gentle courtesy, "And how are you feeling now, Mrs. Donellan? We had all heard of your being ill and unable to join your husband."

"Oh, much better," Lucinda batted her thick bold lashes swiftly. "I'm sure. My doctor in Richmond said the sea air would be good for me and I guess it is, though I still have bad days."

"I trust this isn't one of them?" Halloran asked solicitously as Andrea poured a cup of steaming coffee and handed it to him.

"Well," Lucinda said plaintively, "the heat makes me very weak, but seeing Celia and Mara has given me a lift. And now we really must be going, Mr. Halloran. I've a little shopping to do in Houston before we return home."

"Really, Celia," Donellan said seriously, "I know your and Will's new house in Galveston is completed, and when you move in for the summer months, you must have dinner with us." Amos approached him with his hat and Lucinda's hat and gloves. "By the way, it's a lovely house. I'm sure you'll enjoy it greatly." Then with his broad grin at Halloran, "And yours down the street is very attractive, even without a second story."

"Thanks," Halloran said ironically. "I was hoping for your approval."

"Well, you have it," was the ebullient reply. "At least you won't have to climb any stairs!" And he laughed richly. "Now come along, Lucinda, my love, and we'll get your shopping done while you still feel well. Too bad *Mara Orig-*

inals is closed." He winked at Mara. "But good for my pocketbook, I'm sure!"

Mara thought of the fortune David Donellan had married and repressed a scornful smile.

"Oh, I'm sure you could afford just *one*," she said sweetly.

"I am coming in and will get more than just one," Lucinda said eagerly. "I've seen some of your creations and they are simply divine."

They were moving toward the door and the others followed with last good-byes. As he went through the door Donellan turned a searching look on Celia and said quietly, "We shall be back to see the dear baby, soon. We want to watch her grow."

Celia smiled fixedly and Mara realized that Donellan actually had a paternal interest in the child, more so now that he could have none of his own. She felt cold to her fingertips. Yes, something must be done and very quickly.

When they were seated again, Halloran spoke up. "I came by to catch Will. I've missed him in three offices, including the lumber mills. But my main purpose was to ask Mara if she'd have dinner with me tonight."

"Yes. I'd be delighted." Mara spoke so swiftly that one of his black, slanting brows shot up in surprise. Faintly embarrassed at her quick assent, she added, "I need to talk business with a businessman. Maybe you can advise me, John."

He shrugged. "I know little about *haute couture*, my dear, but my advice, for what it's worth, will be yours."

Andrea, sitting on the sofa and brooding over a last cup of coffee, looked up from under her brows and said bitterly, "Too bad you couldn't have advised my brother not to go to war, John."

"We've had a letter from Branch this morning, John," Celia put in. "It came while the Donellans were here and only Andrea has read it, but it looks like they will see fighting soon, if they haven't already."

Andrea got up slowly and retrieved the letter from her father's enormous mahogany desk in the library. When she returned, she proceeded to read it aloud to the others. It was as rollicking, as merry and full of mischief and excitement as Branch himself. Everything was new to him and he commented on all of it, from the crowded ship to the sandy shores and thick jungles of Santiago. He was not in the least afraid and, with Stuart, was looking forward to avenging the sinking of the *Maine* and to freeing the islands now under the rule of imperial Spain.

"He's a fool," Andrea said gloomily as she read the final lines. "I have the most terrible premonition about them." Her eyes filled with sudden tears and she took a handkerchief from her waist and pressed it to them.

At that moment the front door opened and Will strode in. He glanced at his sister and scowled. "Andrea, for God's sake, what is it now?"

Silently she handed him the letter, but he took it in one hand and went swiftly to kiss Celia and to toss Betsey up in his arms. His face was wreathed in smiles then, but when he read the letter, he grinned broadly.

"You mean *this* has brought you to tears, Andy? I never read a more optimistic and cheerful letter."

"He says they would see fighting in another day or two. You don't think that's bad news?"

"I do not. That's what they went over there for, and the sooner they put down the Spanish, the sooner they'll be home."

Andrea got to her feet and stalked from the room, leaving Will shaking his head at her obstinacy.

Halloran had to discuss two large orders for lumber with Will and that took up most of the conversation. Celia took her departure from the room, as Betsey was demanding attention and crying hungrily. Mara turned to go with her and Halloran broke off his conversation with Will.

"Why don't you wear that red silk dress that makes you look like a spring tulip, Mara? We'll leave about seven. You've never been to the Cotton Exchange Club and I'd like to show it to you."

"Sounds lovely. See you at seven."

Once in Celia's and Will's bedroom, the women faced each other, despair written plainly on Celia's beautiful features.

"Dear God, Mara, who would have thought him capable of such brazen nerve! What in the name of heaven can I do? If Will finds out, or finds him here—oh, and he said he'd come back. He wants us to come to dinner! And you know

Will and I are moving to the new house at Galveston in July to stay the summer!" She sat down, pulling aside her dress, and helped Betsey begin to nurse.

"Don't worry, I'm going to talk to John Halloran about it. I'll have to confide in him, but you know how close-mouthed he is and how close to Will he is. He'll know what to do and how to threaten David so he'll stay away."

"I hate for John to know! He's so skeptical about marriage anyway. He'll surely think the less of me for it."

"I don't believe he will. And it would never do for Will to seek out David and have a brawl with him. It would be all over town then and poor little Betsey would never live it down."

"But what could John threaten him with? How could he shut him up and make them stay away?"

"Don't underestimate John Halloran, Celia," Mara said dryly. "You'd be surprised at how adroit and shrewd he is and he can keep a secret," she finished, thinking about their partnership in *Mara Originals*. Her own bastardy as well, which he never mentioned. "I'm having dinner with him tonight for the sole purpose of putting this matter to him. Bonnie Fairweather told me David was a patron of one of her girls and he had been talking freely and drunkenly about it, implying all sorts of things. So I was deeply worried about it long before I came home this evening and found David in your parlor."

"Oh, it just takes all the joy out of moving to the new house for the summer, knowing they live just blocks away! How can we avoid running into them on the street and in the stores, even?"

"That won't be a problem if John convinces David that discretion is the better part of his loud mouth. *And* his suddenly found paternal feelings." Then in a whisper, "That mealy-mouthed Lucinda! I'll bet she could have a dozen babies, she's just too scared to! Too scared to even be a wife to him. And since Bonnie's going to sell her house and move to Galveston herself this fall—and she will be out of the business because her daughter's coming home—David will have to find a new prostitute."

"Oh, Mara! How can you say that word? How can you have dealings with that woman?"

"Prostitute. I can say it easily. That's what David does,

isn't it? He couldn't have you anymore so he found a prostitute he can pay for favors."

Celia shivered and said brokenly, "I guess that's all I was myself."

"Now that's really stupid. You loved him, or thought you did, and you learned a bitter lesson."

"God, yes. How *could* I have thought I loved him? He's shallow and conceited and monstrously selfish. Oh, he repels me!"

"I could add a lot more to that indictment, sister mine, but I must go bathe and rest awhile before I go out with John and put my—*our*—problem before him." She turned to leave, then swiftly returned to kiss her sister's cheek and touch the baby. "Don't worry and don't say a word to Will about this."

"I'll have to tell him they came calling. Andrea will say something about it and the servants all know."

"Then tell him what David told us. Lucinda was homesick and wanted to see her old Richmond schoolmates."

"That's such a lame excuse. He'll know he came to see the baby."

"He can't be sure and you can tell him you'll *never* reciprocate."

"Still, I'm afraid he'll seek him out to fight with him. Will's a hard man with a furious dark temper which he has a hard time controlling. Believe me, I've seen him fight to control it with me."

"He loves you," Mara said flatly. "What you think is temper is probably unbearable frustration."

"I—I—I'd meet him halfway if only—"

"He doesn't want halfway. He wants you to come to him with love."

"Mara, I just can't do that yet—but—"

"Well, you worry about it, Celia. I must go bathe and get myself ready to match wits with a very hard man myself. You better pray John will be able to do something about it." And she turned and left the room.

As he suggested she wore the red silk. It was a soft, shimmering red and seemed to glow, setting off her dark hair and eyes as she donned the matching wide-brimmed hat, trimmed lavishly with mousseline de soie. Slowly she

drew on her long white gloves and picked up her purse,
which was white like her gloves.

As they mounted Halloran's Victoria he said dryly, "Me-
thinks this business talk is something else again, and a
little more important."

"I'm surprised at your insight, John, but I suppose I
shouldn't be."

"No, you shouldn't be. You and I are a good bit more
alike than you appreciate, my dear." There was a pause as
he clicked to the horses and they rolled down the curved
shell drive. "Is it so important we need discuss it now, or do
you prefer to unburden over a glass of champagne at the
Exchange Club?"

"Will we have any privacy at this Cotton Exchange
Club?"

"They have both large and small private dining rooms.
I'll arrange a small one."

"Then I'll wait and tell you all of it at once. It's not a
very palatable story, especially for dinner."

"Would it surprise you to know that I've sensed part of
it?"

"It certainly would!" She was startled.

"Well, I knew your sister was once in love with Donellan. And I walked into a room where he and his wife were
paying a call, and there were all sorts of undercurrents in
the air."

"You can't know it all!"

"That's true and you can enlighten me later. Anything
concerning my friend Will is more than paramount, it's
personal and deep. Now about your business, you've been
paying me back with great regularity. As a matter of fact,
you're very nearly out of debt and it hasn't been two
months."

"Yes, it's grown beyond my greatest hopes. And truth-
fully, the books are an awful chore. They take up time I
could better spend on my clients. I really need a manager."

"Don't look at me! I wouldn't manage the finances on a
ladies' *haute couture* shop for all the tea in China."

"I must eventually hire someone to do it for me before it
gets entirely out of hand. I'd like it to be a man, for he
could manage the office and the employees better than I
am doing."

"I'll keep an eye out for such a paragon, but I think most men would shy away from a shop such as yours."

"And speaking of the shop, I'd like to knock the walls out between it and that other vacancy next door, if it can be had. We desperately need more room. Since I've taken on those two new seamstresses, we're really crowded and I'd like a larger salon where the ladies can come to browse through the designs and the dresses we're making up to put on models."

He looked at her admiringly in the dusk. "From a seventeen-year-old child, you've certainly grown into a twenty-nine-year-old woman in a hurry."

"I feel twenty-nine, oddly enough. The last months have taught me a great deal and yet I know I still have much to learn."

At the Exchange Club, the groom caught up the reins from Halloran as he turned to assist Mara down the step to the ground. She noted that there was a courtyard to the side where other mounts and carriages were tethered. The groom grinned as Halloran flipped him a quarter. The carbide streetlamps had just come on and the coin gleamed dully in their light. The tall Cotton Exchange Building stood before them, the windows on some of the five floors glowing with light.

"The club encompasses the entire second floor and many a million-dollar deal has been closed in its polished mahogany confines. And I think you'll find the cuisine excellent."

"The deal I hope to close with you is worth a million to me," Mara said, her hand on his arm as they took the heavily carpeted stairs to the club.

"You pique my curiosity even more. Did you know you were the only woman who ever really piqued my curiosity, Mara?"

"No. And I'm not sure how to take that."

They reached the entrance in a broad foyer. The carpet was so thick Mara felt her little white buttoned shoes sink at least an inch with every step. Looking down, she saw it was a floral pattern against a scarlet background. Something about it reminded her of Archer Ashworth's library in Richmond, a reminiscence that deepened as the maître d' led them to a small private dining room. Partly it was because the center of the big room contained a waiting area with big plush and leather chairs and sofas, all as luxurious as Ashworth's had been. It was a man's dining club and every piece of furniture, every oil painting on the walls, drove the fact home. It was richly comfortable, and the elegance had remained along with the comfort. The maître d' took their hats and gloves and placed them on a long polished table at the rear of the small dining room. Then, taking Halloran's order for brandy and champagne, he closed the door to the room and left them alone. Due to the thick mahogany walls and the thicker carpet, the silence was dense. When Halloran pulled a cigar from his vest and struck a match to it, it sounded very loud.

"Well," he said over the first puff, "let's have the problem."

"I—I must confide in you to get your help, I know," she replied hesitantly.

"That's right." His eyes on her were narrow and bright with curiosity.

She drew a long, swift breath and plunged into it. "Betsey is David Donellan's child, but Will married Celia knowing it. I think he must love her very much."

"I *know* he loves her very much," Halloran said grimly. "But I didn't know the fair Celia brought him another man's child to father."

"So now you know," she said flatly and launched into the story Bonnie had told her, ending with, "And he suspects why Ashworth and I quarreled and remarked that bastards seem to run in the family."

"The son of a bitch," Halloran said quietly after a long silence. Then his reaction was remarkably similar to Will's. "The lousy, lying son of a bitch. Telling Celia he loved her, promising divorce and marriage and then refusing to leave his wife."

"It seems," Mara said dryly, "that his wife is not well."

He cut her off with a short laugh. "We both know what that means. She won't sleep with him."

"Anyway, she says they can never have children, she told us that just before you came this evening. And now that David has seen Betsey, he actually seems paternal. You saw him! And he left Celia and me with the definite impression that he intends to see Betsey often." Mara caught her breath and plunged on. "And you know in less than a week, Celia and Will and half the servants will be in their Galveston summer home, making it very easy for him to drop by."

The door opened silently and a dark-skinned waiter appeared carrying a large tray on which stood glasses, a bottle of brandy and a silver bucket of ice from which the neck of the champagne bottle appeared. First he placed the crystal glasses on the table, then opened the champagne with a flourish, poured a little and handed the glass to Halloran.

"You like it, sir?"

After sipping, Halloran nodded and the waiter poured a glass of it for Mara. The ritual was performed again with the brandy before the waiter departed with the empty tray. As he closed the door he said, "I'll be back for your order, sir, in fifteen minutes."

In the silence that followed, Halloran put down his cigar and took up the brandy. Then he said, "And you want me to shut Donellan up, keep him away so Will won't tangle with him, eh?"

"I don't know what you could threaten him with," Mara said, with a thread of desperation in her voice, "but I hoped you could think of something. The baby's legally Will's daughter, isn't she?"

"That's right. Donellan hasn't a leg to stand on. But if Will gets wind of his claim, and he will, he'll kill him and there isn't a jury in Texas that will convict him."

"Oh, but that's just what I—we—Celia and I would avoid! Think of the scandal! Think of Betsey growing up under such a cloud."

"I am thinking of it. You know, of course, that Will may have already heard it and be planning to take action."

"No, no! Bonnie swore she wouldn't let a word of it get out. Her house is going up for sale in July and most of her girls are already gone, she says."

He smiled. "I know. And I know how to shut Donellan up, too." His eyes were wintry.

"For goodness sake, John, nothing violent. That would cause talk!"

"I can't promise that, too."

"You wouldn't—you couldn't—try to take his life!" Ma-

ra's eyes grew black and enormous. "Oh, please, I didn't
mean *that!*"

"He's willing to wreck Celia's, Will's and Betsey's life,
isn't he?"

Mara was silent. Halloran waited. She looked into the
champagne glass to see the diamondlike bubbles still
ascending the crystal glass. "I guess he is," she said miserably.

"And we can't have that, can we?"

"No."

"Then why not leave the method and means to me,
Mara? I'm known for being neat and tidy in my affairs,
with no loose ends left flapping."

"That sound so—final."

"I guarantee it will be final. But if Donellan's a reasonable man, and I'm sure he is, perhaps your worst fears can
be avoided."

"You wouldn't have the motive for killing him that Will
would. No jury in Texas would let *you* off," Mara said low,
swallowing the terrible fear that rose with the thought of
John Halloran hanging for the murder of David Donellan.

"Would that cause you grief?" he asked softly.

"You know it would." She refused to lift her lashes.
"You know I consider you a—an exasperating but dear
friend."

"Dear friend, eh? I'm making some progress. Now drink
your champagne. You're as tense as a coiled spring. You
need to relax."

Obediently she took up the glass and swallowed more
deeply than she intended. She coughed and looked at him
with watering eyes to find him observing her with amusement. She flushed.

"You're teasing me. You'd never kill him."

"But no jury in Texas would convict me for killing him
in self-defense."

"Oh," she said blankly. "How could you—would you—
David would never attack you! He's much too cautious and
self-preserving."

"You don't know how provoking I can be." His eyes were
still amused. "I killed a man in Shanghai in self-defense
once."

Her eyes widened further. "You did! Did you provoke him into attacking you?"

"Let's say it was mutual. The authorities let it go, he was a known cutthroat and thief."

Mara digested this in silence, carefully taking smaller sips of champagne. This was a dark side of John Halloran she had never seen before and it made her a little afraid of him.

"How did you kill him?" she asked cautiously.

"He drew a knife on me. I've another scar you can't see, my curious pretty. He didn't know I had a knife, too."

She shivered, visualizing the smoky darkness of a far-off seaport room filled with swarthy men of violence. She knew she was looking into the black abyss of men in mortal conflict and realized she had set in motion events for which she would not want to be responsible. But she squared her shoulders, and sensing her turmoil, Halloran smiled at her. It was a warm, reassuring smile and the thin cruel scar disappeared completely.

"Don't worry, Mara. None of this is your fault, you know."

She knew that, but she knew she had somehow become part of it by enlisting Halloran. She had involved him in it. And no matter that he would have stood by his friend Mac-Adam, under any circumstances, it was still of her doing.

She couldn't enjoy the delicious meal that followed, for the feeling of dread that persisted in her heart.

On the way home in the warm June night, he said lightly, "Cheer up, beautiful Mara. You haven't signed his death warrant. I plan to reason with Donellan, give him a chance to see where he's making a bad mistake."

"And if he won't reason with you?"

"Then I'll have to show him where he's wrong. Look, Mara, I'm doing this as a favor to you as much as for Will and Celia."

"I know it," she said moodily. "You've already done so many favors for me, I feel terribly obligated. In fact, I'm weighed down by my obligations to you."

"Aha! That's good. So when I ask you for a favor, perhaps you'll grant it more readily." He chuckled.

"I thought so!" she flared. "We're back to that again. Marriage is the only way I'd ever do what you want."

"And I thought you no longer believed in marriage. Look, even Will and Celia! Do you think they're happy?"

"I don't believe in marriage for me," she said paradoxically, "but I think Celia is coming to love Will and I think it may be a happy marriage eventually, if we can just get David out of the picture."

He heaved a mock sigh. "I suppose I'll have to go on doing you favors, then, and hope your sense of fair play will eventually take over."

She laughed dryly. Really, the man was irrepressible, and all he offered was satisfaction to urges that had plagued her only when he was nearby.

As they pulled up before the MacAdam mansion he drew the horse to a halt and turned to her. "Now, Mara, don't you think you owe me a kiss—a willing kiss—for the trouble you're putting me to?"

"Your kisses are—have a way of—they're very disturbing. And you don't know when to stop."

"Good. I want to disturb you. Disturb you so much you'll finally do something about it. Now how about it?"

"Very well. A small thank-you kiss," she said primly, turning her face up to his.

Slowly he took off her hat and pulled the pins from her mass of curling dark hair to run his fingers through it. She made a halfhearted effort to stop him, but he had an arm about her waist and was pressing her bosom against his and her resistance faded. When he had thoroughly disorganized her hair, he kissed her temples lightly.

Then his lips moved to her cheeks and excitement built in her. Her heart was drumming fast as his hand caught her chin and pulled it up to his lips. They were tender on hers at first, exploratory and warm. The scented night had closed about them and the soft leather upholstery of the Victoria felt good and soft against her back, as his lips grew more demanding.

Suddenly a thrill sharper than pain slashed through her and her mouth parted under his as her stiffness melted against his hard body. She felt dizzy and light-headed and as if she might faint as his mouth clung to hers. Languor crept over her and washed out pride and determination, and she held to him as if she were drowning.

When at last he lifted his head, it was he who broke the kiss and not she. She lay against the seat, spent with the turbulence that filled her.

"You see?" he asked and his voice was husky. "It could be like that for us, Mara, only more fulfilling."

She drew a deep trembling breath and whispered, "I'll admit you're a powerfully attractive man to me—you've just proved it. But I can't. I can't do what you want."

"Not yet. But you will," he said grimly, handing her hat to her and helping her to the drive and up the flagstoned walk.

Mara went silently to her room, where she sat on the bed a long time, unhappy and troubled, for herself, for her sister and dimly for Branch and Stuart, who were so far away in a war that had no reality for her. Life could be very complicated, she thought, as she wearily undressed and crept into her bed.

Chapter 14.

✣ JULY first came on Friday and Mara took the day off to help her sister and the family move to Galveston.

"You know well and good that Will had the big room on the south built just for you, Mara. And even though I've hired Rosita's niece, Elena, to come in during the day to help Amos keep the house up, the nights will be long and lonely. Remember, it only takes ninety minutes on the train to get back to Houston."

"But Celia, I'm only twenty minutes from the house here to my shop and—"

"And you know how you love Galveston! Surely you'll come Friday evenings and stay until Monday morning."

Andrea came into Will's big bedroom where Mara and Celia were packing a tall steamer trunk with Celia's and Betsey's clothes.

"I'm depressed," she said gloomily. "We haven't heard from Stuart or Branch in days now."

"Don't be blue, Andrea," Celia said cheerfully, folding diapers neatly. "The boys can't write *every* day and you know only yesterday the *Post* reported that Colonel Roosevelt's Rough Riders helped win the battle at Las Guasimas. The boys must be all right. They weren't listed as casualties."

"Poor Stuart," Andrea persisted mournfully. "He's an orphan with no one but us to worry about him."

"He has two cousins in Dallas."

"You know he says they never write," she said reproachfully, "or even see each other."

"He has the whole law office he works with rooting for him, sending him letters, besides us," Celia said doggedly.

"If you're through packing your things, Andrea, I wish you would help Maria and Rosita pack the last of the sheets I bought for the summer house."

"Thank God we won't have to make that part of the move again," Andrea replied coldly, turning back into the hall.

"Sometimes it's hard living with Andrea everpresent," Celia said, her voice low. "Naturally, Will is very protective of her—as he is of all of us—and I feel sorry for her. She goes out with men so rarely and still grieves for her father."

"Andrea's let her love for her father ruin other men for her," Mara said quietly.

Celia, folding a tiny batiste dress, cast her sister a mischievous glance. "She goes out with men as much as you do, and it's not for the lack of invitations for either of you."

"But I've the shop. I must see that it prospers. You know how much that means to me, Celia."

"I know," Celia replied, her sympathy touched by exasperation. "But it's an obsession, just like Andrea's love for her dead father."

"Surely it's not an *obsession,*" Mara said defensively. "What I'm doing is *constructive.* I make women happy. There's a big difference. There are so many kinds of love," she added uneasily, thinking of John Halloran.

"That's true, Celia answered. "And Andrea does have her clubs and social groups and heaven knows she's insistent enough about my playing with the Ladies' Musical Society. I guess we shouldn't talk of her as if she did nothing but love and worry about her family."

Mara suddenly wanted to ask her about her feelings regarding Will MacAdam, but a glance at Celia's now reserved face changed her mind and the two sisters finished packing the trunk in companionable silence.

Mara spent that night in the big south room upstairs in the Galveston house. As she lay in bed beside a row of windows with their net curtains blowing like belled skirts in a strong south wind, it seemed to her she could hear the surf where it struck the shore with a caressing whisper. It had been a long tiring day and the house was quiet, though it was only ten o'clock.

By all rights, Mara should have been worn out and sleeping soundly, but she moved restlessly in the broad soft bed, thinking of many things. One thought no sooner milled through her mind than another followed it.

She thought first of the shop. All this Friday she had left it to Sudie. Sudie's newly acquired dignity, indisputable knowledge of fashion and calm presence had come to be accepted wholeheartedly by Mara's clients and most of them were as pleased to be served by and consult with Sudie as by Mara herself. And an even better thought was that she would soon have paid John Halloran back his entire investment.

John Halloran. It would be so easy to love him and she faced that fact with what she felt were cool, clinical eyes. Though he mocked her and offered a thoroughly despicable alliance to her, he had honored her confidences, lent her money and was always stimulating company. She would not allow herself to think of the weakness and desire that filled her at his touch.

Had he confronted David Donellan yet? David, after talking so warmly last week of helping them move into their new surroundings, had been conspicuous by his absence, as had his pretty, pouting wife. Perhaps Halloran *had* seen him and threatened him. Had he done more than that, harmed Donellan in some way?

She rolled over to face the windows. Halloran should have called her by now. It had been nearly a week! The cool, salt-flavored wind from the Gulf poured over her, tempering the heat of her thoughts about the man.

She would be eighteen next month and already she was very nearly independent, a heady thought, that!

And it brought Archer Ashworth to mind. As his handsome, ruddy face loomed behind her closed lids, so did his wife's. Aunt Felice's face carried its customary disdain and contempt in the Bonheur brown eyes.

At least Mara had forestalled Ashworth's attempt to force her to continue the mockery of relationship between them, of forcing her to stay under his roof, she thought grimly. Her threat to tell of his actions and of her unnamed father had been a mighty club to wield. In some curious, dissatisfied way, she was almost grateful to her mother's nameless lover. Mara had never realized what a prisoner she had been all those years, bending this way and that, under the lash of Ashworth's scorn and hatred. In their more recent brief encounters under the MacAdam roof, her passing glance at him had revealed to her a wariness in his bright blue eyes, something akin to fear and to reluctant respect.

Her mind swung unerringly back to Halloran. Close-mouthed, tight-lipped deliberate devil! He should have called as soon as he'd seen Donellan. He knew only too well that she was waiting to hear exactly what had happened between them. Donellan was a malicious, selfish swine and there was no telling what reaction he would have to a warning by someone like the iron-willed Halloran.

God, what if there had been a knockdown, drag-out bloody fight? No. A rumor would have found its way back to her. Where *had* Halloran been these last five days? She had thought he'd help the MacAdams move into their new home. He was as selfish as Donellan in his own way, and with the thought, she saw the man in her mind, tall, powerful, his chiseled features marred by the thin pale scar that somehow added to the arrogance and imperiousness he kept—or *tried* to keep—hidden.

Slowly his image blurred, melted into her brain with the ease of a deeply grooved fantasy. Sleep loosened Mara's hold on the breeze-cooled room, filling her subconscious with the scent of the sea and sweeping her into a lulling, tenuous dream.

Saturday morning, everyone was up very early. Will and Celia had brought only Rosita and Maria with the family to Galveston, leaving the other servants in charge of keeping the Houston house open. Sam Johnson, the coachman, would see to harnessing Mara's little surrey each morning and stabling the horse and surrey in the evenings for her.

His brother Amos, the butler, along with Elena, Rosita's summer replacement, would see that the house was kept dusted and fresh. Bo Jones, the gardener, would continue to care for the beautifully landscaped yard about the house. All of them, with the exception of Elena, occupied the apartments above the coachhouse and stable at the rear of the house.

"You'll be in that big house alone at night except for Amos promising he'll sleep way up in Rosita's room on the third floor, Mara," Celia said at breakfast, with both warning and pleading in her voice. "You'll probably have to fix your own supper unless Elena can be persuaded to do it. You'll have to make your own bed every morning."

"I know, I know! But I'll be at the shop most of the time. Probably pretty late some nights. I may eat at the hotel." Then casually, "What happened to John Halloran, Will? I thought he was coming out yesterday to help you move to Galveston for the summer?"

"He was in and out. Had to go to Beaumont on an oil deal we're interested in yesterday. He'll probably be here later today. He has to see a client about a house he's sold for her. I asked him to drop by tonight for potluck supper." Will smiled at her, the special warm smile he seemed to reserved just for her.

Andrea had looked away then, barely hiding her anger. Because of Will's smile, or because of Mara's asking about Halloran? Perhaps both, because of her proprietary feeling about the two men. There was no explaining Andrea, her premonitions, her superstitions and strange quick looks of guilt.

"We won't be back until the last of September," Celia said, going back persistently to the subject most important to her. "You'd better think over commuting between the shop and Galveston."

"Good heavens! I'd be on that train three hours a day!" Mara protested.

"You could take your sketch pad with you and turn out new styles by the dozens!"

Both girls laughed then, but the words stuck in Mara's mind as she breakfasted at the happy table with the family in the big solarium at the side of the house. They ate on a glass-topped, wrought-iron-based table and the room was full of green plants. There were palms, hibiscus in full bloom, scarlet geraniums and dwarfed fruit trees. The glassed ceiling and screened walls let in a flood of warm, tropic sunlight and sweet air.

"I've got to leave in thirty minutes to make the train back to Houston," Will said, draining his coffee cup.

"It's a pity you must go," Celia said politely. "After we

get things settled we're going down to the beach today. It will probably take most of the morning, but we'll have the afternoon."

"Better arrange for one of those big umbrellas they rent at the Pagoda, or you'll have a bad case of sunburn." He was equally polite.

Mara marveled that they could share the same bed each night and be so distant and cool to each other. She wondered if only she could sense it, or if others felt the distance between Will and his wife. No one had ever commented on it, nor had Andrea seemed aware of any breach between the two.

Later, after Will had gone and Celia and Mara were helping Maria to clear away the breakfast dishes, her sister said, "Why don't you go on to the beach early, Mara? You have only today and tomorrow to enjoy it and we have weeks ahead of us. It's just a short walk to the Pagoda and we'll meet you there this afternoon."

She laughed and added, "And I know how you love it, Mara. Who knows? Maybe the sea will do what I can't do, persuade you to commute. Others who live here do, you know."

Mara smiled. "Ah, Celia, you're as persuasive as the sea could ever be. You know all the right things to make staying in the townhouse a mistake."

"Go on then. Taking your bathing suit and change in the Pagoda or one of the bathhouses. Put your things, money and all, into this little canvas satchel. I bought one for each of us."

Later, as Mara swung along the palm-fronded street on her way to the main boulevard, Broadway, she drank in the cool morning air. It was like some exotic wine, flavored with a thousand scents, all of them pleasing to the senses.

Broadway was, as always, beautiful in the bright morning sunlight, esplanaded with palms and oleanders, with the streetcar lines running down the center. Now there were recently laid sidewalks on either side of the broad street, paved with cement. A streetcar clattered by, filled with merry passengers, and Mara's little heels clicked cheerfully as she walked along.

She observed the palatial Walter Gresham home, reflecting that Nicholas J. Clayton had outdone himself in

designing it. He had done beautifully with the MacAdam
"cottage," as he called it, as well. But now her eyes went to
Bonnie Fairweather's mansion, designed by a Louisiana
creole. All the pink brick had been painted a dazzling
white and the white marble pillars rose up imperially on
the broad gallery. There was a fine stallion, with a glossy
reddish coat gleaming in the sun where it was tied to one of
four hitching posts before the house.

Mara lingered, admiring both the horse and the house,
for the house was gracious as Bonnie, and without any of
the ornate scroll work that decorated so many houses.
Dear Bonnie, Mara thought with a sudden rush of affection. How she wished she could invite her for tea at her sister's new summer home, just blocks away.

Ah, but John Halloran could have Bonnie and her
daughter in for tea, cocktails or dinner as he chose in *his*
new summer home and no doubt would, she thought with a
wry smile. Perhaps he would ask *her* to join them some
time and the thought gave her pleasure.

But she froze in sudden surprise as a tall, familiar linen-
suited figure stepped from the doorway of Bonnie's house,
cream panama in hand. It was he, the man that filled her
thoughts all too often.

Her heart gave a great bound of shock as she stood
rooted to the spot. The tall, wide-shouldered Halloran
swung down the steps and on to the stone walkway that
ran to the curb. He glanced down the street as he caught
the reins to his mount, and the quick stillness of his piercing look told her he had already recognized her.

Too late she tucked her head down and quickened her
pace to a near run. She became sharply aware of the
sounds about her, the rattle of a passing Victoria, the clat-
tering hum of an approaching streetcar, but beneath them
all, she was sensitive to the firm clopping of a powerful
horse's hooves that came down her side of Broadway. She
discerned its rhythm above all the others.

How mortifying to be caught staring like any nastily curious woman at Bonnie's house! The faint laughter and
shrill calling voices came faintly to her ears from the Midway, but they mingled with the sound of passing carriages
and all at once the familiar voice came to her.

"Don't hurry so, Mara, or I'll think you're deliberately

avoiding me." There was laughter in the words as he added, "And I know you recognized me. What were you doing peering so interestedly at Bonnie's house?"

"I was just wishing I could ask her to tea," she flashed, wheeling to face him. Then she blurted words that she could have taken back. "I certainly didn't expect to see you coming out so casually, this early in the morning." Her face heated up and she walked faster.

He laughed aloud and pulled his horse to a halt, dismounting. "That implies a certain criticism. Surely you know I do business with Bonnie—and in more ways than you are now imagining."

Leading his horse in the street, he stepped up beside her on the cement walk. The horse in the street followed with a restless toss of his head.

"I imagine nothing!" She looked at him angrily as, reins in hand, he walked beside her. "Besides, I know Bonnie has quit—she doesn't—she's selling her house in Houston and—"

"And one of these days her daughter, Fleurette, will be coming home. She and Desmond and a bevy of servants are getting the house ready to move into. I was there talking to Brant and Bonnie of her interests in the lumber mills and the sale of her Houston house. Does that satisfy your curiosity?"

"I wasn't curious. I don't care a fig for your comings and goings. Least of all for—*that* part of your life."

"What part of my life?" he asked innocently.

"You know well enough what part, the part you have repeatedly endeavored to have me share." Her chin was up and she did not look at him.

"Did you know Bonnie has sold her house in Houston?"

"No!" She was interested in spite of her irritation. "Who bought it?"

"I sold it for her to William Marsh."

"Good heavens! One of Houston's founding fathers."

"And wealthiest. His wife's in a swoon over it, but he says he's going to completely refurbish it and give it to the Houston Historical Society as a museum. He's donating several of his masterpieces to it as a start. You know, old Fairweather built it as the first real mansion in Houston."

"It *is* a beautiful house," Mara said, smiling suddenly. "I hope Bonnie got her price for it."

"From Marsh! One of her oldest and richest friends? I should say she did. Since I handled the transaction for her, I suppose you're going to ask me the amount."

"I am not! I simply am concerned for Bonnie's sake and her daughter's."

"A hundred thousand. I delivered the check this morning and Brant will put it all in government bonds for her. Bonnie's a very wealthy woman, and since money can buy a certain respect, I look for her to become one of Houston's and Galveston's leading citizens."

"Good for Bonnie! When I build *my* house, she'll certainly be welcome in it."

"Oh? So now you're going to build a house for yourself, a *femme seule* living in lonely splendor?"

"I've very nearly paid you off, smart aleck, and when fifty percent of the profits is all mine, I certainly intend to have my own house."

"If you'd really been smart, Miss, you'd have bargained more. You should have at least seventy-five percent of your profits. Twenty-five percent for a silent partner is plenty. Too bad!"

"You want to change our agreement?" she challenged. "I'd be willing."

"It was your decision." He smiled, then with a lifted brow, "Now if you should say yes to my proposition that—"

"If you had an ounce of decency, you wouldn't make nasty propositions!" she exploded. Between the morning sun and the heat of her anger, she felt she must have turned beet red.

"Why not? You weren't averse to making a nasty proposition to me."

"What do you mean?" She glared at him, slowing her step.

"Didn't you proposition me to scare the pants off David Donellan?"

"Oh," she gasped. She had completely forgotten her sister's *bête noire*, and it had been uppermost in her mind even at breakfast. She seized the initiative and said accusingly, "And that's another thing. You should've known that I'd be on pins and needles about that and called me the moment you'd seen him!"

"You haven't seen him hanging about Celia, have you?" he asked laconically.

"No," she admitted, feeling a touch hypocritical. "Not around Celia anyway."

"Surely not around *you?*" he asked mockingly.

"No." She flushed again. "How did you—what did you do, say?"

"I both did and said. I called on him at his office at the Galveston Wharf Company and told him in private that I would personally slit his throat if he made any further noises about Betsey, or came near the MacAdams."

"How did you convince him that you could do such a thing?" she asked, fascinated by the muscle that tightened in his jaw and the narrow glitter of his eyes.

"My, what a nasty curiosity you have, Mara." He laughed suddenly and the menacing scar disappeared entirely. "Let's leave it at that, my dear." Then abruptly changing the subject he said, "I suppose you've a bathing outfit in that little bag?"

"Yes."

"Can you swim?"

"I—well, no, not really swim. Once Celia and I went to Chesapeake Bay and stayed with Aunt Julia at her summer home. But we never really learned how to swim."

"There's a bad undertow and it's not too far out," he said, suddenly somber. "Stay close to the shore."

All at once the sunlight seemed to dim and she felt a somewhat familiar prickle on the back of her neck. When had she felt that before? Ah, yes, the first time she had come to Galveston, as if her destiny lay in the island. Such foolishness! She was as bad as Andrea, thinking of premonitions and omens and such!

He swung up on his horse, tipping his panama politely, and smiling with the winning charm she knew so well. The sunlight was warm and bright again and she laughed, for the Midway was just beyond them, and people, like colorful flowers, were everywhere. The scent of cotton candy and popcorn floated to meet her and she thought once more how she loved this fairy city by the sea. *My fair isle*, she thought, happy with the music of the words. *My fair isle.* A

band playing far down the busy Midway could be heard
faintly, adding to the festivity.

Halloran turned his horse and rode away. Mara looked
after him thinking, *He always excites and stimulates me,
damn him.* Then she smiled wryly at her mental expletive.
Truly, being independent was a powerful stimulant itself
and it had subtly changed her, matured her, freed her from
many of the day's taboos.

She realized with new insight that Halloran had had a
point when he told her that with independence came a certain freedom from respectability and the day's mores that
might well make his suggestion of an illicit relationship
between them quite possible. The thought frightened her
and she put it resolutely from her mind as she swung
briskly into the Midway, past the laughing babble on the
boardwalk toward the Pagoda.

John Halloran did not come that night for a potluck supper with them. Instead, Will came in late, after they had
all dined, saying that he and Halloran had had supper together in Houston.

Earlier that day, one of the dredges had suffered a dawn
explosion, and in the afternoon, Halloran had gone out on
Buffalo Bayou to examine the damage. It was bad, though
not irreparable. They had been unable to discover the
cause of the explosion so far, but luckily no one was hurt
and the damage would soon be repaired.

So Monday morning at six, both Mara and Will left the
house in his surrey. They were on the train by six-thirty
and on their way to Houston. Will stayed in the smoker
and Mara took out her pad and pencil and rough-sketched
some new ideas that had come to her over the weekend.

Later, when they arrived, Will had called ahead and his
buggy was waiting.

"I'll drop you at your shop and see that Sam picks you up
by five," he told her.

When she entered *Mara Originals*, she found that Sudie
was there before her and greeted her warmly.

"Oh, Mara, last Friday old Mrs. Marsh was in to see
about those two afternoon dresses we're making for her
and she was fit to be tied!"

Mara laughed. "I know why, too. It's because her husband bought Bonnie Fairweather's house for a hundred thousand dollars and is going to turn it into a museum."

Sudie was deflated. "How did you know? It happened while you were in Galveston."

"I ran into John Halloran. He just happened to have sold the house for Bonnie."

Anna and Bella came in the front door and greeted Sudie and Mara. "I do declare, Miss Mara," Bella said, wreathed in smiles, "has Sudie told you we took four more orders on Friday, while you were gone?"

Both seamstresses took off their hats and held them as they looked happily at their employer.

"No," Mara smiled, "only that Mrs. Marsh was in to see about her afternoon dresses."

"I nearly finished one of them Friday," Anna said, putting a hand to her fading blonde hair. "I ought to finish it in a couple of hours this mornin'."

"And I'll be through with the other by the end of the day," Bella put in as the two turned and walked briskly to the working area at the rear of the shop.

The door opened again the two new seamstresses entered. Mara greeted them, "Hello, Millie. Good morning, Jane."

The two were younger than Bella and Anna and they blushed as they returned Mara's smile and hastened to follow the other two.

Mara experienced a warm feeling of satisfaction as the sound of humming sewing machines came from the rear room. She went to check on the stock of materials in the storage room, putting off the moment when she must sit down and bring the ledgers and invoices up to date.

Oh, how she needed a person familiar with figures—bookkeeping, the paying of bills and salaries, the billing of clients—to run her office! Well, that would surely come in time, certainly by the time she expanded, as she intended to do. The building next to her was empty and she knew it was for sale, but that would mean borrowing more money from Halloran which she wanted to avoid if she could. Still, she must expand—the business demanded it. Perhaps she could buy it on time! She would approach the owner as soon as she paid Halloran the last three thousand.

It appeared the war had stimulated the ladies to new heights of fashion and an increasing appetite for Mara's designs. As a result, her receipts had also climbed to new heights. Sudie had told her that even *Ashworth Originals* was meeting with some success, with lower-priced originals and baby layettes.

Mara had regretfully ceased making layettes, because of the demand for fine dresses and ballgowns, but she fully intended to make them again as soon as she expanded and hired two more ladies who would specialize in layettes.

Hiring two more seamstresses posed no problem, for Mara had already had others apply. Even two of Ashworth's French seamstresses, very young women from New Orleans, had secretly approached her about working for *Mara Originals*.

Monday went well, despite the four hours Mara spent wrestling with her ledgers and invoices. Several women came in for fittings and five more came to browse through Mara's books of fashions. Three of them decided to buy and the other two said they would make their decision and come in tomorrow for fittings.

Mara was busy until the moment Sam drove up in her small rig and waited patiently outside until she bade her employees good-bye, locking the shop door after them. Sudie rode with Sam and Mara within a block of the MacAdam house, where she left them and boarded a streetcar that ran within two blocks of the Ashworth house.

That night, though Rosita's niece, Elena, stayed long enough to fix a small supper for Mara, herself and Amos, the house seemed incredibly quiet and lonely. When Elena left, shortly after dark and Amos retired to the upper reaches of the house, Mara realized suddenly that her older sister had been entirely correct when she had said Mara would find the house too large and too empty.

Even though she knew Amos lay a story above her, the noises that lurked in the night unnerved her. She had thought herself impervious to any apprehensions, but the house without the bustle of family and the comings and goings of Will and other men who came often to talk business with him in the evenings was altogether unpleasant. She missed Branch, too, with his rollicking laughter and his penchant for a tart, amusing phrase. It would be good

to have him back *if* war lasted no longer than John Halloran's predicted three months.

Besides, there was Galveston, her fair isle, like a siren
by the sea. She loved it, was excited by it, longed for it. It
called to her and she succumbed.

On Tuesday morning she called her sister from the shop.

"Celia? How are you all?" she asked. She was alone in
her office, having had Amos to bring her at seven-thirty
that morning. She could have driven the surrey in herself,
but Amos had protested it left him with nothing to do. Besides, a young lady needed "pertection."

"Fine! We had a picnic on the beach yesterday. We drove
in the buggy to a spot far down from the bathers and we're
all just a touch sunburned, even Rosita and Maria. How
was it alone in the house last night?"

"You were right," Mara said candidly, "and I was
wrong. I think I can stand it just about long enough to get
my things packed and have Sam drive me to the station
Wednesday evening. I'll commute and gladly."

Celia laughed triumphantly. "Smart girl! Have you
called Will and told him?"

"No. Frankly I'm ashamed to—"

"Don't be. You'll be interested to know that he told Andrea and me that he thought you'd last about four days. He
figured you'd miss Betsey most."

"He was right. I do miss her and I won't even make it to
three nights, let alone four."

"Well, call him, Mara. He can help you with your luggage Wednesday evening. We'll all meet you at the station!"

Mara did call Will that afternoon from her shop and was
relieved that he did not laugh aloud. Instead, he told her
gravely that he thought she was making the right decision. And further, when he knew her to be safely in Galveston, Amos would be glad to sleep in his own bed over
the coachhouse where his brother Sam had remained with
Bo Jones, the gardener.

Wednesday afternoon at four o'clock, John Halloran appeared in her shop, looming large and male among the
frilly dresses she had spread out for the approval of Mrs.
DeHaun, a wealthy cotton merchant's wife.

He bowed to the lady and she returned his greeting with

"Nice to see you again, Mr. Halloran," before he turned to Mara.

"I've some business to discuss with you, Miss Mara. Will you have dinner with me tonight at the hotel?"

"I'm going to Galveston tonight," she informed him. "I've decided to—"

"Yes, Will told me. To commute. I think it's a very wise decision and I'll take your baggage down to the station for you now." He smiled again, "I'll come back and pick you up at five-thirty. We'll have dinner. I can lay my business before you and get you to the eight-thirty train. Will said he'd pick you up at the Galveston station at ten."

"I'll discuss it with you later. Mrs. DeHaun's waiting."

"Oh, I don't mind, dear," chirped that lady, "I'm having a dreadful time making up my mind between the rose velvet and the pale blue satin."

"Come into my office, Mr. Halloran," Mara said coldly.

Following Mara into her small office, he murmured, "The hell you say, madam—*Mister Halloran!* After all we've shared together, the confidences, the emotional crises. What a prig you are."

She closed the door and turned on him like a cat. *"Mr. Halloran* absolutely! I shall never refer to you in any other manner in front of my clients!"

"Even Bonnie?"

"Oh, hush. What in the world is this business about? In three more months I should have paid you off."

"Is that your luggage there in the corner?"

"Yes, it is," she retorted. "Now what business have you to discuss with me?"

"I'll tell you over dinner," he relied imperturbably, catching up the two large suitcases and putting the wide valise under his arm. "I'll pick you up here at five-thirty." Shifting the bags, he opened the door and went out swiftly.

She followed after him and Mrs. DeHaun looked up from some strips of fabric she held and smiled at the two, as Halloran nodded and went out the front door.

Sudie came from the back room and said, "Miss Mara, we've finished all Miss Lane's lingerie and we can start on her wedding dress this afternoon, if she can come in for a fitting."

"Fine," Mara said absently, looking out the long win-

dow as John Halloran put her luggage in the back of his
Victoria and leapt easily into the driver's seat, reins in
hand. "I'll call her as soon as Mrs. DeHaun has come to a
decision."

Although preoccupied with Halloran's words, Mara
turned a sweet and persuasive smile on her client, who immediately pointed to the rose velvet dress and began to
question her about other materials.

That evening after she had locked the shop door and
Halloran had escorted her to a seat in the Victoria, she demanded suspiciously, "Now this business you—"

"Later, my dear. Over dinner," he interrupted, then
asked, "Have you seen the afternoon paper?"

"No. Why?"

"There's been heavy fighting in Cuba and in Santiago
Bay."

"That means Branch and Stuart and all the Phillips
brothers are in the thick of it," she replied slowly, her
heart lurching downward. "I hope they're all right."

"I hope so, too. But they're big boys and I expect they'll
weather it," he said and launched into a discourse on the
merits of the Spanish fleet versus the American fleet. He
seemed optimistic, but Mara was silent with worry for the
young men she knew who must surely have been in the
fighting.

Later, when dinner was served them under a cooling ro-
tary ceiling fan in the spacious dining room of the Houston
Hotel, he veered suddenly from talk of the war.

"I've bought the building next to the shop, Mara, and
you can start your enlargement as soon as you like." His
eyes on her were expectant.

"Oh!" she cried in dismay. "*I* was going to buy that
building."

"With what? You'd have to borrow money from me."

"No, I wouldn't," she said stormily. "I was going to contact the owner and buy it on time."

"As a fifty percent silent partner with money, it's all the
same. Just quicker."

"No, it's not the same. I'm so entangled with you financially now that I don't know where my part begins and
yours leaves off."

He grinned engagingly. "I want you entangled with me and you know well enough why, but this doesn't complicate matters. Even if you'd bought it on a dragged-out note, fifty percent would have been mine anyway. This is just quicker."

"No," she said, somewhat confused, "I could have someway kept that part of it out of our partnership." Then angrily, "I want to buy out. What will it take?"

"You can't buy me out, my pretty. I won't sell at any price. I *like* doing business with you. You *need* me. And you'll be eighteen next month—a little riper and you're changing every day. One day you're going to *like* living with me."

She looked down at her crab bisque and then up at his amused dark face. "You're wrong, John. I don't intend to wind up like my sister, pregnant by one man and having to marry another." Her voice was level and cool. She put her fork to the bisque and slowly, deliberately, put the delicacy into her mouth.

He shrugged. "And suppose you didn't get pregnant? There are ways—"

"That's a chance I'll never take."

"For one so young, you're remarkably determined. Do you expect me to marry you?"

"I thought we'd settled that long ago. You're not a marrying man, and I've come to the conclusion I'm not a marrying woman."

"Yes, you are," he said mockingly. "You're about the most marriageable woman I've ever met."

She widened her eyes derisively. "Can you possibly be wavering in your determination to stay a single man?"

"Not as long as there's a chance that I'll get what I want without it." He laughed. Then sobering, "When do you want to start knocking out walls and making *Mara Originals* a more sumptuous parlor of seduction for ladies of fashion?"

"As soon as possible, though I hate the disruption of business when it's going so well."

"No need for that. We'll simply fix the new building, you can decorate it in your own inimitable way, *then* we'll knock the walls out. It won't take two days of discomfort for your many customers."

"You think of everything," she said dryly. "It's so nice to have a silent partner who's so knowledgeable."

"It's my business to be knowledgeable about such things," he replied, matching her dryness. Then with a slight smile, "Our mutual friend, Donellan, has struck back. Had you heard?"

Her heart gave a quick startled bound. "No. How?"

"I think he was back of the explosion on one of our dredges in Buffalo Bayou over the weekend."

"Will mentioned you stayed in town because of an explosion," she said slowly. "He didn't say that David had anything to do with it."

"I don't suppose he knows yet. The Deepwater Committee hired a private detective and today he reported to me that he'd traced a piece of a box found on shore. It had held dynamite and it had come from a storehouse for such things belonging to the Galveston Wharf Company. It was dynamite that exploded on the dredge, we found traces of it. I expect Donellan paid one of the Wharf Company stevedores to do the job for him. But we've nothing in the way of proof. And if we did, it wouldn't be Donellan we could prosecute."

"That sounds like David Donellan. Letting someone else do it for him and getting off scot-free himself. Won't he try again?"

"We've doubled the guard on the dredges at night now. We'll catch the next one who shows up. And I just may pay Donellan another visit, but a more forceful one this time." He paused, then, "Now when do you want to start enlarging *Mara Originals?*"

"Next month," she said thoughtfully. "I think my birthday would be a good day to start."

"Eighteen going on twenty-nine," he said, smiling again.

"I wish you wouldn't say that!" she retorted angrily. "What's so magical about twenty-nine anyway?"

"Nothing. But there's something very magical about being eighteen *and* successful."

"I'll grant you being successful is very satisfying," she replied, mollified. But she could never have done it without his backing, she thought guiltily. Then she assuaged herself with the comforting knowledge that he was going to make money for a long time on his investment.

"I'm going to move into my house in Galveston next weekend," he said conversationally as the waiter entered, pushing a glass cart full of French pastries and other desserts. "We'll all be commuting together—you, Will and I.".

"Celia has promised to get me up each day in time to catch the six-thirty morning train with Will so I can be in the shop before eight."

"I know. Will plans to drive you to the train in his rig and pick me up on the way."

When they left the hotel dining room and stepped outside, newsboys were hawking an extra of the *Houston Post* on the streets and Halloran stopped to buy one from a cheery lad.

"Y'know there's been hard fightin', sir, in Cuba. Somewheres call San Juan an' Kettle Hill. The casualties is comin' in now. Read all about it," he said pocketing the dime that Halloran told him he could keep for the three-cent paper.

Halloran and Mara paused under a carbide light as he shook out the paper. Though it was late twilight, the streetlights had come on and he scanned the news stories quickly.

"They say over fourteen hundred of our men have been killed and over a hundred officers, but they took San Juan and Kettle Hill. And we know they've won the battle of Santiago Bay. They say the battleship *Texas* did yeoman service in the bay." Halloran folded the paper and put it under his arm as the young stable boy for the hotel brought his Victoria to the curb.

"I'll be so glad when it's over," Mara said, "and Branch and all the boys come home. I've missed them."

"It won't be more than a month now before Spain will be suing for peace," Halloran said as he helped her into the carriage.

As Will had arranged, he met the train at the Galveston Station at ten o'clock that night. It was dark as they drove home together, conversing companionably about their day. The streetlights were bright, but not too numerous along Broadway, and lamps glowed in windows of the big houses.

Will did not mention the explosion on the dredge, nor the suspect in that disaster, though Mara knew the dredge had been put out of action until repairs could be made to the engine. Instead, he told her of the day at the lumber mill and the cotton exchange and she told him of her busy morning and afternoon at the shop. Then they spoke of the newspaper extra regarding the casualties in Cuba and Mara reiterated her feelings regarding it.

"I'll be so glad to see Branch and Stuart, too, of course, and even those madcap Phillips boys. But I miss Branch's wonderful humor most. He always managed to put things in perspective."

"I miss him, too," Will said somberly as they turned in the drive beside the MacAdam house. "And I know he'll be back despite Andrea's dire pronouncements."

Mara smiled. "I do, too, Will," she said impulsively. "Nothing can beat the MacAdam brothers!"

He gave her a brotherly squeeze as he helped her from the carriage. "That's my Mara, you're a bright spot in my world, you know."

She stood waiting as he unharnessed the horse and put hay in the bin for him. Then they walked to the back door of the house, where the lights shone a welcome.

It was Friday night about eight that the door knocker sounded. Mara sat in a wicker rocker with the family about her, rocking Betsey in her arms. Dinner had been especially good with Rosita's crisply fried chicken and fresh garden black-eyed peas and tomatoes, which Rosita and Maria had bought at the grocery down from the Strand only that morning. And Rosita was as expert as Pleasance in making hot rolls.

The loud knock startled them all, including Will who was in the act of relighting his pipe. Andrea put her hand to her throat as she rose in one fluid movement, making her way to the door. Mara glimpsed her strained, white face as she passed her on her way into the hall.

Will rose more leisurely and followed her as the murmur of a young male voice came to them on the sweet Gulf air that coursed through the house. They heard the screen door slam and Andrea's muffled cry. Will's stride length-ened, but Andrea met him at the hall door, her eyes wide and terrified. She held an envelope in her hand.

"It's a telegram," she said in a strangled voice as Will reached out and took it from her. "Branch is dead. I know it. I feel it." She stood rigid as her brother swiftly opened the envelope.

"Tell me," she whispered. "Tell me what it says."

Mara had stopped rocking. Betsey waved her arms and cooed. Celia sat poised in her chair.

"Branch has been severely wounded, his left leg and arm. He's had surgery in the hospital in Tampa," Will said slowly. "It's Stuart who died in the battle for Kettle Hill."

Chapter 15.

THAT summer in Galveston was never as joyous for Mara after that. Another telegram followed the first, informing the MacAdams that Branch had not only lost his left leg at the knee, but they had been unable to save his left arm, having to remove it at the elbow.

A mortar shell had caught him as he was attempting to save his fallen friend, Stuart Kennedy. The mortar had blown Stuart to pieces as well as mangling Branch's left arm and leg. And Stuart had been buried, like his other unfortunate countrymen, in a spreading Cuban meadow. The doctor who wired them from the hospital said that Branch had been specific in his request that the family not come to Tampa to see him, but he gave no reason.

It had saddened them all deeply. Andrea took no comfort from the fact that Branch's life had been spared. She was certain he would suffer complications that would eventually result in his death, long before he could reach home. And it took the combined efforts of the family to keep her from boarding the train for Tampa to see him, as she said, "One last time."

"He'll write us when he's ready for that, Andrea," Will said forcefully and Andrea had subsided, though she still wore gloom like a shroud.

The days dragged by without a letter from Branch. Will had found his address at St. Joseph's Hospital in Tampa and each of them had written him long, cheerful letters with the exception of Andrea. Hers were tearstained and full of recrimination, not about her doleful predictions, but because she had not made a stronger effort to keep

303

him from joining Colonel Roosevelt's Rough Riders. She blamed herself entirely for failing to make him see the foolhardiness of his actions. According to her, his crippling wounds had been inevitable, there was nothing either she or he could have done about that. They had been a foregone conclusion from the moment of his enlistment. She took pride in reading these rambling letters aloud to Will and it did not matter to her when the others were present.

By July twenty-eighth, General Ponce had surrendered Puerto Rico to General Nelson Miles, who commanded the American Army there. And later, on August thirteenth, after Mara had worked late at the shop, John Halloran came by for her and took her to dinner for a belated celebration of her eighteenth birthday.

When they were seated at a snowy-linened table at the Cotton Exchange Club, he spread the *Houston Post* before her. According to the headlines, a peace protocol had been signed the day before with the Spanish and the fighting was over.

"I told you it wouldn't last more than three months. Though with all the pompousness that goes with ending a war, it won't be formally ended for a few more months. At least, the fighting's over and Spain has lost."

"Thank God it's over," Mara murmured, scanning the article. "Hmmm. It looks as though Spain will be giving up all her dominions in the Americas."

"That's true, but there'll be many a document and much negotiating before all the loose ends are tied. Cuba will get her independence, in the end. And America will get the Philippines and Puerto Rico, though we'll pay plenty in coin for them before it's over." He picked up the menu and looked at it idly. "Sorry you couldn't get off to celebrate your birthday, but we'll make up for it now."

And they did. Mara felt quite giddy from three glasses of champagne and even the large delicious meal did not quite dim her euphoria. Later, as they got into Halloran's Victoria, he turned to her.

"Now when are you going to make *Mara Originals* larger? I've long ago closed the deal on the building next door."

"Tomorrow," she said happily. "I think tomorrow would be a good day to start."

And when she came in from Galveston the following

morning, she was surprised to see workmen and carpenters swarming next door. Halloran was there himself, clad in an open-throated plaid shirt and coarse jeans which clung to his legs and small buttocks like a second skin, as he moved lithely among his work crew.

As the days went by, he supervised the construction himself to Mara's surprise, and it went swiftly toward completion.

The first of September, Bonnie Fairweather came in to see her. Mara greeted her gladly and took her to her own private office where they could talk unhindered by the three disapproving women who were thumbing through Mara's new designs. The three had studiously lifted their noses at Bonnie's entry.

"I've called by to visit you three times, since you've moved to Galveston, Bonnie. You're never home!"

"I'm so sorry! Dominique told me you had called, but I have been so busy." Bonnie's green eyes sparkled and her smile was open and endearing. "I'm so excited, Mara! Fleurette had written that she wants me to meet her in Paris, where we can properly say good-bye to France. We will come home together."

"How wonderful!"

"We'll stay a month in Paris and then take the ship home. We'll dock at New York, of course, but we don't plan to stay there long. Fleurette says she is anxious to come home." Bonnie's face fell into pensive lines. "She was only six when I took her abroad for schooling. She's been at the Académie in Chartres ever since, except for little trips about the continent." Then with quick compassion, "I've heard about Branch, of course, and I'm sick at heart for him. Do you know when he's coming home?"

"No. He won't answer our letters. He's told the doctor he doesn't want any of us coming to Tampa to see him and that he'll come home when they finish patching him up."

"He was such a wonderful young man. Even with the loss of his arm and leg, he can lead a very useful and full life."

"Evidently he doesn't feel that way about it, Bonnie," Mara replied with a troubled frown.

"And he was such a good manager for *MacAdam & Hal-*

loran. I know Will told me it really doubled his work when
Branch enlisted. Surely he'll adjust when he gets home."

"If he comes home," Mara said. "He's so silent. He just
may stay in Florida and settle there."

Bonnie sighed. "Well, darling, I really came in to order
two fall frocks, a traveling suit for the boat trip to France
and a ballgown for the time I'm in Paris. I think I have
enough others to see me through until we return."

"Wonderful! I have just the designs for you," Mara
smiled, relieved that she had her work to take her mind off
Branch's tragedy. She reached for her most recent fashion
sketches.

By October first, Halloran had completed the expansion
of *Mara Originals* and was ready to remove the wall that
separated the shop from the new addition. Mara was busy
having the new portion decorated to match the original.
She was thankful that the family had moved back to Houston the middle of September, for she was kept at the shop,
supervising, arranging furniture, overseeing the place-
ment of the machines across the long workroom at the
back, both morning and night. Often she did not leave for
home until after ten in the evening, skipping supper and arriving at the big MacAdam house starved. Rosita always
stayed up for her on these nights and had a good supper
put aside for her.

Celia scolded and Will frowned at her long hours, but
she mollified both of them with promises that it wasn't for
long that she would be so busy.

The only one who didn't seem to be disapproving of her
late hours, besides Andrea, was Halloran. Often he arranged to meet her on some of the long evenings as she finally turned away the last draper and decorator and he
drove her home in either his buggy or his Victoria, de-
pending on the weather. He complimented her on her
taste, on her perseverance and her determination.

One crisp, cool October night after nine, Halloran came
in and told her, "I've called and gotten word to Sam that
I'm picking you up tonight and taking you to a late supper
at the Cotton Exchange Club."

At first, she was resentful of his presumption that he
could call on such short notice, but she was very hungry,

and more, she was tired for the move was now complete and she had just settled a wrangle between the seamstresses over which spot each had wanted her machine placed.

She rode along beside him in the darkness as they passed several buggies and two or three men on horseback. The carbide lights cast pools of light in the misty night.

Later, when the two of them had been seated in one of the small private dining rooms, Halloran said, "Will had made up his mind he was going to Tampa to see Branch this morning, when a letter finally came from him—the first—and it was sent to the office."

"Thank God he's written! What did he say?"

"It was a bitter letter with none of Branch's old wit and humor," he said, looking at her. "It seems he blames himself for not snatching Stuart from under the mortar fire in time. He said Stuart would be alive today if he had been a fraction of a second quicker."

"He and Stuart were boyhood friends, of course," Mara murmured. "It's only natural that he would grieve over his loss."

"Well, he ended his letter by saying he didn't give a damn what happened to him now. In fact, he said, and I quote, 'For God's sake don't do anything stupid like trying to come and see me, any of you. I'll be home as soon as they can put me together—if they can.' His handwriting was steady as a rock and quite readable and Will decided to abide by his decision." He put aside his menu and said abruptly, "I think *Mara Originals* has outgrown the term 'shop.' It qualifies as a house of fashion now. When do you plan to have your second grand opening?"

"I thought November first." Mara sighed a little wearily, and Halloran silently picked up the menu again.

Mara looked at hers unseeingly. Women were giving their daughters "Mara Originals" for birthdays and the coming holidays. Even men came in, with carefully noted measurements, ordering opulent negligees and nightclothes for their wives. Some of them, Mara suspected, were ordering for women other than their wives. Daughters ordered lacy underthings for mothers and girl friends. Mara had never been so busy.

The result was that she had at last, only a week ago,

hired two more young Mexican girls who had brought with them samples of their expertise to show her. One of these girls was none other than Elena, Rosita's niece, who had worked in her aunt's place briefly last summer at the Mac-Adam house. In her soft, accented voice she murmured that she had always felt she could do better than house-work. After seeing her dainty stitches, Mara heartily agreed with her and hired her on the spot, along with her friend, Catania Lopez, who was also expert with the needle. They would come to work November first, the day of the new opening.

She sighed again and Halloran's dark brows drew to-gether. "You sound dead tired. How about a short brandy before we order? A pick-me-up."

"I could use it, but I'll settle for white wine. I'm so tired, brandy might do me in."

"What's made you so tired, Mara?" he asked, his voice softening slightly.

"Oh, nothing much. The girls have been wrangling over whose machine goes where."

"You have how many now?"

"Sudie, of course, is in a class by herself, she's so good, but there's Bella, Anna, Millie and Jane, each as Irish as a shamrock. And I've just hired Elena and Catania, Span-ish, and terribly good at baby clothes, and very volatile."

"Seven employees can be quite a handful. Do you want me to try to find a clerk-manager for you?"

"No," she said sharply. "I don't want a *clerk*. I want someone who'll be more than a clerk. An office manager, who'll take some interest in the excellence of our products and handle any complaints from the help or the custom-ers."

"Have you had to handle many of those?"

"Not from the customers yet. But I'm sure the day will come. And I'm constantly keeping peace between the seamstresses. So I want someone with compassion and un-derstanding of human nature."

"You don't want much," he said dryly, sipping his brandy, as the waiter reentered. Mara had drunk but little of her wine as he took their order.

When he had disappeared, closing the door behind him after replenishing the small log fire in the fireplace beyond their table, Mara sipped her wine and said, "Never you mind, John Halloran. I shall find someone. And meantime I'll wrestle with my problems myself."

"I wouldn't think of encroaching on that independence of yours, Mara, but had you thought about Branch?"

She looked at him blankly. Then, "Of course. Every day since he went away."

"I mean for your office manager. He's a man with compassion and a real talent for bookkeeping and invoices."

She stared at him open mouthed.

"Well," he said impatiently, "you knew he was office manager for our lumber company and both stores. Kept the books on them, too. Damned well. So much so that we had a crisis before we filled the position with not one, but three young men after Branch enlisted. Of course, he doesn't need the money. The Colonel's fortune is immense and he's an inheritor."

Her eyes began to shine as the waiter returned with fresh crabmeat cocktails and a luscious crisp salad topped with roquefort dressing.

"I'll bet he wouldn't think of doing such a thing, working in women's high fashion! Besides, you and Will want him back, I'm sure."

"He sounds like a man whose life has changed and his attitude toward it as well. I got the impression he thinks he's lost his usefulness. Will and I can't *make* him come back, though you know we'll try. Anyway, it's an idea and I think it might do him some good to know he has a choice."

"He'll certainly have a choice," Mara replied, falling to the crabmeat with a suddenly increased appetite.

November came and with it Mara's second grand opening. This time, she served champagne and hors d'oeuvres to the ladies who crowded the spacious salon. She had pressed Rosita and Maria into service, and even Amos, tall and stately, carried a large silver tray full of sparkling champagne glasses about to the ladies.

One or two men came at the insistence of their wives, but they left early. Mara smiled, for she knew they would be back before Christmas, ordering more frocks, lingerie and accessories, a department which she had just put in for their wives.

The opening was a great success and post war prosperity swept into December on a tidal wave of orders. Mara had to be careful with her promises now that her designs were at a high premium.

Mid December, she had a letter from Bonnie Fairweather in Paris. In it, she told Mara of the glamorous places she and Fleurette had been and what a wonderful time they were having, but, she said, none of the clothes, even at the great and famous fashion houses, could compare with *Mara Originals*. She said she and her daughter would be back in Galveston in January after Christmas in Paris. Her final paragraph was a touch wistful and made Mara's heart ache for her.

Ah, Mara dear, I fear for my baby when we return. My baby, at eighteen! People can be so cruel and I have left only fifty miles between me and my past. I dread the day my Fleurette discovers how her mother got her start, businesswoman though I may now be. Will she forgive me and love me still? Oh, my dear, if you could help me by being kind to my daughter. How foolish of me! Of course you'll be kind. You could never be otherwise.

Much love,
Your Bonnie

I shall call on her, Mara vowed, *the minute she and Fleurette return.*

But before Bonnie Fairweather and Fleurette returned, Branch MacAdam came home. He told no one he was coming and took a hack from the station to the house, arriving in the cold, late December evening, just before dinner. Mara herself had only just come from her busy fashion house and was taking off her coat and gloves when the door knocker sounded.

Amos answered it and his glad cry echoed back to those in the parlor. Will, who had arrived thirty minutes before, was the first to sprint into the hall, followed by a swift-running Andrea. Celia, with Betsey in her arms, followed.

Mara was the last to join them. Will was pounding Branch on the back and his eyes were moist. Andrea clung to her younger brother like a leech and Celia was tiptoeing to kiss his tanned cheek. Evidently the hospital staff had kept him out in the Flordia sunshine as much as possible. He was unchanged outwardly, except for the twin lines from nose to mouth that indicated pain and suffering. And his eyes no longer held the mischievous twinkle. They were old, wise eyes in a young face.

When the others started talking among themselves and the servants joined them in the hall, Mara went to him quietly and kissed his cheek, murmuring, "Branch, welcome home. I'm so glad you're here, that the war's over and peace has at last been negotiated."

"The war's not over for me. I'll carry it to my grave," he said, low voiced.

"It *is* over for you. You will *not* carry it to your grave. You're going to live a long useful life. You wait and see," she whispered, her cheek to his.

He shook his head, his lip twisting in a cynical smile. "I'm good for nothing." His empty coat sleeve was neatly pinned up and he stood straight in his long trousers, for he had been fitted with a wooden leg at his knee. His limp was quite noticeable for he had not yet become accustomed to balancing himself on the wooden leg. "I'll never be able to ride as I used to," he muttered more to himself than to her.

After the servants had all shaken his hand and welcomed him, Amos picked up Branch's one small suitcase and took it up the stairs to his old room. Then the family drifted into the parlor with Will talking eagerly of Branch returning to the lumber and cotton business.

"You'll never know how much we've missed you! You knew I had to hire three men to take your place, Branch," he said with a laugh. "Thank God you can take over again."

"I'm not taking over. I'm not needed. You've got the three men. Let them do it," Branch said flatly as he seated himself on the large divan. "Nor do I intend to dabble in cotton." Because the night was cold, Will had started a warm blaze in the fireplace.

"My God, Branch," Will burst out, "just what are you going to do?"

"I'll let you know when the time comes," his younger brother said obliquely, but his voice was firm and Mara sensed that he had long ago come to a decision. Her heart fell for she had hoped to entice him into the business end of *Mara Originals.* "Don't worry," Branch added with a touch of sarcasm, "I won't live off my inheritance and be a rich loafer."

"Now listen here, Branch," Will began, "you're a rich man and you owe it to yourself to—"

"Let him alone," Andrea cut in swiftly. "He needs a little time to himself, to make his peace with what he's done and the consequences of what has happened to him as a result of it." She paused, then looking at Branch with a strange mixture of triumph and compassion, she added, "You and Stuart would both be here, safe and whole, if you'd listened to me and the Colonel. It's going to take time to heal your conscience."

"Look to your own soul, my sister," Branch's voice crackled with bitter passion. "You carry a load heavier than I—the promise you exacted from us at the Colonel's deathbed—the secret *you* carry!"

"We all carry it!" Andrea's voice shook slightly and her eyes sought Will's, but he was looking at the wooden leg that extended just below Branch's trousers, a sad partner to the neat black shoe beside it.

"We're not going to quarrel the minute Branch has come home," Celia spoke up firmly, her face hot with anger as her dark eyes flashed at Andrea. She rose and deposited Betsey firmly on Branch's knees. "Here, get acquainted with your niece, Branch, dear, while I fix you a good toddy. I'll wager you could use one."

"I certainly could," he replied, holding the baby awkwardly as her slate blue eyes fixed on his. "I see you are all ready for Christmas," he added, his eyes leaving the baby and fixing on the tall, ornament-covered spruce that glittered in the corner.

Then cuddling the small bundle in his good arm, he stood upright and limping only slightly, walked to the tree, saying, "Look, Betsey. I'll bet Santa brings you a fuzzy little bear. Do you know fuzzy little bears?"

The seven-month-old cooed and reached up her dimpled hands to pat Branch's cheeks. Her little mouth was pursed for a kiss and Branch looked at her a moment, then buried his face in the soft sweet curve between shoulder and neck. "Merry Christmas, little one," he said thickly.

Mara felt her own throat tighten. If ever a broken heart showed, Branch's did. He had come home maimed, crippled, bereft of his best friend, only to be told by his sister that it was, in essence, his own fault, that he had brought it all on himself.

Damn Andrea and her sanctimonious superstitious self-righteousness! What was the secret she had imposed on Branch and Will? It had to do with their father. One of her premonitions, no doubt, Mara thought furiously. Stupid woman! Branch was a hero and should be greeted as one.

Will rose and went to stand beside his brother before the tree. He put an arm about his shoulder and spoke to him in a low voice. Mara could not make out what he said, but Branch shook his head and said clearly, "No, bud. I know what I'm going to do, and nothing will change my mind."

Will's voice rumbled argumentatively, then coaxingly, but Branch merely shook his head and spoke firmly, "I had to come back to see you all once more. And Andrea hasn't changed. Ah, well, she'll take some satisfaction when she knows the course I've chosen."

Supper that evening was subdued, though Christmas was only five days away. Andrea's glances at her crippled brother were full of love and compassion. The indefinable tincture of triumph was either well hidden or had vanished. Branch told them a little of the war, bitter anecdotes and pitiful tragedies, and for a little while he spoke of their victory, saying it would make the Americas more peaceful, with less danger from interference by a strong foreign power. But he told none of the amusing stories of which he had been a past master.

"You won't be leaving before Christmas, will you, Branch?" Will asked.

"No, I won't be leaving before Christmas," Branch replied with an enigmatic little smile.

"You should stay right here. You don't need to work," Andrea said vigorously. "You could read and you might write a book about the war."

It was the first constructive thing Mara had heard Andrea say and she looked at her searchingly.

"Yes, I could write a book," Branch said acidly, "but I don't think I will, Andrea." All traces of his good humor, his wit and charm had left him and Mara had the feeling she was looking at the empty shell of a man.

He was dextrous with his right hand and seemed to manage very well without the left one. She thought, *He could become quite independent again. He could even ride again, if he would only try.* It was simply a matter of balance and adjustment to his handicaps. Where was he going? Somewhere far away, she sensed, and a deep depression settled over her as she thought of it. She hadn't realized how deep-rooted had become her desire to have Branch in charge of finances and employees in *Mara Originals.* Too late for that, she thought dismally. He's made other plans, apparently ironclad.

The week before Christmas was frantic at *Mara Originals.* All of them worked overtime, the seamstresses willingly because it meant Christmas bonuses for them and Mara because she loved the business. Besides, at the end of December, she would make her final payment on the original loan Halloran had made her through the Houston National Bank.

Her ledger was not up to date and she dreaded the moment when she would have to sit down to the books and try to put all her invoices on paper. Like many artists and creators, Mara had a poor head for figures and it was all she could do to manage the single ledger she kept.

Christmas Eve, when the last satisfied customer went out into the late evening and the seamstresses departed, shiny eyed with their generous checks in hand, Mara sank down in the chair before her desk. It was littered with notes, bits of paper with figures on them. She only hoped she could remember them all. At least, she had put a name on each one, as the dress or piece of lingerie was completed. She had a separate box full of notes for baby clothes and layettes and it was full, too. She would have to enter them all in her single ledger. It was a good thing she had been able to meet each installment on her loan, she thought dismally, for her haphazard records would truly madden a banker or a lawyer.

Sudie had been the last to depart, protesting, "Mara, you

are too good to all of us and to me especially. You got to remember, though, that you're in business and you got to make a profit."

Mara hugged her and sent her on her way, with a larger check than the others, but Sudie's responsibilites were heavier. Mara depended on her more, and all the clients had come to rely on Sudie's nimble fingers and instinctive sense of fashion.

Looking at the paperwork that must be done filled her with sudden revulsion and she rose from the desk and went into the darkened Selection Parlor, where she sank down on a satin sofa. She looked at the mannequin in the window before her, gently lighted by bulbs hidden behind shades. The model wore an ivory satin evening dress, cut low over the bosom. Long, close-fitting satin sleeves clung to the model's arms, ending in little points over the backs of the extended hands. The model was half turned, her golden head tilted, and there was a suggestion of a train at the back of the draped and shirred satin skirt. The shirring above the hips softened the long slim lines.

It was a ballgown, but it could easily become a wedding dress by the simple addition of a veil. Mara visualized it dreamily. She had designed it with a wedding dress in mind, before her practical side asserted itself so she could have it both ways. She would let Elena sew encrusted pearls across the bosom and on the shirring if some young thing wanted it for her wedding. Mara never drew a dress without visualizing herself in it; even special orders from the dumpy Mrs. Marsh and the dumpier Mrs. Seagram, or even the lanky Mrs. Mellon, she drew with her own figure in mind. Perhaps that was why she was so brilliantly successful in slimming Mrs. Marsh and Mrs. Seagram and softening the bony Mrs. Mellon.

She looked beyond the window at the Christmas lights that lit the length of Congress Street. Any minute Sam would come rattling up in her small buggy to drive her home.

Then suddenly a strange sound assaulted her ears, growing in volume until it caused her to sit up in alarm. It sounded like one of Halloran's dredges in Buffalo Bayou, only faintly subdued.

Two lights appeared in the darkness beyond the windows and she saw the shape of something she had seen but once before when Will had taken them all to town to see what was called a horseless carriage. It was! It was a horseless carriage!

In the glow of the Christmas lights, she saw a familiar form climb out of it and walk swiftly to her door. Halloran, of course, she thought. He would be the one to ride about in a horseless carriage. Will had threatened to buy one himself, but Andrea had raised such a tumult about the inherent danger of such things that they had all read about in the papers. A French racing driver named Jenatzy had driven a French car at nearly seventy miles an hour, which seemed impossible. Both Andrea and Celia had begged Will not to buy such a dangerous vehicle.

But Mara had said nothing. She was vastly curious about the new means of transportation and only wished she had the money to buy one for herself.

Halloran pulled the bell and Mara switched on the light as she went to unlock the glass door.

"Good evening, Mara," he said, eyes gleaming with anticipation. "I called home and told Celia to cancel Sam's plans to come for you. I told her I had a surprise for all of them."

"I see," she said enviously. "You're driving one of the new horseless carriages."

"It's from Detroit, Michigan. It came in on the train just hours ago, with three others. William Marsh, Tom Henderson and John Delaney took delivery on the same model. The town will be full of them soon."

"I don't doubt it," Mara replied, going to her office to get her coat, hat and gloves. "How fast will it go?"

He had followed her into the spacious, but littered office. "It'll do better than twenty-five miles an hour, but that's fast enough for you, my dear. My God, this office looks like a twister hit it full on."

"We've done too much business too fast," she said defensively. "I couldn't keep up with the old ledger, and heaven knows how I'll get all those bills sent next month."

"You'd better let me ask around for an accountant for you."

"Not yet. I'm still going to ask Branch even though he'll probably turn me down. He's been home nearly a week and

I don't think he's smiled even once." Thinking of Branch's drawn face depressed her and took the glow of Christmas from her heart. She added doggedly, "But I intend to ask him anyway."

"You may be able to do what Will and I can't seem to do," he said soberly.

"I think he means to go away, back to Florida or somewhere."

"Has he said that?"

"Not in so many words. All he'll say is he's decided on his course of action. Whatever that is." She put on her coat and hat and took up her gloves.

"Well, don't sound so down about it. He's young and he'll come around, whatever he does. Come on and let me take you for a spin in my Winston Motorcar."

"Wait!" she cried, turning back. "I have two last packages to take home." And she caught up the gaily wrapped boxes from a chair in her office.

As they stepped out into the chill, damp night air, Mara turned and locked the door behind her, taking a last fleeting look at the mannequin in her Christmas windows. The whole length of windows was beautiful and it was hers, she exulted silently. Well, hers and Halloran's.

He assisted her up into the car and she removed a glove to run her hand over the cold leather cushions and put her packages on the floor. She could see the complicated panel before her. A tiller, such as she had seen on sailboats, protruded from it. Beyond that was the front of the car itself, a long piece of metal with a hinge running down the middle.

Halloran had taken up a strange twisted iron handle from the floor under the tiller and had gone to the front of the vehicle, where he thrust it into the motorcar and began turning it swiftly. The thing coughed to life under his efforts and Mara clung to the door as it vibrated under her.

Halloran leapt into the seat beside her and seized the tiller, turning it slowly, and the car moved away from the curb. Picking up speed they traveled down Congress Street bumpily. She hadn't realized the street paving was so rough and it seemed to her they were moving with increasing speed. She reached a hand up to her hat and the cold night wind blew her hair where it could reach it. She clung to the door. It seemed very noisy.

"Relax!" Halloran shouted. "I've had two hours instruction with the factory representative on how to drive. I'm an expert."

"Expert indeed," she shouted back. "Slow down!"

He threw back his head and laughed. "And you asked how fast it would go!"

"I don't want a demonstration—go slower!"

He slowed the car until they were traveling no faster than a brisk trot. "Don't you like it, Mara?"

"Oh, yes!" she said breathlessly. "It's takes a little getting use to, though."

He drove her up and down the city streets so they could admire the decorations in the shop windows and storefronts, the wreathed doors and the tinsel-wrapped light standards. So entranced was Mara with this new mode of travel that she did not even notice the chill wind that blew around them and her cheeks were becomingly pink when he drew to a stop in front of the Cotton Exchange Club.

"I also told the MacAdams I was taking you to Christmas Eve dinner," he grinned, helping her out of the car.

Inside the dining room, the air was fragrant with pine boughs and lighted bayberry candles along the window sills and mantels. Fresh holly decorated each table. Without thinking, she followed him into their usual private dining room and absently ordered from the long menu handed to her.

Mara had not noticed as the days hurriedly passed into weeks and months that she had not had time for any male company but that of John Halloran. Nor had she considered that she never saw him in the company of any woman other than herself. It did not occur to her that she had come to depend upon him for whatever diversion she had, for advice in her business, for consolation in her smallest disappointments and worries. If she had, she would have shrugged it off and said it was too minor to have any meaning.

When they drove up in the circular drive to the MacAdam house, lights shone warmly from almost every window and the brass chandelier on the porch flung spangles of light on the great holly wreath that hung in the center of the broad front door, which flew open as Halloran turned off the motor in the new car.

Will towered in the doorway and beside him were Celia and Andrea. Over their shoulders could be seen the servants, wide eyed as they all poured out onto the gallery.

"I see it arrived," shouted Will and they all streamed down the steps to the motorcar. Mara looked up to see Branch leaning in the doorway, unsmiling as always and with little interest in his blue eyes.

Halloran went to the back of the car and unlocked a luggage boot at the rear and began removing packages. "Here, Celia, Andrea, Will, all of you help me. You, too, Sam and Amos, and everybody. All my last minute Christmas is in here."

The smiling servants reached out to help and in a little while Halloran had emptied the boot, closed and locked it once more.

"By God, that's a fine piece of machinery, John!" Will said, running a hand over the upholstery, opening the door, then closing it again. "In the front seat and back seat you can carry six, John?"

"Yep. And the factory is sending down a top that can be attached by uprights, here, here and on the other side."

"They're very dangerous contraptions, John," Andrea said reprovingly. "I certainly don't intend to ever get in one."

"Ah, I'll have you in it in less than a week, Andrea," Halloran laughed.

"No, you won't," she retorted. "I just hope to heaven you don't get killed in it. I read about that man in France who drove one more than a mile a minute. That's terrible!"

The servants had gone all around the car, touching its different parts gingerly. "Reckon I might git inter one o' them things, if I had the chance," Sam said, grinning.

"Get ready to learn how to drive one, Sam," Will Mac-Adam said, grinning back at the coachman. "You'll be chauffeuring Mrs. MacAdam around in one of them one of these days."

"Better put your order in now," Halloran said. "It's taken them four months to deliver mine, Rice's, Marsh's and Delaney's."

"You mean those three came in today, too?" Will asked incredulously.

"Yep. The town'll be alive with 'em soon."

"I'll bet it won't," Andrea said derisively. "It's a fad and you'll be stuck with it after the new wears off."

"What makes it run without a horse?" Amos asked. "Electricity, like the trolley cars?"

"No, Amos, gasoline. It's a gasoline-combustion engine."

"Where you get this gasoline?" Amos asked.

"It's refined from oil, Will, that's why I'm after that little hill called Spindletop over at Beaumont. This country's going to need plenty of oil."

"I know, I know. You've convinced me. I'm going to invest more in that land with you, I swear it. Now, come on in out of the night air and have a drink," Will said, his laughter warm and welcoming.

They all trooped back into the house and the presents were put at the base of the tall tree, where there was already a small mountain of them. Mara noticed that Branch followed them and stood looking at the tree and the presents, a curious grief in his eyes and the set of his fine mouth.

Mara suddenly sensed that he had come home to say good-bye to all of this, that he had gone over home in his mind a thousand times, yearningly, lovingly while he lay on his hospital bed and that now he looked on it for one last time. As she surreptitiously observed him his eyes swung to the Colonel above the mantel, tall, imperious but kindly withal. What was he thinking as he looked at that handsome soldier, the man they had all loved so devotedly?

The excitement of Christmas Eve had gripped them all and the servants were loathe to leave the room. They hung about, picking up the packages with their names on them, shaking them, laughing with each other in anticipation.

Will gave each of them a brandy and everyone toasted the season before they left for their quarters. He tried to get Halloran to spend the night with them as it was already near midnight. Betsey had been in her crib for hours, Celia remarked.

"No. I'll be here early in the morning, but I've got to get my new mortorcar into my stable. It looks like rain and I don't want the upholstery to get wet, even though the manufacturer says a certain amount of the elements won't harm it."

And when he was gone, the family lingered in the parlor, looking at the ornamented tree. Will had forbidden the usual lighted candles because, he said firmly, the danger of fire was too great, but Andrea had complained.

"It just doesn't look right without the candles on Christmas Eve, Will. I think you're a killjoy."

"No, Andrea. No lighted candles. I've seen too many bad burns in houses at Christmas."

"The Colonel always let us have lighted candles," she replied sharply, her eyes going to the portrait.

"I'm not the Colonel," Will replied slowly. "And if you remember further, he was always very careful about it."

"In fact, the worst whipping I ever got was for taking a candle off the tree and putting it back on crooked," Branch said, his mouth twisting in a sardonic smile.

"Branch, there's an awful lot under this tree with your name on it," Celia said, putting out a hand and drawing him into the group about the tree.

"I'm sorry, Celia," he replied, swallowing hard, "but there's only one present from me under the tree and it's for Betsey."

"That was thoughtful of you," Celia said, standing on tiptoe to kiss his cheek. "And it's quite enough of a present to have you with us again. None of us could ask for a better one."

"You're a kind person, Celia," he replied low. "I wonder how my brother—I hope he deserves you."

Celia blushed hotly and her eyes flew to Will, who smiled at her blandly and said, "I try, Branch, I try."

"I don't suppose you'll ever marry now, Branch," Andrea said with unconscious cruelty. "I mean with your arm gone and your leg gone."

"You're right, of course, Andrea. No one would have half a man. My courting days are over, but it doesn't matter much anyway." Branch's blue eyes looked unseeingly at Mara and she knew that in his mind he had already fled to some far country.

"Well, you certainly brought it on yourself, Branch," Andrea said flatly. "I tried to warn you. Even the Colonel tried to warn you, but you were uncaring and bullheaded. And now you'll have to live with the consequences."

"You're wrong about that, Andrea," Branch replied quietly and he turned and left the room.

"I guess he's going to bed. I didn't know cripples could be so touchy and grouchy. Branch is a different man than the one who left here last spring," Andrea said as he disappeared.

"You don't help much, Andrea," Will said, his voice hard. "I want you to lay off that kind of talk to Branch, always reminding him about your warnings." His black frown at her was forbidding, and she shrugged, spreading her hands.

"He's got to face up to the fact he's handicapped and can never lead a normal life again," she said.

"He *can* lead a normal life and he will! You just lay off. You hear me? I mean it, Andrea. I can make your life rather unpleasant," her brother said and there was iron in the words. "And I promise I will if you keep picking at Branch."

"Well, I love him, too," she said plaintively, "and you know it."

"Then show it by being cheerful and constructive with him," her brother retorted. "I think it's time we all went to bed."

As Mara went to her room uneasiness spread through her. Something was very wrong and she did not know what it was. Her chest felt constricted and her throat was dry and she couldn't get Branch's whitening face out of her mind. She slowly disrobed and put on her peach velvet dressing gown, feeling driven by unseen furies, and her turmoil grew. She was breathing fast as she went into the bathroom and brushed her teeth.

She hadn't finished when the compulsion to go to Branch and ask him to come into *Mara Originals* clamped her in a vise. She rinsed her mouth, putting the brush aside. Haste was suddenly imperative.

Drying her hands quickly, she belted the robe tightly and almost ran from her room. She sped down the hall to Branch's door. She was under such compulsion, she did not knock, but flung the door open and burst into the room.

Branch sat on the bed. One lamp was burning. He held a

pistol in his hand and was slowly drawing it up to his head. He seemed oblivious to Mara, who poised in the open door.

So this was why he had told Andrea he wouldn't have to live with it! He intended to die with it. He had come home to bid his family good-bye and take his life!

Mara flung herself headlong across the room and he looked at her with wide unseeing eyes as she sprang forward, seizing his arm. It seemed to waken him, for he began to struggle with her and he was strong. His right arm was like iron and slowly he drew it up again to his temple, even with Mara hanging on it with her full weight.

"Get out of here, Mara," he said thickly. "I've waited a long time for this."

He was still fully clothed and Mara knew he meant the family to find his body so.

Chapter 16.

❧ "You can't do this, Branch," she said low, struggling to pull his arm down.

"You little fool! Get away from me. Don't you know this gun could go off with you pulling on me, and kill *you?*"

"I won't let you shoot yourself, Branch. I need you too much!" She clung to his right arm tenaciously.

Suddenly it loosened in her grasp, hung down, but still his hand gripped the pistol.

"You need me?" The words were incredulous and his blue eyes narrowed on her face. His curved mouth twisted down. "What kind of a joke is this, Mara?"

"It's no joke," she replied fiercely, panting from her desperate exertion. She tried to keep her voice down because Andrea's room was next to Branch's. "Besides, do you want Andrea running in here and hysterically proclaiming the Colonel's portrait falling had foretold your death?"

His mouth twisted deeper and a bitter little laugh shook him. "And she would, too," he said, his voice mocking. "But you needn't add a lie to her hysteria."

"What lie?" she asked in quiet violence. "Don't you know what a mess the financial end of *Mara Originals* is? I can't keep books, send out invoices, keep peace among my seamstresses *and* design dresses and lingerie at the same time! I desperately need a partner with a business head who can manage the money while I fashion clothes." Out of breath she stopped, and as she did, a sharp rap sounded on the door.

"Branch? Branch?" It was Andrea's imperious voice. "What's going on in there?" She turned the knob and entered to find Mara seated on the bed beside Branch. He had swiftly tucked the gun beneath the pillow. "What are you two doing? Branch, you know you can't—"

"Never mind what I can't do, sister dear," Branch retorted, a faint trace of his old insouciance creeping into his voice. "Mara and I are having a *business talk*. It includes you *out*, Andrea." Then with downturned lip and bitter sarcasm, *"If* you don't mind, of course."

"But I—"

"Really, Andrea," Mara spoke up with tart anger, "I'm discussing *Mara Originals* with Branch. Does that satisfy you?"

Andrea stood a moment longer, staring at her fully clad brother and Mara's beautiful warm dressing gown. Then stiffly, "I should think you'd find the library a more appropriate place for such a discussion."

"Andrea, I'll do business where I choose," Branch returned and then brutally, "get yourself out of here."

She closed the door with a bang behind her, and Branch rose, went to it and turned the key in the lock. "Just in case she changes her mind, as she is so prone to do." He grinned, and in the lamplight, Mara recognized a trace of wonder in the light blue eyes fixed on her dark ones.

Smiling, she casually put her hand over the gun under the pillow.

"Never mind, missy," he said sharply. "I won't use it. You've done what I thought no one or nothing in the world could ever do again. You've interested me."

Mara drew a deep breath. "Then sit down and let me tell you what I want to offer you."

He took the gun and seated himself across from her in a broad cushioned chair and leaned back stiffly. "I'm listening."

"I need a manager, someone who can keep books, someone who knows how to bill people and to help me make up my mind what price the public will pay for the types of things I produce. Someone to keep peace between four fighting Irish women and two Mexican spitfires. Oh, they're not mean, just temperamental like all creative people. Only Sudie can get along with all of them." She paused. "I'm going to Europe next year, to buy materials and accessories and I need someone to go with me, to squire me through the great fashion designer houses of

Paris and London. I haven't told that to a soul, Branch, so don't mention it yet. I've always admired your taste and I think you could be of inestimable help to me."

His ice blue eyes were clear and sharp now and the lines that held his face drawn had loosened. Magically, he looked once more the twenty-five-year-old man that he was.

"How fortunate for me," he said softly, "to have a little sister, pardon me, a little sister-in-law—with such talents and with such *needs*. You've almost convinced me."

She spread her hands. "What would it take to convince you? I'll tell you another well-kept secret you must never tell. John Halloran set me up in business and he owns fifty percent of it. I've paid him back the original fifteen thousand it took to get started. But I know he'll go along with me. In fact, we've already discussed it."

"You discussed *me?*"

"We did."

"You mean this wasn't done just off the top of your head to stop me from—"

"Absolutely not. You can ask John himself. He knows I was going to tell you about the arrangement and he's willing to pay his share of whatever it takes to persuade you to help me."

Branch was silent, his stare unwavering. "You mean you'll hire someone with half a body for such a beautiful establishment? Take half a body on buying trips with you under the delusion that a cripple can escort you with safety?" His questions held all the old, bitter grief.

"You might as well face it, Branch," she said, as matter-of-factly as the sharp businesswoman she was, "most people will look on you as a romantic figure, a hero home from the war. You're a handsome man and you have a *whole* head, full of education and common sense, and business experience."

"I'll be damned," he said softly. "I'll be damned if you haven't convinced me. But I'll talk to John Halloran just the same, if you don't mind."

"I'll be glad for you to talk to him," she replied, rising and crossing the room before him. "Now if you'll give me that gun, I'll go to bed. We can tell the family over break-

fast in the morning that you've taken a job managing
Mara Originals."

"Thanks," he laughed dryly, "but I'll keep my gun. Oh,
don't worry. I give you my word that I've lost all interest in
using it as a means of exit from this world." He rose and
unlocked the door for her. His walk had been with only the
barest trace of a limp, and as she went through the opening he bent his tall body and dropped a kiss on her tumbled
hair.

"Good-night—and Merry Christmas, little sister."

"Good-night, Branch—and thanks."

That Christmas morning had been the merriest Mara
could ever remember. All of them were surprised and delighted over Branch's new position at *Mara Originals,*
even the astonished Andrea.

And even the fact that Celia had invited Ashworth and
Aunt Felice to dinner did not dampen Mara's joy.

Sudie had kept Mara informed about Ashworth and Felice during the long months. She knew that Aunt Felice
had made herself indispensable to him since Celia and
Mara had left. *I think he's gone an' fallen in love with her,
Mara,* Sudie had said, *an' Miss Felice isn't the same at all.
She's plumb sweet an' kind most of the time. And she give
up all her society doin's an' goes to the store with him every
day.*

Ashworth's was doing well, too. Mara had heard that
from several sources. Halloran had told her that Ashworth
was contemplating construction of a modest mansion in
Houston Heights, so Mara knew money was being made,
now that the aunts and uncles were paid off. Mara herself
had contributed more than half of that pay-off.

Still, in her heart lay that cold hard memory of what he
had done to her, the things he had said about her mother,
the names he had called Mara herself, and the anguished
years of his cold watchfulness. No, she could not forgive or
forget, but it was Christmas and she let the warm pleasure
of the season take her

Besides, Ashworth and Felice did not arrive until noon
and the morning hours had been filled with laughter and
jokes, for Branch had returned to them on a tidal wave of
humor. He teased Andrea. He even seized her with his

right arm and made her do a small dervish with him, while Celia played Christmas carols after all the presents were opened.

"Andy," he told her merrily, "if you'd forget your grief over the Colonel half a minute, James Phillips would sure come a-courting you," then sobering slightly, "and all three of the Phillips brothers came back with nary a scratch on 'em."

He let her go, then caught up Betsey, who squealed with delight, holding the small stuffed brown bear Branch had given her, the favorite of all the toys she had received.

Andrea, watching them, fingered her chin, frowning. She was on the verge of speaking, when Will's warning glance caught her and she shrugged, turning away.

The servants had opened their presents earlier with the family and were now in the kitchen, heartened by a dollop of Christmas brandy, preparing the feast to come.

Celia played on until Halloran knocked at the door about ten in the morning. And more merriment followed as his many gifts were unwrapped.

After the sumptuous Christmas dinner which Ashworth and Aunt Felice attended, Mara left with Halloran and Branch, ostensibly to try out the new automobile, but actually to get their heads together over *Mara Originals* and the addition of Branch MacAdam to its staff. That Mara did not have to endure the company of the Ashworths added further to her pleasure as they drove away.

Branch was properly awed by Halloran's new car but declined to try it at the tiller. Halloran laughed and said, "In another couple of years, I'll lay you a thousand dollars to one that you'll be driving one of these, Branch."

"I'll need to gain a little more confidence in my capabilities before that, John," he said honestly. "Right now, I'm not sure I could sit a horse well."

When they reached *Mara Originals*, Mara showed Branch her office.

"It will be yours from now on, Branch. I'll stay in the room I had blocked off where I do my sketches and have my draft boards and easels. All my paper and colored inks are kept there, too." As they entered it, she added, "See? It's not as large as the office, but I furnished it quite well, I think."

Branch looked down at her with a little smile, his eyes twinkling. "I think the whole layout is positively sensational. The addition you put in while I was gone makes it quite a posh establishment. I think it qualifies as a fashion house." He laughed suddenly. "You know, I always did have the secret idea that I was a frustrated artist."

"I know you have a streak of art in you, Branch," Mara said earnestly. "I remember when you used to comment on the clothes at the opera openings and the balls you attended. You were quite succinct and on the mark."

"Branch MacAdam, couturier par excellence," grinned Halloran. "Frankly, I don't know a damn thing about it, but I sure as hell know when a woman looks good to me in something."

"And you sure as hell have the money to dabble in the business," Mara said bitingly. Sometimes the things he said irritated her beyond measure. So he looked at other women and knew when they looked desirable to him. She wondered fleetingly where he went for such pleasures now that Bonnie's house was sold. To her further annoyance, she flushed unexpectedly.

He was looking at her in some surprise, having never heard her swear, but he said nothing. *He should know the things I sometimes think!* And Mara turned to Branch.

"You're sure five hundred a month will be enough for all that you will be doing, Branch?" she asked anxiously.

"You know I don't need the money as much as I need the job, Mara my dear. But you and John have given me more than I expected. And I intend to invest in the business if you'll let me. Ten percent of a business as lucrative as this would be great. Do you realize, Mara, that you could have shops in Dallas and San Antonio, perhaps someday in New York?"

Mara laughed aloud. "Now how would I ever manage *that?*"

"You wouldn't. I would. Your originals would still be originals in distant cities."

"You make me doubly glad that you're in with me, Branch. My visions didn't extend so far." Mara shook her head doubtfully, and Halloran unexpectedly caught her small hand in his big warm one.

"Just don't become too obsessed with it, Mara. Take

time to live. It can be fun, you know." His black eyes were fastened on hers and she recognized the brief flame of desire that was at once hidden in their depths.

But she extricated her hand, still feeling his rough warmth after she slipped her glove on. "It *is* my life," she said firmly. "And I *am* living every minute that I'm involved in it."

He shrugged and his eyes went blank and courteous. "You know what you want, I guess. In fact, you're the only woman I ever met who knew exactly what she wanted and got it." There was not a trace of humor in his voice as he said it and she felt oddly uneasy the balance of the day.

During the month of January, after Branch took over her office duties, things went amazingly well. Mara was astounded at how much she was able to increase her volume. She had never had time actually to sell her designs before.

Now, with Branch taking care of the many receipts, bills and ledgers, she found more time to consult with her customers and personally advise them.

Branch put innovative advertisements with her sketches in the *Post* and this increased her clientele. But it all meant extra work for her seamstresses, who were delighted by the increased bonuses they received as a result. Further, they had developed a warm camaraderie among themselves under Branch's gentle and humorous prodding.

Houston was growing prodigiously and *Mara Originals* was growing with it. Fortunes were being made in cattle, cotton, lumber and merchandising. There was even a respectable amount of shipping, which had to be carried on through Galveston.

In this latter, John Halloran had succeeded in prodding the Congressional Commission on Rivers and Harbors into coming and examining Buffalo Bayou with a view to government help in making it into a ship channel. Fortuitously, it rained a deluge just before they came, making the little bayou into quite a respectable river and the commission went away with glowing reports, which the Houston Committee for Deep Water celebrated for several days.

Meantime, money from these newly rich men, and their

women in Houston flowed into *Mara Originals* in an increasing flood. Mara, with her own sewing machine beside her drawing boards, lost herself and her sense of time as she created special confections with her own fingers.

Bonnie Fairweather came by in the middle of February. She had Dominique with her, and Desmond Brant sat in the driver's seat of the Victoria, which she kept in Houston for her special trips to the city from her Galveston home. Desmond had to double-park on the broad street before Mara's shop. The salon of the shop was extraordinarily crowded with women this day, who lifted their brows and moved studiedly away from Bonnie's proximity.

But they did not leave the shop, not even when Mara greeted Bonnie warmly and escorted her back into her personal designing room.

"I thought sure you'd bring Fleurette, Bonnie. I'm so anxious to meet her! She did come home with you, didn't she?"

Bonnie made a wry face. "Of course she did, but you saw those old cats in your salon, looking as if a rattler had somehow slipped in. I hated to even leave Dominique among them."

Mara rose immediately and stepped into the hall, calling Dominique to join them, and Branch MacAdam opened the door of his office curiously. He watched as the little black French Haitian smiled gratefully before passing him and going into Mara's office.

"Hi, Dominique," Branch said, following her in, where he went straight to Bonnie and brushed her cheek with a kiss. "Welcome home, Bonnie, dear," he said.

Bonnie reached up and pulled him back down for a sound kiss. "Just as handsome as ever, I see." She laughed. "The war didn't change you at all."

"Thanks," he said dryly, his face darkening, "for not being maudlin and telling me how sorry you are about my leg and arm."

"What leg and arm? You look wholly yourself, Branch MacAdam, only more of a *man* now."

"Thank God *you* haven't changed, Bonnie," he said and with his barely discernible limp, he left abruptly, closing the door on the three women.

"Now tell me about your trip and Fleurette," Mara began after seating herself on the large sofa beside Bonnie.

"Fleurette's at home, my dear, in Galveston. She knows nothing of my past here in Houston. I'm at my wits end how to keep her there. She's dying to come to Houston to shop."

"Bring her here, Bonnie."

"Oh, Mara, I can't bear for her to face these women, as they look at me with such loathing, pulling their skirts aside!"

"Bring her next Sunday then. I'll open the shop just for you and Fleurette." She smiled at Dominique. "And Dominique, of course."

"That would be too much trouble for you, Mara."

"Don't be contrary, Bonnie. Nothing would be too much trouble for you and Fleurette. You can explain to your daughter that I do it for a very special friendship between us."

Bonnie sighed. "You are the sort of girl I want her to know, to associate with, bright, independent, talented. Did you know she won several honors for her paintings?"

"Why, no! You never told me."

"You are very nearly the same age. She was eighteen on August fifth."

"And I was eighteen on August second! We are virtually the same age. Oh, I do look forward to meeting her! Perhaps we can go to Sunday dinner at the Houston Hotel together after you choose your fashions. You saw my new accessory corner, didn't you?"

"I caught a glimpse as we went by. It looks delicious!"

"You should recognize some of the belts and scarves and jewelry. They were shipped in from France—Paris, no less."

Dominique spoke up in a burst of French, smiling and gesturing.

Bonnie said, "Dominique went with me everywhere in Europe. She knew your accessories were from France. She and Fleurette converse in French all the time. I know only a little of the language." She launched then into a description of the places they had been, the sights and adventures that had awaited them. Bonnie had many friends in Paris, where she was respected greatly as a wealthy American widow.

"Did Desmond go along, too?" Mara asked delicately.

"Of course not, darling! Desmond is my financial manager. He stayed home to manage my investments and interests. He doles me out an allowance each month." She laughed merrily. "That is, until I tell him to give me more, which he promptly does. If you are wondering about our relationship, let me assure you it is strictly platonic and has been for years. To be sure, he lives in my house, but what house is safe without a man in it? But he is an employee, just as Dominique is."

"I think he loves you, Bonnie, and you're too young and too beautiful not to remarry."

"My dear, I assure you that if I ever find the right man— and it isn't Desmond—I would marry in a moment." She shrugged lightly and her voice lowered. "For ladies my age, all the right men are already married."

"Personally, I don't intend to ever marry," Mara said briskly. "I like my independence too well." But as she said it something deep and hurtful turned slowly inside her and her hands grew moist. To her dismay, she found Halloran's handsome face behind her eyes and she put it aside determinedly. "Yes, it's a single life for me. I'm in love with my business."

Bonnie looked at her cryptically and her little smile was only faintly cynical as she said, "Independence is fine. I know. But don't wait too long, darling Mara. Don't wait too long."

When Bonnie had gone, Mara took up her pen and sketchpad with a vigor that had a touch of desperation to it. She could lose herself in designing. She *knew* she could. She had done it! And without the unwelcome thoughts of Halloran intruding. She had been a fool to let the man become such an integral part of her life, but how could she have avoided it?

He was always *there*, at every turn. He had been the first to encourage her about designing on that long-ago train trip to Houston. He had been the one who convinced Ashworth to let her run *Ashworth Originals.* He had been there to rescue her from the storm, when she had been shattered by the knowledge that Archer Ashworth was not her father—and worse—had raped her. He had taken her to Bonnie where she had recovered, mind and body, and he had lent her the money for this very spot where she so successfully sat. More than that, he had anticipated her need for more room and had arranged that very neatly.

Oh, yes, she thought bitterly, John Halloran had made himself very nearly indispensable, but where had he been the last few weeks? In any case he didn't want marriage and she certainly didn't want what he was offering instead.

She flung her pen aside and pushed the sketch beside it. Rising, she swept from the room and went into Branch's office, where he was bent over the double entry bookkeeping ledger.

"I've a headache, Branch. I'm going home early. I may be coming down with a cold."

He leaned back and surveyed her. "You look very healthy," he drawled. "In fact, quite beautiful, little sister, but a day off would do you good. You've been at this business hammer and tongs too much lately. Take the buggy and you can send Sam after me at five."

She turned, but before she closed the door, she said, "I'll see you at dinner tonight, Branch."

When she pulled up in the drive of the MacAdam house, she saw a fine Victoria, with two glossy bays in harness, tied to the iron horsehead post. Celia had visitors, she thought. Well, maybe they would divert her. She was thinking still that it had been nearly three weeks since she had seen John Halloran.

Sam, hearing the buggy on the gravel, came out of the house at a lope and took the reins from her hands, then assisted her down.

"Sam, Branch is at the shop. He'd appreciate it if you came for him about five in the buggy."

"Yes'm. I will." He grinned broadly. "Can't you smell spring in this air, Miss Mara, an' look at them jonquils an' them sprangling forsythia bushes. Like ladies in full yeller skirts."

She was delighted by the poetry in the coachman's words. "You're right, Sam. I drove all the way home without noticing. Guess I've had my nose to the grindstone too long." Then as he started away, "Sam, who's visiting us?"

He looked uncomfortable. "Your paw, Mister Ashworth, come by to see Miss Celia, but she's gone to th' Ladies' Musical an' he's a-waitin'." Even the servants were keenly aware of the estrangement between Mara and the man they believed to be her father.

"Aunt Felice with him?" she asked shortly.

"No'm. Not this time."

As Sam took the vehicle around the side drive, she took the steps to the porch and opened the door resolutely, determined to pass the parlor as swiftly as possible. As she did so, Ashworth saw her and rose, calling out, "Mara—wait!"

"What is it?" she asked curtly, but her heart beat hard with the echo of fears, old apprehensions she had known even as she had loved him with a child's singlemindedness. He was holding a bourbon and water in one hand and had just lit a long slim cigar. She noticed that there was more gray at the temples of his springy copper-bright hair and a slight tremor in the big hand holding the bourbon.

"I want to talk to you. Celia and I have discussed our quarrel and she is determined to make it up between us." He hesitated as her icy glance flicked him. "In fact, I was coming to the shop—your shop—to talk to you about it. She's persuaded me that enough time has passed by—over a year—and after all, you are my daughter."

She burst out laughing. "I didn't think you'd ever have the gall to call me *that!*"

"Legally, you're my daughter," he said doggedly. "And you belong at home with your aunt and me." He hesitated and reached out to grasp her arm, adding, "Come sit down and talk with me."

She pulled her arm away. "We have nothing to say to each other. You said it all, the night I left. And we finished it the day you had the incredible nerve to come to my hotel room." But the old pull asserted itself and she followed him reluctantly into the parlor, where he seated himself on one of the broad divans. She took a chair across from him.

"We might as well get it over," she said slowly and deliberately. "Our quarrel will never be resolved and I shall never set foot under your roof again."

"Now, Mara, hear me out! Madame Choisse has gone back to New Orleans and taken her flighty brood of seamstresses with her. *Ashworth Originals* is shut down. I have a business proposition for you, Mara." He became persuasive. "I'll buy the store next to mine, the one old Mrs. Winters owns, but her husband's died and she wants to sell it. I'll buy it and fix you the finest fashion salon in the country. You can keep your name, *Mara Originals,* and be associated with *Ashworth's.*"

She was silent, astonished by his wheedling tone and his apparent humbleness. Her heart had slowed but it still beat heavily.

"I *need* you, Mara. *Ashworth's* needs you. Oh, I'm doing a *good* business but with *Mara Originals* bringing in the cream of Houston's wealth, we could become the biggest, most prestigious store in Texas." He smiled at her, his teeth white against his coppery mustache and muttonchop whiskers. Still she made no answer.

"Mara, I was drunk the night you ran away," he said coaxingly. "You must believe me, my dear. I was so drunk I have no recollection of what I said or did to make you take such drastic actions." His voice was soft and as paternally kind as it was when he spoke to Celia. "Honestly, Mara, I've been really under a strain, trying to remember what happened. I have only a vague remembrance of my brandy bottle falling and—I—do remember you coming into the library. Beyond that—" He let out a gusty sigh and leaned back on the divan. "It's all a blank in my mind. Felice says she went to Julius after you left and between them they got me to bed. I remember nothing until I wakened the next morning."

She studied him thoughtfully trying to stem the tide of uneasiness, and as the silence between them began to draw out he shifted and reddened under her scrutiny. "Felice showed me your torn dressing robe and gown, said she found it in your room after you'd left. If I struck you hard enough to do that, I can understand your anger, but I swear to you I didn't mean it. I was so torn up over Celia's elopement—and that's all you can call her marriage at the time—an elopement, that I got blind drunk." He spread his hands. "That's all there is to it. Surely you're old enough now to understand and forgive a father for that."

"You aren't my father." The words were low and strangled.

"Did I say that? All right. I'll admit your mother was pregnant when I returned from my buying trip abroad, but that doesn't matter. You've been my daughter all these years."

"Have you told Celia I'm her half sister?"

"No," he said swiftly, "and I'd appreciate it if *you* wouldn't."

"I have no intention of telling it to anyone *unless you try to force me to return to your business or your home.*" There! She had got out the words, but they did not ease her nameless fears.

"Now, Mara, I'm offering you what amounts to a great deal of money."

"I'm making a great deal of money." Her voice was steadier now.

"But I can offer you more now that my sisters are paid off."

"I don't see how, Mr. Ashworth."

He winced. "Must you be so unkind?"

"We've been over this before. You didn't strike me the night I left your house. I've told you exactly what you did to me that night." She looked at him fleetingly and realized her voice was sounding faintly shaken again.

He put down his glass and laid the cigar on a porcelain dish to put a hand to his eyes. "No, no." His voice was muffled. "Don't say it again. I can't bear it!"

"You can believe it. *I* wasn't drunk that night. And I'll tell it, I swear, if you try to force me to return to your house." This time the words sounded stronger, more defiant.

His face was pained. "I'm not trying to force you, Mara. I'm trying to *reason* with you. You loved me once, I know you did."

"So I did. You destroyed it completely."

"Mara, for God's sake be reasonable! As God is my witness, I don't remember any of that night. Can't you—is there no forgiveness in you?"

The sound of wheels on the gravel drive came to them,

and from nowhere, Rosita appeared and glided to the front door, opening it to Celia. How much of her conversation with Ashworth had Rosita overheard? Probably all of it. Well, she thought bitterly, it should afford the servants an interesting diversion.

"Oh, it was a lovely concert, Rosita! Where's Betsey?"

"She ees upstairs een her leetle bed, asleep like an angel, Mees Celia. Your padre an' seester are een zee parlor."

"Oh!" It was a cry of pure gladness, and without removing her hat and gloves or her cape, Celia ran into the parlor. "You two have been talking! Oh, Mara—Papa. I'll bet you've made up your silly quarrel!"

"I've been trying," Ashworth said with a fair approximation of wistful hope.

"Oh, Mara, surely now that you've talked—" She stood poised, her lovely face wreathed in a smile of joy. "It would make me so happy!"

Mara rose. She, too, still wore her hat, with her coat over her arm, her gloves in one clenched hand. "Celia, dear, I'm afraid things are still the same between us. Now if you both will excuse me, I'm going upstairs. I have a beastly headache." She moved away.

As she went through the door she heard Celia say, "Oh, Pa, don't look so heartbroken! At least you talked."

"Celia, darling, I offered her practically half the store if she'd come home."

Mara slowed, listening. A feeling of oppression shortened her breath.

"Papa, dearest, she'll think about it. I just know she will." Then with quick vehemence, "I'll *never* give up trying to get my family all together again. Never!"

Mara moved on down the hall. Oppression grew and became a sense of dread. She loved Celia dearly and she understood her eagerness for a family reconciliation. But if she knew the truth of the matter, it would alter Celia's feelings forever. Mara wondered fleetingly if Celia would love her less as a half sister. No, she thought with a little smile, it would likely make Celia all the more protective of her.

Anyway the confrontation with Ashworth had driven Halloran out of her mind and now he returned forcefully. Why hadn't he come around to *Mara Originals* lately?

Well, she thought grimly, I've paid off his original investment and Branch can just mail him his percentage of the profits.

As for Ashworth, perhaps he *didn't* remember all that clearly. Perhaps she should give him the benefit of a doubt. For Celia's sake, she decided to be more courteous to him, but that would be all.

She drew a deep breath as she took the stairs. Why she should be suffocating under a feeling of doom was ridiculous. She squared her shoulders and assured herself that nothing bad could happen. She had weathered the worst Ashworth could do. Yet it was as if the dim future held some unbearable disaster, and it was waiting patiently for her.

At the end of February, Branch took Halloran a check for his half of the receipts and came back with the news that Halloran was ready to board the train for New York on a million-dollar lumber deal for *MacAdam & Halloran.* He would be gone a month.

Then late in March, when spring perfumed by oleander and jasmine whispered along every greening limb, Bonnie Fairweather called and asked if she and Fleurette could come see *Mara Originals* the next Sunday.

When Mara announced to the family that she would not be home for Sunday dinner but was instead going to the shop first, then to dine with Mrs. Fairweather and her daughter afterward, Celia looked at her with pleading eyes.

"Darling," she said from the sofa where she played with Betsey, "you know what the town thinks of that woman—I mean, of Mrs. Fairweather. Please don't make a friend of her."

Will looked over the edge of the Sunday *Post* and his blue eyes were narrow and watchful, but he said nothing.

"Celia, you know Mrs. Fairweather is one of my best customers. I expect her daughter, Fleurette, to be one, too. Besides, dear, *if* Bonnie Fairweather ever engaged in what all the good ladies think, she doesn't do such now. She's moved to Galveston and you can't make me believe such things of her there."

Celia's delicate dark brows drew together. "But Mara—"

"Besides, whoever heard of a bordello becoming a museum?" Mara smiled. "And really, darling, you know the old Fairweather mansion is becoming famous as a museum." She noticed Will's broad shoulders shaking imperceptibly behind the paper as he concealed a sudden laugh.

Branch did not bother to conceal his. "Sis," he said to Celia, "she has you there. Bonnie entertained in that museum all right, but it was all a matter of business, investments and the like."

Andrea spoke up. "I'm sure it *was* business," she said with cold sarcasm. "And I'm sure she *entertained* all her male guests. And Mara, of course, will do as she always does, just as she chooses." Her pale eyes flicked Mara contemptuously.

"Let me drive you to the shop, Mara," Branch said with an angry glance at his sister. "I need to go over the books. Then, if I wouldn't be intruding, I'd like to escort you ladies to dine at the Cotton Exchange Club."

"I'll bet they won't admit Mrs. Fairweather and her daughter," Andrea said bitingly.

"Admit her, hell. She could *buy* the place," Branch exploded.

"Besides, Andrea," Will said casually, turning a page of the paper with a rustle, "I've seen Mrs. Fairweather at the Exchange Club many times."

Celia looked at him searchingly, and Mara thought she detected something like hurt in her dark-fringed eyes, but she said nothing to her husband.

Instead, Andrea said caustically, "I'm sure *you* have indeed, Will."

"Come on, Mara," Branch said roughly, taking her arm. "Let's go."

Mara was relieved when they reached the shop to find that Bonnie and her daughter had not yet arrived. Branch unlocked the door with his key and they entered, closing the screen door behind them and leaving the glass door with its delicate gold lettering, *Mara Originals,* open to the cooling Gulf breeze. Mara moved quietly to turn on the whispering ceiling fans throughout the rooms and a gentle fragrance permeated the silk and velveted rooms.

Branch crossed the main salon, and paused with his hand on his office door. He said, "Mara, you know Bonnie's a good person. She couldn't help what happened to her after she got to Houston and had to make her own way at seventeen. She never told me, but she told Will that her family had thrown her out on her own because—well, because of Fleurette."

"You don't need to explain to me," Mara said softly. "I know. I think she's brave and very kind."

"You're one in a million, Mara," he said, with an oblique smile, "but then I knew that the moment I met you." And he turned and went into his office, closing the door.

When Bonnie and Fleurette arrived, Mara met them at the door with a warm smile, looking over their shoulders at Desmond, where he sat at the reins of Bonnie's Victoria by the curb. After greeting the two, she said, "Do you want to have Desmond come on in, too?"

"No," Bonnie smiled, waving to him, "he's going to the local saloon and enjoy himself for an hour or two. He'll lunch there, too." The Victoria moved off under Desmond's direction as she spoke.

Once inside, Mara turned a frank gaze on Fleurette. Her features were aquiline and sculptured as finely as Bonnie's, but her hair was a rich, chestnut brown. There was one word that came to Mara's mind as she looked at the girl. Sparkling. That was the only way to describe her, the flash in her green eyes, her dazzling smile and white, white teeth in a faintly olive-skinned face.

"You're beautiful, Fleurette," Mara said honestly, "but being Bonnie's daughter, I knew you would be."

"And Mama told me you were exquisite. She was right." Fleurette's smile was as genuine and warm as Mara's. It faded and her lips parted slightly as her eyes widened, going beyond Mara. *"Mon Dieu,"* she whispered.

Mara turned swiftly to see that Branch had come out of the office and stood leaning in the door, looking at the girl. Even as Mara watched she saw the old defensive cynicism close over his features and end in a downtwisted smile. Yet she caught the sudden hunger and fire that lit his eyes in the instant he looked at the daughter before smiling at Bonnie.

"Oh, Branch!" Bonnie cried. "How good to see you! Come and meet Fleurette." She turned to her daughter,

"This is the young man I told you I knew who won't go let President McKinley give him the Medal of Honor."

Mara was dumbfounded. "Medal of Honor? But Branch never said—we didn't know—Bonnie, how did you find out?"

"Yes, Bonnie," Branch said cynically. "How *did* you find out?"

"When we were in Washington, I had dinner one night with an old friend, Congressman Lightfoot, from the next district. He told me all about Branch's medals, his gallantry in action, his commendations from Colonel Roosevelt himself, and that he had refused to come to Washington and accept them." She shook her finger at the tall man. "What a naughty boy you are, my dear."

"To tell you the truth, Bonnie, they didn't seem worth much at the time, and not now either. None of them can bring Stuart back."

"Branch MacAdam," Mara said in sharp astonishment. "You *are* going to Washington and accept your medals if I have to drag you there myself!"

"Good for you, Mara," Bonnie said warmly. "What is he doing here at your shop, Mara?"

"He is a partner and a manager, too. Heaven knows how I did without him. My business has almost doubled in the two and a half months he has been with me. Honestly, Bonnie." She laughed. "I'm terrible with figures—the arithmetic kind—and I never sent a bill that I was sure of!"

"Ah, but you're perfect with the kind of figures Fleurette and I have, thank heaven. Now do show us your summer fashions. My mouth is watering—" She broke off abruptly for she had glanced at her daughter.

Fleurette had not taken her eyes from Branch's face, and Mara was astonished to see reflected in them, not sympathy or curiosity, but a surprised, quick heat. Under her innocently revealed desire, Branch's tanned face reddened slightly. He had been riding again in February and by now wore the perennial tan of most South Texas men. Mara was further startled when Fleurette spoke.

"Magnifique," she breathed. "You are wonderful"—she hesitated a moment, then chose to call him by his first name—"Branch."

It was suddenly as if the two of them were in the room alone together, for Branch's hot eyes narrowed as he said roughly, "You don't know what you're saying, Fleurette. I'm only half a man. I've lost my left leg and left arm—this is a wooden leg I'm standing on." And he lifted his shortened left arm, with the pinned-up sleeve.

"*Non, non,*" she cried in a burst of passionate, rapid French, ending with, "you are a whole man, *mon cher* and you are *trés beau*—the handsomest man I ever saw."

There was a piercing moment of silence before Branch turned and went back into his office without a word. He did not limp. Fleurette's face was desolate.

"He is so *hurt,*" she murmured and there was a deep sympathy in her voice now. Then, "But he is so fine a person, so great a *man.* I will make him see it someday. I will, I will!"

"Now, darling," Bonnie said with a laugh, but her suddenly frightened glance swept past Mara's own wide dark eyes, to the empty door where Branch had stood. "You're so precipitate! I'm sure Branch will run for the hills, if he learns you plan to remake him."

"I would never remake him, Mama," the girl said quietly. Her sparkling smile was subdued, but the green eyes flashed with determination. "He is perfect, just as he is. I would only *comfort* him." But there was a promise of much more than comfort in the rich, faintly accented voice.

Later when Fleurette was in Mara's designing room, poring over the sketchbooks, some of them with only half-finished designs, Bonnie pulled Mara aside.

"Dear God, Mara," she whispered, "what can I do? Fleurette has done just as I did, fallen completely in love—all at once and forever—and with a man who belongs to one of Houston's best families!" There was agony in the words.

Chapter 17.

৩৬ BONNIE and her daughter had picked out nearly five thousand dollars worth of summer frocks and ballgowns, peignoirs and lace undergarments, when Bonnie complained of a headache.

"It is one of those migraines that I sometimes have, Mara darling. You will please forgive us, if we bypass dinner this trip and just go on back to Galveston. I'm comfortable only in bed with the medication I must take."

Fleurette had given her mother a quick, disappointed glance but had rallied to her side. Mara called Branch and asked him to drive down to Finian's Saloon and get Desmond, which he had done without glancing again at Fleurette. Mara recognized the old bitterness that his face had worn when he first returned home, a bitterness that had behind it hopelessness.

He and Mara stood in the shop door and watched Desmond drive Bonnie and Fleurette away. Branch turned to Mara and said mockingly, "Well, you can see how it goes even with such a fine person as Bonnie. She'd fake a headache before she'd let her daughter dine with a cripple or show interest in him. Come on, Mara, you don't mind dining with me. Let's go."

"Branch, you're wrong. Bonnie doesn't want her daughter hurt. As a member of one of Houston's most prestigious families, she feels you are unattainable. You know how Houston society looks on Bonnie. What makes you think it would be different for Bonnie's daughter? Why do you think we came here on Sunday? So Fleurette wouldn't have to face the contemptuous disapproval of the ladies who frequent my establishment."

344

Branch stared at her. "By God, I think you have a point."

"I know I do. Can you imagine the reception Fleurette would receive at a ladies' musicale or the Lyceum, or any of the balls the wealthy matrons sponsor?"

"Damn," he swore silently under his breath. "I can't believe it!"

"Bonnie would be glad for Fleurette to go with you anywhere. She'd be proud of you as an escort for her daughter and *you know it.* It's Fleurette's happiness she's trying to protect." She paused. "Did you know she even thought of living abroad, as a protection for Fleurette to try to get completely away from her past?"

"No!" he said with poignant swiftness. "She couldn't do that! All her interests and business connections are here in Texas."

"That's what decided her to build in Galveston. I think she has hopes that Galveston society may accept her accomplished daughter eventually."

His face hardened again and he muttered, "I couldn't court her anyway—a cripple. She deserves better than that. Besides, she probably has already had second thoughts about me!" He laughed harshly. "Well, come on, little one. Let's go to the Grand Central and I'll buy you a ten-course dinner."

And unaware of what waited her there, Mara locked up the shop, and with Branch at the reins, they drove to the Hotel. As he looped the reins over a vacant hitching post, Mara noted that a horseless carriage very much like the one Halloran had purchased, was parked along the curb.

To her dismay, her heartbeat quickened, for it had been such a long time since she had seen the man. Since Branch had joined *Mara Originals,* he had not been by, not since Christmas day when the three of them went to the shop together. With the memory came the remembered words, *Just don't become too obsessed with it, Mara. Take time to live. It can be fun, you know.* At her flippant reply the little flame in the back of his eyes had winked out and suddenly turned flat and cool.

Branch took her elbow and together they entered the luxurious hotel. The windows were all open and the ceiling fans swung lazily, stirring the fragrant air. As they went through the lobby to the dining room the scent of delicious food came to them.

The dining room was extraordinarily crowded, and for a moment Mara was afraid they could not find a table, but the maître d' approached and, recognizing Branch, bowed swiftly and led them to a secluded table near a row of windows banked with richly green-fronded Boston fern.

When they were seated, Mara permitted herself to look surreptitiously from behind the tall menu. She saw several of her customers, both male and female, and as they caught her eye each nodded and smiled, returning her own acknowledgment. But Halloran was not among those she could see. She moved uncomfortably. There was nothing but to turn and examine the faces behind her, but before she did so, Branch spoke.

"I see John's here, and with an old friend."

"Where?" She turned eagerly. "I haven't seen him since Chris—" She broke off with a near gasp as recognition spread through her. She knew that beautiful blonde woman—girl, really. She had seen her but once, yet Tosca's was not the sort of face easily forgotten. John Halloran was leaning toward her, smiling the smile that always caught Mara's heart.

Abruptly a scalding jealousy filled her and she swallowed thickly. Her heart beat in heavy, irregular jumps, and she was appalled at her helplessness to stem the tide of angry misery sweeping her. As she was frozen in her stare she saw Tosca reach a slender hand out toward him and catch his hand, and her smile was meltingly lovely, full of admiration and genuine charm.

"That's an old friend?" Mara blurted involuntarily.

"Yep. You wouldn't know her, Mara, but she's known John a long time."

Wouldn't know her? She'd never forget her, standing in the hall at Bonnie's sumptuous Houston mansion, smiling and chatting with her before Mara went on down to the kitchen.

"Who is she?" Mara asked, unable to keep the catch out of her voice.

Branch looked at her sharply, then his eyes softened suddenly, the pale blue as gentle as a summer sky. "Her name's Tosca Latrelle and she's from New Orleans. I thought she'd gone back there to stay when Bonnie sold—uh, well," he finished lamely, "she has a lot of friends in New Orleans."

"Evidently she has some, or at least one very affluent one in Houston," Mara said huskily. She had never seen John Halloran with another woman since she had met him back in Richmond and now she realized the galling fact that she had taken him for granted—and worse, much worse, she had unwittingly fallen in love with him.

She was miserable through the meal, forcing herself to talk to Branch about the shop, toying with her food, anxious only to be gone without having to speak to Halloran or Tosca Latrelle. But she was not to get off so easily.

The two were having an after-dinner liqueur and Branch insisted that he and Mara have one, so the two couples rose from their tables almost simultaneously and, naturally, met on the way out.

"Ah, Branch and Mara." Halloran's deep voice was pleasant. "How nice to see you. Mara, allow me to introduce my friend, Tosca Latrelle of New Orleans. She's just returned to Houston."

"How do you do," Mara said coldly, but Branch thrust out his hand and said, "Hello, again, Tosca, glad to see you're back in town."

"Yes, I just got in last week. I find I like Houston much better." She laughed merrily. "There's more money to be made in Houston. And I've met you before, Miss Ashworth, though you've probably forgotten. We only talked a minute."

"Oh, yes, I remember," Mara said tonelessly. This girl was taking full advantage of John Halloran's infamous proposals, she knew. She was very fashionably dressed. No doubt she would be coming to *Mara Originals* for Mara's highest-priced designs any day now and Halloran would pick up the tab. So Mara stood smiling fixedly while in her heart she longed to claw that beautiful face bloody. Oh, God, how had she come to this pass? How *could* she have let John Halloran come to mean so much to her? Frantically she tried to retrieve her resolve not to marry, but it slid from her mind like an eel. She realized that marriage with Halloran was something she wanted more desperately than anything in the world. All emotion paled beside her burning desire for this tall, lean man.

"How have you been these past months, Mara?" Halloran asked blandly.

"Better than I dreamed. But I'm sure you know about that." Certainly he knew about that. He received his check from Branch every month.

"Yes, we hear great things about *Mara Originals,*" he said, smiling so winningly that the scar disappeared completely. "You're very good for the economy, Mara. Are you ready to branch out to other cities yet?"

"I will be soon, I'm sure," she replied, smiling so steadily her face ached with it.

"It was good to see you again," he said, still smiling and Mara looked directly into his eyes to find them alert as a cat's, anticipating and somehow accusing. "Come along, Tosca," Halloran said, "it's time I got you home."

Home, thought Mara. Probably to one of his houses. Bonnie had said he came to her "girls," and no doubt Tosca was his favorite. In her mind she saw them arrive and go into his house and up to the bedroom together and her misery was complete. Oh, what a fool she was to have let him come into her heart! It was all the things he had done for her that had broken through her reserve, she told herself. She knew he was a full-blooded male and she had spurned him—*there!* She was making excuses for him! That's how besotted she was.

Halfway home, Branch said gently, "You haven't spoken a word since we saw them, Mara. Did it hurt you that badly?"

"I shall never have anything to do with John Halloran again, other than business," she said clearly.

"I thought it was always business."

"It was, but there was friendship, too."

"And because of Tosca Latrelle you're going to pitch friendship out the window? Tosca's a pretty good girl—"

"In bed, I'm sure." She whirled on him. "You needn't look so surprised Branch MacAdam. I'm not the ignorant girl I was when I first reached Houston. And I shan't be dining and wining with John Halloran again—*ever.*"

"Now, Mara, that's unreasonable. A man has to find comfort somewhere and Tosca—"

"I don't want to talk about it anymore. I know what Tosca is."

He laughed low. "Yet you fight tooth and nail for Bonnie. What's the difference? You're not joining the blue noses in our social circle, are you, Mara?"

"I'm no blue nose," she retorted furiously, "and you know it damn well, but for John Halloran to flaunt her in public is—is an insult to me."

He was silent awhile, then slowly, "Had you staked your claim on John? You sound like a betrayed wife to me and that's not like the independent Mara I know."

Tears stung her eyes and her throat was unbearably thick as she fought them down. That's exactly how she felt. Betrayed. And the combination of jealousy and betrayal made her feel actually sick.

"It's nothing but wounded vanity, Branch. I—I guess I thought John Halloran was above all that." Her forced laugh was husky.

"No man's 'above all that,' darling little Mara. I must confess to you that I've been with Tosca myself and it was—ahem, most satisfactory. She always made me feel like such a *man.*" His own laugh was bitter.

Mara reached over and caught one of his hands on the reins. "You are a man, every inch a man, Branch dear. It's just that—well, I guess I'm not in Tosca's league," then hurriedly, "nor do I wish to be—which I guess is a contradictory statement and makes me something of a fool." Then with false cheer, "Anyway, thanks for the delicious dinner."

"How do you know?" There was a smile in his voice. "You didn't eat a bite after you glimpsed John and the company he was keeping."

"Now Branch, I—"

"Mara, I love you more than I love Andrea and Will and in the same way—and I know you're *in* love with John Halloran—whether you know it or not."

"It's a good thing you're wrong, Branch, because John Halloran will never marry. He's told me so himself."

"I'm not wrong. And Halloran *thinks* he'll never marry, but in the end, he will."

Her laugh was short and angry. "You're the last person I would have suspected of being an unrealistic dreamer.

Anyway," she continued with feigned indifference, "I do not love him and that should close an unpleasant subject."

"Right, boss," was the jaunty reply and he began to whistle "There'll Be a Hot Time in the Old Town Tonight."

And when they drew up in the MacAdam drive, he called, "Sam? You there?" Then before the coachman came to take the horse and buggy to the stable, Branch assisted Mara down and whispered in her ear, "Don't worry, little one. Your secret is safe with me. I swear it."

When Sam came around the corner of the house and greeted them, he caught up the reins and began leading the horse and vehicle around to the rear.

"There's no secret—" she began angrily.

But Branch took her elbow and escorted her up the steps to the gallery, and under the brass chandelier suspended above them she looked into his irrepressible smile in the late afternoon sunlight.

She wanted to explode in a dozen angry denials of his acute insight, but she had said enough already, enough for Branch to have reached his conclusion and anything more she might say would only confirm it.

John Halloran came by for his check himself at the end of each month after she had seen him with Tosca Latrelle, but Mara was studiously cool with him and very business-like and she refused his invitations to dine with him.

He did not seem the slightest concerned about her cold-ness, and his cynical, mocking eyes were a source of great discomfort to Mara. During the long spring nights and into summer, she had fought a good fight in trying to convince herself that his attraction was purely physical, but she lost. She knew she loved him and would always love him and would never marry him, or know his intimate touch.

In June, when the household was readying for the move to Galveston for the summer, she informed the family that she was going to Paris. She wanted to study the great fash-ion shops and their products there. More, she wanted to buy exquisite and expensive Paris silks, satins and chif-fons. Branch was to accompany her and she told her anx-ious sister she would be well chaperoned by him.

At the last minute, she discovered that Bonnie, Fleurette and Dominique were booking passage on the same ship for Paris. This happy coincidence was uncovered when she stopped by Bonnie's imperial, snowy mansion for tea one Saturday afternoon.

"Fleurette is so restless and she wants to go into Houston all the time. I thought a trip to Paris might divert her. I can't bear her to learn of my past. We've booked passage on the *Saratania* leaving June fifteenth."

"Why, Bonnie!" Mara said joyfully. "That's the ship we've booked passage on!"

"We?" Bonnie looked bewildered.

"My brother-in-law, Branch MacAdam, is coming with me. He's so knowledgeable about materials and style now, even with all the office work he does. I'm leaving Sudie in charge of everything. Oh, Bonnie, Paris will be so much more fun with you and Fleurette and Dominique to show us around."

"Branch is coming?"

"Yes. He's my right hand. Besides, it's so much better to have a man along."

"Mara, I must tell you something. Fleurette talks of him constantly. I do not know what possesses the child, but I know all Houston would be outraged if they should fall in love and marry. A madame's daughter and the son of Colonel William Hunter MacAdam!"

"I don't think you need to worry," Mara said sadly. "Branch says he'll never marry her because he is a cripple. He couldn't bear to do that to her."

"Good lord!" Bonnie ejaculated. "That's the last objection I'd have. It's my reputation that hangs like a black cloud over my darling Fleurette. I have concluded that the only escape is to go to the continent where I'm known only as the wealthy widow of Clive Fairweather. Then perhaps my Fleurette will meet and marry some personable young French gentleman."

"I think you and Branch are both wrong. But I'm interfering. Forgive me, Bonnie."

"There's nothing to forgive, Mara. I know you wish me and Fleurette only good things. But I'm right about Houston society. And I would hate for my Fleurette to ever learn of—well, you know what I mean." Then at Mara's woeful look, Bonnie laughed irrepressibly. "Not that I regret a minute of it. I'm like the little girl who stole the cookie jar and not at all sorry about the cookies I ate. Just sorry as the devil I got caught."

"Ah, Bonnie, you are so delightful. It's hard for me to believe you stole the cookie jar. You're such a *lady.*" Mara was fervent.

"Well, I plan to return all the cookies with good deeds. Perhaps someday I'll be forgiven my sins. If not by Houston, then by some other good people who know less about me."

Mara brightened. "For three whole months we don't have to worry about Houston, and Sudie will be running *Mara Originals* for me so I don't have to worry about that. The bills can wait until Branch returns. And we're all going to Europe together. What fun it will be!" She hugged Bonnie impulsively.

And the fifteenth of June found all five of them aboard the *Saratania,* Mara trying hard to hide her wild excitement and congratulating herself that she wouldn't have to see or think about John Halloran during the weeks ahead.

Fleurette sparkled in a white silk suit dress, and though he tried, Branch could not keep from looking at her. Branch had been to Europe on a grand tour when he was eighteen, but he vowed he remembered little of it and was prepared to be impressed all over again.

The train trip to New York had been long and tiring, but the *Saratania* promised to more than make up for it and it did. The food was delicious, there were games to be played on deck and chairs for lounging. There was dancing in the great ballroom inside and a bar on each deck for the men. There was even a swimming pool on deck for the more daring of the passengers and Mara and Fleurette took full advantage of it, with Bonnie and Branch and the ubiquitous Dominique watching indulgently.

When they arrived in Marseilles, they were rested and refreshed for the train trip to Paris. Mara, looking out the windows at the smoothly passing scenes, thought it not much different from the beautiful countrysides in Virginia. But she deeply regretted not having studied French in the Richmond school for young women. She had, instead, taken Spanish, thinking it the more romantic language. Though it had come in handy at the shop with Catania and Elena, the Mexican seamstresses, now she was dependent on Dominique and Fleurette for translations, for Bonnie was nearly as ignorant of the language as she.

Branch made no bones of his lack of knowledge and reluctantly asked Fleurette to translate for him. She was quick to respond and was so warm and gracious that before they reached Paris he had been persuaded to take a crash course in French, which necessitated their heads being together more than ever. Bonnie had given up trying to separate them, but Mara saw the anxiety in her sea green eyes when they rested on the two.

When the train pulled into the enormous Paris station, with what looked to be hundreds of other trains, Mara was properly awed. And Paris itself awed her further.

She stared in amazement at the recently constructed Eiffel Tower, all nine hundred and eighty-four feet of it, aware that there was still controversy among Parisians as to the aesthetics of the wrought iron lattice work that Alexandre-Gustave Eiffel had built to commemorate the French Revolution. It was the tallest building in the world and Mara thought it perfectly beautiful, rising so slenderly and majestically over the city.

The rest of Paris was equally entrancing and Mara marveled at the broad streets and the myriad vehicles being pulled or propelled through them. Horseless carriages were infrequent and they looked strange among the elegant, horsedrawn carriages.

On the way to the hotel, they passed a flower market and Mara made the driver halt his horse while she bought an armful of blossoms of every hue, some strange to her Virginia-bred eyes. Bonnie, Fleurette and Dominique were indulgent of Mara's constant "oh's" and "ah's" and her evident admiration of everything the French city offered.

As they passed by Notre Dame on their way to the hotel, Bonnie leaned over to Mara and whispered, "Look up at the gargoyles. They always remind me of Archer when he couldn't have his way about something." And she burst into a cascade of giggles.

Mara, looking up at the glowering monsters, smiled

grimly. There was no resemblance, but there was something reminiscent of Archer Ashworth in their expressions. She had seen it more often herself than any other
member of the Ashworth family.

Reaching the hotel, they each were shown their separate
rooms, and Mara had the maid bring up vases for her flowers. She sat for an hour at the window in her flower-filled
room, looking out at the roofs of Paris and drinking in the
sights and sounds that came to her.

In the distance, she could see the hill on which stood the
Church of the Sacre Coeur and she let the distant beauty
sink into her very depths. She silently promised herself
that she would not miss a single building of note while she
spent her three months there.

She was true to her promise. But first, she and Branch
went to every famous couturier in the city, and after the
showings, she would rush back to the hotel and her
sketchpad and swiftly outline the shapes and styles she
wished to make, or change or embellish in some new or different way.

They went to the great material houses and bought
yards and yards of exquisite silks, satins, velvets, shan-
tungs (which were fairly new on the market), voiles, organ-
dies and wools as well as crepes, chiffons and mousseline
de soie. Sometimes Fleurette went with them, but she and
Bonnie knew a number of fine families in Paris and were
often invited out to afternoon soirées and dinner parties.

Bonnie had offered to introduce Branch and Mara to
these friends and they did meet some of them, but for the
most part Mara and her partner adhered strictly to the
routine of the shops and material markets.

But before the summer ended, Mara saw the glittering
palace of Versailles, with its sculptured gardens and
painted ceilings with cherubs entwined among portraits,
its enormous hall of mirrors where the aristocrats had
danced before the tumbrils claimed them. Fontainbleu
was equally beautiful and she spent long hours with
Branch in the Louvre, while Bonnie and Fleurette went
shopping with Dominique.

Mara drank in the huge oil paintings, the vivid pano-
ramas, gold framed on the gray walls, the smaller paint-

ings with their exquisite colors and the hundreds of fabulously sculptured figures.

Between visits to the famed couturiers, she dawdled in the perfume shops, buying indiscriminately anything that pleased her nose. And she ate, sometimes with Branch, sometimes with Bonnie and Fleurette and sometimes with all of them in the little restaurants along the Champs-Elysées. She reveled in the beautiful gardens that filled the city, and from the vantage point of the top of the Eiffel Tower, she gasped at the vastness of the metropolis below her. At night she would sit at her window and marvel at the lighted city, twinkling beyond.

Yet when she went to bed each night, John Halloran's face would steal across her mind, and no matter how many things she had seen to exult over, his face was what she saw before sleep took her. She was unable to reconcile herself to the fact that she loved the man. She refused to accept such an anomaly in her life, she who had everything any girl could want.

She loved her work. She was nineteen, and youth and beauty were hers. She was that incredible phenomenon in a man's world, a financially successful woman. And she had done it all herself. Well, whispered that small voice behind the thought of Halloran, *almost* all by herself.

During her trips to the great fashion houses, she concentrated fiercely upon styles and colors, and her baggage grew enormously as she added the crates of materials and accessories to the growing number being sent to their port of embarkation.

Then two days before they were to take the *Saratania* back to New York, the five of them made one more sortie. As a favor to Fleurette, they took the train to Chartres, so that she might see her old school friends and the teachers there, as it was late August and school was starting up. While the trip was ostensibly for Fleurette, Mara was the unexpected beneficiary for she saw the Cathedral of Chartres and was enraptured.

In the dim recesses of the old church, she looked up at the famous windows and an audible sigh of enchantment escaped her. It was a brilliantly sunny day outside and so the windows were an angelic, vivid blue in the ancient walls.

"That's the color—the exact color," Mara whispered to Branch. "It's as though ecstasy itself had a hue and was caught in the glass."

"I remember seeing *this,*" Branch was low voiced beside her. "I have yet to see that shade of blue anywhere else in the world."

"Then I can never find it in a satin or silk?" she murmured in disappointment.

"I think not, Mara. When I first saw these windows, I was eighteen, and for two years or more, I always searched for a girl with eyes just this color of blue." His little laugh was whimsical. "I never found her."

Bonnie and Dominique had chosen to go to the school with Fleurette and greet her teachers, so Branch and Mara were alone in their admiration of the cathedral. And now Branch moved restlessly and Mara sensed his desire to be with Fleurette.

"Go on and find the others at school, Branch. Then you all come back for me here. I want to sit and dream a bit, and perhaps thank God for my blessings."

Branch's sudden laugh was mirthless. "You won't mind if I skip that? My blessings don't seem to include the things I want most in life." Turning, he strode away in the cathedral gloom toward the crack of brilliant white light that was the broad, high door, standing ajar. Mara looked after him, her heart aching, for she knew he would never ask Fleurette to marry a cripple.

Branch was of inestimable help in supervising the loading and unloading of the crates of materials and ladies' accessories. There were boxes and boxes of them and each time she looked at them, Mara's head spun with ideas for fresh and new creations of her own.

From Branch's experience with *MacAdam & Halloran,* he knew exactly how to get the quickest service from the stevedores and wharf men as well as the baggage and freight men on the trains, even in France and despite the language barrier.

And when at last they boarded the train bound from New York to Houston, Mara took hold of Branch's right

arm and said warmly, "Branch, one of the blessings I
thanked God for at the Cathedral of Chartres was that you
agreed to work with me. You are a very marvel."

Fleurette, drawing up behind them, came around the
left side, where his empty sleeve was pinned neatly. Without hesitation, she caught the upper portion of the arm and
squeezed it tightly.

"Il est magnifique. I keep telling him he is unique. One
man in a million!"

Branch turned a slow red beneath his tan. "Fleurette,
you know well and good I'm only half a man. You can't—"

"Can't I? You are a hero, *mon cher,* twice the man of any
I ever met." Her twinkling green eyes were warm and
embracing and Bonnie shot Mara a glance of frustration.

"She's right, you know," Mara told him. "You're twice
the man for this job. You have done so much that none
other could do for me on this trip. I shall be eternally grateful to you." She sent Bonnie a reassuring glance, one tinctured with pleading.

He said with angry sarcasm, "You ladies are being too
kind. Where is your conscience?"

"Not a word of flattery in what we say," Fleurette said
pertly, ignoring his scowl. "Strictly fact."

He laughed unwillingly then, and they began to seat
themselves in the Pullman.

Without hesitation, Fleurette clung to Branch. "Here,
you must sit with me, *mon cher.* You need more coaching
in *la belle Française.* After all, you and Mara will have to
go back there often. Think how convenient, to be able to
chatter away like magpies. You could argue prices down,
mon grand bon homme. I will teach you."

Bonnie and Mara sat together and Dominique occupied
the seat facing them, her slim brown fingers flashing in
and out with knitting needles as she created a fluffy pale
green afghan.

"I fear for my little girl," Bonnie murmured to Mara. "I
fear she has set her heart on a man who will never marry
her."

"It's not because he doesn't *want* to," Mara retorted
quickly and somewhat bitterly as Halloran flashed
through her mind. "It's only because he won't saddle her
with what he fancies are his deformities."

Bonnie looked at her young friend with anger. "It's because she's the daughter of a woman who housed a brothel."

Mara seized her hand and clenched it tightly. "Bonnie, don't say that. Don't ever say that again. You did what you had to do to get along and it's all past now."

"What a little dreamer you are, Mara." Bonnie laughed softly and laid her head back against the Pullman seat. "The past is with us always. It will never be forgotten, nor will the good ladies of Houston ever forgive it. There can be no happiness for my Fleurette among them."

"Bonnie, forgive me, but you are a fool. Fleurette could marry Branch, if she can persuade him she doesn't care about his losses—and she would be accepted by Houston. It might take a little time, but she would be accepted."

"I should have to tell her about me before she married Branch." Her voice was low and fraught with pain. "And that I could *never* do."

"How can you so bravely carry such a burden?" Mara's own voice was low and torn with sympathy. Unbidden, into her mind flashed a vision, a child with Halloran's sculptured lips and strong chin, a child with her own dark, long eyes and heavy lashes. A child that could not claim its father, a bastard like herself, the only kind of child she could ever have by the man she loved.

"I do not carry it bravely," Bonnie murmured. "I carry it because I must and my heart breaks each day."

"But you're through with your old life! You'll never have to think of it again."

Bonnie sighed deeply. "I tell you, Mara, the past is never fully gone and you will learn that someday. Some dark day you will realize, darling Mara, what I mean."

As expected, when she and Branch arrived in Houston, they were met at the station by Sam, whose dark face was wreathed in smiles.

"The folks is still in Galveston, Miss Mara, Mister Branch. They're goin' to stay till the middle of September. You all are back just in time to help them move."

Branch groaned. "What a welcome, Sam. I've got to come back to the freight depot tomorrow and supervise the moving of half of Paris to Miss Mara's shop. No rest for the wicked!"

Bonnie and Fleurette and Dominique were met by Desmond who had parked only a few feet from the MacAdam carriage. With waves and smiles, they left the curb before Mara and Branch.

"We'll go to Galveston tomorrow, Sam," Branch said. "Miss Mara wants to see the shop before we go."

At *Mara Originals,* Sudie was particularly glad to see them. It was late afternoon and near time to close.

"Before God, Mara, it seems like you've been gone a year," she said, after they embraced.

Mara shook hands with the seamstresses crowding around them, then she opened the shopping bag she carried, handing each of them a gift from Paris. Most were perfumes, but for Elena and for Catania she had purchased broad silk scarves, multicolored and gay. All were very pleased and even Branch's roar of dismay at his paper-strewn desk failed to dampen their spirits.

The following night, Mara luxuriated in the big porcelain tub in Will MacAdam's Galveston house, and afterward, though she had put in a full and busy day at the shop, she lay restlessly in the big bed by the windows.

It seemed to her that autumn hovered in the warm gusts of Gulf wind that blew through the many windows in her room. An impending excitement gripped her stomach and with it a kind of anxious uneasiness. And she knew it was because she would soon see John Halloran again.

She endured the feeling for over two hours until, flushed and angry, she got out of her bed and made her way down the hall and staircase, through the foyer and into the kitchen. There, she switched on the light and opened the icebox to pour herself a glass of milk.

She had just seated herself at the kitchen table when she looked up, astonished to see a tousled-haired Celia looking at her with big, dark eyes. Her face was pink and the peignoir she wore was one of Mara's most seductive creations.

Seeing Mara's surprise, Celia blurted, "I bought it while you were gone to Europe. I had hoped to please Will by wearing it."

"Please Will?"

Celia rushed to her and gathered her into her arms. "Oh, I'm so glad you're home, Mara."

Mara put down the glass of milk to keep from spilling it and held her sister by the arms. The red-gold hair spilled riotously about her shoulders and Mara had never seen her look lovelier.

"Now what's this about pleasing Will? I thought you wanted to keep him at a distance."

"Mara." Her head fell and her lashes were inky fans against pink cheeks. "Mara, you'll think I'm utterly mad, but I've done the old familiar thing in dime novels, I've fallen in love with my husband, and I can't find the courage to tell him."

"So you've been trying to seduce him?" Mara asked with a wry smile.

"How," asked Celia dryly, "did you guess?"

Mara's smile vanished. Hadn't she thought often enough of seducing, or being seduced by Halloran? And with the thought followed its counterpart: He must be in his house, just down the street, or in his townhouse, in Tosca's arms, no doubt. She felt the hot blood in her own cheeks.

"When did this great love of yours for Will spring up?"

"I'm not sure," Celia said slowly, carefully. "It was slow, but one night when we went to bed, I—oh, Mara, I want him so! So much more than I ever wanted David. What a silly fool I was and David was such a—"

"A mule," Mara said, "and when he smiles he looks like a mule eating barbed wire."

Celia laughed with a touch of hysteria. "I remember you saying that. Just now, though, I went to your room, found you gone, and I came looking for you. I had to talk to you about it."

"You know I've always thought Will loved you, Celia. Why else would he marry you, make David's child as beloved as if it were his own?"

"I don't know," Celia replied, tears welling up in her eyes. "I thought that at first, too. And he's always so courteous and kind, but I lie there beside him in bed like a stick of wood. And it's such a *big* bed. We never touch—well, hardly ever. And I feel I can't bear it if he doesn't take me in his arms." She paused, then tragically, "He never does."

"I don't know what makes you think I can tell you any love secret," Mara said bitterly. "I don't know how to make a man love me," she paused, then under her breath, "enough to make him marry me."

"Just telling you has made me feel better," Celia said, wiping her eyes on the back of her hands. "Just knowing you know, helps."

Mara smiled, hard put to keep derision out of it. If she were married to John Halloran, she'd find a way to let him know she loved him! Her problem was in keeping him from ever knowing it.

"You'll find away, Celia," she said reassuringly. "I know you will. After all, you're beautiful and you want him."

Celia drooped. "It's a terrible thing," she said forlornly, "when you have to find a way to seduce your own husband."

Mara picked up her glass of milk and put the other arm about her sister. "You'll think of a way."

"I feel so forward! It's so embarrassing—"

"You'll find a way," Mara reiterated firmly, turning off the light. They took the dark stairs together. "I'll bet he's awake when you get back, and then all you have to do is take him in your arms and kiss him."

"Oh, Mara, I could never do such! What a fool I'd feel if he turned away and made apologies for my behavior!" Then enviously, "You've always been so impulsive and impetuous, it would come naturally with you. But I'd die before I could make such a move."

They stopped at Mara's bedroom door and she said, "Well, then patience is your best course. Maybe he'll take you in his arms himself and then you can certainly kiss him."

Despite the milk and her midnight sortie, Mara did not go to sleep quickly. The knowledge that it was the thought of Halloran that kept her awake was of no comfort at all, for his face rose up before her, smiling cynically, the thin white scar almost hidden.

* * *

But it was near the end of September before she saw him again. The family had moved, bag and baggage back to the big house in Houston, and Mara, terribly busy in her shop, realized that she was going to need a still larger place of business. She could use a great deal more show room and some extra fitting rooms, she concluded, but the six seam-stresses and herself and Sudie could still handle the vol-ume of selections that came through the store each week. Increasing the size of her shop would necessarily involve Halloran and secretly she welcomed the idea.

Branch had seen to it that all her boxes of materials and accessories were warehoused, for there was no room for them all in the confines of the shop. There were only two large crates of materials and she had made room for an-other glass case for accessories in the Selection Parlor, which further cut down on the room the ladies had for cir-culating among the fashion books.

Late Friday afternoon, after the seamstresses, including Sudie, had left for the day, Mara was still poring over her sketches and the samples of cloth she was trying to match with each one. She had told Branch to go on to Finian's Sa-loon for his evening drink and to return in a hour with the surrey. She had locked the door and was surprised back in her small nook to hear a firm knocking coming from the front.

Frowning, she looked back down at the gown she was sketching. Her open hours were printed in curling gold let-ters on the door, plainly readable to all. But the knocking persisted and at last she rose.

Midway to the door she halted abruptly. Through the glass, the lean hips and broad shoulders in the late twi-light were undeniably those of John Halloran. It was the end of the month, she thought going forward. He had prob-ably come for his check.

Opening the door she said coldly, "Hello, John. I'll see if Branch has made out your monthly share of the profits," and turned to go.

He caught her arm, swinging her around to face him. "I didn't come for my check," he said lightly. "And I expected a warmer greeting. After all, it's been over four months."

"Has it? I hadn't noticed." But her heart was pounding

furiously and she knew that in the soft lamp shine of the Selection Parlor, her color was high.

"Not even a handshake?" His voice lifted mockingly.

"By all means," she said in a businesslike tone as she thrust out her hand.

He took it warmly in both his and then brought it up to his lips, turning it over so that his mouth pressed her soft inner palm before she could snatch it away.

"I'm really glad you stopped by," she said, struggling to sound casual. It annoyed her that her voice shook slightly. "I was going to call you anyway. We're going to have to enlarge the shop again to accommodate our volume of business. Or do you think we ought to move to another location?"

"I anticipated your need, my dear, and I bought Larmer's Gun and Sports Store next door, or didn't you notice he'd moved out during your absence?"

"Yes, but I didn't dream *you'd* bought him out!"

"Always thinking ahead—with you in mind, of course." He bowed slightly and his little smile did not reach the thin scar. Then abruptly, "And who celebrated your nineteenth birthday with you over in Paris, my very businesslike little friend?"

"Bonnie and her daughter and Branch, of course," she replied coolly, wishing they had invited at least one of Bonnie's titled friends to their private party. That would show him she'd gotten about socially, instead of being the sightseer and businesswoman she was during the entire trip.

"I have a present for you."

"You know you shouldn't give me a birthday present! We're business partners *only.*"

"My affiliation with you has been so lucrative, I felt a rather elegant present was due. Anyway, it's my custom to give all my business associates Christmas bonuses and birthday presents." His eyes matched hers in studied coolness.

"Well," she said briskly, "if it's a business practice, I suppose I—" She halted as he drew from his pocket a long, slender velvet-covered box.

She took it gingerly and opened it to find a string of perfect pearls glowing richly in the ivory satin interior and caught her breath. How clever he was with his generosity, and when she was so vulnerable!

"This is too much," she said firmly, closing the box and handing it back. Had he hoped for a kiss, an embrace of gratitude?

"I think not." His voice was hard as he took the box and reopened it. "Here. Let me put them on for you. The dealer tells me they take on a luster from the skin of the wearer, and your skin, Mara, is very lustrous."

Mara wore a low-necked pale rose voile dress, for the late September weather was unusually warm, and she turned reluctantly to allow Halloran to place the pearls about her throat. She felt her breath constrict as the big, hard hands brushed the back of her neck. Damn the man and his effect on her!

She went over to one of the big gold-framed mirrors that hung on the inner walls of the parlor. The pearls glowed with a luminous and mysterious beauty against her ivory throat.

He followed, placing his hands on her shoulders, and she cursed him for his cleverness in coming while she was alone, for trading on the powerful physical pull that he knew he held for her.

He murmured into her hair, "Since that night I was with Tosca and met you, I—"

She whirled about and faced him, all the rage and hurt that had built up since that long ago moment in the Grand Central Hotel choked her. She flung away from him and said huskily, "I was glad to see you'd found some outlet for your animal instincts."

"Not the one I want, of course," he said lazily, observing her with alert black eyes. "Now that you've seen life abroad, perhaps you'll look more tolerantly on my—er—animal instincts."

"I'll *never* look tolerantly on living with you, John Halloran! When I live with a man, it will be because we're married."

"I thought we both agreed that marriage is a bad investment."

"I must have been crazy, then!" To her horror she found that tears stung her eyes and she fought them down with fury. She reached back to unfasten the pearls, speaking with choked anger. "Take your gift to Tosca. She's earned it, I'm sure, and—"

He seized her before she could touch the catch on the strand and his arms closed about her, one hand thrusting its way up into the hair at the back of her head. He brought her face up to his. With a slow and deliberate rage, he put his mouth over hers in a long, angry and hungry kiss. As her lips parted under his pressure, his hand slipped from the back of her head to her hips, pressing them against the hardness of his thighs and the source of his hunger for her.

She was fluid with desire, even her bones were melting to him, her breasts against him throbbing with urgency. Oh, if he would only stop, if he would never stop! She was powerless against his greater strength and the increasing urgency in his touch.

He put his head down to her breasts and she felt his quick, hot breath in his kisses through the fragile voile, and her heart beat with thick, passionate bursts. In another moment she would be lost. She would let him take her here on the plush audubon rug in the middle of her shop.

With sudden violent effort, she broke away and they stood staring at each other across two feet of space, like adversaries, like swimmers rescued at the moment of sweet drowning.

"You know damn well you want me as badly as I want you, Mara," he said between his teeth, his black eyes narrow, the dark hair tumbled on his forehead.

"I'll never do it. Do you understand? *Never.*" The words were ragged but pulsing with cold will. "You go back to your Tosca. From now on, it'll be business—strictly—between us. I won't want to see or hear of you outside the business of this shop. Do you understand? You stay away from me!"

His face hardened to granite, and the narrow black-fringed eyes blazed with fury and frustration.

"You *will* come to me one day and on my terms, Mara. Remember it."

He turned and strode out of the parlor, closing the door carefully behind him.

Chapter 18.

‽ JOHN Halloran did not personally supervise the second addition to *Mara Originals*. Instead, his second-in-command at Halloran Construction Company, a burly man with a crop of red hair and Scotland in his burring voice, came in and with excellent manners presented the plans and drawings of the addition to Mara and Branch, received their approval and fell to work with astonishing speed and accuracy.

In fact, Halloran did not come for dinner so frequently at the MacAdam house the balance of the year, causing Andrea and Celia to comment on his absence. Will shrugged it off, saying that their friend was so busy with his many interests he scarcely had time for rest, let alone socializing.

But Mara held her tongue. She had hidden his gift of pearls in the far back of a bureau drawer and had sworn never to wear them. She knew she was responsible for Halloran's obvious absences and she not only felt guilty, she felt—well, to describe it accurately—bereft, and she resented it. So she threw herself into her work with renewed fury, and under her long, slender fingers, the designs that emerged were exquisite and quite unique, unmatched in the field of fashion, and her reputation and fame spread.

And as the century came to an end *Mara Originals* came to full flower, a long row of glittering windows in a gray brick front with white trim. The name and business hours were limned in gold on the broad glass door and discreetly along the lower case of two of the six enormous silk-draped display windows. Mara's Selection Parlor was sweeping, the rugs on the polished oak floors plush, in texture and

design. Her decor was impeccable and all the ladies of the
new year of nineteen hundred were properly awed and impressed. And her third grand opening in the middle of January was complete with champagne and caviar on little
crackers.

Indeed, Mara stayed so busy that she did not have time
to notice the remarkable change in her sister. Will was the
same, courteous and thoughtful to the three women in his
house, loving and tenderly patient with the toddling Betsey, but Celia blossomed and played the magnificent piano
he had bought her with crashing enthusiasm, sending mel-
ody coursing through the house in waves.

Aunt Felice and Ashworth came frequently to dine at
the MacAdams during this time. Mara had inured herself
to it and dined with them, listening to Ashworth and Felice extoll the business that was flourishing at his store.
They had started construction on their new house in Houston Heights, which Will's and Halloran's construction
company was building for them, and they were unusually
enthusiastic about it.

Only the faintest trace of Aunt Felice's sharpness remained. She was, as Sudie had told Mara, a new woman
since her marriage to Ashworth and she was positively
gracious at the dining table. She was even kind—no, re-
spectful of Mara, herself. But the thing that impressed
Mara most was the way Ashworth deferred to Aunt Felice.
It was plain to see that he had come to depend on her and
her advice, and there seemed to be real affection between
them at last.

Still, Mara was always glad when she was able to excuse
herself and go up to her drawing board in the big bedroom
above. These cold winter days and nights were ideal for the
sketching of her spring designs and she made the most of
her time.

Indeed, she was up in her room one Saturday afternoon
in March, sketching a new ballgown for Mrs. Marsh when
Celia burst in on her, eyes sparkling, hair perfectly coiffed.

"I've just come back with Andrea; we've been to the musicale at the Houston Women's Club. I played *Kamenoi
Ostrow* and *Liebestraum.*"

Mara stretched her arms above her head and yawned.

"You look like you just won the grand prize, if there is one." She smiled at her vivid sister.

Celia ran to her, pulled her up from the chair before her drawing board and hugged her with uncharacteristic abandon.

"I *have* won the grand prize, Mara," she whispered in her sister's ear. "Will loves me and I'm three months pregnant."

Through Mara's surprise there flashed a hundred small vignettes. Will's hand on Celia's shoulder, lingering tenderly as they rose from the table, his light kiss on the top of her red-bronze hair as he left a room, his eyes as they touched her downcast lashes when they all sat together in the evening.

"I should have known," she said, brushing Celia's cheek with her lips. "It's been written all over you. How did it come about, Celia?"

Celia blushed furiously and looked away. For a long moment there was silence between them.

"I did what you said one night in bed. I—I pushed myself up to him, curled my arm across his chest and put my lips against his." She shivered with sudden delight. "And he kissed me then. Oh, Mara, it was heaven!"

"I'm sure it was," Mara said quietly, remembering, always remembering John Halloran's last kiss and the delight that had shivered through her own body at his touch.

"When is the baby due?"

"Early September. Oh, Mara, d'you suppose it'll be a boy, like Will?"

"Or a girl, like you. Like Betsey, maybe."

"Oh, no," Celia said positively. "He'll be dark like Will with those remarkable blue eyes of the Colonel. All the MacAdams have those wonderful clear light eyes."

She was wrong about that, but neither of them knew it then. Mara would remember it with great shock and a strange and wonderful satisfaction months later.

In April, Mara invited Bonnie to have lunch with her at the Grand Central Hotel after she had come for a fitting. Bonnie was distressed because Fleurette was unhappy in Galveston. They had met but a few people and the girl had to spend much time alone.

"I would've brought her with me today, but for the first time, Amy Medlock Brown—you've heard of James M. Brown? His is the Italianate Villa just up from my new house. Well, she invited Fleurette to go on a boat excursion and picnic with them, since the weather's so nice."

"As a matter of fact, Bonnie, it's Fleurette I wanted to talk to you about. I have great need of someone, besides myself, to show my clients the fashion books, to take notes, and I'm putting in a line of dresses we've already made up. I have room for two racks of them behind mirrored doors in the new section. I need a sales consultant to help with them. Would you consider letting Fleurette work with us at the *Originals?*"

Bonnie's beautiful face was a study in doubt, gratitude and concern. "It would throw her with Branch constantly," she said thoughtfully.

"I'm counting on that. He's dying of love for her and it's his stiff-necked pride that won't let him come courting. He'd be at your doorstep every minute he could get away, if he could stop hating himself for the loss of his leg and arm for five minutes."

"You think Fleurette could really be of help?"

"With her sense of style and that faint French accent, it wouldn't surprise me if she took over the shop in a few months." Mara laughed. "I knew when we were in Paris last year that I would give a pretty penny to have her in the business with me."

"Mara, you are wonderful!" Bonnie burst out. "It would give the people in Houston a chance to know my daughter without my background being part of her. At least some of them, the ones with any understanding in their hearts."

"I'll introduce her as Miss Fleurette Fairweather, from France. I'll throw in that exclusive school of hers, too, and that ought to impress them. Celia can take her to some of the musicales and we'll all go to the Lyceum and the Orpheum together. She can become part of the city herself."

"She can live in my hotel during the week. Thank God I own enough of it to see that she gets a nice suite," Bonnie said, then pensively, "Does your sister play that wonderful piano of your mother's often? Johnnie told me about what a marvelous musician she is."

"Ashworth didn't give her Mama's piano when she married. She has a new Steinway that Will bought her."

"You mean to tell me that oaf didn't give his daughter those things that Johnnie bought for you to have in—" Her hand flew to her lips and her green eyes rounded as Mara's dark ones narrowed on her.

"You mean it was *John Halloran* who bought Mama's piano and other things in Ashworth's library at the auction in Richmond and sent them to us here in Houston?"

"Oh, Mara," Bonnie said contritely, "I promised Johnnie I wouldn't ever tell anyone and I haven't until now."

"That's one more thing I owe him," Mara said without expression.

"You mustn't feel that way! *That's* why he told me never to tell. But that's the way Johnnie is. He does things for people—I could tell you more, you'd be amazed—and he never lets them know. He wouldn't have told me about this, except he was at my house when the freight people called and told them the furniture arrived and they needed instructions for delivery."

"He brought me to you, out of the storm when I couldn't have made it. He practically put me in business from the start. He's partner to me and he's anticipated both my additions to the shop," she said angrily. "And yet there's no way I can repay him unless it's to do as he wants me to—to live with him."

"So that's it, is it? His old taboo, marriage. Damn his mother and father for mistreating that child!" Bonnie's voice shook with rage. "Make no mistake, his mother would have killed him." She hesitated, then in a rush, "Oh, Mara, don't live with him out of gratitude!"

"I wouldn't live with him out of gratitude, Bonnie," Mara said evenly. "It would be for love."

Bonnie's sea green eyes widened, then twinkled with understanding. "You've fallen in love with him, then," she murmured.

"And you have another secret, one you must keep for *me.*"

Bonnie's hand closed convulsively on her napkin and her face held an ineffable sadness. "Mara, darling, don't give in to John Halloran. He is a fine and good man, but you, you, my darling, like my Fleurette, you must *marry* for love." Her voice fell lower still. "Of all the many things I have learned in a long, hard life, this is the most important. Marry for love. I could not marry the man I loved and I have never been truly happy. Only when I think of his daughter, my Fleurette, have I had happiness."

"I have told John I will not live with him," Mara said, squaring her shoulders. "So you and I have in common the fact that we could not marry the men we loved. But I believe your Fleurette will marry the man she loves. In fact, I *know* it." She smiled a brave half-smile. "Now about Fleurette becoming our sales consultant. Have I your permission to ask her if she will do it?"

"You and Branch come to dinner Sunday at the house and talk it over with her. I think she will jump at the chance."

And jump at it, she did. She was ecstatic over the idea, and as the months flew by, Mara knew she had made another shrewd move, for Fleurette was not only accepted, she was sought after by the young women who shopped at *Mara Originals*. There were three or four of the older women who knew she was Bonnie's daughter, but even they were coolly polite to the girl, though they asked for Mara when they came to have dresses designed and fabricated.

As a by-product of her addition to the staff was the cheerfulness of Branch. Fleurette was where he could watch her every day and occasionally dine with her. He even drove her about in the buggy when she went to call on clients who were unable to come and see about their dresses due to illness. Mara watched them with an almost maternal eye, for she could see the icy pride of Branch MacAdam melting a little each day under the irresistible onslaughts of Fleurette's warm and sparkling charm.

By the time the MacAdam family made its annual move to Galveston in June of the summer of 1900, Branch was a caller at Bonnie's great white-columned house. And while he made it plain that he was calling on both Bonnie and Fleurette, it was Fleurette who met his cynical smiles and argued with him that he was twice the man of any other she had ever met.

By August, all of them had a golden tan. Will was the
darkest for he never sought the shade of the large umbrella that Rosita and he set up on the beach for the others
during the hot weekends.

Once, John Halloran joined them and he was as darkly
tanned as Will, with whom he spent all his time talking.
Andrea pouted at him for this and he merely laughed at
her, the strong Gulf wind whipping his crisp dark hair
over his forehead.

"Andy, you ought to let Jim Phillips come court you, instead of holding on to your grief over the Colonel. He and
the others have been lovesick over you for years." Andrea
turned red, but Halloran went on. "Besides, you girls
should be bored to death with my talk of the bayou, the
dredges and the oil land Will and I have invested in."

"I should think you'd at least have something to talk
about with Mara," Andrea said maliciously. "Goodness
knows you used to see enough of each other."

Mara felt his speculative eyes on her. It was Sunday and
he was going to make one of his rare dinner appearances at
the MacAdams' that evening, as well as picnicking on the
beach with all of them today.

"Mara's a busy girl," he drawled lazily. "Surely you've
seen her vast new emporium. Why don't you buy a frock
from her, Andrea?"

Andrea, under the umbrella beside Celia, frowned. She
had never even entered *Mara Originals*. "I'm the tailored
type and—"

"She makes some sharp-looking tailored suits for
women, Andrea," he interrupted.

"I—just the same they're too—too flossy for me. I prefer
those of *Ashworth's*. And I'm sure Mara doesn't care one
way or the other."

"And *Ashworth's* appreciates her business, John," Mara
said, dropping a kiss on Betsey's gold curls. She held the
child in her lap and before them was rising a rather lop-
sided sand castle. She had long ago become inured to Andrea's hostility. At least her brothers didn't share it and
that was enough for Mara.

"And I'm sure Mara doesn't miss my business," Andrea
added, spite in her voice. "Not with all of Houston's ladies
clamoring at her door."

"They *do* clamor," murmured Fleurette, where she sat beside a fully dressed Branch. "That is just the right word for it, Andrea." Her smile was sweet and bland. "Clamor. *C'est comme il faut, Mara's Originals.*"

Rosita and Maria were sitting under a second umbrella, with empty baskets that had contained the picnic. Lunch had been delicious and eaten with gusto, and the two servants were a little impatient. The sky was rather hazy, a good sky for a bad sunburn, and it was very hot. Now Rosita spoke.

"Eez veree hot for zee babee, Mees Celia, don' you theenk?"

"I do indeed, Rosita. I think we've made a morning of it and too much afternoon. We should all go home." Celia was clad in a most becoming beach shift that Mara had created for her of multicolored silk and long loose sleeves. It hid her bulk admirably and was extremely comfortable.

The men rose first and began taking down the umbrellas, picking up the baskets and carrying them to the two buggies where the horses stood patiently waiting among the dunes. The women picked up their carrying bags and followed more slowly with Mara walking beside her sister. One buggy was the big MacAdam buggy and the other Halloran's. The two vehicles held all ten of them, plus the equipment with ease.

Arriving home, Celia immediately bathed herself and the baby and rubbed the little one's pink skin down with lotion. The others followed suit. But Halloran left them at the house and drove the short block to his own where he would make several telephone calls and return in time for dinner.

Over the table that night, the conversation was spirited, and even Andrea seemed to have forgotten her pique at the beach. Rosita and Maria were repeatedly complimented on the fried chicken, the fat hot rolls and mashed potatoes, the fresh green spring beans, the tossed salad and the delicious coconut cake that topped it all off.

"Rosita, you always spoil me when I come to dinner with Will," John Halloran teased. "Nothing ever tastes as good anywhere else."

"Then you mus' come more times, Meester John. We mees you."

"You know, everything here would be perfect tonight but for one thing." Celia glowed, as the Gulf wind blew fragrantly through the solarium. The scent of all the tropical flowers was seductively sweet on the air, and Mara, despite her constant and frustrated desire to look at Halloran, felt a certain peace herself, full of good food and fresh air and sunshine.

"What do you lack, honey?" Will asked interestedly. "I'll get it for you."

"No one can get this for me. I must get it myself and I have big plans for it." She looked at Mara mysteriously. "It's going to be the sweet healing of old wounds and I'm going to bring it about, or die trying." She did not know how close she was to come to that latter, as she continued, "My dearest wish is to see Papa and Mara friends again. No, wait, Mara, don't say anything. Papa's changed. Vastly changed. He looked on you as a child and the cause of Mother's death, but he knows better now. You have matured—why, you were twenty just this month and he knows you're a grown woman and a brilliant success. He's *proud* of you, and he told me so himself."

When she paused, Mara looked at her steadily, her face still as stone. Eventually this passion for healing the chasm between Archer Ashworth and Mara would drive Mara from the MacAdam home, loving those in it as she did. How could she ever tell this warm, loving, imploring sister of hers this bitter truth?

"But never mind," Celia smiled, waving a slender hand. "We won't talk about it anymore. I have a plan and when it's ready, I'm sure it will put an end to a long, hurtful period in our lives. I'm certain of it."

Still, Mara did not speak and Will took it up, gently as was his way, but strong as the man himself. "Darling, you must be very sure of this. Perhaps it's something we really shouldn't mix in."

"We're all mixed in it anyway," Celia spoke with sudden passion. "I adore my sister and I adore our papa. I've wept many a night over it."

Mara spoke suddenly, "Do what you will, Celia dear." She was touched by the deep emotion in her sister's voice. "I promise to go along as far as I can"—which would be to

speak to him and Aunt Felice and nothing more. But let
Celia be happy, making her plans for reconciliation.

That night, before they retired and after Halloran had
kissed the ladies' hands in gallant good-byes, Celia came
to Mara's room.

"You still are taking off that first week in September to
spend with us?"

"Oh, yes, I need a vacation! I shan't put a pen to a
sketch, and all the designs will fly out of my head on the
Midway, in the shops and at the restaurants, and while
I'm playing with my darling little niece!"

"That's good," Celia said contentedly. "I have lots of
plans for things we can do together."

"Your time will be so close, Celia. I hope you haven't
planned very active things for us to do. After all, you'll
have this baby just as soon as we get back to Houston."

"Maybe sooner," Celia said with an impish grin. "I've a
good doctor here in Galveston; he's as good as old Doctor
Samuels. He's been checking on me and says I'm a perfect
picture of a healthy mother. He said I'd probably have the
prettiest and smartest baby in Texas."

"That's good, but I don't want you taking any extra
chances." Mara felt vaguely uneasy, as uneasy as she had
that long-ago first trip to Galveston, when the sun seemed
to dim on what she called her "fair isle." She pushed the
sensation to the back of her mind, but even after Celia left
her and she lay on the cool bed with the wind and its sweet
tang of salt caressing her, she was uncomfortable.

It was as if she had said something she shouldn't have
said, inadvertently wounding, or worse, shaming herself,
and she could not name it nor when it happened, but it
stayed with her until she slept. And when she slept, she
dreamed of the feeling and Halloran was in the dream,
vivid and unattainable, and she awakened tired.

He never again came by for his check, not after she had
stormed that she never wanted to see or hear of him outside of their business dealings. Oh, yes, she thought bitterly, he had seen to it that they did not even have
business dealings together. The check was either mailed to

him or carried over by Branch on one of his trips to *Mac-Adam & Halloran.*

But she remembered and carried in her heart like a fatal talisman his final words: *You will come to me one dảy and on my terms, Mara. Remember it.* And in trying to shore up her defenses, she told herself, *Never!*

She took off the week of September third, leaving *Mara Originals* in the competent hands of Branch, Fleurette and Sudie. The seamstresses, including Sudie, who had been promoted to head seamstress, clustered about her early that Monday afternoon, bidding her good-bye and telling her to relax.

"You rest, Mara," Sudie said firmly. "I been worried about you. You got circles under your eyes, like you ain't—haven't been sleeping so good."

"Truth to tell, Sudie, I haven't. But the sand and sun will bake all the miseries out of my bones." She grinned at her lifetime friend. Sudie and her parents had bought three houses in the last two years. They rented them out now, and Julius, shrewd manager that he was, stayed with his Mister Arch and put his money into more real estate. He and his family were well on their way to becoming part of the black wealth that Houston already claimed.

Branch and Fleurette took her to the Houston Grand Central Station, full of admonishments about having a good time and not worrying about *Mara Originals.*

"I guess you took John's August check over to him this morning, didn't you, Branch?"

"Sure did. He said give you his regards and to let him know when you got ready to expand to Dallas."

Fleurette looked at him mystified, then questioningly at Mara.

"I think you're the one he should take that up with, Branch. Such an expansion involves you more than me," Mara retorted, which seemed to answer Fleurette's questions, for she had looked up at Branch adoringly and Mara knew she was thinking that Branch was the man to handle such decisions.

But Mara knew she would have the final word and tried to draw comfort from it as she took her Pullman seat alone. Hers was the genius that made *Mara Originals* the huge success that it was. She had conceived it, labored long hours over it and saw her bank balance grow each month. In fact, she should have a house of her own by now. She could well afford it.

As the train rocked easily out of the station and down the tracks toward the Gulf, she told herself this might well be her last summer in the home of Will and Celia Mac-Adam.

She thought of Andrea and her constant small pricks with a kind of indifference. Indeed, the dreaminess that always overcame her when she approached the city of palms and white-lace houses drifted in through the open window. Below ran the narrow sandy road from Houston to the island. Sometimes it was under water, sometimes after a dry summer, like now, it could be seen threading its earthbound way to the sea.

As with all her daydreams, John Halloran loomed large in her thoughts. She could see his big, hard body in the coppery sunlight, as it had been that last Sunday in August. And as always, uncertainty lay behind the vision. How long could she hold out against the man? She wanted to shout *Forever!* but wisdom hushed the word and she moved restlessly. Looking ahead at the hot bright rim of the earth where the water lay, a semblance of peace crept into her heart. Blue sky and blue water melded together and the horizon was a glimmer of blue-whiteness.

Rosita and Maria met her at the station with the big MacAdam buggy.

"Mees Celia, she want to come weeth us," Rosita smiled as they all mounted the buggy, "but I tell her 'no.' Zat babee eez too close to come now." She clucked to the horse, and holding the reins, she steered them through the small crush of vehicles and horses that met each train from Houston.

"I think maybe she'll have twins, Mama," Maria said, her white teeth flashing.

"No, no!" laughed Rosita and Mara in unison.

"Well," Mara said as they rolled onto Broadway after waiting for the streetcar that ran down the center of the broad street to pass, "if she has it this week, at least I'll be in on it. I was there when she had Betsey, you know. I'd like to make it a family tradition."

"Ees good. A tradition. Meester Will ees home more and

that ees a tradition, no? Eef he do it after zee babee come."
Rosita smiled.

And Will was home early that afternoon, coming in on
the train after Mara's. He caught a ride home in Halloran's surrey and persuaded him to come in for a tall, iced
drink, garnished with mint.

"Best bourbon in Texas," he said to Halloran after all of
them had greeted him.

They went out into the solarium, where the wind could
get full play over them. The men took off their coats and
Mara had changed to a white silk blouse and matching
skirt. She had brought Celia a new shift, another of pale
rose silk, full gathered and her sister had donned it immediately. She was unmistakably nine months along, even in
the rose silk, where she now sat in a white wicker chair
near Will.

"John, I do hope you'll come to dinner next Friday night.
It's the night I plan my big surprise," Celia said as Maria
served tall cold glasses of iced tea to Andrea, Mara and
Celia.

"Sorry, Celia. I must be in Beaumont next Thursday and
Friday. I won't be back until Saturday morning."

Mara looked at him from beneath her thick black lashes.
He was smiling at Celia, his winning smile that hid the
scar. Damn that scar, thought Mara bitterly, damn the
woman who had borne him, had hated him, had driven
him from home, and worst of all, who had made him
unmarriageable.

Even his deeds of kindness he hid behind an armor of
cynicism, and she would never be able to thank him for her
mother's piano, the beloved books and furniture. Yet he
had bought them because of her own torment, the torment
she had let escape at the ice cream parlor in Richmond
three years ago over an idle dish of sherbet. She had been
sixteen then and she had looked at him with all the innocence and impulsiveness of a child and had found him so
appealing that she could never forget him.

They talked on for over an hour and then he rose from
his chair and said courteously, "I must be going home.
Luke will have fixed dinner by now. He's a good man,

Luke, he doesn't mind switching from house to house when
I move from one to another."

"I think you're a gypsy at heart, John." Celia smiled. "I
don't think you *can* stay in one place longer than a
month."

"You may be right," he said ruefully, rubbing his chin.
"Someday, though, I may surprise you all and stay in one
of my houses instead of selling it."

"That I'd like to see," scoffed Andrea. "And I don't think
you're as respectable as a gypsy. You're a will-o'-the-wisp,
neither caring nor pretending to care about anything. Except perhaps old friends—like Will—like us."

"I do care about old friends," he said seriously. "And
being a will-o'-the-wisp isn't all champagne and roses. It
can be very lonely."

"Bosh." Andrea laughed. "You, lonely? There's not an
unmarried woman in Houston who wouldn't marry you except me, and that only because the Colonel has spoiled
lesser men for me." The grief for her father crept over her
face and there was an uncomfortable moment before John
spoke again.

"Your father was a wonderful man. I'll never forget the
kindness he did me. Nor can I ever repay it."

Mara wondered fleetingly if that was why, as Bonnie
had told her, John Halloran was always doing someone a
carefully anonymous kindness.

"The Colonel wouldn't let you repay him, ever. He was
that kind of man," Andrea said, her voice thicker now with
old grief.

"We all knew the Colonel well, loved him well, but I
think you might do better to dwell less on his death, Andrea," Will said. It was kindly said but there was a touch of
iron in it. "James Phillips would be only too glad to comfort you and you know it well."

Andrea turned and left the solarium without a word, but
Mara saw that her eyes were bright with tears. Poor
twisted, superstitious Andrea, guarding her father's memory like a faithful dog! Mara was suddenly sorry for her despite her strange hostility.

When she was back in her room, Mara looked out to the
south. Though the wind was off the water, it was hot, humid and somehow oppressive. The sky was that cloudless

blue vault that so often was over the Gulf. Yet Mara had a
sense of impending disaster. It had come over her more
strongly when Andrea spoke of the Colonel, but it had
really started days ago when Celia mentioned her "surprise."

Mara knew Celia was going to have Archer Ashworth
and Aunt Felice over for dinner next weekend. She was
going to maneuver things in such a manner as to bring
Ashworth and his other "daughter" back together again.
She *knew* it, though Celia had said not a word to her of her
plans. It depressed Mara terribly. She could never think of
Ashworth without hearing again his hateful words about
Mama, without remembering the violence he had done
her. Could she be civil to him to please Celia? She knew
she must make the effort for her sister, for Celia was
Mama's child, too.

The week flew by on the gossamer wings of a dragonfly,
despite Mara's depression over the coming weekend. She
took long walks down the Midway. She put on her bathing
suit and flounced about in the surf, without learning to
swim a stroke. She ate at Murdoch's and watched the gulls
swoop after tidbits she flung out the window to them.

For a few halcyon days she did not think of a single dress
design, or any of her clamoring clients. She did not even allow herself to think of the Dallas expansion, which she
knew Branch was eager to see happen. He and Halloran
were farsighted men who thought in millions, not thousands as she did.

And she knew *Mara Originals* had the potential of millions. Expansion to other cities was the answer, but she
would not think of that now. Not among the palms, the
sand and sun, the riotous hibiscus flaunting their glory in
dashing reds and yellows. The everpresent oleanders flung
their perfume wantonly on the air and Mara drank it all
in, while her sister let her do as she pleased, which was
mostly to walk or bathe in the Gulf alone. Andrea ignored
her completely as always.

Friday came at last and with it Archer Ashworth and
Aunt Felice. Only one thing marred Celia's plans for the
reconciliation dinner. Will had called from Houston and

said he was going to have to go to Dallas and would be gone until Sunday. Some cotton deal, Celia told Mara and Andrea vaguely.

So Andrea, Celia, Mara, Archer Ashworth and Felice sat in the parlor sipping iced wine and speaking very civilly, even warmly to each other. Over Rosita's and Maria's excellent dinner there was more jollity. Ashworth was particularly courteous and solicitous of Mara, asking her about her business, comparing notes companionably with her regarding his own efforts to have an original couturier. It seemed he had gone through three but was enthusiastic about a new one, coming from New Orleans once more. But this one had had experience in a great Parisian fashion house. Ashworth lauded Mara's success in florid terms and his obvious efforts to ingratiate himself by doing so chilled her further.

They were all to stay the weekend and return to Houston on Sunday, September ninth. And Mara knew instinctively that her sister would get the three of them alone together to make her move. Celia could not know, Mara thought despairingly, that they had never been a family. Only Ashworth and Celia and for a brief time their mama had made up that family. Mara had never been, could never be, a part of it.

Her oppression seemed to go farther than this meeting with the man she once thought her father, down into the deeps of her soul, and Friday night she tossed and turned and sleep would not come because of it. Was it Halloran, as always? Yes, that and more. She felt she was under a terrible burden that would never be lifted and she could not name it.

She rose Saturday morning since she could not sleep and watched the dawn sky over Galveston. She pulled a chair up to one of the big south windows and looked at it in wonder. The sky was like the inside of a gorgeous seashell, gloriously pink, but with tiny serrated clouds which reflected all the colors of the rainbow. The net curtains hung limp. There was little wind, oddly. She had never seen such a beautiful sky. It was going to be a wonderful day, she told herself, despite her oppression and the dim feeling of potential disaster. And she would spend all of it at the beach. Then there would be no falsely pleasant conversations with Ashworth, for he and Felice would not want to go to the beach.

But her spirits did not lift, and as if to corroborate her sense of doom, by the time they had all gathered around the breakfast table the beautiful sky had turned a leaden gray and great drops of rain were falling. Mara was deeply disappointed. It meant an entire day spent in odious company.

Ashworth was jovial at the table and he was holding forth on the weather. "I heard in Houston yesterday that the weather forecaster in Galveston was saying that we'd have a little blow this weekend. A hurricane that's far out in the Gulf may touch the city."

"I've never seen anything but the tail end of one in Houston," Aunt Felice said brightly. "It ought to be fun. Perhaps we could all take our umbrellas and go down to the beach and look at the big waves as they roll in. That would be exciting!"

"I wouldn't want to take the horse and buggy out in such a rain. Especially without Will here to dry him off and curry him down afterward," Celia said slowly.

"We could catch a streetcar and go down to the Midway," Andrea volunteered. "I've often watched bad weather come on. If it's a good blow, the waves should be spectacular."

Aunt Felice clapped her hands childishly. "What a wonderful idea!"

"It's only two blocks we'd have to walk to catch the car, but we could take umbrellas," Andrea said, relishing the doubt and worry on Mara's face.

"There's an awfully strong wind," Celia said dubiously. "I don't mind getting wet, but with the baby due and all—"

"You won't set foot out of this house, Celia," Mara said sharply.

"It's only two blocks to the car line," Andrea repeated. "I always walk that far anyway and sometimes all the way to the Midway."

In the silence that followed her remarks, surf booming

blocks away could already be heard and the winds seemed to grow ever stronger.

"I feel venturesome." Aunt Felice's little laugh was light. "I think watching the waves would be fun!" Her voice was high and Mara realized suddenly that Aunt Felice was trying to be youthful. It shone in the long, dark eyes that touched her ruddy-haired husband.

"Then I must escort all of you," he responded gallantly. "Surely you're not afraid to come, Mara?" he asked, for she was the only one not excited by the prospect. "I know my other daughter, my Celia, isn't afraid." He gave her a fond glance.

"I'll go if Celia promises to stay here," Mara replied with a look of warning mixed with pleading at her sister.

"I shall miss the fun," Celia agreed, smiling. "But you can all tell me about it when you return."

Thus, an hour after breakfast the four of them, Andrea, Mara, Archer Ashworth and his wife, sloshed out into the slanting rain, with raincoats flapping and umbrellas held against the increasing velocity of the wind. They caught the streetcar at the end of the block and it was packed with people who were in a holiday mood, refusing to let a little weather spoil their weekend on the island. They laughed and joked with each other in a spirit of excitement, some with umbrellas and a few hardy souls in bathing suits under their raincoats.

When the car arrived at the beach, spilling out its highly stimulated cargo, the waves beyond were towering, throwing white spume into the air. The portable bathhouses, which had been trundled into position as they were on every morning to receive their human cargoes, were a gay sight, their brightly painted walls the only festive note on a gray, threatening horizon.

With umbrellas tossing furiously, the quartet made their way cautiously through the heavy rain to a spot where they could watch the monstrous waves come rolling in.

These towering, curved slashes of water were already coming up very near the flooring of the giant, wood-constructed Pagoda, the bath and dining house of enormous size. Mara knew her first thrill of real terror at that moment. It looked to her to be only a matter of time until the waves would start smashing all those structures, which were still open in the wildly holiday spirit. These were the little wooden shacks where merchants sold seashells, salt-water taffy, kewpie dolls, satin pillows and myriads of cheap souvenirs. Crowds were heaviest along this ten-block area of the Midway and all seemed highly exhila-rated by the unleashed elements.

By now all four of them, Andrea, Ashworth, Felice and Mara, were soaking wet, their umbrellas turned wrong-side out by the increasing wind, but they paid little serious heed to the strange elations that gripped them.

"Look, look, girls! That one almost smashed into the Pa-goda. Do you suppose they will really get that high?" Aunt Felice asked. She turned to Ashworth and said, "You don't think this storm will really be dangerous, do you, Archer?"

"Of course not," he said reassuringly, patting her hand that held the useless umbrella.

They did not speak again, for all were transfixed by the sight of the stormy seas rolling in, one wave on top of the other. It was a sight of such grandeur that all were awed. Even the rattling Aunt Felice did not speak again, hushed by the overpowering storm.

Suddenly, Mara became aware of the telephone wires' eerie whine that rose and fell in a sort of singsong, and her fear grew. Then as they watched, a giant wall of water surged forward, caught the brightly painted bathcarts and tumbled them like children's toys against the shore and other buildings close to the beach.

In a few more minutes, the thrillseekers were astounded to see the giant Pagoda begin to sway as the waves contin-ued their remorseless advance. Suddenly the whole struc-ture collapsed into so much kindling, with people seen floundering, struggling to make it to shore. There were those inside the Pagoda not so lucky, sucked out to sea or crushed beneath the falling building.

The concessionaires began hurriedly to close their shops, but still the stunned crowd lingered, hypnotized by the de-struction of the beach buildings and by the ever-increasing height of the waves. Far down the Midway, Mara glimpsed Murdoch's Pier Restaurant beginning to sway as the waves reached above the giant pilings and crashed against the floor of the restaurant.

All four onlookers, like all the others about them, were drenched, and though it was quite warm, Mara was uncomfortable and the sight of possible deaths about her made her heart pound with fear. She knew Celia must be waiting anxiously as the fury of the storm increased by the moment.

"Oh, I shall always remember this terrible thing," Aunt Felice quavered uncertainly. "The sight of nature on the rampage is terrifying."

"I think we should go home as fast as we can. The wind's still rising," Mara said firmly, turning away. She looked back at the street and saw it was covered with rainwater. The streetcars were no longer running. The tracks had disappeared under the water. Mara realized that they had stopped running because they would be shorted out by the high water. "We're going to have to walk all the way back in the rain and we'd better get going," she finished, her voice hard, to keep from quavering as Aunt Felice's had done.

As they left they were aware that walking in the high winds and sheets of rain was harder than ever. Andrea had not spoken once and her face was very pale. Ashworth took her arm, asking solicitously, "Are you all right, Andrea?"

"This is my fault, I'm afraid. I know this is my punishment."

It was such a strange remark that no one answered her.

As they sloshed and pushed against the wind, the water above their ankles and ruining their shoes, Aunt Felice spoke again in her trembling voice, "Just look at the streets. The rain is doing what the waves can't—completely flood Galveston. Oh, Archer, I'm frightened!"

"You needn't worry about high water," Ashworth said confidently. "Will told me that his house was built to withstand flood. It's high on a brick foundation. The water will never come up that far anyway."

Mara, head down against the driving rain, said nothing. Andrea, beside her, lifted her head to the rain and let it beat against her upturned face, which looked curiously bloodless.

"I'll never forget the way the Gulf looked," she said in a strange voice. "As if God had raised his fist, determined to punish, to bring down retribution."

Mara looked at her sharply. It had occurred to her suddenly that all the wildly exhilarated people still straggling along the streets had no conception of what this storm might bring. They had not realized that the roaring elements might not be an entertainment, but an executioner.

As Mara and the bedraggled trio of sightseers about her splashed their way along the few blocks, with the surf booming ever louder behind them, the rain driving in heavier sheets, every nerve in her body had tightened with this terrifying knowledge.

They were thoroughly soaked, and the previous excitement of Aunt Felice had given way to real apprehension when they reached the MacAdam house.

Rosie met them at the door, round face screwed up with anxiety. "Eeeh! So glad you 'ave return. Mees Celia call the weatherman, Meester Cline, an' he say the worst is yet to come! Oh, eef only Meester Weel was coming. I'm afraid for Mees Celia, so close to her time."

"Oh, it can't get much worse than this," Ashworth laughed, still hearty. He was the only one still trying to belittle the raging storm. "We probably won't even have to batten down the shutters."

"I theenk Maria an' me, we do zat right now, Meester Ashworth," Rosita said, "just to be on zee safe side."

Ashworth shrugged, helping his wife remove her sopping raincoat. The others had pulled off theirs and were going up to change into dry clothing, as he added, "I think you're unduly alarmed, Rosita."

They were all taking the stairs now and Celia appeared at the top.

"Oh, Papa—Mara—Aunt Felice and Andrea," she cried, reaching out to them, "I've been terrified for you out in this weather! Thank God, you are all back safely!"

Below, Maria came from the kitchen and looked up at those on the staircase. Her little face was pale and she said, "I've just called over to the Marsh house and their cook, Tina, says that Mr. Marsh says the bay back of us is a cauldron under the wind from the north and they've had to close down the port and let the workers go home." Maria was second-generation American and had lost her Mexican accent. She looked so terrified that Celia came down the stairs to her.

"You all go on up and get dry clothes on, Papa," she said

soothingly, her voice light. "Be quiet, for despite all the wind and roaring about, Betsey's asleep. Now Maria dear, let's see what we have for lunch in the kitchen. We surely won't be going to market today."

As the two went toward the kitchen, Mara, the last to start upward, heard Maria say, "And Mr. Marsh told Tina that there can't be any trains come across to Galveston from Houston now, 'cause the trestle's mighty shaky and the water's getting higher. He told her one train had to back up—all the way to Houston, I guess. *If* it got back."

Celia's calming answer faded as Mara climbed the stairs. She could hear a faint banging from the parlor and knew that Rosita had begun closing and latching the shutters that would protect each window from the fierce gusts and flying debris. Reaching her room, she stood a moment very still. The house seemed firm enough under the onslaught, although she could tell by the increased roaring outside that the wind was still rising.

She slipped out of her wet, clinging skirt and blouse first, then her petticoats and corselet. Last came her limp kid shoes and she paused, nude, listening. One of the shutters outside her room had popped loose from the latch that held it back from the window and was banging noisily against first the window, then the wall. She slid into fresh underwear, not bothering with the dry corselet and went to the window.

She was newly alarmed by the sight that met her eyes. The rain was blowing in heavy vaporous veils across the yard, down the street before the house. It was a pale curtain of violence between Mara and the house next door. Already there was a sheet of water in the streets, flowing like a river and in some cases creeping up into the lawns of the houses down from the MacAdams'.

Mara knew with a sinking heart a promise of terror and of death. Over her crept the feeling she had experienced when first she looked at this fair isle, and this time her breath grew short and her heart pounded.

She was in a houseful of helpless women, with only the man she despised to protect them. Did she dare open the window and seize the loose shutter before it broke the windowpanes?

She tugged at the sash and heaved the window upward.

She was immediately drenched by the solid rain. Her already wet hair was soaked anew before she could catch the banging shutter and pull it toward her. She wrestled about, reaching for the opposite shutter so she could close the two together. She found a slippery purchase on the latch, unfastened it and brought the wooden slats toward her as she was blinded by the rain. There was a strong suction and she fought against it. She could not see what she was doing in the beating rain and had to perform the chore by feel alone. Then hastily, she dragged at the sash, pulled the window back down.

She stepped back, blinking water from her thick lashes, running her wet hands over her equally wet face. She looked down to find that her camisole and knee-length silk drawers were soaked, clinging to her body like the ones she had just removed.

"Damn!" she muttered, skinning out of the garments and flinging them atop the ones she had taken off before. At the bureau drawer, she pulled out the third pair that morning and put them on. Then she went to the bathroom down the hall and got a towel, came back to her room and toweled her heavy dark hair repeatedly. It was still damp, so she shook it out and let it tumble in soft, curling waves down her back.

A firm rap came on her door, followed by Rosita. "To pull zee shutters together, chiquita," and Mara looked at the drenched little Mexican woman.

"I've done just one and it was a bruiser. Think you can do the rest alone, Rosita?"

"*Sí.* I do all zee rest of them alone. I am not afraid of zee beeg wind."

"You're very brave."

"*Sí,* an' very wet, too," she said, going to the south windows and beginning to raise them, pull the shutters together, latch them and close the windows once more, one by one. With each one, the wind, though still driving from the north, sucked out and blew in like some giant, warm-breathing monster. Finishing, Rosita turned, "Zis was zee last room. I go now and put on dry clothes."

As she opened the door Celia stepped in and Rosita smiled at her woebegone face. "Don' you worry, Mees

Celia. I feex a good lunch as soon as I put on zee dry clothes."

"Thank you, Rosita," Celia replied, her white face turning to Mara as the door closed. Mara put aside her towel and put her arms about her sister.

"What is it, Celia?"

"I'm afraid my baby might come in this storm."

"Of course it won't!" Mara said firmly, though she had harbored this fear herself. "These storms never last more than twenty-four hours and most of them even less."

Celia began to cry softly. "And this has spoiled my surprise. I was going to get you, Papa and me off alone together in the solarium so we would be a family again."

"I know, darling," Mara said swiftly. "Don't think about that now. Papa and I will be friends." There! She had sworn never to call him "Papa" again. Well, this was one lie well told for her sister's sake.

Celia took a lace-trimmed handkerchief from her shift pocket and blew her nose. "I'm such a fool," she apologized, "but you know pregnant women are supposed to be a little foolish." She essayed a laugh and Mara joined her. "But oh, Mara, how it warms me to hear you call him Papa again. I can weather this storm and anything now!"

"Of course you can. Together, we'll—"

The door opened without a rap and Andrea stood there. She had the curious look of a sleepwalker.

"Your Aunt Felice is having hysterics," Andrea said, "and lunch will be served in ten minutes, so Maria says." She was looking at Mara oddly, her eyes like pale blue flames.

"Let's all go down then," Celia said hastily. "Perhaps I can calm Aunt Felice."

"Your papa is trying that," Andrea said, following them down the steps, "apparently without success."

Mara had donned a pale pink cambric frock, the waist of which was very tight because she had scorned the corselet in her haste. The trio entered the parlor to find the Ashworths dry clothed now, but Felice was wet eyed and her voice a piercing squeak. ". . . And I think we'll all be blown away, Archer. Blown away, do you hear? House and all!"

"Now that's not true," Ashworth said, looking at the

girls as they entered. He gestured helplessly over his wife. "Celia, I made the mistake of calling the weather bureau again and Mr. Cline himself answered. The man's a fool, saying the worst is yet to come. Why, this thing is blowing itself out right now. And to think he even advised going to a higher place on the island!" Ashworth's voice hoarsened slightly. "I know Will built this house over four feet of brick foundation and I know the water won't come nearly that high." He snorted angrily, "Him and his talk about the barometer falling so low! Felice, for God's sake, quit crying!"

Rosita came in and said, "I feex lunch in zee dining room, Mees Celia. Zee solarium—" She shrugged eloquently. "Eet eez een zee storm."

"Yes, I know. Thank you, Rosita," Celia said, putting an arm about her Aunt Felice. "Come, Aunt Felice, a cup of hot coffee and some of Rosita's and Maria's fine chicken and avocado salad will cheer you up."

From the dining room, they looked out through the French doors into the glass and screened solarium. The ferns and caladiums, the dwarf orange and lemon trees were whipping wildly in the wind and rain while the white wicker furniture was tumbled about.

The meal was eaten in silence except for Aunt Felice's quiet but steady weeping and she ate nothing. Andrea joined her in this latter. She picked at her salad, and while she buttered a roll, she did not eat it. And her pale eyes were fixed most of the time on Mara's strained face. After the dishes were taken away, Ashworth spoke up firmly.

"Celia dear, I think a good stiff brandy would do us all a world of good. Have you any?"

"Of course," Celia said, moving her bulk out of the chair with surprising agility and going to the liquor cabinet. "Rosita," she called, "bring in the brandy snifters for all of us, except me." She gave a little laugh in the direction of her sister and said, "I don't want to give any brandy to Will's boy yet!"

After two brandies, Ashworth grew expansive. "Believe me, dear ladies, this house is built to withstand any weather. We're all quite safe."

"Just the same, I wish Will could have come," Celia said

wistfully. "He knows all about hurricanes and what to do when they strike."

As she spoke, the electricity suddenly winked out. All the lamps darkened and the shuttered house was filled with gloom. In a few moments, Rosita and Maria had lit kerosene lamps, kept on hand for just such emergencies, but still they were not as cheerful as the electric lights had been.

All of them had gathered in the parlor, each one trying to speak of something cheerful. Only Andrea and Felice remained silent.

With the kerosene lanterns perched on the false mantel and each table, it was not quite so dark, but the house was being steadily buffeted. While it stood firm on its high foundation, it creaked and groaned under the onslaughts. The fury of the storm was so intense that those in the parlor gave up trying to talk and finally fell silent, listening to the rain and wind beat upon the house.

The wind was still from the north, Mara knew, blowing rain and water back toward the sea. She prayed silently that it did not change direction, for if it should swing from the south, those towering, spuming waves would be pushed toward Galveston, and Mara had a sinking intuition they might roll into the city itself.

Betsey had awakened and Mara could sense the restlessness in Celia as she tried to play with her little girl. Mara suspected she was thinking of Will, just as she herself was thinking of John Halloran. He had always turned up just when she needed him most, but there would be no Halloran for her to turn to now.

The kerosene lanterns added to the stuffiness in the rooms. It was not terribly dark outside, but the drawn shutters cast the house into darkness. The windows that were protected by the roof of the porch had been left unshuttered, and occasionally each of them went to look out into the streets through the blowing rain.

And the rain was unremitting. The wind velocity did not decrease as Ashworth kept saying it would. In fact, it was obvious that it was increasing steadily. They began to see shutters torn from other houses, skating through the air, along with other debris.

At four o'clock, Ashworth called the weather bureau

again but got no answer. There was no way the people in
the MacAdam house could know it, but the weather bureau was too busy to answer calls. People had waded to the
bureau in the Levy Building and were asking what they
could do to escape the devastation that was being wrought.
All of them, as Ashworth had earlier been told, were advised to seek higher ground.

Mara herself at that moment was trying to imagine
where higher ground might be, but she could not imagine
higher ground on an island that had all appeared flat to
her. Broadway, where the mansions were built, might be a
little higher, but not much. Still, it was a thought and she
spoke it.

"I wonder if we shouldn't all make our way to the great
houses on Broadway. We could go to the Walter Gresham's
or to Bonnie Fairweather's mansion. That seems to be the
backbone of the island and those homes have five-and six-
foot foundations."

Ashworth gave her a look in which contempt fought
with his newly pretended affection. What resulted was patronizing. "This house is as sturdy as any on Broadway,
Mara dear. You're borrowing trouble. It will soon be over,
and besides, your sister is in no condition to walk that far
in such weather.

Well, he was right about Celia, but she knew he was
wrong about this house. Rosita and Maria came into the
parlor frequently to look out the parlor windows at the
flooding streets through the veils of rain. They would look
a moment and then swiftly make the sign of the cross.

After one such trip, Rosita said, "Mees Celia, the 'lec-
tricity eez not all zat's gone. Zee gas won't come on, too."

Celia tried to reassure her. "Rosita, they both will come
back on after the storm. You'll see."

Rosita was not comforted, but she took Maria's hand and
they went back to the kitchen, where they tried to prepare
a cold supper.

Mara, herself, went to the windows and saw that the
water had risen still more in the streets, over the curb, and
was now creeping toward the house. Would the four-foot
foundation Ashworth spoke of so confidently be enough?
Those behind her had given up trying to talk and only
Celia made an effort to play with Betsey, who was unper-

turbed by the noise and fury of the storm. It was when Mara took her seat once more that she realized Andrea was looking at her fixedly, the pale blue of her eyes gleaming in the poor light of the kerosene lanterns. She tried to ignore those eyes, but after an hour she turned to Andrea.

"What is it, Andrea? Why do you stare at me so?"

"Branch told me I'd have to wrestle with my own soul," Andrea said in a queer hoarse voice, "and I am."

Mara bit her tongue on a sharp rejoinder that she would better spend her time wrestling with the problem that faced them all—what they would do if the house flooded. Instead, she got to her feet and passed the dozing Ashworth and her stiffly terrified aunt and went to the window once more. She barely restrained a cry.

It was five o'clock in the evening and the wind was screaming about the house with slowly, but steadily increasing velocity. Mara saw the water had risen to the top of the foundation and was just below the porch on the front of the house.

Real fear crawled through her, and in the dim, humid light, she could feel perspiration on her upper lip. It crept from under her arms and she felt sticky in the suffocating air.

She noticed the house was vibrating slightly under her feet now and she realized with a sudden spurt of terror that the wind had changed and was blowing from the south. That meant it was pushing those block-high waves toward Galveston. She tried to remind herself of the experts who said the beaches sloped so gradually to the sea that waves could never reach into the city. She wondered suddenly if any of the deep water now surrounding the house was salt. Or was it all rainwater? It had rained so long and so fiercely that surely it must be rain water! It was falling in such heavy sheets, too fast to run off.

She turned away to see Ashworth stretching and yawning. "Has it lessened? Or do I just imagine it?"

"I think it's blowing harder," Celia said starkly, and Aunt Felice began to whimper softly.

Mara turned back to the window again, and through the opaque veil of rain she saw a house being carried along the street, floating on its side.

"Oh!" It was startled out of her. "Come see! Someone's house has been blown down."

They all clustered to the windows and stood watching silently as the house vanished down the street. But after that, they saw bits and pieces of houses floating by regularly. The wind and the constant heavy rain were toppling the houses one by one—who knew? Perhaps by the dozens, those not so sturdily built as this one.

As the evening wore on, a chilling premonition filled Mara. Mr. Cline of the weather bureau had told them the truth. The worst was yet to come, and thousands, herself among them—her sister and Betsey—could well die during the violent night to come.

The pale light from the sky was dimming further and water was creeping slowly across the front porch under Mara's disbelieving eyes when the front door was flung open and her name was cried in a roaring baritone.

She ran into the foyer and shrank back from the half-naked man looming blackly before her, who slammed the door shut with a powerful thrust. At first she did not recognize him, but as her eyes adjusted she saw that it was Halloran, dripping and bruised, his shirt in shreds and his trousers torn off at the thigh.

His feet were bare and he caught Mara to him before she could move.

Chapter 19.

🙠 "THANK God you're alive and still here!" he said huskily. His body against hers was cold from the wind and rain and he loosened his arms immediately, asking, "The others?" and looked up.

The others were already in the hall staring at him, open mouthed.

Ashworth spoke first. "My God, man, you look like an apparition. How did you get here?"

"I caught the last train to Galveston, and when they decided to back up to Houston again, I got off. I made it across the trestle and alternately fought the wind and swam here."

Mara saw now that there was a dark bruise on his forehead and one of his bare shoulders bore a long, wicked scratch which had ceased bleeding. He was looking at her again now, the black eyes sharp on her white face.

"Whatever made you come?" she asked in a small voice, her heart unbearably relieved at the sight of his powerful figure in the foyer. "It's so dangerous now."

"I called Will when the weather news broke and he's caught the first train out of Dallas for Houston. He'll be here, Celia, as soon as he can make it, if he has to swim or row a boat all the way." The black eyes began to twinkle at Mara. "As to why I came, my pretty, after all, we've got too much invested in Galveston to risk letting it float away. Have you tried to call anyone?"

"Not lately," Celia said, holding Betsey on her hip, "not since Papa talked to the weather bureau earlier."

"If you had, you'd know the lines are down. I wanted to call when I reached the Strand, to let you know I was coming. Even the poles are down, and the wind has switched. It's coming from the south—"

"You need dry clothing, young man," Ashworth interrupted, as if wind from the south was a matter of no consequence. "Mine won't fit you, but they'll be better than what you have."

The door behind them burst open once more and another drenched figure stood in the opening. The wind from the south was blowing so fiercely now that a sheet of rain swept like a living curtain into the house before he could slam the door closed.

It was David Donellan, dripping from head to toe, but his clothing was yet intact, with only a rip in the coat. But like Halloran, he also was barefooted.

"You're all still here!" he said half hysterically. "I was so afraid the storm had taken Betsey and Celia, too."

The others looked at him silently. It was Celia who spoke first. "Where is Lucinda?" she asked coldly.

"Our house—it tipped over, fell apart about us. I caught her hand and pulled her up as I scrambled out of the wreckage. She was unconscious—something had struck her head." His voice caught, choked and he swallowed convulsively. "Just as we surfaced, part of the porch broke loose. I—I—my God! I couldn't believe it was happening! It caught her, tore her from my grasp and swept her under and down the street. I waded—or tried to wade—it's much deeper on our street than yours. I swam after her and searched and searched." He looked at them all hopelessly. "I couldn't find her—and I began to worry about you and Betsey, Celia—and you, Archer, and—and all the rest, so I made my way here." Blood from a deep cut on his temple was still welling, mingling with the water running from his hair.

"Well," Halloran said sharply, "since you're here, let's get to work and see if we can keep this house upright. Where are the tools kept, Celia, axes and sledgehammers and pickaxes?"

"Will keeps such in the storage room off the kitchen— My God, I just remembered the horse!"

"He wasn't locked in the stable, was he?" Halloran asked quickly.

"No," Rosita said. "I put heem in zee stable, but he could come out eento zee corral around zee stable."

"Then don't worry about him, Celia. He can swim to higher ground. Now about those axes and tools, come show us where they are, Rosita." Over his shoulder he said, "Never mind the dry clothes, Ashworth. If we can stabilize the house, I'll worry about it then." He turned and followed Rosita and Maria through the foyer, into the hall and the kitchen, with Donellan trailing him.

Mara looked out the glass of the front door and noted that the tall house across the street was canted at a strange angle. The vibration of the MacAdam house about her was greater now, filling her with fresh apprehension. But John Halloran was here. He would do something about it, thank God. She turned to the white-faced Celia and spoke.

"Here, Celia, let me hold Betsey. You look ready to drop."

"I'm too frightened to be tired, Mara. Oh, God, if John can just stop this vibrating, and if Will can only come soon!"

"He's coming as fast as he can," Ashworth said. "Meantime, your papa is here, Celia. I'm not going to let anything happen to my girls." He did not glance at Mara and she knew unerringly that he referred to no one but Celia and Betsey. They would come first with him always and for the first time she felt a twinge of pity for Aunt Felice. If Ashworth had to choose whom he could save, Felice would not be the one.

They waited tensely in the foyer for the two men to return. Before they did, Ashworth murmured something that could not be heard over the noise of the storm and followed after them and the two servants.

"Do you think," Celia asked loudly, "that he really waded and swam trying to find Lucinda?" Her eyes sought Mara's with strange desperation.

"I don't know—," Mara began, but her sister cut her off.

"Of course not. He simply waded and swam to what he hoped would be safety for himself." The baby tipped her coppery curls backward and looked up into her mother's face and laughed aloud. *"You* don't know why he came splashing in here, do you, my darling? I pray God you never do."

Mara gave her a quick warning glance, but Celia was looking at her child with renewed fear and Andrea still wore the glazed look of a sleepwalker, unhearing, unheedful of the holocaust around her.

In moments Halloran was back, a large pickaxe in his hand. Donellan carried an axe and looked helpless. Ashworth carried nothing, but his ruddy face had gone white for the first time, as if the danger of their position had at last been driven home to him.

"Back off, everyone," Halloran said, swinging the pickaxe high above his head and bringing it down with a crash on the bare floor.

"What are you doing?" Celia cried, her terror mounting.

"My dear, I'm trying to equalize the pressures on this house, so it won't do as the others are and float off its foundation, tip over and drown us all." He glanced at Donellan, who hesitated.

"Get to work, man," Halloran shouted. "If you can engineer blowing holes in my dredges, you can certainly engineer chopping a hole in this floor."

Donellan reddened and swung the axe with sudden vicious force. In seconds, water was gushing up through the openings the two men had made. It spread with appalling rapidity about their feet and flooded into the adjoining rooms. In minutes, it was well above everyone's ankles, but the shivering vibration of the house had steadied.

"We might as well sit in the parlor until the water runs us out," Halloran said cheerfully.

The rest of them followed him into the room, wading in the slowly deepening water, which was well up under the sofas and chairs now. Halloran flung himself down on a large sofa and closed his eyes wearily. To Mara's astonishment, he was asleep immediately. She started to wake him, but Celia shook her head.

"Let him rest. If he's come by foot all the way from the trestle and through town, he must be half-dead."

Mara settled herself into a chair and watched John Halloran and the water in the room with tense anxiety. "I wonder," she said, "how hard the wind is blowing now?" And as she spoke, two of the shutters popped loose and the glass in the windows beside the fireplace shattered inward, splintering against a marble table and knocking a vase off into the water, which swept it all away silently.

Later, Mara was to learn that at that moment, the anemometer of the Levy Building was ripped loose from its strong moorings and Mr. Cline of the weather bureau, estimating the gusts of wind at one hundred and twenty miles per hour, determined to go home to his family at once. But he was to be too late, for all of them, wife and children, had perished.

All of those in the room and Rosita and her daughter had rejoined them, looked at the gaping openings in silent horror as the rain blew unimpeded through the windows, drenching everything within its reach, making small dimples in the water swirling on the floor. Only Halloran slept through it, but he was awakened soon enough.

The house trembled suddenly and a great crash shook it from rooftop to bottom floor. The splintering shatter brought Halloran upright as Celia cried out.

"The solarium—it's blown off the house!"

The house was vibrating again. The noise could not be distinguished from the roar of the storm now that the first collapse had sounded. Rosita and Maria had brought in two more kerosene lamps, to add to the two on the mantel and the one on the dining table in the next room.

The two French doors before the solarium blew open and shattered as they banged against furniture and wall and more water gushed in. The tumbling white wicker chairs and table could be seen whirling among the debris of plants and glass, screens and small wooden sections.

As they all stood transfixed, Rosita reached down, put a finger in the water and touched it to her mouth. Her face crumpled.

"Madre de Dios, eez salt water—eez salt water!" she cried out.

"Come now, Rosita," Halloran said gently. "Of course it's salt. I told you the wind is from the sea now and so is the water."

The darkness outside was complete now and Andrea reached to the mantel and turned up the two kerosene lamps there. By their light, it could be seen that the water was now well above their ankles. Mara could *see* it rising, swirling in small eddies, curling hungrily about the furniture. And still the screaming winds blew from the south.

Mara thought again of the monstrous waves, casting spume over a hundred feet in the air and knew they must be higher now. She remembered again last summer's conversations about the gentle beaches that extended so shallowly out to sea that wise men vowed no wave could ever gather force enough to inundate Galveston. How wrong they were!

Betsey, beginning to feel the agitation among them at last, looked at her mother with round eyes and her lip began to quiver. Donellan looking at her, as he had been doing steadily, spoke up.

"Let me hold her awhile, Celia. You must be very tired."

"No," Celia said sharply. "If I grow tired Rosita can relieve me."

Felice had ceased whimpering and now clung like a leech to her husband's arm, her bloodless face imploring Halloran silently.

"No trouble," David Donellan insisted, reaching for the baby. "And I know you need rest in your condition."

"I'll take her," Mara said swiftly, plucking the baby from Celia's arms. Donellan's look at her was so full of malevolence that she would have quailed had her anger at him been less. By now the water was up to their knees.

"Come on," Halloran said roughly. "We'd better all go upstairs. The house seems to be holding onto the foundation but if the water rises much higher we're going to have to get above it anyway."

Wading into the foyer and climbing the stairs, Ashworth spoke loudly. "The foundation better hold. Will MacAdam paid enough for it and one of the best architects in the country designed it."

"Nothing's guaranteed," Halloran said flatly, "in a storm like this."

Rosita and Maria carried the lanterns high and Andrea clutched one with white, tense fingers. The upstairs was dry, but they were all wet and uncomfortable as they reached the hallway above.

"We'll all stay together. It's safer," Halloran said briefly as they stood there, amid the howling and banging noises that could be heard over the constant drumming of rain.

Mara noticed that Andrea's eyes sought her constantly and she could not fathom the strange expression in them. That the young woman was in a kind of mental agony was plain to see, but Mara could not understand why she directed it at her.

"We'll stay in the south bedroom, because if the house goes, we'll have a better chance when we leave it through the windows," Halloran spoke matter-of-factly but at his words, Felice gave a great cry of anguish.

"I can't swim!" she wailed.

"Neither can I or Celia," Mara said sharply, hoping to stem her aunt's hysteria. "We'll just have to depend on those who can."

"I can," Andrea said, her voice torn as they all entered Mara's bedroom.

The shutters had blown off and the windows were blown out. The rain and wind were pouring in every opening, most of the furniture was soaked, the bed especially since it was beside the row of windows. Wind coursed freely through the room, and while it was not cold, the cyclonic force of it chilled them all to the marrow. No one moved to change into dry clothes, realizing it was a hopeless task.

Celia reached over and took the baby from Mara. "It comforts me," she said, "to hold her."

All of them tried to find a comfortable place to sit down but it was impossible. Mara sat on the wet bed, and Andrea, holding the lantern, took a seat beside her. Its reflection gleamed back at them from the thousands of droplets blowing in through the windows. A shudder ripped through the house as something struck it forcefully and everyone lurched to keep their balance.

"What is it? What is it?" Felice shrilled.

"Probably part of another house struck us," Halloran told her. "That's our greatest danger. The foundation might hold us, but the debris and the current are other matters. A hard enough blow and this house could be dislodged. That's why I want us all to stay together. We've a better chance for survival."

Rosita went out into the hall and held her lamp high as

she looked down the stairs. Then she returned. "Eet's still rising. Eez up to above the landing."

"Still rising," Mara echoed. "What can we do if it rises enough to fill the house?"

"We'll get out of these windows, my pretty," Halloran said with his irrepressible grin. "I may have the chance to save your life and no telling what form your gratitude might take."

Mara marveled that he could speak so lightly, when they were all in such dire straits, with death all around them, death on the wind, death in the darkly rising water, death riding the debris that was hurled against the house. Irregular thumps and jarrings told her that more and more of the flotsam and jetsam of the storm was lodging against the house.

"You know," Halloran went on seriously, "there's enough debris floating about us now that we could cling to it and wait out the storm if we must."

Andrea gave a piercing cry, startling all of them. "And we will all drown. God is punishing me! Will said I'd be punished for it—Branch told me to look to my soul! And I am being punished."

Mara stared at her in amazement and Andrea's pale eyes looked unflinchingly and without their usual malice into hers. It astonished Mara that the young woman could put such a general holocaust into a personal punishment for herself.

"I'm sure nothing you've ever done would warrant such a storm as this coming down on you," Mara said encouragingly. "Don't think of such, don't worry, Andrea."

They were all watching Andrea now, for her face was contorted with anguish and regret and her voice was shrill above the storm.

"You don't know what I've done, Mara! And I've done it to you. Denied you your birthright. The Colonel told us on his deathbed that you were his daughter, that he loved your mother and she loved him, but she would not leave Archer Ashworth and Celia." Her voice rose higher still, above the rain, the roaring wind. "And I made my brothers swear never to tell you. I denied you your own kin!" She put her face in her hands and wept. "Oh, I shall be punished for that. I *am* being punished for it."

No word was spoken among those in the room and Archer Ashworth's face went as pasty as the belly of a dead fish. Mara was speechless with shock and Aunt Felice kept opening and closing her mouth as if she could not breathe.

Celia's already white face went whiter. Her long dark eyes, so like Mara's, widened enormously. She looked as though she had received a stunning blow and could not fully comprehend what had happened to her. Then, as realization flooded her she reached out a hand to Mara in supplication.

"But you're still my sister!" she cried, her voice thin in the roar of the storm.

Andrea lifted her head at Celia's cry and said, "The Colonel was so *good,* so honorable, so wonderful that—I never wanted a bit of scandal to touch his memory and so I denied you, my own sister. Will told me I should tell you when you had the quarrel with Mr. Ashworth, but no! I was too proud to admit it." She raised her white, tear-stained face and cried out again, "Oh, I'm going to be punished! I shall die in this storm."

Ashworth's face was working, the cords in his neck stood out and his eyes bulged. He had worshipped the Colonel and had been cuckolded by him, the man he admired most in the world. And Celesté could have left him, it would have been so easy. They could have come to Houston together twenty years ago.

Mara, looking at him, knew what was coursing through his mind. All these years he had wondered who Mara's father was and now, in the midst of a roaring storm, with death at his heels he knew the truth of it. Words someone had spoken to her echoed in her mind. Who had said, *I tell you, Mara, the past is never fully gone.* Bonnie! Bonnie Fairweather had warned her and now, in this hell of wind and water, she knew that the past had reached out and touched her, touched her with warm, loving fingers. She was the Colonel's natural daughter and through the years he had loved her and had claimed her at the end.

Suddenly there was a grinding, a deep fundamental movement, and Mara realized the house was shifting at last on its foundations. Looking swiftly at the door, she saw water creeping into the room, rising, rising, ever rising.

It began to look as though they might all be punished, most without cause, Mara thought grimly. The sea was sweeping into Galveston and destroying it. In less than an hour, they might find themselves up against the ceilings in water.

There was another ominous groan as the house shifted in the flood. Mara could feel the sway and she said to Andrea beside her, "Don't think of it anymore. God's not going to punish you. I know we're sisters now and your slate's wiped clean." It was all she could think of to try to soothe the distraught young woman, who clutched her hands and put them to her tear-wet face, muttering over and over, "Forgive me, Mara."

Ashworth had not spoken a word, his face still ashen. But he had flung Felice's clutching hands from his arm and his look at Mara was one of unimaginable pain and hurt. Gone was the old familiar contempt and in its place a look of such agony that Mara had to look away from him.

She had wanted vengeance and she had wanted to know her father. Now she knew both, but her heart ached painfully. It was too late.

She seemed unable to console Andrea, who wept convulsively even as the water continued to rise above their legs and reach the bed itself.

"We're all going to die—and because of my cruelty—my refusal to accept you, Mara." Andrea was unable to stem the torrent of words. "Did you all know that winds of a hundred and fifty miles per hour exert a force of one hundred pounds per square foot?" she babbled. "Math was my best subject in school, so I'll tell you all something. This means that an exposed wall measuring twelve by forty feet would have a total pressure exerted against it equal to, let's see—twenty-four tons. *Tons!* That's why we're going to die in this frame house, no matter how well Will built it. It can't stand that kind of pressure!"

As she finished the words the house canted precariously under a heavy blow from the south. Something big and solid had struck it just outside Mara's bedroom window and the house was tilting northward.

"Is there anything in the house that floats?" Donellan asked hopelessly. "Something we can all hang onto?"

The furniture was slipping across the floor and another grinding crash jarred it speedily to the other side of the room. Everyone was hanging to the battered window frames. The kerosene lanterns went into the water, all but the one Rosita held.

"Come on, Andrea," Halloran said forcefully, "confession time's over and we've got to get out of this house, every last one of us." He was peering into the rain-lashed darkness out the far window. "By God, there's something broad—out of the water and just beneath the south windows. A roof, I think, from some other house. Come on, all of you—here, Celia, give Betsey to Mara while Donellan and I help you over the window sill. Ashworth, you go first and help her get a hold on it."

Ashworth, who had not spoken a word since Andrea's revelation, went silently out the window and disappeared. The house was slanting steeply now and water was at their waists.

Rosita, holding the last lantern, gave a sudden cry as it slipped from her hand and disappeared in the water with a hiss. Darkness like death closed about them. A violent shudder shook the house and water climbed above Mara's waist. She held the baby high, but the child was dripping wet as were they all from the sheets of rain sweeping through the row of broken windows. There was not a sliver of glass left in any one of them, for which Mara silently thanked God.

"Come, Maria," Rosita cried. "Take my hand. We jump out these window an' swim to Mees Celia."

Now that her eyes had adjusted to the night, Mara could see their figures as they leapt out the window beyond. No splash was heard, such was the noise of the storm.

As the shuddering of the house increased, Andrea gasped, "I'm going under . . ."

Mara turned, searching for her, and holding the baby with one arm, she seized her newly found half sister with the other, pulling her up to the slanting window. "No, you aren't. Get out! You can swim, and that piece of wooden house, or whatever it is, is just below!"

But Andrea fought against her. "I should die. The Colonel himself would condemn me for what I've done. He wanted you to have a fourth of his fortune and I've cheated you—"

"Shut up, Andrea," Halloran snarled, seizing her shoulder, "and get out this window. Here, Mara, give me the baby and I'll hand her down to Ashworth. Come, Felice, you follow Andrea. I'll bring Mara myself, since she can't swim."

Betsey began to cry, a faint mewing sound against the storm as Halloran lifted her out the window. Then Andrea, still weeping, followed the baby out.

After her, Halloran half lifted, half carried the fainting Felice to the opening and let her down. He turned swiftly to Mara, caught her up in his arms as the shivering house slid further on its side. The two of them, with Halloran holding her strongly, slipped out the window, fell some three or four feet, and in the water, they caught an angled purchase on the flotsam below.

Mara looked around, and as her eyes adjusted further she could see dimly by a pale light from a storm-swept, phosphorescent sky. They were all on the steeply slanted wooden roof of some lost structure. It rocked with sudden violence and she saw the MacAdam house turn on its side and begin to drift in the currents about them.

She was suddenly aware that she was still pressed tightly against the broad bare chest of Halloran. It was rough under her cheek, with a thick mat of curling black hair.

Despite the threat of death that surrounded them all, she felt her body respond to his and she wound her arms about his chest more tightly, pressing her face harder against his broadness. How strange to know that she could die any minute now and yet feel passion surge through her that was stronger than the winds that blew constantly about them.

She could hear Betsey crying dimly and she knew she should ask about her sister, Celia, who might go into labor any minute now. Still, she clung to her rescuer and he made no move to let her go. She felt the weakness in her thighs that his touch always engendered, the pounding of her heart and a desire to press closer, ever closer until they were one flesh.

Reluctantly, she pulled away in order to see about the others. "Celia!" she called out, "are you all right?"

"Yes. It's hard to hold on, and the rain beats so. But I'm here and Betsey's beside me with Papa and Aunt Felice."

"Andrea!" she called, "are you all right?" Strange to suddenly have two sisters to be concerned about. Poor Andrea, what a price to pay for pride and fear that scandal would touch her adored father. The price had been the complete humility she had shown back in the house. That, and a willingness to die. And Ashworth, who had not spoken since learning her father's name, was silent still.

"I'm here with Mr. Donellan, though God knows I shouldn't be," Andrea answered.

Ashworth spoke at last, "The night isn't over yet. You may not be alive before it's over—*you* and the *Colonel.*" The venom in his voice was shocking.

"Don't say that, Meester Ashworth," Rosita spoke up suddenly. "We mus' all try to save each one of us. You weel be all right, Mees Andrea. Maria an' me, we say much prayers every minute."

The rain beat down with such unremitting force, that Mara felt her body yielding to it, shrinking from it, and her clothing was already ripping from the rough shingles as well as the elements. Soon she would be as naked as Halloran, who still had an arm about her.

They sat on the peak of the strange roof and it was an uneasy hold. Mara tried to clutch at the shingles, but their splintery surface slipped from her grasp. As the roof turned and moved with the eddies and waves, they banged into other debris. In the nightmarish light from the sky, she could see that all the houses on the block had vanished. Some of them were floating on their sides, some must have disintegrated into the vast expanse of loose boards that covered much of the choppy water about them.

Suddenly, she felt something whiz past her head, then twice more she was aware of projectiles in the wind about them as they all held to the piece of roofing with both hands.

All at once she was consumed with worry about Celia. What if a flying shutter or board were to strike her sister's unprotected abdomen? It would surely kill her no matter where it struck her. Flying debris could kill any of them for that matter, but Mara was mainly concerned with Celia's condition, which she knew could well result in her death.

Again something whizzed past her head, narrowly missing it. She did not know it, but it was a slate shingle, one that had replaced the wooden shingles on roofs after the fire of 1885. These tiles, ripped from roofs by the screaming winds, were like projectiles fired from guns, with the velocity and cutting power of scythes. They had already wrought havoc downtown, decapitating and killing those who waded through the streets seeking higher ground or trying to enter the brick buildings still upright.

She caught Halloran's arm and pulled him with her, nearer to where Celia was clinging with her father and Betsey, in an effort to shield Celia's body with her own and Halloran's.

"Celia?" she asked again, unable to keep fear out of her voice.

"I'm not in labor yet, Mara," Celia called loudly over the velocity of the wind and rain with an attempt at humor.

Thank God, Mara thought, she wasn't prostrate with terror, either.

Only Aunt Felice seemed to be that. Ashworth was holding the baby with one arm and Felice with the other, forcibly urging her to try to hold on herself, but she was whimpering piteously.

Curiously, Donellan and Andrea were seated together on the large piece of flotsam, but neither tried to aid the other. Donellan was silent as he clung to the roof, and from the shape of his form in the gloom, terror was in every line of it.

Now the roof gave a mighty lurch as it struck another, heavier piece of storm-tossed wreckage, which was settling slowly into the water.

Mara kept slipping and Halloran caught her up each time. The others were having an equally hard time maintaining their hold on the slanting roof and Mara noted with horror that pieces of it were breaking off in the water. It was disintegrating underneath them even at this moment.

Bits of wreckage kept flying past them on the mighty wind and some object struck Mara's cheek with stinging force, even as the rain beat upon her with bulletlike, stinging droplets. She could feel that she was cut and when she put her hand up, she found warm blood mingling with cold rain. Though the temperature must have been above seventy degrees, the velocity of the wind chilled them all.

It was at that moment that Aunt Felice buckled without a sound and slid toward the water. Only Ashworth's swift move caught her. In the pale gloom, Mara could see she was limp and her head hung at a strange angle.

"My God!" Ashworth shouted. "She's been struck in the back of the neck—it's a—it's—Jesus! It was a slate roof tile and it's damn near severed her head."

Mara could see then that her head remained attached by a slender strand of flesh and she realized suddenly that her aunt was dead. Though Mara had never had cause to love her, and much cause to resent her, she nevertheless felt a piercing regret. She hadn't deserved this! And it increased her fears for Celia, unprotected on the peak of the roof beside her father and her aunt.

Ashworth appeared to be stunned. Mara knew he had not yet recovered from the blow Andrea's revelation had dealt him and he kept holding to his wife's limp body and trying to brace Celia at the same time.

It was Donellan who spoke up first. To Mara's surprise, he said in a desolate voice, "Archer, you may as well let her go. She'll be found after the water recedes. Celia and Betsey need all your strength." Then pleadingly, "Please let me help you, too, Celia—let me have Betsey. I'll hold her."

"No!" Celia said fiercely. "You look after Andrea. Papa will help Betsey and me."

Thus Aunt Felice was the first of them to slide from the roof into the torrent surging about them and Ashworth devoted himself to Celia and Betsey. Betsey had stopped crying and had burrowed her face into her mother's breast.

Oh, Mara thought desperately, if Celia just had some protection around her. If there were only walls of some sort about her vulnerable body. If those flying tiles were to strike her anywhere—Mara shuddered and clung fast to Halloran.

As they swept along in the current, there abruptly appeared beside them a large, empty steamer trunk without

a lid. It was like a flat-bottomed boat and the high sides
protected the interior from the water. Mara pulled away
from Halloran and reached out to it, sliding dangerously
as she did so. Halloran caught her and the trunk at the
same time, drawing it to the side of the roof.

"Celia!" he called, anticipating Mara's thought. "Come
get into it. It'll protect you from the flying slate shingles
and the other debris!"

"You can crouch down inside!" Mara yelled.

"I won't leave Betsey!"

"Then bring her," Mara screamed. "There's room for
both of you. You can't risk sitting on this disintegrating
roof. You'll be safer. Besides, John and I and your papa
will hold it close to the roof—we'll stay together!"

"That's a good idea, Celia," Ashworth said rapidly. "I'll
hold it beside us, darling, and you two will have some protection."

Celia, with Ashworth's help and holding Betsey to her,
moved awkwardly toward the trunk. Her bulk slowed her
as she put one leg into the trunk, which rocked drunkenly.
By now, her silk shift was sadly torn and her legs were
bare above the knee. All of them had long ago given up
their shoes.

She turned as she seated herself in the broad trunk,
barely able to peer over the side and then only when she
lifted her head high. With both Betsey and herself safely
in the depths of the trunk, Ashworth lay flat on the
slanting roof for a better grip on it. He clamped his two
hands desperately on the edge of the waterborn vehicle.
Halloran, holding Mara tightly with one arm and hand,
grasped an edge of the trunk.

At that instant, the floating roof lodged against a three-
story house that was still standing. Mara couldn't place
where they were by now, but they were even with a top gallery porch that ran around the third floor. It seemed to be
standing firm against the current and another large piece
of their raft broke off, causing Rosita and Maria to scram-
ble up until they were against Andrea.

There was no sway to the house and the raft hung poised
against it for what seemed an interminable time.

Suddenly Rosita lurched toward it, crying, "I'm goin' to
get off here. Thees raft, she eez get smaller an' smaller—

come weeth me, my chiquita!" She tugged at Maria's hand.

"It'll just go in a few hours, Rosita," Ashworth called to her wearily, but she shook her head stubbornly as she edged her way to the balustrade, pulling Maria with her.

"Some of thees houses mus' stand. Maybe thees one. Anyway, soon there will not be room on thees roof for all of us anymore." As she spoke, another small section of the roof broke away and Andrea and Donellan were forced to move closer together.

Rosita and Maria reeled in the wind as they threw their legs over the bannister and stepped onto the gallery where Rosita opened a door and the two of them vanished inside, closing it against the storm.

"Maybe we better all get off here," Donellan said uncertainly. "Like Rosita says, some of these wrecks are bound to stand and this hurricane can't last forever." The wind from the south tore his words away and they sounded useless and puny.

Halloran's arm closed tighter around Mara. "If it should go, we might not be lucky enough to get out of it this time," he said in her ear.

"I can't risk Celia in another flooded house," Ashworth yelled. "She's comparatively safe now, but she might not escape when this one's swept away, as it surely will be."

"As it surely will!" Andrea screamed suddenly. "Let me off this thing! I'm going with Rosita and Maria. I'd hate to die alone."

She staggered up and then fell to her knees, crawling toward the house. The roof swung uncertainly and Mara saw for the first time that the elements had torn most of Andrea's clothing from her. Her dress was shredded and her brassiered bosom almost bare. As she flung her leg over the bannister she looked back in the gloom toward Mara.

"Forgive me, Mara," she screamed. "I should have accepted you when the Colonel showed your mother's letter to us as he lay dying. Instead I tore it up and made my brothers swear—oh, God, forgive me!" She staggered toward the door and flung it open, disappeared into the black maw of the flooded house.

The wavering roof, caught by a violent new current, swung away from the house and back out into the mainstream. It was all Halloran and Ashworth could do to hold the steamer trunk against the edge of it.

The wind was so strong and the rain so slashing that Mara, when she looked down at herself, saw that her own clothing was in shreds; her breasts were bare under the thin filaments left. Another hour and she would not be left with a stitch to protect her from the stinging bullets of wind-driven rain. She pushed closer to Halloran as he held the steamer trunk with one hand and Mara with the other. She was half naked, but she felt no shame in the pale light beside the man she loved.

The force of the wind was unbelievable, and Mara was forced to the conclusion that it was still rising. She stared back at the doomed house as they spun away. *We'll all be drowned,* she thought clearly. *This hurricane is going to kill us all and I will never know the sweet consummation of my love for John Halloran.*

Her thick hair had long ago come loose and it whipped wetly about her face and she had difficulty keeping it out of her eyes. The roof took a sudden swerve, but Halloran's hold on her tightened and kept her from sliding into the water, which was much nearer now that so much of their raft had broken off.

As their bit of wreckage swept along, she saw other houses, some toppled, some floating. She looked at them longingly in the pale and ghastly light from the sky. They looked much more secure than the piece of flotsam to which they were clinging.

Donellan sat alone on the peak of the roof, making no effort to hold the trunk. He seemed dazed and uncertain and the elements had at last beaten most of his clothing from his body.

Suddenly a large house rose up before them. It was partially intact and their floating roof crashed against it with unbelievable force. Donellan was knocked from his perch into the water where he began swimming with all his strength to seize the swirling roof. At the same time, Ashworth's and Halloran's hands were torn from the trunk, which seemed to fly forward in the water with Celia and Betsy inside.

Celia, peering over the side, gave a piercing shriek.

Mara was numb with shock and the speed of the mishap,

and in a matter of seconds, the trunk was far ahead of them.

Ashworth slid into the water and began swimming after them, calling out desperately, "I'm coming Celia! Don't be afraid—I'll save you!"

Donellan, unable to reach the roof for the current against him, got his bearings suddenly and struck out after Ashworth. The two left on the roof could hear him calling, "Hold on to Betsey! Hold on, Celia! I'm coming—"

The last Mara and Halloran saw of Donellan—Ashworth had already disappeared—he was swimming strongly in the direction of the trunk and Ashworth. Her heart took a sickening plunge as she thought of Celia, as unable to swim as she, herself. With Betsey in her arms and the baby she carried, if the trunk should hit a snag and turn over—Mara shrank from the picture behind her eyes.

Halloran, holding her close, felt her shiver and he pulled her a little higher on the peak of the roof. The rapid movement of the further-diminished raft through the water now was terrifying, and objects kept whistling through the air all around them as they banged repeatedly into other pieces of disintegrated buildings. A bit of flying wood struck Halloran forcibly and he grunted, then muttered a curse.

"I'm all right," he added swiftly. "Are you, Mara?"

"Yes, but with this wind," she cried back, "we're bound to be struck again and again."

"Try to hold to this ridge," he said in her ear, "and curl as flat against it with me as you can."

They careened along for what seemed hours, wordless in the screaming storm about them. Mara knew their piece of speeding flotsam was being knocked to pieces slowly but surely, for now her legs and feet were in the water.

She could feel it rushing past, the current strong against her flesh. She cringed as unknown objects brushed her ankles. Too, she could feel what was left of her clothing tear against the rough shingles beneath her, but she was unaware of pain. Her cheek felt numb where it had been struck. The frenzy in which she was caught up was almost an anesthesia in itself.

The submerging roof spun around in a wide circle and a giant blackness loomed up before them in the pale luminosity. Another house? Their floating roof was held against it by the strong south wind and the current. Mara's hair streamed about her face and shoulders, clinging coldly to her bare skin. She brushed it back briefly and seized the peak of the roof once more. She was chilled to the bone, yet it was still summer in Galveston, still warm. It was the wind, she thought, the awful wind against her wet skin.

Halloran feeling her shiver again, drew her nearer and where their bodies touched in their near nakedness, heat emanated. He spoke into her ear.

"This house before us is still standing, though God knows it must fall eventually. Nothing can stand in these hurricane winds and water. But our roof is sinking, Mara, and we must risk it. Come—"

He half lifted, half carried her, across the now rapidly sinking roof and stepped over the balustrade that ran across the upper porch of the tall house.

He still held her close against him as he let her bare feet touch the soaked planking. They stood staring together at the pale luminescence over the devastation before them. The wide spread of water was filled with large and small objects, bits and pieces of buildings, bushes, trees, and Mara turned away suddenly as she saw the white arm and leg of a drowned human being.

"Can't we—we g-go inside and get out of this wind?" she asked, her lips against his bare shoulder.

"I guess it can't be any more dangerous in there than it is out here," he agreed. "When it starts to go, we'll have to chance it anyway."

They went into the house. It was pitch black inside and they collided with various pieces of furniture in ankle deep water. Halloran called out loudly, thinking others might be there, but there was no answer to his deep-voiced "Hello!" The occupants were long since gone.

"Here," he said, pulling at her hand. "It's a chair and it's amazingly dry."

Though the winds coursed through the blown-out windows in the room, they could speak without screaming at each other. The house, though it creaked loudly, did not vibrate with the terrible shiver that presaged collapse.

"I'm so c-c-cold," Mara said and his arms went around her again, before she could seat herself. "And so t-tired."

"There's a bed over there in that blind corner," he said carefully. "It's standing in a foot of water, but it's dry, too."

"Let's lie down, then," Mara said with equal care. "We—we can rest until this house begins to go like all the others."

In the dark they sank down on the bed with no words between them. The winds continued their death-dealing velocity, ever rising to new crescendos.

Mara thought, *It's like the end of the world.*

The world was ending for her and with it all her hopes and dreams of love and success, of springs to come and winters ahead. All the life force in her rose to beat back the loss. She turned to Halloran, pressed herself against him.

"You once told me I'd come to you—and on your own terms. You told me to remember it." Her hand crept up the back of his neck, into the thick, faintly curling wet hair there. "Well, I'm remembering. And on your own terms, John."

She didn't say *I love you,* though it cried out in her. Those words went with marriage and it would chill the sudden heat that enclosed them as they lay down on the bed together.

Chapter 20.

༄ AT first, his touch was gentle and his mouth as soft against hers, as hers was against his while they lay face to face. Her camisole was in thin wisps about her bare breasts. Only the straps remained. He took them in the dark, pulling first one aside to kiss her shoulder with warming lips, then the other as he swiftly laid her flat so his big, hard body covered hers lightly.

He kissed her then with mounting passion, until her lips parted under his. His breath was warm and clean as it mingled with hers. The wonderful weakness burned in her thighs, parting them to him even as her lips had parted, fervently and mindlessly.

He kissed her eyelids, her cheeks, then her mouth again, and once more her breasts tingled, for this time they knew the rough touch of springy hair on his bare chest as he let his weight down upon her.

Heat kindled brightly in her, wiping out the chill, wiping out the storm that raged beyond them with a storm of rapture belonging to them alone. For they were alone in the world. There was no one, and no time beyond this single fiery moment between the two of them.

It rose and rose, shaking them unbearably until it burst in a shower of intensity and Mara experienced a sweetness sharp as pain. Glory suffused her and she reveled in it.

Suddenly she was part of the wildness that was the destroying night, and like the storm about them she knew it could not last forever. So she clung to him, drawing out the aching delight that shook them.

And it lingered, as if reluctant to melt away into reality. She didn't want to think, only to feel, and she slipped her hands up and down his bare back, then up to his face as he rolled off her with a slow-drawn breath. Her fingertips caressed the chiseled curve of his lips, slid over the roughness of his growth of beard to the smoothness that was the thin scar that ran from below his eye to the corner of his upper lip.

The words in her bubbled up spontaneously, "Oh, John —I lo—I think you're wonderful." She had almost said it!

His answering laugh was husky. "You made me forget it all, Mara. *All.*"

What did he mean by that? The storm, or his unhappy, dangerous childhood? Turning her head she looked at the windows, strange grayish luminosities against the furious night. *I must think*, she told herself with a touch of panic. But she was so warm now—almost dry—lying in his arms like this. Even relaxed as they were, she could feel the supple ripple of muscle in them. Was that his heart beating in her ears, or her own?

She was jarred out of her dreaminess by a shiver in the body of the house. The whole of it shook under the blow of some huge floating object that had struck the very corner in which they lay.

Both of them sat upright, swinging their feet into the inches of water that covered the floor. Through it could be felt that ominous vibration that Mara knew so well, though she had never felt it before this night. The house was grinding off its foundations, preparing to join its neighbors in the deep Gulf waters that covered Galveston now.

Mara ran to the window and looked out into the still, white face of a woman she did not know. The woman lay in the eddying water on the balcony faceup, eyes blind in death. Mara turned swiftly to Halloran, who stood beside her now.

"Ought we to get her?" she asked.

"It's too late to help her," he said and with his words the floor beneath their feet slid dangerously upward. As they stepped out onto the balcony they were struck by such a blast of wind they could not move.

The supports for the roof of the balcony suddenly blew away, one striking Mara a glancing blow on her right hand. But she felt nothing as she watched the woman's body disappear in a circling current, while the porch roof, no longer held by the tall wooden columns, took off like a gull and sailed away in the pale light.

Slowly, laboriously, she tried to move, but she, like Halloran, was caught and pinned by the wind to the wall. The house was tilting, slowly, ever so slowly, and she strained her head about to look back down a slanting black hall. She was transfixed by one of nature's phenomena.

The drops of rain became luminous as they struck the black wall, the phosphoresence glowing brightly. She found herself watching a display of glittering diamonds that burst like fireworks against the darkness, beautiful and deadly. It was a visual expression of all the sensations she had known in Halloran's arms so short a time ago. Beautiful and *deadly.* She would pay with her reputation for her decision about Halloran this night. *If* she lived through it.

The house spun and tilted. The view was gone. Mara cried out into the wind.

"It's falling and I can't get loose from the wall." She screamed against the incredible pressure of the wind. But Halloran's arms came out slowly to close about her.

The tilting house seemed to hover, to hang, until Mara thought it would never crash into the water. But then suddenly it was on its side and she and Halloran were hurled into the maelstrom once more.

She came up sputtering, floundering helplessly in the wind-flattened water. There were no waves and she had the sense to kick away from the fallen house, as Halloran was doing even as he held her. Even so, sunken wreckage rose to surface around them.

A piece came up directly under them, like an answer to her unspoken prayer. It was the flat broad surface of a wooden door. It was much safer and easier to cling to than the peaked roof that had served them all earlier.

Mara was once again chilled and this time her teeth began to chatter. Halloran lifted her onto his lap and held her close to his own wet and chilled body in an effort to warm and protect her from the shrieking gusts. Debris had ceased sailing through the air, and Mara silently thanked God. It had all been torn away long since and there was nothing left but the swirling, eddying deep around them.

She saw a dead cow and two horses floating by, before she saw the children. She cried out and clung to Halloran ever tighter as they slid up beside their raft. Three small bodies were looped together with what appeared to be a piece of clothesline rope. For an interminable time, they all slipped through the water together, the bodies sweeping along beside them. Then at last a vagrant current carried them ahead and off to the left.

"We're heading north at an angle, Mara," Halloran said in her ear when he spoke at last. "The backbone of the island and all the bigger mansions are north of us—even downtown where some four-and five-story brick buildings are. Maybe some of them are still standing."

"Surely everyone can't be drowned!" she cried.

But belying her words, a man and a woman, clasped together face down in the water slid by them. But nowhere in the pale darkness did they see another living soul. She wished desperately that she knew how long this hell had endured, but it was still night so she knew it could not be more than a few short hours.

She thought of her sister, Celia. The water coursed along almost evenly, still blown flat by the gusts. That would give the trunk Celia and Betsey were in more stability. She forced herself to believe that Celia and Betsey were still afloat. Had Ashworth reached them?

She knew he had not. He was not that good a swimmer. But Donellan might have. What irony that would be!

And Rosita and Maria—and what of poor guilt-ridden Andrea? Was the house they were in still standing, or were they, like herself and Halloran, afloat once more on some shattered hulk of a building?

What was the average length of time a hurricane wrought its havoc? she wondered. But then this, she knew, was no ordinary hurricane. It was a killer and only God knew how much longer it would live.

But strangely, her desperate fear and panic had disappeared when she and Halloran had come together. That moment had wiped out everything but his nearness and the comfort of his big body. She was warmer, too, now, where they touched and they touched constantly. His hands, in the storm, caressed her breasts, her bare stomach, her thighs, and it stirred her blood. But they did not try to talk again over the tumultuous winds and constant driving rain.

At last Mara spoke into Halloran's ear. "What if we're being blown out to sea? What if we drown at last like all these other . . ."

He kissed her mouth swiftly and hard. Then pressing her head to his chest, he said, "I've only just got you. Do you think for a moment I'll let you go—ever? We aren't going to die. We've a lifetime to live."

Her courage rose to meet his and hope flared afresh. She could think about the future. What would her elegant clients say when word got out that she was living with John Halloran? A wry smile twisted her lips. How little that mattered now, when her sister Celia and both her babies, the born and unborn, might well be lost in the salty sea that covered Galveston Island.

Suddenly salt tears mingled with the salt spray that blew about them. They were hot on her face and stung the injured spot on her cheek. A little sob caught at her throat, shook her shoulders where they lay against Halloran's broad bare chest. His arms tightened about her, hands closing on her wet arms, which were folded tightly against the wind.

"What's the matter?" he asked in her ear.

"My sister," she said tearfully.

"Which one?" he asked dryly. "It seems you have two, you know."

"Both of them, if it comes to that. But mostly Celia because Celia needs help most. Oh, if only that trunk stayed afloat!"

"It was a very seaworthy vehicle, Mara, and as long as Celia and Betsey don't tip it, it should carry them safely until the water recedes." He paused, then added, "Will and Branch are going to be so relieved, now that you know they're your brothers. I didn't know *what* it was, but I've known for the last two years something's been bothering them, and, you must admit, their attitude toward you was one of unusual warmth. I was a shade jealous of Branch."

"You? Jealous? I didn't think it mattered that much," she said, snuggling closer.

"You know I've wanted you ever since I laid eyes on you, you minx."

She couldn't believe that they were jousting with words in the midst of a hurricane, but she couldn't repress a laugh.

"That's better. Stay cheerful. This can't last much longer."

"It's already lasted a lifetime."

"So it has," he replied somberly. "Lifetimes for many."

She looked down at her hand where it had been struck and it was dark and tender to touch. The door frame and its surrounding wall whirled and scudded along the wind-whipped water for an eternity, while Mara and Halloran saw nothing but the shattered remains of buildings, bodies of animals and occasionally people, from whom Mara hid her face against Halloran's broad chest.

Then suddenly their piece of wreckage swirled at an angle and carried them up a street. Mara knew it was a street for there were actually houses still standing. They were bigger, more solidly built houses. And far up the street, she saw light emanating from the cracks of still shuttered windows that had weathered the blow so far.

All at once it came to her. They were on Broadway, the wide street that so many of the mansions were on, including Bonnie Fairweather's! Hope blazed up in her.

"Oh, John, look! Look where we are!"

"Yes, I know," he replied. "We're on Broadway and it's higher here. We can make it to the Greshams' or to Bonnie's now and we'll be safe while we wait out the storm."

They sat anxiously on the door frame as it slowed in traveling up the broad street. She saw Bonnie's mansion, looming white and clean in the dim light, and beyond it, the Greshams' rose-granite palace.

"I believe we can wade from here," Halloran said. "Let me slide off and see." He did so quickly and the water came up to his waist. The rain had plastered his dark hair to his skull and all he wore was the top of his pants. "Come, darling, let me help you off."

The endearment was the first he had ever spoken to her and there was possession in the word. She drew a deep breath, for just the sound of it warmed her as she slipped off into his arms. The water came well up over her bare breasts, but as they began to wade toward Bonnie's house and the lights that beckoned from it, Halloran put an arm

about her and braced her against the eddying currents
which swept first one way, then another.

It took them half an hour to reach the house. Mara saw
that all the kitchens under the main body of the house
built of hardy brick, were inundated. The two of them felt
their way in through the water-covered gate. Then they
felt the granite steps under the water as their feet touched
them. Slowly, they mounted each step.

On the gallery, which ran around the colonial house,
there was only rain beating against it. It was above the
Gulf waters. As they made it to the broad door, Halloran
stopped her.

"Mara, wait here a moment. Let me go in and get a blan-
ket or a wrap for you."

She looked down to see that she was nude except for a
fragment of petticoat that hung about her waist and she
shrank back against the wall.

"Oh, do! Please. I can't go in like this."

He knocked on the door, which was opened immediately,
and Mara heard Desmond Brant's baritone.

"By God! Bonnie! Dominique! Come here, it's John Halloran. Come in, man, come in." And the door shut with a
bang against the gusting night.

Mara stood shivering in the faint light of the storm,
waiting. But almost instantly the door opened again and
Halloran stepped out, wrapped her thoroughly in a large
bedspread and lifted her up into his arms.

Bonnie was waiting in the foyer. "Oh, my dear! My dear,
dear Mara! I thank God for your safety! Desmond says this
house will ride out the storm because of the high foundations and all the brick and cement. Oh, my dear, you must
let me help you!"

Mara looked around at what appeared to be hundreds of
people, black and white and brown, all refugees from the
storm. She smelled hot coffee in the air, a fragrance that
made her instantly aware of hunger.

"Oh, your cheek is cut—and your poor little hand. And
Johnnie's got an ugly scratch and bruise on his shoulder.
Do sit down, dear. We'll bring each of you some hot coffee
and a sandwich before I take you upstairs, Mara, and put
clothes on you."

It was so comforting to have Bonnie fussing over her as

she had done on that long ago night when Halloran had carried Mara to her for refuge. She felt for the first time a faint sense of safety, even with the wind and rain howling outside. Not even the storm could demolish this immense mansion of Bonnie Fairweather's. Mara tightened the thick bedspread about her and looked at the dozens of people around her. The storm had made brothers of them all and the blessed dry warmth of the bedspread made her suddenly sleepy.

Black workmen and women, white laborers and several children sat on the damask couches and in the exquisite French chairs in Bonnie's main salon. Mara was later to learn that all the big houses that still stood had welcomed each victim like a kinsman. Mara realized at last that these mansions stood on the highest point on the low-lying island. The crowded room was singularly quiet, the many voices subdued and sober. All seemed stunned to silence by the enormity of the disaster. But it suddenly came to Mara as she sat there on the couch between two Mexican women that the wind howling about the house was just a touch less violent.

Desmond Brant confirmed this by coming in with a pot of fresh coffee and announcing, "I think the blow is diminishing. The wind from the south is lessening."

Bonnie bustled up and put a chicken sandwich and a cup of the coffee in Mara's hands, where she sat with the bedspread wound about her. Halloran had vanished into the back of the house.

Yes, Mara thought, that wind from the south had blown the Gulf of Mexico into Galveston, covering every inch of the island, and now it was decreasing slowly. But she did not know that with the cessation of the wind, the water pushed in from the sea would have nothing to hold it on the island.

The vast rush of those waters back to the sea would be of much greater intensity than the blown water that came in with the hurricane. And even as she sat there, utterly weary and nodding with fatigue as she drank the restoring coffee and ate her sandwich, the water was preparing to rush back to the Gulf, carrying with it the few remaining wooden houses that had withstood the storm and those unfortunate survivors who were in them.

No, Mara did not know these things and her weary mind was taken up with worry about Celia and those others who had left the roof at the height of the storm. Where were Rosita and Maria and Andrea now? Ashworth and Donellan? Had they found something to hold to, or were they among the pitiful drowned people she and Halloran had seen as they spun with the currents on their makeshift raft?

Where had Halloran gone? She knew the house was full of people. There were more upstairs and in all the rooms on the lower floor. Was he searching for others he knew who might have been saved?

Bonnie came and took her cup, beckoning her to follow. "I'll take you to my room and you can put on some clothes and rest on my bed. It's the only room in the house not filled with wounded and sick victims of this terrible storm."

Mara followed her silently and wearily and silently dressed in the shirtwaist and skirt Bonnie gave her. It was a little too large for her, but Bonnie had pinned it neatly around her slender waist.

"Don't worry about Johnnie, dear. He's eating like a horse. And here, I must treat that cheek with medicine and wrap your little hand." She did so, quickly and efficiently. Dominique stood by with the medicines and bandages.

"I am so happee zat you escape, Mademoiselle Mara," the little black French girl said warmly. "Now you rest in Madame's beeg bed, yes?"

"No," Mara replied. "I want to be downstairs. I must see if my sister—sisters—will be found."

And so she went back downstairs and sat on the couch with the two dozing Mexican women. Slowly, quietness spread through the house as the winds continued to drop. There was no banging of shutters, no howling about the eaves and Mara felt strange without the wild requiem so long endured. It had seemed an eternity—that it would never stop. She had been in the living hell of the storm so long she could not believe it was almost over.

People were stretching out on Bonnie's thick plush rug and falling asleep all about her and she yearned to do the same. But she denied herself sleep. Now with the storm over, surely they would find Celia and Betsey, and the others.

She looked at the clock on Bonnie's graceful marble mantel and noted with disbelief that it was just a little past ten o'clock. She could have sworn that it was the dead hour just before dawn. She could have sworn her ordeal had lasted through the night. But no, it had started only this morning and it had lasted only a little more than fourteen hours.

All the pent-up waters were now ready to begin their disastrous rush back to the sea, and throughout what remained of the city were people clinging in houses, or to the wreckage in the water, and giving thanks for their survival all too soon. For in minutes the gushing water sucked and scythed down those remaining.

But Mara did not hear it then, nor did she know it. Sleep had claimed her at last. While she slept the water level outside dropped four feet in forty minutes and the drenched lawn, shrubs and fences could be seen in the pale light.

The tattered survivors about her heard of it when a black man came in and announced that the downstairs kitchen and rooms were ruined, but the water had drained away.

There were murmured, "Thank God," "Thank the almighty," and "We're safe!"

But Mara did not hear them.

It was the scent of fresh hot coffee once more that woke her. Everyone was up, or getting up from their makeshift sleeping areas. Many of those who had been in the house when Mara arrived had already gone, hoping to find what they could of the homes they had abandoned. It was broad daylight outside, as fair and clear as if there had been no storming skies.

Mara looked about for Halloran but she did not see him. Those remaining about her were readying themselves to leave. Bonnie stood beside her front door, Desmond nearby, shaking hands with her departing guests. Alone, Mara sat up on the couch, the two Mexican women who had shared it with her had disappeared.

She put a hand to her tumbling hair. It was quite dry

and the clock on the mantel proclaimed the hour as ten in the morning. She had slept nearly the clock around.

Dominique came up to her with a cup of coffee and a plateful of sliced, hot buttered bread. Mara took a slice of the bread in one hand and the cup of coffee in the other, realizing that she was stiff and sore and the muscles along her back throbbed angrily as she sat upright.

"Eet's homemade bread, Madame Gresham send it ovair to us weeth more food from her keetchen. Everybody eez share weeth everybody." Dominique's white smile was broad. Her pretty face was wreathed in happiness as she added, "Mademoiselle Mara, the storm eez ovair. The sky, she eez beautiful!"

"Thank God," Mara said, with her mouth full. "Where is Mr. Halloran?"

"He's waked up at last, too. He eats een zee upstairs leetle kitchen weeth madame. Desmond geeve him clothes. They fit good. You weel see."

Neither Mara nor Dominique, nor any of those still in Bonnie's big salon, had any inkling of the horror that awaited Galveston in the morning light.

So she ate cheerfully, keeping an eye on the door to the hall leading to the small upstairs pantry-kitchen and hoping Halloran would come out of it soon.

Bonnie joined her and Mara saw her lovely face was troubled. Mara's heart sank. Had she heard bad news?

"Have you heard anything of Celia?"

"No, but Jim, who takes care of my horses, has been out. He was told that the eastern section of town was swept clean of frame houses, leaving only piles of loose planking as far as the eye can see. And, my dear, I'm sorry to tell you that the death toll is much greater than anyone knows. They are trying even now to identify them and give them proper burial."

"But my sister and Betsey were in a trunk. I believe she made it to some place of safety . . ."

"I had Jim go and ask if she was at the Greshams' and further up at the Brown's villa and she wasn't." Then hastily, "But that doesn't mean she isn't safe somewhere else. Several of the larger buildings in town have survived. She could well be in one of them." Bonnie's brows lifted in distress as she added, "It is so very hot and the sun is out with a vengeance. It is necessary that they bury the dead as soon as possible."

Mara swallowed and blinked back tears as she set her coffee cup down on the table at the end of the couch. "And there's Andrea and Rosita and Maria—and Ashworth and Donellan."

"Yes, Johnnie told me that Archer and David were with you. I think Archer's too mean to die. I'll wager he grabbed hold of something and survived. David, I'm not too sure of, but from what Johnnie says, it'll be no great loss to lose either of them. Now perk up, Mara, please don't cry. I've sent Jim out again, this time to look for food as well as survivors and—"

Halloran drew up before them. Desmond's shirt fit his big shoulders tightly and looked as if it might tear if he flexed them. The pants fit tightly too, but he had shaved and he looked so dear to Mara it was all she could do to keep from throwing her arms around him. But he gave her a strangely preoccupied glance as he spoke to Bonnie.

"Bonnie-girl, Will MacAdam's going to be here shortly, or I miss my guess. He'll come if he has to swim, and I know he's made it back from Dallas hours ago. He'll be looking for Celia and his babies. I'm going out now and see if I can find any word of them—or Andrea and the two who were with her."

"I'm going with you," Mara said low and hard. "They're *my* kin and I'll not sit here idly and wait for them to be—"

"Mara," Halloran said quickly, "you don't know what it's like out there. Mr. Gresham's already worried about looters and there are things you, as a woman, shouldn't see—"

"Shouldn't see, be damned," she said passionately. "If I could see and live through last night, there should be *nothing* I shouldn't see."

He shrugged. "I was only trying to spare you."

Bonnie put her hand on Mara's shoulder. "Darling, stay here with me! Men will be coming and going all day and you'll get word just as fast. Desmond's going out to see if any of our friends have survived, too."

"No, Bonnie. I'm going with John, whether he wants me to or not." She felt touchy and resentful because Halloran did not seem as tender as he had last night. The bright

Sunday morning seemed to have wiped out all remembrance in him.

"Come on then," he said grimly.

Bonnie made one more protest. "Mara, dear, Jim tells me the dead are scattered everywhere and there are things—sights—a young woman like you doesn't *need* to witness."

"No, Bonnie." Mara rose to her feet. Bonnie's shoes were a little wide on her slender feet and slipped up and down as she moved. But they were comfortable now. "No, Bonnie, darling, I must do it," she said resolutely. "My sister—Celia is very dear to me and I'm sure Andrea will be with time. I *must* try to find them."

When Mara stepped down from the mansion's gray granite steps onto the ruined walk leading to them, her hand on the balustrade beside them, she looked about with disbelief.

"Why—why—from here it looks as though nothing had happened, only a hard rain." She spoke in an awed voice. "All the great houses are standing yet." She was quite right. Only the drooping shrubs, a residue of sand and a few steamy puddles of water under the burning sun indicated that water had stood four feet deep here last night.

"The wind was blowing from the south when we lost the trunk with Celia and Betsey in it," Halloran said sharply. "We'll start looking toward the north."

They walked carefully down the street. The sidewalks had shifted and in her borrowed shoes, which were none too comfortable now, Mara preferred the street. And in two short blocks, the whole view changed. Suddenly they were in the midst of utter chaos and carnage.

Piles of wreckage loomed everywhere, houses that had been telescoped, buildings destroyed, and nowhere was there a street to be seen. Men were pulling at the wreckage in some places, frantically with death in their faces. But it was the helpless forms of the dead that very nearly destroyed Mara's resolution.

There were nude and seminude bodies lying among the wreckage and some had been carefully laid out upon the sand by men who were working among the debris. In some cases, those who had the means to do so had thrown covers over some of the naked corpses. But there were all too many pitiful hands, feet and legs sticking out among the shattered boards that had been houses.

Slowly, the enormity of the loss of life was borne in on Mara. She was sickened by it and she fought down the visceral urge to retch. Depression and sorrow choked her. Were Celia and her child lying somewhere in the steaming and pitiless sunlight, sightless eyes under the brassy bowl of the sky?

Halloran looked at her white face and took her arm firmly. "You *would* come, Mara."

She lifted her chin. "Yes. I would come. I have a right to look for my sisters and my niece."

He said no more, but his hand on her arm was warm and somehow impersonally comforting. Mara knew she looked pale and drawn. Her hair hanging from her shoulders to her waist, she felt, completed her wretched appearance, but she strode along beside Halloran undeterred. Bonnie's shoes were rubbing a blister on one of her heels now.

As they approached the Strand they saw that much of it had survived the storm. Still, it was littered with evidence of the storm's destructive power. Other women and men, even children, were wandering from building to building, asking those inside if there was a James Grady or a Johnathan Calhoun—or, as Halloran asked, a Mrs. Will MacAdam and her child among them?

The answer from the exhausted and pitiful people they encountered was always *no*. No, with compassion from some. No, dully from others. No, with gratitude from some that they themselves were saved by whatever miracle.

"We'll not walk down to the wharves, Mara. I won't risk taking you there. We'll go back by way of the other buildings still standing and then, by God, I'm taking you back to Bonnie. You're limping and you'll be good and sick if I don't get you out of this heat."

So he walked her slowly back by way of the Medical Building, which was still standing, but no one there had heard of Celia or Betsey, or any of the others they asked about. There were other buildings still standing but they were all too far away.

"You'd never last until we reached them, Mara, and you

may as well face it. This sun is broiling and you look as if you just might pass out any minute."

Mara was exhausted but she refused to admit it. "Then I'm coming back later and look at those places that are too far. I've *got* to find Celia and Betsey—and—and the others."

"Will should be coming into Bonnie's at any minute now."

"How can you tell? The island's completely cut off from the mainland. No telephones, no wireless and no way to get from here to there."

"Don't underestimate Will. He'll get here. I *know* it. And he'll find Celia and Betsey. He and I, you may be sure."

"Of course you will," she said automatically, sure now they would never find her sisters and the servants and child in this sea of devastation. They were lost, she told herself, and was filled with bitter grief.

They passed dead horses and other dead stock, swelling in the steamy heat. A faint sickening odor drifted on the still air and sudden panic struck her. My God! If all these bodies lay out in the sun long enough—she drew closer to Halloran and he stepped up their pace.

It seemed a much longer trip going back through the twisted paths of wreckage. The heat brought perspiration to her face and she could feel it, moist and disagreeable under and along her arms. As they picked their way through the dead and the living searchers among them, of which there were many more now than when they had first started, she had time to think.

She thought of good Rosita and her loving daughter, Maria. She thought of poor Andrea, who after her confession last night, had seemed to accept Mara. Curiously, there had even been love in her voice.

She thought of Ashworth and Donellan, swimming hopelessly after the trunk, which spun along on the current too fast for them. Were they buried under the kindling that had been houses?

And where was Aunt Felice's body—and that of Lucinda Donellan? In her ignorance, Mara thought of the dead in terms of hundreds, which seemed ghastly enough. She was to learn later that between six and eight *thousand* had perished. The exact toll would never be known.

By the time they reached the Fairweather mansion, her feet were painfully sore. She looked at Halloran's bare feet and envied him.

Bonnie greeted them cheerfully, despite Mara's long face. "Celia will be found," she assured her young friend. "You just wait until Will gets here. He'll turn this island upside down until he finds her."

"I cannot believe that now," Mara replied, her voice quivering. "The city is in ruins and hundreds have perished. And I fear my sisters and Betsey are among them. I would have covered the island from one end to the other if I'd had a horse."

"You're such a little thing, Mara," Bonnie said kindly. "Leave the searching to the men. Johnnie, come in and eat a little before you go out again. Surely Mara isn't going back out with you?"

Halloran gave Mara a curious look. "Are you, Mara?" Was there a challenge behind his glance? She didn't know and she was too tired and depressed to care. It seemed to her that he had forgotten all about the tender moments they had shared in the storm. He had forgotten how she lay in his arms, forgotten the glory they had known.

"No," she said wearily. "I'll stay here until Will comes— *if* he can come."

"He'll come," Halloran said shortly. "You can bank on that. Now how about something to eat, Bonnie, before I cover the west end of town?"

"Go to the kitchen-pantry, Johnnie. The cook and Dominique will give you whatever we have. I don't suppose you'd run across any food supplies on this trip that you could bring back?"

"Not likely. I'll be more liable to run across looters. Do you have a gun I could take with me and a little ammunition?"

"Desmond has an arsenal. Ask him for one." Then as he disappeared, "Come up with me to my room, Mara, dear. All my guests have gone, hoping to find kin of their own. And you look like you need more rest."

Upstairs in Bonnie's room, untouched as it was by the fury of the hurricane, Mara felt curiously disembodied.

The fragile French furniture, the deep rugs and gold-framed mirrors, the white ruffled organdy curtains at the now open windows were dreamlike. But Bonnie stood at one of those windows looking out as Mara slipped out of her shoes.

"You can see it from here," Bonnie said somberly.

"What can you see?"

"The smashed houses beyond and the shattered buildings. Only these big houses on Broadway escaped the worst of it. Only a handful of bigger buildings scattered out from downtown and a few downtown weathered it."

"Oh, Bonnie, I can't bear it! Andrea told us last night, just as the house was going under that the Colonel was my father," Mara blurted, unable to stem the tide of words. She poured it all out to Bonnie, the shock, the disbelief that had shaken her—not only at Andrea's revelations, but at the raging storm itself.

They sat together on the bed, Bonnie's slim white hand holding Mara's tanned one, while the younger woman wept her heart out. Exhausted at last, her words died and Bonnie soothed her, stroking her hair and murmuring softly.

"Here, pull off these stockings, dear, and lie down. You're still worn out, even more so now. Don't think about any of it any longer. Are you hungry?"

"No, and I think I shall never be hungry again."

"Yes, you will, Mara," Bonnie smiled. "And dear," she paused at the door, "I'd much rather the Colonel was my father than Archer. My brother is an egotistical, selfish swine and swollen with false pride. Your mother knew it herself and stayed with him anyway, after she discovered what he was. I think she was brave and courageous."

Mara sighed. Her head on the down pillow felt strange, swollen yet light. As the door closed quietly, she closed her eyes and a fitful sleep took her.

She roused, wide awake at the sound of the light rap on the door. It opened slowly on Will MacAdam. His hair was rough and tumbled. The crystal blue eyes were red rimmed and his face dark with two days' growth of beard.

Mara leapt from the bed and flew to him, throwing her

arms about his waist and putting her head on his chest, fighting back tears.

"Oh, Will—Will! Celia and Betsey are lost out there somewhere. We looked and looked. John and I both looked. The whole city's dead—dead!"

He held her strongly, and when she pulled away, she looked up into his drawn face. He looked as if he hadn't slept for days.

"How did you get here, Will? I heard the train trestles were down and I know all the wires are down. We can't call anyone from anywhere. We've been shut off from the world."

"I rowed over in a boat with four other frantic men before daylight. We just got here. I walked up and down this street asking at every door for any of you, and the Greshams told me you were at Bonnie's. What makes you so sure Celia and Betsey are lost?"

"I didn't mean they were dead! Never that! Just lost from us—the rest of us last night—"

"Tell it to me. All of it."

"We were all together yesterday when the storm struck and last night after the house went under . . ." She told him then about all of them clinging to the roof and Celia and Betsey climbing into the trunk to avoid the flying slate shingles, which had killed Aunt Felice. She told him how they had lost them, and of Andrea, Rosita and Maria trusting to God, and of a house that was still standing. She told him of Donellan and Ashworth swimming after the trunk when it broke away from them, and of the wild lashing night that she and Halloran had endured. She told him all, except the spun-gold moments in Halloran's arms during the night—and Andrea's fear-driven revelation.

He had put his head into his hands and now slowly raised it, looking at her somberly. "I'll find them," he said low. "I'll find them if I have to scour every inch of the island."

"Of course you'll find them!" Mara said with suddenly reviving hope. "I know they found safety somewhere. There are bound to be other places like this one where people were saved. It can't all be devastated."

"I don't know, Mara. I saw a lot of the devastation, just getting here. The wharves are smashed in on one side.

They've all been unroofed and shattered all the way down quayside. Piles of rotting vegetables are littering the streets and small boats and tugs are driven into some buildings far back from the bay."

"Then Galveston as a port must have suffered a terrible loss."

"After we moored our rowboat, we saw hundreds of thousands of dollars worth of flour, grain, cotton and other produce scattered in piles around miles of uprooted train tracks and smashed freight cars. Galveston as a port may well be finished. Tell me, how in the name of God, did John get here before the worst of it? He called me in Dallas and he was still Houston, but he said he was going to make a run for it."

"He caught the last train out from Houston, but it had to back up before it got here because of the storm. John said he got out and walked the trestle and swam a lot of the way. All his clothes were torn off except the top of his pants."

Will laughed grimly. "Well, he saved the thing he loved most—and I'd have done the same if I'd had the chance." Then with eyes blazing suddenly, "There's something you've got to know, Mara. I think this tragedy releases me from a deathbed promise to Andrea—"

Mara lifted her hands, palms upward in supplication. "Andrea told me, Will, while we were in the house, as it was being torn apart by the hurricane. She asked my forgiveness and I gave it."

Will was up in a flash and caught her to him, his arms a vise, squeezing the breath from her. "Thank God," he murmured in a choked voice. "To know that you were our sister and be unable to tell you has been a kind of hell for Branch and me, and Andrea, too, though she wouldn't admit it."

"As I look back, Branch as good as told me half a dozen times. I don't know why I didn't suspect it."

"And I came close to it myself more often than you know." He kissed her cheek swiftly. "Our littlest sister—and such a successful one, too. Ah Mara, you're so much like the Colonel. Impetuous, full of optimism and charm and ready laughter, when finally you got from under Ashworth's squashing domination."

Mara's little laugh was half sob. "You can't imagine how good it feels to know I *belong*. All I had before was Celia—and I guess I can count my niece, Betsey. But now I've a whole family."

"You certainly have and one that will see you're loved and welcomed." He paused, drew a deep breath and added, "Now, little sister, can you tell me which way that trunk carrying all my darlings was headed? God—I'm so afraid for Celia—I don't need to tell you it's time our baby was due."

"I know, I know! But one of the last things she said to me was 'Don't worry, Mara, I'm not in labor yet!' and she managed a laugh. The wind was blowing from the south and you can't imagine how fierce it was, Will. The trunk was being blown northward."

He moved to the door. "I'm going then to search the north half of the island first." He paused, then, "Oh, one thing I must tell you. Branch and Fleurette took me to the landing to find a boat, and Fleurette sent you a message. She said to be sure and tell you she had chased Branch until he caught her—said you'd understand—and the wedding will be on Thanksgiving day."

Mara laughed aloud, her first real laugh since the storm. "Good for Fleurette!" Then sobering she said, "Shouldn't you rest a bit first? You look like you haven't eaten or slept in days."

"I haven't since John telephoned me." His little smile was crooked and his reddened eyes narrowed to chips of ice. "And I can't. There'll be no rest for me ever until I find Celia and our babies." He closed the door quietly and swiftly behind him, leaving Mara alone, yet somehow comforted.

Overnight she had acquired two big brothers, another older sister, and more. She had made up her mind at last that she belonged to John Halloran body and mind, now and forever, and she meant to be *his* anyway he would have her.

Chapter 21.

$\mathcal{CV}$ LATER that Sunday afternoon, Bonnie's big colonial house became headquarters for a number of city officials including John Halloran, who had recruited other surviving men. Bonnie and her servants with Mara's help served coffee and homemade bread and whatever else in the way of canned goods that could be salvaged from the drenched main kitchen below the first floor.

Mara, on the periphery of all the activity, caught most of the conversations.

At first, burying the dead had been attempted. Then, as their ranks increased a thousandfold, the men had become desperate and were now putting them in makeshift morgues near the docks.

Identification was a moiling nightmare. Looters were beginning to make sporadic raids and Desmond's arsenal was soon emptied as the men armed themselves.

That night, Will and Halloran returned, red eyed and more exhausted. Will's search for his family had been in vain. Halloran, who had been with him, with the combined help of Bonnie and Mara, prevailed on him to sleep that night at Bonnie's, since nothing could be done in the dark. The house had emptied of all except the servants and Bonnie's three friends, and all slept the deep sleep of utter fatigue.

But early Monday morning, September tenth, Halloran, Will and Desmond left again to help in the stricken city and seek others still missing.

At noon, only Will returned briefly to tell them that contact with the outside world was still nonexistent, but that a temporary headquarters for the town's administration

had been set up in the damaged Tremont Hotel downtown.
He had come to give this news to the women and the servants and to eat quickly.

"A man named L. R. D. Fayling has, at the Mayor's request, raised a volunteer force to maintain law and order
in town," he told them as they served him hot coffee,
beans and cornbread, all of which Gertrude, the cook, had
prepared over the kerosene stove. "And a man named
Richard Spillane, a commercial editor of the *Galveston
Tribune*, has been sent with two other men in a small boat
across the bay to Houston, with details of this disaster.
And he's to telegraph all of it to Washington."

As he finished the last of his coffee, he added, "I've got to
get back. That make-do morgue they've created near the
docks, with the sun beating down on the corrugated tin
roof, has turned the place into an oven, so they tell me. But
I've got to see if Celia and Betsey—" His voice trailed off
and he shook his head. "Then there's Andrea and her
companions—" Again he broke off.

They all followed Will to the front door, including Bonnie's servants and Dominique. As he opened it John Halloran and Desmond came up the steps, their faces gray with
fatigue and revulsion. Jim, Bonnie's coachman and stablehand, was with them. Perspiration was rolling down his
dark forehead.

Halloran looked at Will with compassion and he said,
"We've already covered the morgue dockside, Will, and
none of them are there."

"Thank God!" Will's ejaculation was heartfelt.

"The place is foul," Halloran added grimly. "Blue bottle
flies are swarming over those decomposing bodies. Some of
them already almost unrecognizable and more coming in
by the drayful."

Mara shrank inwardly, her stomach churning as Halloran added low, "Wait until I've had a bite and washed up,
Will. I'll go with you. We'll make it toward the Ursuline
Convent next. It's the only thing left standing for blocks
around it." He paused, then even lower, "You've your gun
and plenty of ammunition? Looting is widespread now."

"Yes," Will replied, turning to accompany them all back
into the house. "Brought it with me from Houston."

Mara's heart pounded as she remembered the lonely

corpses, the ravaged town she and Halloran had walked through only yesterday morning. They had been too early. Looters had not yet begun. Now, in the aftermath of the tragedy, they had risen like vultures to pick at the dead.

Mara brushed against Halloran as they made their way to the pantry kitchen and looked up quickly, seeing his eyes. He gave her only a passing glance before turning to Will again.

Didn't he remember anything of their time together, she wondered desolately. Will had said Halloran had "saved the thing he loved most" and she was sure he had meant her. The thought did not comfort her now and she left them abruptly and went upstairs to the room where she had slept.

Like the communications system, the water system of the city was ruined, but Bonnie Fairweather had an old hand pump over a well in back of her house, which she had ordered the builders to leave because it was picturesque with oleanders and bougainvillea around it. Now, after much priming and pumping by Jim, it gave forth a weak stream of somewhat acrid water.

With it, they had all made separate attempts to bathe themselves. Dominique had refilled the pitcher on the washstand in Mara's room. Feeling almost crusty with salt and sorely in need of a full bath, Mara made another effort to bathe out of the bowl on the washstand, while she thought wrathfully of John Halloran.

In their whispered night sessions back at school in Richmond, Mara's schoolmates had talked of girls who let boys "go all the way," and they had said in hushed voices to each other, "And he *never* called on her again." Was that the way it was to be? Had conquering her been all Halloran had ever had in mind? She tried to remember all that he had said to her during those frenzied moments of lovemaking and afterward as they whirled through the maelstrom on their bit of flotsam. It had seemed so comforting to her then, but now his words were like moths, flickering away under her efforts to catch them.

She thought of it all through her attempts to bathe again and strained to hear his deep voice from downstairs as he ate and drank with the others. No. Bonnie's house was too big, too richly constructed and carpeted to carry voices so far.

In the scanty chemise that belonged to Bonnie, she flung herself across the bed and lay there dry eyed. She would *not* cry again. No matter what the future held, she would not cry.

For the first time, her thoughts turned to *Mara Originals.* How had Houston fared during the storm? Had the great glass windows which displayed her designs so beautifully been blown in, like the windows in Galveston? No. Branch would have ordered them boarded up before the heavy winds hit. Branch would have seen to everything. And Fleurette. They had more than weathered the storm, she knew. Will's message had confirmed that.

Earlier, Bonnie had told Mara, she thanked God that she had been letting Fleurette stay in her suite at the Houston Hotel, even though she had previously been disapproving of her weekends spent in Houston. But Bonnie didn't realize how deeply Branch cared for Fleurette. Now he would marry her long before he would take her in the wild night, as Halloran had so passionately taken Mara.

She buried her head in the pillow, and to her surprise she slept.

She wakened in the late afternoon to a vagrant breeze pushing in through the open, but screened windows across the north wall. It carried the pervasive and unmistakable smell of death.

Mara put down an urge to gag. It was far too hot to close the windows, but the scents on the wind were terrifying, and in the distance, Mara could hear the crack of gunfire. Looters! She rose and went to the windows and looked out, but she could see nothing but the devastation beyond Broadway, the tottering lean of a few houses and the acres of jumbled planking.

She dressed hurriedly and went below to be met in the small kitchen-pantry by Bonnie and Dominique.

"I came up to see about you, but you were sleeping so sweetly I tiptoed away." Bonnie smiled. "Are you hungry?"

"I was—until I smelled the breeze. Now I don't know if I can eat."

"Eet ees dreadful," Dominique said, wrinkling her dark, narrow French nose.

"I'd give anything for a bucket of ice and a bottle of champagne in it," Bonnie sighed, going to a cupboard and taking out a bottle of whiskey. She took up three napkins from a table nearby and soaked them in the whiskey. Turning, she handed one each to Dominique and Mara.

"When the scent gets too strong, put this to your noses, my dears. It should help." And she put her own pert nose into the whiskey-soaked napkin, bringing it up again quickly. "I don't know which is worse, the smell of raw whiskey or that awful smell in the breeze."

"The whiskey helps," Mara said, breathing it in. It seemed to clear her nostrils of the cloying, clogging putrescence that clung in them.

She ate very little of the food that Bonnie's cook prepared for them. It was meager enough fare. More of the boiled beans, cornbread and canned tomatoes. All washed down with the acrid well water.

The women, the servants, even the big luxurious house seemed to wait through the long, late afternoon. Twice strangers stopped by, asking for water. Then two men stopped and asked for a little food. They were armed volunteers on their way to patrol the neighborhood to the north. They could tell them nothing except more of the horror stories that were circulating through Galveston.

"Before God," said the rougher of the two men, a bearded giant, as the two seated themselves before bowls of beans and a pan of cornbread, "I ain't seen nothin' like this in all of my life. I seen five men tryin' to rob a body—cuttin' off the fingers and ears of a dead lady for her jewelry. About that time, the militia come up, and before you could say Jack Robinson, they shot and killed all five of them men."

"Yeah, Jeb," said the other, a clean-shaven younger man, "an' 'fore I joined you, I seen people arguin' with an Eye-talian lady standin' in the middle of the street holdin' the foot an' leg of her little baby, what was cut off from the body. She didn't have on enough clothes to cover a jay-bird, but she was alive an' crazy as a loon. I went down to see could I help but couldn't none of us persuade her to leave that pile of kindlin' what was coverin' the rest of her baby.

She's been there night and day, they say, an' done got a turrible sunburn."

Gertrude offered them more beans and cornbread and they accepted readily. Under Bonnie's forthright questions, they opened up further and told the women more.

"Lordy, lady, that ain't nothin' to what it was like at the wharves," the bearded one said, "where they're loadin' them dead bodies on barges. They're comin' in by the drayful an' ain't stiff no more. God help me, when I seen them men slinging them ever whichaway onter the barges lined up there, to be towed out to sea, I liked to lost my breakfast."

Mara felt herself pale and, looking at Bonnie, saw that the blood had left her face, too. From the windows, the faint crack of gunfire could be heard more often now.

"At least they're trying to do something about the situation," Bonnie said bravely.

Dominique turned and left the kitchen swiftly as the men continued.

"Lady, I heard the head man say at the barges, 'You men get with it. The life of ever' man, woman an' child left livin' in Galveston depends on gettin' rid of these dead. Pestilence is gonna kill us all if we don't. We ain't got time to give 'em a proper Christian burial.' Lady, you got a little whiskey we could wash this cornbread down with?"

Silently, Bonnie went to the cupboard and poured out a half glassful of whiskey for each man.

"We're part of Fayling's volunteers for law an' order, ma'am," said the younger one, patting the revolver at his hip. "Thank God we ain't on that burial detail. Them men was gaggin' and retchin' an' smokin' big black cigars an' takin' big belts of whiskey to help 'em get on with the job. And lordy, the sound of them soft, swollen bodies when they hit them barges—"

"That's enough," Bonnie said in a strangled voice. "We can imagine the rest."

"Hope we didn't upset you nice ladies," the bearded one said, wiping his mouth with his hand after swallowing some of the whiskey. "But are you ladies protected here? Have you some firearms?"

"No," replied Bonnie, "but we have men who will be returning tonight to sleep here. They have guns."

"That's good," replied the younger man, rising. "I don't think any of the robbers and looters will come up this far, especially in the daylight. Me an' my partner, Jeb, will swing by here on the way back to check on you again."

"Do you know if word has reached the outside world about the plight of Galveston yet?" Mara asked them as they walked back through the foyer to the front door.

"I dunno yet, lady. Won't be much longer though. I'm sure of that."

At the door, they turned and smiled, singularly kind smiles, saying, "We thank you ladies for your hospitality."

The cook and Bonnie's second maid, Betty, stood behind Mara, Bonnie and Dominique, who had returned, and all three servants looked ill. None of them spoke a word before retreating to the back of the house once more.

It had been a scorching day, and as it drew to a close the faint breeze carrying a thousand stinks that seemed to settle in Mara's hair and clothing, clogging her nostrils, grew stronger. Three times, she and Bonnie resoaked their whiskey-wet napkins in their fight against the nauseous stenches. Even when darkness fell and the Gulf wind grew stronger, it, too, carried the smells of death.

It was just after dark that the men returned. Halloran came in first, followed by Jim and Desmond. Will was not with them.

Mara wanted to run and fling herself into Halloran's arms as he came into the glow from the kerosene lamp. His face was grimy, so grimy that his day's growth of beard could scarcely be seen. Even the thin scar was obliterated by smoke and dirt. But all three of the men were smiling.

"Don't get too close to any of us, ladies," Halloran said, his grin broadening, his white teeth standing out in bold relief against his sooty face. "We're somewhat gamy after today's work."

"But you're smiling!" Mara burst out, unable to restrain her own smile. "Oh, surely you bring good news—"

"We do, we do," responded Desmond, his dark gaze on his green-eyed employer. Jim, the stablehand, was looking at Bonnie, too, all three men were so dark they might have been brothers.

Gertrude, the corpulent black cook, said, "You all ain't gettin' a bite to eat till you tells us all."

"Will found Celia and the babies this evening," Halloran said, wiping his forehead and leaving a lighter smear across it.

"Did you say 'babies'?" Mara cried joyously.

"Sure did," replied Halloran. "Betsey and Will the third. Looks enough like the Colonel himself to be another one just like him. Head full of black hair and eyes just like his pa's."

"Johnnie, if you don't sit down and tell us all everything at once, I'll—I'll never speak to you again," Bonnie said, close to tears.

"Bonnie, we're too dirty and smell too bad to sit down on your pretty furniture," Halloran replied. "But we'll sit in your little kitchen and tell all of you about it over some beans and cornbread."

He was as good as his word. Better, considering that he began telling the women with interpolations from his two companions on the way to the kitchen.

Not only had they found Celia and the two babies at the Ursuline Convent on the far east side of town, but they found Andrea with Rosita and Maria, walking toward town from an old schoolhouse in which they had finished weathering the storm. These last three, on learning about Celia and the babies, had insisted on going to the convent, determined to stay there with them, until all were able to leave the island.

At the Ursuline Convent, the nuns told Will they had manned poles and ropes from the second floor of the Convent during the storm. They succeeded in pulling victims from the water as they floated by during the night and the early dawn.

A little nun named Sister Theresa, with the face of a griffin like those at the Gresham's gate, had manhandled the trunk containing Celia and Betsey to the wall of the convent and, with the help of two other nuns and an old man just plucked from the waters, pulled the two up through the window and into the convent. The entire lower floors were submerged, but the sisters of mercy had made a hospital out of the remaining floor and were responsible for saving dozens of lives.

No sooner had Celia been pulled from the trunk and put into one of the nun's cells than she gave birth to Will's son. Now Will was reunited with them and the nuns had arranged for quarters for all of them in the crowded convent. The lower floors were now being cleaned out and they would have additional room as soon as it dried out a little more.

Halloran looked at Mara from under his brows and her heart contracted because she could not read the meaning in their dark expression.

"Celia was mighty glad when I told her that you and I had made it safely to Bonnie's that night," he said. "She told me to give you her love." He paused, a forkful of beans in his hand. "And Andrea sent you a rather tentative message."

"Andrea?"

"Yes. She said to tell you she hopes you're as glad that she made it as she is that you are safe. And the first person she's going to call when she gets back to Houston is her old beau, James Phillips." He put the beans into his mouth and chewed during the silence that followed, then added, "And she sent you her love—a strange thing coming from Andrea, eh?"

"Strange. But not unwelcome." Mara lowered her thick curling lashes, refusing to meet his suddenly penetrating glance.

"Now, Bonnie, dear," Halloran said, stretching suddenly and yawning prodigiously, "if you'll let us get some of that miserable water out of your pump and clean up a bit, I feel that eight hours of sleep might help us all."

"I'll git the water fer all of us, Mister John," Jim said, getting to his feet. "I'm the one knows best how to coax the water out'a that mean pump."

"I hate to go to bed without a full bath," Desmond said in his resonant voice, distaste running a strong thread through it. Desmond was a fastidious man and Mara had never seen him anything but perfectly groomed and turned out, until this moment, and she sent him a glance of sympathy. Despite her bowl baths, she, too, felt grimy on retiring.

"Oh, Des, you're such a dandy," Bonnie said lightly.

"This ought to do you a world of good, make you appreciate running water when we get it back."

"And Galveston will get it back sooner than you think. By the way, communication with the outside world's been established again and word is that the whole country is rushing to send aid to us," Halloran said, leaning back and sipping his coffee. "Two small steamers came in today and delivered foodstuffs to the ruined docks below the Strand. It should be distributed in the morning."

"We need some," Bonnie said quickly. "I'm so tired of beans and cornbread, I could gag."

"Bonnie," Desmond said somberly, "there are those a lot worse off than we are. We've seen them today."

"And you'll get supplies soon, I'll see to it," Halloran said. Then looking at Mara in that strange way once again, he added, "I know you're anxious to get back to Houston and your shop, but I'm afraid it'll be another day before there can be a steamer in for that. The hardest hit victims, the ones most seriously wounded, are being taken back to Houston hospitals on the boats that delivered the food."

"One or two more days won't matter," Mara said evenly. Something had changed Halloran. She could not be sure what it was, but their relationship, so sweet the night of the hurricane, was not the same. It was in his eyes, the set of his jaw. What was it in his eyes? Conflict? Anger? Yes, both of those, and something else she could not put a name to.

The following day, they learned that looting was still widespread, despite the harsh punishment for it. And bodies were still being found, even though the loaded barges had been towed out to sea to dump their pitiful cargoes.

The men, Halloran, Desmond and Jim, had left early to help police the city and to aid victims in finding a place to stay. Desmond came home briefly to eat and told them that the sea was returning its victims. The barges that had been towed out and emptied of their cargo were useless, for the tide had washed the bodies back on the beaches where they lay rotting in the broiling sun. The desperate men on the burial details had determined to burn the bodies in the effort to prevent the spread of disease.

Thus the pall of burning bodies was added to the murk that hung over Galveston. And along with the smell of death, the vagrant breezes carried the odor of burning flesh. It was almost more than Mara and the women could bear. Once more the whiskey-soaked napkins were used.

Once in the small kitchen, where Mara was again soaking her napkin, Gertrude turned a troubled black face to Mara and said low, "Miss Mara, Jim done come in the back way a while ago ter get a bite to eat, an' he tol' me they said two women was raped in broad daylight, while searchin' for their famblies."

"He *saw* it?" Mara hid her shock.

"No'm, but he say the black woman who tol' him seen it."

"Saw what?" Bonnie asked, rustling in, her fresh starched skirts defying the sticky humid weather and unbelievable stenches in the air.

Mara told her, succinctly.

"That's only a rumor, I'm sure, Gertrude. But I'm glad Jim's come back."

"He says Mister Halloran sent him back to watch out fer us women," Gertrude said darkly. "Mister Halloran give him more ammunition fer his gun, too. He's out back now, pumpin' water for all us and fer when the men get home."

"Well," said Bonnie cheerfully, "with Jim here, we'll all be quite safe. Now do make up a pot of coffee for us, Gertrude. I know it's hotter than a flatiron today, but coffee does smell good and it makes that water bearable."

And so the women endured the third day in the house, guarded now by the armed Jim, while Desmond and Halloran helped the harried men of Galveston in their efforts to find and reunite the broken families, and in their other, more dismal, activities.

Mara, with the napkin to her nose, felt that she had been forever in the misery of the storm's aftermath. Her heart ached with the love she bore John Halloran and his strange attitude toward her now. And in her heart, she tried to turn her mind to *Mara Originals* and take comfort from her love of the art involved in fashioning beautiful clothing. But it turned inward once more, to Halloran and the confusion he had stirred in her.

* * *

That night, the two men returned, washed their hands and faces in the bucket on the drain and sat down in the small kitchen to the inevitable cornbread and beans. This time, Jim had once more scoured the soaked kitchen below and come up with a dozen or more cans with the labels washed off. So when they all sat down at the table together, canned peaches and pears were served with the usual fare.

As they took their places Halloran, grimy and fatigued as Desmond, bore more grim news.

"I went out to the convent to tell Celia," he began, with an oblique look at Mara, "and I'm hoping this news won't hit you as hard as it did her, Mara."

"What news?"

"Today we found Ashworth's body, as well as Donellan's, but no sign of Donellan's wife nor your Aunt Felice's body. I'm sorry, but I'm sure they had to be burned, as will Ashworth and Donellan. There's no other way, if we're to keep disease from spreading over the rest of us who are left."

"I'm sorry for them," Mara said slowly, aware dimly that some heavy burden she had carried for years lessened suddenly and was gone. "Ashworth was a bitter, selfish, angry man, but I don't think they deserved this kind of end."

"That's debatable," Halloran said, his voice hard and uncompromising.

"And poor Lucinda, I know she didn't deserve it." Mara did not speak of Donellan for she felt she could not be guilty of such hypocrisy.

"No. Poor, lightweight little Lucinda, like thousands of others last Saturday night, deserved better than winding up as fish bait out in the Gulf." His voice was still hard but there was a touch of sorrow in it.

"I'm sorry that they couldn't be buried properly—"

"Hell! We're all sorry for every one of them that couldn't be buried properly. But a disaster like this calls for disastrous action and, God knows, all the men and women left alive on this island have worked like dogs to make it better. It just wasn't to be."

"Now you're sounding bitter, Johnnie," Bonnie said reprovingly. "That's not like you—to let it show, anyway," she amended.

"Well, I haven't quite been myself since I rode out this blow," he replied, shooting a quick look at Mara. "A lot of things I thought all my life have undergone a change."

"Into something rich and strange?" Bonnie asked lightly.

"Perhaps. Only time can tell that." And abruptly Halloran got to his feet. "Jim!" he called into the storage room next to the kitchen. "Have you brought in the water?"

Jim came in carrying two dripping buckets. "Yes, sir, plenty. I got two big tubs full in the storage room. If you want ter wait, Gertrude'll heat enough fer you to put in the upstairs tub, fer an all-over bath. Mister Desmond's gonter do that."

"Good for you, Des." Halloran grinned at Bonnie's so-called business manager, who reddened slightly. "But I'm becoming very expert with cold water and a bar of soap, so if you'll bring the water, Jim, and now, if you ladies will excuse me, I'm very tired and very dirty."

Mara watched him stride out of the room, followed by Jim and the two waterbuckets he carried. He had eaten very little. The blue smudges beneath his black eyes attested to his weariness. She ached to follow him, touch him, plead her love. Yet she could not, for it was as if he had suddenly withdrawn a protective shield that had been around her from the day they met and she was left naked and vulnerable in a hostile world.

And in that crucial moment, she came to sudden realization. She could never tell him again that she would come to him on his terms. She could never again pocket her pride and repeat her offer. For she was certain now that he had rejected her—even as a mistress.

She was conscious suddenly of Bonnie's and Desmond's eyes. They were looking at her and there was pity in each of their faces.

Desmond cleared his throat and said briefly, "I heard at the Mayor's Headquarters that the steamers will take on passengers for Houston tomorrow. They've evacuated all the critical survivors."

"That's wonderful," Mara said quickly. "I'll take passage on the first one out tomorrow."

"Aren't you going to wait for your sister—sisters—to return home with you, Mara?" Bonnie asked.

Though Bonnie was her friend and confidante, Mara had no wish to confess that it hurt too much to stay near Halloran.

"No, Bonnie. Now that I know they're all right, I want to get back to my shop. Branch and Fleurette will think I've abandoned them."

"From what Will told me, the word Fleurette and Branch sent you, I don't imagine they care if you stay a few more days," Bonnie said dryly. "And I suppose I must start planning for a Thanksgiving wedding."

"Yes, you must," Mara smiled. "Be glad for them, Bonnie. I am."

"And so am I," Desmond said obliquely, his eyes on Bonnie.

"I *am* glad," Bonnie said, but the worry in her voice belied the words. "It's only people, and how they might whisper, or openly talk. They can be so cruel."

"Bonnie, if I can get away with being Colonel William Hunter MacAdam's natural daughter—and the word *will* get out as it seems Will and Branch and Andrea are all determined—certainly your daughter can get away with marrying one of Houston's richest, most respectable and eligible young men. After all, he's a hero besides."

"How can she lose?" Desmond said lightly.

"That's what Will says," Bonnie replied. "And Johnnie, too. I guess I'm a fool to worry."

"No," Mara said softly. "You're just a good mother, and once more I'm deeply in your debt." She looked down at the clean skirt and blouse she wore. Bonnie apparently had an inexhaustible supply of them. Bonnie, following her eyes, laughed.

"You're so slender, I'm afraid they don't fit too well."

"They fit very well and I'm so grateful for them, Bonnie."

Bonnie rose and came around the table to hug her. "My dear, having you here is the one pleasant thing that came out of that hurricane. But I'm sure the boys will be glad to escort you to the dock tomorrow morning."

"When does the first steamer leave, Desmond?" Mara asked.

"Nine in the morning," he replied.

"You can sleep late, darling," Bonnie said with a cheerful laugh, "because you have little to pack."

She had nothing to pack, but she rose at six and dressed in the fresh clothes Bonnie had given her last night. It was a fitted dress of white poplin with a high round neckline of white lace that fitted the slender column of her throat, as did the gathered sleeves her arms. They were full to the elbow, then fitted down to her narrow wrists. Mara had designed it herself. While the waist was too loose, Bonnie had given her a white poplin belt and she belted it firmly about her narrow midriff.

When she looked into the mirror to put up her hair, she found that the outfit was very becoming. She had taken a full hot bath last night and washed her hair as well. She looked at her face critically.

An oval with a slight indentation in the chin, full, passionate mouth and the famous Bonheur eyes, big, tipped at the corners with lashes thicker than a privet hedge.

Where was the Colonel in that face? The nose, straight and thin? Yes. The jaw, where it was firm and uncompromising? Yes. The dark curling hair where it grew to a narrow peak centering her forehead? Yes. Strange that she had not noticed that when she looked so often at the portrait over the mantel.

What was there in that face to hold John Halloran? She sighed. Nothing, obviously.

She went downstairs to the small first-floor kitchen where a sleepy Gertrude was making coffee. The heavy-set cook had on a fresh, starched white apron over her starched blue dress.

"Mercy," she declared, "Miss Mara, you're up mighty early."

"Yes, Gertrude. I'm excited to be going back to Houston, I guess." She took the cup of coffee the black woman poured and sat down in one of the two kitchen chairs.

"You got lots to git back to. I hear so much about your beautiful shop. From both Madame Fairweather an' Miss Fleurette, an' I see them beautiful clothes they brings home."

"Thank you, Gertrude. Yes, I've got a lot to get back to."

Strange, for the first time her life seemed emptier and even the thought of the shop held little comfort. "I just wonder if my—my fair isle will ever be the same again."

"Yes'm, it sure will! Us Galveston folks is hard to discourage. My mammy and pappy was borned on this island an' I was brung up here. Ain't no storm, no matter how bad, gonna run us off!"

Mara felt a faint lift of spirit. "You make me feel better about it, Gertrude. I love this place."

"Mister Will do, too. He and Mister Johnnie will rebuild their houses an' so will all the rest of the city. Jim says they're talkin' downtown about buildin' a—a—seawall, so this here thing can't never happen again."

"A seawall," Mara echoed, visualizing a great structure near the beaches. "That sounds good."

"An' Jim say they're talkin' 'bout raisin' the whole city up. Dredging up sand and makin' everything sit higher."

"That sounds harder to do," Mara said doubtfully.

"I bet you they do it, Miss Mara. They ain't nothin' Galveston people can't do once they set their mind to it."

Mara laughed. "And I bet you're right Gertrude."

"Sure I am— Oh, good mornin', Madame Fairweather," Gertrude broke off as Bonnie entered the kitchen.

"Aren't you both early birds!" Bonnie laughed. "Gertrude do give me a cup of that coffee. The boys will be down for breakfast soon. I saw Des in the hall upstairs."

Later, they all had breakfast in the dining salon for the first time, at Bonnie's insistence. As they were finishing up a strange mélange of grits, canned peaches and boiled pinto beans with the inevitable cornbread, Halloran spoke up.

"I'll see that Mara gets to the steamer, Desmond. You can report for duty and tell them I'll join you later." His voice carried something of command and both Desmond Brant and Bonnie looked at him curiously. Mara said nothing, and he continued, "Sorry I can't get a horse, Mara. But all the animals that survived the storm are doing double duty, hauling the—debris of the storm and pulling lumber off demolished buildings."

"I don't mind the walk. It's not as warm today as it has been. I could enjoy it, except for the terrible smells."

"It's a good mile and a half down there. Bonnie, can you spare a brimmed hat for her?"

"Of course," Bonnie replied readily.

And thus when the two of them left the house, Mara wore a broad-brimmed summer hat trimmed with green satin ribbons tied neatly under her chin. She had on a pair of Fleurette's shoes, which she and Bonnie discovered fit her feet much better than Bonnie's.

In silence, they took the granite steps, with Bonnie and her household waving good-byes. And in silence they walked the first block. Suddenly Halloran spoke.

"I took advantage of you during the storm, Mara, and I—"

"I think not," she interrupted with bitter honesty. "I made the overture. It would have been very ungallant of you to refuse."

"On the contrary. It would have been the decent thing to do—you were under such stress. Decent and honorable." He spoke with a bitterness of his own. "But you see, I don't seem to be much of either. I'm thirty years old and there's not much I believe in. I'm not a good bet, Mara, and I have a feeling that Bonnie, my kindhearted friend, has enlightened you about my—shall we say, unfortunate?—childhood and early youth."

"She also told me it was you who bought and sent my mother's piano to us and all of Archer Ashworth's library, not to mention mother's beautiful tables and ornaments. I can thank you now. It meant a great deal to all of us at the time."

He shrugged. "It doesn't matter now. Will tells me that you'll have a fourth of the MacAdam fortune. So you're not just a successful designer of clothes, but a very, very wealthy woman. You don't need me and my gifts or loans any longer. You're not just independent, Mara. You're an heiress."

So that was the source of his withdrawal, for her feeling that she had lost her shield against the world!

She tilted her head and looked up at his set face. It was so much browner now from the hot September suns that had scorched Galveston the last five days. But he did not look down at her.

"I just wanted to apologize for the night of the storm,"

he said, and the words sounded rehearsed. "If you had been yourself, I know it would never have happened."

They were passing through recently cleared streets, heavily sanded, with tall piles of lumber in neat stacks on either side.

"It would have happened," Mara said, breaking her vow. "It would have happened because I wanted it to happen. Even on your terms." Then even while swearing she would never say it again, "Even as your mistress."

There was a long silence as they swung along side by side. All around them was the evidence of a ruined but unbeaten city. The half-destroyed buildings, the horses pulling drays filled with debris, the people working in the shattered buildings, shoring up what was left.

When he finally spoke, his voice was oddly husky. "I don't want you on my terms any longer."

"Oh, I know that now. You've made it painfully clear in the last few days. We'll trade apologies. I apologize for lov—for making overtures to you."

"Mara, can you possibly love me? A cynic, a man with no background, no heritage to offer you? A mental freebooter who scratched his way up?"

She stopped and he stopped and they stood staring into each other's eyes. "What are you saying, John?"

"I've never said it before—to anyone in any circumstances and I swore an oath I never would—but I love you." He drew a deep breath and his voice was thick. "And I want to marry you. But you don't need me now."

A surge of blood pounded in her veins and a joy that cut into her like a shining knife.

"Oh, John." She did not try to keep the trembling out of her voice. "I've loved you so long and so much, I was willing to throw away my own honor. And I need you now, more than I ever did when you were helping me to make a success of the shop—of my very life."

"I was so proud of you and your shop . . ."

"Was? You still are, I hope. Because we both belong to you. Without you, neither of us is worth a snap."

He caught her hand hard and they walked silently through the half-destroyed Strand and to the dock, where the steamer waited and people were walking in twos and threes up the gangplank into the small vessel.

454 *Ann Forman Barron*

His hand tightened on hers, swinging her to a stop, and she looked up into an anxious face.

"No big wedding," he said firmly. "No hundreds of staring people like that thing in Richmond when Donellan married Lucinda."

Her little laugh caught in her throat and she fought back tears. "We'll do it like Will and Celia did. Just a quick trip to the courthouse."

"I'll take you anywhere you want to go on your honeymoon, but no big wedding." He sounded greatly relieved. "Just Will and Celia as witnesses, maybe." Then anxiously, "God, I wish I were going with you, but they need every man here. I've got to stay until a replacement can come. Even Will is sticking with it, though his heart's with Celia and his babies."

Then as she stood at the gangplank he caught her in his arms. The dear familiar and delicious weakness spread through her as their lips came together.

"Oh," she breathed, "I do love you—more than you know."

"You can spend the rest of your life teaching me how much, because there'll never be a more willing pupil." He did not smile and the thin white scar was clearly visible.

She ran her finger along it. "I love everything about you," she murmured, "even this."

Later, she stood at the railing of the vessel as it pulled slowly away from dockside. She stood there looking at him, where he was standing, straight and tall, long legs slightly apart, his endearing smile just for her until the dock dwindled and she could no longer see him.

She went and sat down on one of the long benches on deck under a flat roof. He loved her. How wonderful life could be! A sudden gust of euphoria swept her. As her fair isle grew dim in the distance, she knew with sweet certainty that the future waited, a wide and untapped vein of gold. Love, success and joy waited. They would all be hers, Mara—not Ashworth—Mara MacAdam Halloran's. None of the grief and humiliation she had known could ever touch her again.

And, she thought with sudden pleasure, *I'll wear the pearls he gave me on—our wedding day.*